Julia Wedgwood

The Moral Ideal

An Historic Study

Julia Wedgwood

The Moral Ideal
An Historic Study

ISBN/EAN: 9783337032746

Printed in Europe, USA, Canada, Australia, Japan

Cover: Foto ©Andreas Hilbeck / pixelio.de

More available books at **www.hansebooks.com**

THE
MORAL IDEAL

A Historic Study

BY

JULIA WEDGWOOD

Second Edition

LONDON
TRÜBNER & CO., LUDGATE HILL
1889

NOTE TO SECOND EDITION.

THE only change made in this edition is, that I have added one or two out of the many additional references I should have wished to give, and that I have tried to make clearer one or two passages which had either been thought obscure or misunderstood.

TO AN OLD FRIEND.

———•———

THE following pages, little as they justify such
a description, represent the thoughts and endeavours of more than twenty years. When, after
so long an effort, we have reached a stage where
we are forced to recognize, with however little
satisfaction to ourselves, that something is con-
cluded which must stand as the goal of endeavour,
and take its chance as a chapter of achievement,
we look around for some sympathizing spectator
of our work, some criticism tinged with the desire
to approve. You will not wonder that at such
a moment I turn to an old friend ; you will recognize it as natural that I should address words
meant for the public, in the first instance to you.

The title I have chosen, though I can find none
better, does not cover the ground I have sought
to explore. I should better have described my
aim had I called the book a History of Human
Aspiration ; but while such a title would have

seemed an ironic introduction to any volume of
its size and informal character, the sketches which
follow cannot be called a *History* of anything.
To an ordinary reader, the mere list of headings
will suggest the débris of a gigantic scheme, without a centre and without a scale, begun at intervals here and there, and abandoned as often.
The review of human thought which, starting from
an attempt to follow the moral development of
the Aryan race in its early branches, lingers over
the utterance of an individual, or quits all limitation of race and nation to describe the feelings of an age and the speculations roused by
a dawning faith—such a review may well be
thought, in its neglect of all obvious method, to
embody the mere fancies of a dreamer. I am
not afraid that it will bear that aspect to you. In
the execution of my design you will certainly find
much failure and probably some blunders, while
you will look in vain for a suggestion or an idea
not already familiar to you; but you will not be
offended by the apparent desultoriness of the
scheme. Where the space given to description
keeps a common measure with the period of
time described, there, we may be sure, but little
of the inner life is revealed to the reader. In

the perspective of an individual memory, years dwindle to a point, and moments expand to an age. A true biography, were such a one possible, would measure its progress by some other standard than the dates which mark advance from the cradle to the tomb; and the historian can hardly more than the biographer afford to forget that, as it has been finely said, " God has so arranged the chronometry of our spirits that there shall be thousands of silent moments between the striking hours." The criticism that the writer of a moral history follows no obvious scale and respects no obvious limits is in fact a recognition that he has ignored all that would shackle him in recording those throbs and pulsations which make up the true life of Man.

The true life of Man! there you at least will be with me. In asserting that the history of aspiration is the clue to all history, I shall not appear to you to make any extravagant claim for the Unseen. You believe, even more firmly than I do, that a partial and incomplete revelation of what men have sought to be, tells us more of their true nature, than does the most exhaustive record possible of what they have accomplished. " The word outlasts the deed," says a singer who

saw the greatest deeds of Greece. The member
of a less vocal race may expand that saying; the
thought outlasts the word. Aspiration exceeds
utterance, as utterance exceeds achievement. The
endeavour to illustrate this truth for those who
believe it, to set beside the picture of human
action the suggestion of those feelings in which
it finds its spring—this·is an aim in which I have
no doubt of your approval. As I lay down the
pen I find that conviction ènough for me; and
although your sympathy perchance be given
rather to the worker than the work, I know that
if you can care for what I have written, sooner
or later one or two others will feel its meaning,.
and enter into the vast consolation and hope
bound up in the thoughts I have striven to
follow, and the convictions which they have
strengthened, deepened, and purified.

CONTENTS.

———•———

THE MORAL IDEAL.

CHAPTER I.

INDIA AND THE PRIMAL UNITY.

No deeper cleft divides human spirits than that which separates the faith possible to men for whom Evil means a mere negation, a mere shadow, a form of ignorance, from that which regards it as an actual existence, a real antagonism to good. A clearer light, it may be, revealing in each division its line of cleavage from its opposite, will show each alone as the half of a truth too large for our minds, at their present stage, to take in ; but here and now it remains true that almost all other antitheses which divide human spirits either involve or spring from this contrast. So far as men are capable of logical thought, so far as their ideas are combined in any coherent whole (and these quali-fications cover many apparent exceptions), those who diverge here will be found to arrive at different conclu-sions on almost all the important questions which can exercise the mind of man. Their logical and obvious antagonism will prove the smallest part of that which is actual ; on each side separate assumptions will colour common belief ; the two parties will draw different con-

A

clusions from premises apparently the same, and dis-cover unconquerable divergence, where both seem to seek a common goal.

The issue, as it is one of the deepest by which human spirits are kept apart, so it is apparently one of the oldest. Almost the earliest event discernible to the straining eye of history in the dim twilight of the world's dawn is the schism which consummated what must have been the long experience of this divergence—which showed the twin children of young humanity that their paths lay in different directions and led them to part company and increase their remoteness at every step. The faiths of Persia and India, in their complete develop-ment, afford typical specimens, respectively, of that which looks upon Evil as an antagonistic principle to good, and that which sees it as a mere illusion; and during the centuries which the twin tribes who after-wards held these beliefs spent together in the high-lands of Western Asia they must have discovered the profound and far-reaching character of the moral differ-ences which, culminating in religion, influence the whole of life and thought. The Rig-Veda,[1] the oldest sacred book in the world, appears in parts at all events a record of this earlier condition, though its existence as

---

[1] The hymns of which the Rig-Veda is composed were collected about 1000 B.C., and must, of course, be themselves considerably older. Some of them are even supposed to express the beliefs of the Indo-Persian branch of the Aryan race before the separation of its two members, a view which would take back these utterances to the dim dawn of civilization on our planet. Their age is brought home to the mind by the fact that they contain not a single allusion to writing, a fact the significance of which, as Prof. Max Müller observes ("History of Sanscrit Literature," p. 497), will be obvious to the reader who recalls the frequent allusions to writing, "the book," &c., in the Old Testament. The geographical scene of these hymns is the Indus. "In India," says Dr. Roth in his address to the meeting of orientalists at Darmstadt, 1845 (translated by John Muir and published at Calcutta by Government), "the Veda occupies the place of Homer." This comparison gathers up the whole contrast of Indian and Hellenic life.

a scripture is subsequent to the separation. It depicts the dawning aspirations of young humanity, and would not, to one who knew no further development of the feelings there chronicled, suggest any latent divergence among those whose spiritual life it expressed ; but looking back from the developed faiths of a later day, we may find them both here in germ, though not with equal distinctness. If we take our stand on the religion of the Veda, we may regard the Pantheism of later India as the plant fully developed on its native soil ; while the dualism of Persia is a young shoot transplanted to another climate, and bearing evidence of changed circumstance and new influences. But both lay in embryo in one seed, and we find within the earliest religion of man the inchoate expression of the deepest divergence of these two ideals, as perchance we shall find in the most complete and perfected religion of man an expression of their fullest harmony. A primeval race finding in Light the symbol of all that is Divine was divided by the development of these tendencies into two branches, one of which found in Darkness the symbolic expression of evil, while the other saw in Darkness no more than the passing shadow which symbolizes man's weakness and illusion, and looked upon all creation as the outcome of one vast Unity. The two religions are perennial forms of human faith, but the symbolism by which they were expressed belongs to the circumstances of the infant race ; and for us, in so different a condition, it is not to be entered into without an effort of imagination.

Light and darkness form the great contrast of the outward world for all races and all generations, but the contrast, as it is exhibited to civilized eyes in the rhythmic succession of day and night, is no contrast of good and evil. A darkness which we can dispel at will, and which comes upon us amid the safety and conveniences of modern civilization, is a type rather of rest than of evil. But to a race for whom darkness meant helplessness in peril, the possible approach of the most dreaded foe, the alternation of light and darkness would repeat the familiar imagery of conflict, and associate the unseen powers of nature with recollections of defeat and victory. The dawn of a new day, to men who had no light but daylight, was the return into safety from a plunge into an abyss of peril ; the joy which hailed the morning must have gathered up into itself every association of deliverance, and become the type of all thankfulness and all worship. The different representations of this triumph were, by their very variety, fitted to give breadth and solidity to the impersonations which they created ; the one unique daily victory of light over darkness had its more gradual, more variable repetition in the return of spring ; and the combat was represented before the imaginative eyes of those early races in a still more vivid form, when in the dark thunder-cloud the principle of light seemed imprisoned, and then burst forth with dazzling suddenness. But the typical event representing the triumph of beneficent power was the dawn of day, and the hymns which greet it gather up all that a young and vigorous race can express of thankfulness, relief, and hope.[1] They breathe in every line the exuberant gladness of young life, unfettered by inherited ills, untrammelled by ancestral error, free to delight in all exercise of energetic strength, and abounding in effervescent power of enjoyment and of action. The vivid sense of life finds its exact and

---

[1] The translation of the Rig-Veda always quoted here is the latest, and the only complete one with any pretension to accuracy—" Der Rigveda, oder die heiligen Hymnen der Brâhmana, zum ersten Male vollständig ins Deutsche übersetzt mit Commentar und Einleitung von Alfred Ludwig, Prag, 1876."

expressive symbol in the birth of every new day out of the darkness, and seems to passo ver into a sort of surprise that the recall into activity and consciousness which the Dawn brought to the slumbering earth should not penetrate to the world of the dead. "She awakens to movement all living," [1] and that wide picture of rising activity in which the human and infra-human worlds combine reminds the singer of its limitations. "Yet the dead she revives not." [2] How expressive of eager reverence is that exception! Aurora, it seems, might be expected to have called back to life the inhabitants of the underworld. She is invoked by men to whom the distinction between sleep and death is not sufficiently familiar to be passed over in silence. She wakens the sleepers on earth—why not sleepers below earth? Light pursues its orderly and periodic victory over darkness; how is it that the mysterious principle which light symbolizes is baffled in the encounter with Death? Why, beside the transient shadow from which life emerges refreshed and reinvigorated, have we this supreme darkness from which there is no dawn? These thoughts, or others allied to them, repeat themselves in dreams, and the Dawn is invoked to banish them, [3] along with the other terrors of the night. The gladness of her approach is symbolized by the kindling of the morning sacrifice, and to the imaginative ear of the worshipper [4] the crackling flames greeted her with a joyous song, the flaming altar seeming to mirror and concentrate the flaming East; Agni, the god of Fire, is a divinity equal in importance to Ushas, the goddess of Dawn. Her healing, reviving power associated itself at once with the images of homely, naïve enjoyment, natural to a pastoral people, and the ideas of radiant

[1] Ludwig, 4, 9.   [2] *Ibid.*, 5, 8.
[3] *Ibid.*, 125, 18.   [4] *Ibid.*, 18, 2.

beauty belonging to awakening powers in an unspoilt
earth. The white radiance streams upon a world palpitating with welcome as the milk [1] is poured from the cow,
while the bold image, " with her advent the eye is born," [2]
sets before us the recurrent vision of beauty which she
seems almost as much to create as to reveal. Her approach is hymned in strains of glowing richness, which
suggests Guido's well-known picture of the classic
Aurora.[3] Other associations, equally familiar, touch on
her moral aspect ; the prayer to become the " Sons of the
Dawn " [4] reminds us that from the first the expression
" children of light " had its present typical significance.
For the most part, however, the desires of the young race
were child-like and unmoral ; their prayer to the new day
was for "joy in heroes, cattle, steeds ; " [5] their desire for
wealth is expressed with a fearless confidence impossible
to a race familiarized by long inheritance with the temptations and abuses of wealth. It had then none but pure
and healthful associations, and seems always connected
with desire for a numerous posterity. Earth had a
welcome for each new-comer, and the hopes of new
life balanced and compensated for the terrors of death.
All images of child-like enjoyment, of manly hope, of
moral inspiration and picturesque beauty, are united
in the hymn to the new Day ; [6] and the association of
the light with all that is most worthy of reverence has
remained ever since indelibly impressed upon the very
structure of language. Heaven means both the world
of light above us and the world of hope within us, and

---

[1] Ludwig, 9, 8.   [2] *Ibid.*, 16, 1.
[3] *Ibid.*, 18, 4, " Betreten hat sie den Wagen, den leicht angefügte Rosse
führen."   [4] *Ibid.*, 21, 4.
[5] *e.g.*, 15, 8 ; but the expression recurs often.
[6] See especially the whole of 5. Ver. 9 shows the mutual relations of gods
and men, "als du" (Ushas) "die Menschen, die opfern sollten, wecktest,
thatest du den Göttern damit ein gutes Werk."

the earliest name [1] of the Divine beings is simply " the bright ones." Such names are more than metaphors. But if they were simply metaphors they would show how closely the world without is adapted to express and render definite the yearnings and the fears of the world within.

The antagonism between Light and Darkness, though it was adopted later by the Persian faith as the symbol of that between Good and Evil, does not truly lend itself to a principle of dualism. Light is a full and adequate type of all that is felt as desirable by the spirit of man, so full and adequate, that it seems something more than a type ; it would appear rather the common expression of the needs of our dual nature than the description of any bodily need or satisfaction transferred to the realm of spirit. But the opposite of all this is not true of Darkness. However vividly the return of day brought back the sense of safety, however close was the association of darkness and peril, still it remains that the difference between light and darkness, as far as ordinary experience extends, is a difference only of degree. Absolute darkness is known only to the artificial arrangements of man and the ideal of the supernatural, it is a part of the horror of the dungeon, it is a characteristic of the imaginary underworld ; it has no part in the whole realm of nature. The symbolism of Light and Darkness, in a genial clime, measures truly the ideal of good and evil in the later Indian creed. But the Vedic belief took in instincts and emotions which later seem to have withered away, and uttered aspirations and desires belonging to the realm of the Conscience. We find ourselves here in contact with a race that felt the antagonism

---

[1] *Deva*, from the root *div*, to shine, meant originally bright. "The same word lives on in the Latin *deus*" (Professor Max Müller, "Lectures on the Origin and Growth of Religion as illustrated by the Religions of India ").

of duty, a race to whom Sin was a reality sufficiently
definite to associate the Divine power with the idea of
Redemption. The prayer for long life passes naturally
into the entreaty,[1] "extinguish our sins," as though sin
and death were already connected; we find even that
mysterious idea of inherited guilt[2] which is so perplexing to the moral sense. But the yearning thoughts
which turn to God[3] "as kine move on to their pastures" are speedily delivered from all that is oppressive
in that yearning. The pain of unsatisfied desire, already
familiar, is recognised as a mere subjective delusion.[4]
"Thirst came upon the worshipper, though he stood
in the midst of the waters."[5] Nothing was needed for
his satisfaction but the removal of his own blindness.
The doubt which interrupts prayer is transient,[6] the God
reveals himself at once—"Here am I, behold me! in
might I surpass all things." "Did I see the God who
is to be seen by all?" exclaims the worshipper,[7] with

---

[1] "Laszt fortdauern unser Leben, löscht aus unser Gebrechen" (32, 4
Ludwig). These expressions are found mainly in the prayers to Varuna, 81-90
Ludwig.

[2] "Die Verschuldungen, die ich mir zugezogen, sende weithin, nicht, mög'
ich büszen, was ein anderer gethan hat" (83, 9). "Lasz uns nach, was unsere
Väter Untreues gethan und was wir selber in eigner Person" (85, 5). This last
hymn appears in an English version by Max Müller, in the lecture on the Vedas
republished in the Selected Essays already quoted. M. Ludwig's translations
appear crabbed and often barely intelligible after the graceful rendering of his
countryman, to which, it must be added, he has always enabled the reader to
refer them, by a double index.

[3] MM. Rv. i. 25, 16; Ludwig, 82, 16. The meaning is much more defined
in the former.

[4] MM. Rv. i. 41, 4; Ludwig, 88, 4.

[5] Ludwig, 88, 4.

[6] MM. Rv. viii. 100, 3; Ludwig, 983, 3. Here the German seems to me the
more expressive—"Es gibt keinen Indra, so hat der eine und der andere gesagt,
wer hat ihn gesehn?" There is something very striking in the modern form
which doubt here assumes. The answer comes immediately, ver. 4—"Hier bin
ich, o Sänger, schau mich an hier, alles Geborene übertreff ich an Grösze."

[7] MM. i. 25, 18; Ludwig, 82, 18, "Dasz man sehe den Allsichtbaren, sehe
den Wagen über die Erde hin, finde er Gefallen an diesen Liedern mein."

joyous triumph. "Did I see his chariot above the earth ? He must have accepted my prayer." The prayer of the transgressor ascends with a sense of confidence to a God eager to forgive and awaiting only the justification of humble entreaty; while the human expiation is no arduous penance, only the trustful utterance of the psalm in which penitence is found as a mere parenthesis. We feel in perusing it as though listening to the confessions of children, with whom the penitent tear is forgotten almost before it is dry. The few chords in the plaintive minor succeed, and are followed by, a strain of which its inter-ruption only enhances the vivid hopefulness; and the dread of evil seems only just enough to intensify the leaning on supernatural power, to bind man to God. Life is strong, joyous, hopeful, full of activity, full of scope for activity; all natural desire is innocent, the object of Divine sympathy, or indeed, for a great part, of Divine participation. The Gods delight in the Soma drink, the psalms of the worshippers soothe them with placid enjoyment;[1] they hear without scorn the eager petitions for wealth, for children, for cattle; they show at moments the severity of the wise father to the erring son, but never the alienation of the monarch towards the rebel, never the blank hostility of the ruler towards the traitor. The sense of sin in these scriptures is fitful, evanescent, fragmentary; it finds no large consistent symbol, it is the expression of a small part of the nature, and it threw no dark shadow into the unseen. Evil appeared as an exceptional, fragmentary, fitful influence, the Gods could make it as though it had not been.[2] Man looked to the world of supernatural power

---

[1] "Wie der Wagenlenker das angebundene Ross, so lösen wir zur Gnade Varuna deinen Sinn mit Liedern" (Ludwig, 82, 3). Prayer is welcome to the god as rest to the weary steed.

[2] "'Deos fecit timor' dit le poëte latin. C'est une assertion que l'histoire ne confirme pas. . . . Il est possible de trouver une religion sans terreurs; telle

as wholly one of deliverance from evil. Varuna is able
to deliver man even from the sins which he has committed. The earliest litany of the human race[1] that has
come down to us confesses transgressions, but pleads
with the "strong and bright God" that through want
of strength his worshipper has gone astray. "If I
move along trembling, like a cloud driven by the wind
—have mercy, Varuna, have mercy." "It was not our
doing, Varuna," pleads the worshipper; "it was a slip,
an intoxicating draught, thoughtlessness"—never the
prompting of a mighty rival. Human frailty was subject
to error, but all that was strong was elevating.

It is interesting to trace this feeling in the symbolism
of Light and Darkness. While day was an object of
rapturous welcome, night was not an object of unmixed
horror. Side by side with the sense of peril in darkness we find certain inconsistent indications of what we
may call a more modern feeling towards it.[2] Though
sometimes the foe, it appears often as the sister of
Dawn; a sister whose dark steeds prepare[3] the pathway
for the glowing chariot of the Day; and who has, more-
over, her own revelation of light. Her coming unveils
the stars which fly away "as a thief" at the return of
morning.[4] "These constellations which are placed on
high, by night alone may we discern them; whither have

a été la religion de nos ancêtres Aryans" (Emile Burnouf, "Essai sur le Veda").
The allusion to a future hell is so rare in the Rig-Veda that it has been found
possible to deny, erroneously I believe, the existence of such an idea.

[1] Given in Max Müller's Lecture on the Vedas, republished in his Selected
Essays. Rv. i. 41, 9; Ludwig, 88, 2.

[2] "Usas kommt mit dem Lichte, . . . wegdrängend alle unheilvolle Fins-
ternisz" (Ludwig, 18, 2). But Night and Dawn are associated, 55, 1, "Weg
von ihrer Schwester Usas geht die Nacht;" 236, 1, "Usas und Nacht, die
beiden Hohen, Schönen;" and they are often named together as mutually
friendly powers.

[3] "Weg von ihrer Schwester Usas geht die Nacht, es macht frei die Schwarze
der Rothen die Bahn" (Ludwig, 55, 1).

[4] Ludwig, 127, 2.

they fled by day."[1]　Varuna commands the darkness as
well as the light in Heaven.[2]　Night is invoked as
the bringer of rest.[3]　Even the awful last night from
which the welcomers of the Dawn turned in terror was
not wholly devoid of gentle and gracious associations.
Night was the bringer of rest ; might it not be that Death
was also ?[4]　The beloved Dead was laid in the arms of
Earth as a child on the mother's breast ; she is entreated
to make room for him with an embrace, to enfold him in
her garment with the tenderness with which the mother
enwraps the child.　There is supreme desire in the
living to live, but there is no horror in the thought of
death.　Darkness, and all that darkness symbolized,
was a transitory phenomenon ; the light seemed the great
reality ; it was positive, actual ; where it was interrupted
it was not opposed by any antithetic influence, only
checked and hindered by something that was little more
than a symbol of the imperfection, the failure, the doubts
of humanity.　If we seem to make inconsistent assertions, it is because we are speaking of a state of mind
not perfectly consistent, of the rich confusion of an
awakening civilization, as yet uncommitted to definite
exclusions and distinct alternatives.　The Vedic faith
embodied two divergent ideas—the sense of conflict and
the sense of order ;—the moral life which centres in the
conscience and confronts an antagonism of being—the
spiritual life which finds its counterpart in nature, and
feels everywhere after one vast Unity.　But the two

---

[1] Ludwig, 81, 10.　　　　　[2] *Ibid.*, 87, 2.

[3] *Ibid.*, 131, 1, "Ich rufe zum Heile Ratri (die Nacht) die das Lebende zur
Ruhe bringt."

[4] " Begib dich hin zur Mutter Erde da, der weit geräumigen, heilbringen-
den, weich wie Wolle. . . . Spring auf, o Erde, press dich nicht nieder, gib
leichten Zutritt diesem, freundlich hieran dich krümmend, wie die Mutter den
Sohn mit dem Saume so, o Erde, bedecke diesen" (943. 10, 11). M. Burnouf
gives a more graceful translation of this hymn in his " Essai sur le Veda," p. 92 ;
it is perhaps the best known in the whole collection.

ideals were not equivalent.   The joyous spirit of the young race gave to the one a hasty, passing recognition, and lingered over the other, as expressing its deepest thought.   The sense of Evil, though it was distinct, was faint, and occupied but a small space in thought and utterance ; we somewhat exaggerate the general impression when we speak of it as a sense of Sin.

Perhaps it was the development of civilization which strengthened the belief in Evil.   Certainly there is something in the mere evolution of industrial activity to bring forward the part of life that belongs to disaster.   As nomad tribes became stationary and herdsmen tillers of the soil, the passage into a more arduous form of civilization brings with it a greater sense of all the opposition that nature sets up to the careful toil of man, and a wider illustration of all that thwarts and disappoints patient effort.   Even to a pastoral people the order of nature cannot have been entirely beneficent.   In the return of the seasons there must have been many a misfit between anticipation and result ; the visits of the celestial herds whom the storm gods drove onwards to yield their milk to the thirsty earth would not be so regular as the need for their presence ; the earthly herds sometimes failed to find their pasture because the heavenly ones failed to visit the empty sky.[1]   In this earlier condition order would be felt as infinitely greater than disorder ; but agriculture must always bring a different element into the feeling with which man regards nature.   He has, as it were, entered into partnership with the powers of the earth and sky, he regards their doings with a keener interest ; the general order, which was almost enough

---

[1] " The Iranians," says Dr. Martin Haug, " forsaking the pastoral life of their ancestors, became agriculturists.   Hence inevitable feuds between these tribes, for the settled agricultural races would be the sure mark for the freebooters among these nomads " (Haug's " Essays on the Sacred Language, &c., of the Parsis," second edition, 1878, edited by E. W. West).

while he had made no effort to modify the face of the land, discovers grievous want of adjustment of anticipation to event, when once he had embarked on this endeavour. The storm which would only have refreshed the pastures lays the crops low ; the drought of which a wandering people could have escaped the worst effects makes the harvest a melancholy record of wasted effort. Nor would this change take effect in the world of nature alone ; the mere growth of agriculture brings out the ideas of pro- perty and right, and with them gives occasion for new offences, of which an earlier civilization knows nothing. It is a far more advanced stage of honesty which respects the waving crops, their near and similar kindred the growing pastures being still accepted public property, than that which refrains from driving off the half-personal beings so closely associated with the home, and, as is evident in all early legends, playing a large part in mythic representations of orderly power in conflict with lawless power. The inconstant Heavens and the hostile brethren would thus become agencies of evil together. And thus the sense of conflict which had been there from the first, finding a developed symbolism in the world of nature, and a more frequent illustration in the world of man, passed into the sense of wrong.

We are thus driven to recognize in this early faith two ideas which, in their full development, are mutually hostile. No idea is more characteristic of the Veda than the conception of the Order of Nature as a Holy Order. The expression recurs constantly. The Gods are the " increasers and guardians of the holy order,"[1] a signi- ficant expression ; they are not its originators. The worshipper prays that he may share with them this

<hr/>

[1] The Açvina are addressed as " Mehrer der heil'gen Ordnung " (Ludwig, 68, 5). The reader is reminded of the " Mehrer des Reichs" of the Holy Roman Empire. So Mitra and Varuna are " Behüter der Ordnung," 100, 1.

Divine work.[1] Varuna, the god who stands in the
nearest connection to moral ideas, is the leader of the
Holy Order. These passages, and many in harmony
with them, breathe the spirit of an elevated monotheism.
If it be not literally true in human affairs that one law
implies one law-giver, we cannot conceive it to be
otherwise in the Divine world. The law may be, as we
often see in our own day, a more ultimate conception
than the law-giver; in fact, it was so in this dawn of
thought to which we recur. But a universal law and
a perennial conflict are inconsistent ideas. Yet the
Vedic belief embodies the idea of an original Unity, expressed in the Holy Order, and also dwells constantly
on the fact of a great continuous conflict, a strife
between the God of Light and some hostile power which
opposes itself to all the beneficent action of the warrior
god, Indra, who is Supreme God of the Vedic period.
The thunder is his voice, his aid is sought in the din of
war. Images of conflict are always associated with him;
it is by his darts that the black clouds which collect
before the annual rains are forced to let loose their
flow of longed-for water; and while the growling thunder
would seem his shout of victory, the flashing of the
lightning would express in some confused way the
triumphant principle of Light, wresting the treasure from
the dark power which was, by a symbolism not very comprehensible to our mind, represented as the withholder
of the precious floods which we should more naturally
regard as its gift. This power seemed to hold the
water-bag; Indra's flashing spear rent it open, and gave
the thirsty land its need, and the event most desired
by a people of shepherds and herdsmen was always
associated with images of conflict. In these latitudes

---

[1] "Mögen wir mehren, Varuna, des Gesetzes Brunnen" (Ludwig, 83, 5).

Heaven gave its longed-for boon only with the, storm. The blessed gift of nature, the life-giving rain, never known to India except with the accompaniment of thunder, seemed wrung from some reluctant and hostile power, of whose overthrow the re-emergence of the sun was a witness, the antithesis of light as good and darkness as evil being thus retained even under those aspects where to us it appears unnatural. The idea of a conflict thus inherent within the very being of nature is fundamentally inconsistent with that of a Holy Order, and the symbolism of nature expresses the development of the inward life. The progress of thought was towards the idea of the Unity of the Divine, and there can be no worship further in its spirit from monotheism than that of a warrior god. A prolonged struggle implies an adversary —not a mere disorderly mob of vague mutinous beings —but a rival. And so far as this idea was logically carried out, the conflict in the Heavens would change its character from the incessant triumph of a mighty monarch over the mutiny of a rebel crowd, to the duel between two great potentates equal in distinctness and analogous in claim. The Persian element in Vedism would thus detach itself from the parent stem. The halving of the Divine kingdom between hostile powers was abhorrent to the spirit which sought for Unity, and it would seem as though it were in the recoil produced by the discovery of this tendency within itself, that India plunged into the mystic Pantheism which belongs to her completed thought. History shows us Aryan faith in its infancy as an eager personification of the variety of nature, a glad, reverent recognition of the Powers expressed in nature as harmonious and convergent in their action; and then, again, it shows Indian thought in its completeness as recoiling from the idea of any multiplicity, any variety, and, above all, from any dualism, not only in the Divine Being, but in any being at all. We cannot but believe that in the interval something has rendered this particular branch of the Aryan race more a unity within itself, detaching from it some foreign element, and intensifying all that remained with a sense of contrast. We know, at all events, that in the interval the creed which ranges all Being under two heads had taken its rise, and when we add that the creed of India embodies a latent protest against this ethical antithesis, we do little more than interpret the hints that remain of remote events by the experience of all time.

For it is, after all, this interpretation which forms our chief material. We can know but little of the ethical development of the races that precede history, we could know nothing of it if it were a process confined to the experience of the infant world. But perennial experience lights up the dim records of the past, and the process here suggested by history is always going on among the human beings we know. A man may repeat the words of a creed with unhesitating sincerity, he would say at a certain stage that it expressed his entire conviction. Then suddenly its influence on another character flashes upon him its true meaning, and he repudiates it. He sees side by side his inconsistent admissions and his characteristic beliefs, and learning what it is that he denies, he first knows what it is that he asserts. To others he seems to have undergone a violent change. He himself, perhaps, is not conscious of any change, only of learning to know his own mind. But he is changed, a shock has influenced his direction ; he diverges from his old path, though often unawares. The shock has precipitated some element dissolved in his unconscious thought, and that which is left is a new thing, though it may seem to him only the old purified. The moral evolution is twofold. It is not only that the new faith is different from the old, but antagonism to it makes the old faith different from what it has been. Because the one party turns to the right, the other will turn to the left; latent tendencies become distinct, protest changes the proportion of belief, denial gives new meaning to assertion, and thus the varying aspects of a single creed become hostile faiths opposed at every point, and moulding life, where life shows no obvious connection with faith.

The primeval Aryan faith held in solution the religion of the conscience, and that of nature, combined in a seemingly homogeneous unity. The religion of nature recognized imperfection, the religion of conscience did not emphasize sin. But the union was an unstable one, and while one race awoke to the energetic definiteness of organized conflict, the other plunged deeper and deeper into the mystic repose of a vast unity accepted as the ground of all Being, and therefore as the harmony of all opposites and the end of all strife. The religion of nature was not Pantheistic in its origin, but as it recoiled from Dualism it moved towards Pantheism. The religion of conscience was not dualistic in its origin, but as it recoiled from Pantheism it moved towards Dualism. The latent Pantheism of the earlier creed would seem idolatry to those who believed that the rule of the supernatural was shared by a Power which it was a sin to adore, a Power which in all its manifestations should be the object of unfading hostility and protest. The definite dualism of the new creed would seem deadly heresy to those who believed that a Divine world surrounded and interpenetrated the human world, and that all good and evil were mere phenomenal distinctions, destined to fade in the light of a new knowledge. We can imagine how,[1] to the more ethical

---

[1] This view, brought forward in the most definite and historic form by

believers of the new creed, the faint distinction of good
and evil which marked the old, roused a fierce Puritan
zeal, while to the defenders of the old Faith this ignoring
of the Holy Order as the one ultimate reality would
seem the worst impiety and the most fatal heresy. We
know that the twin tribes separated ; the relation between
their separation and their difference of religion is a matter
of controversy. It is asserted by some students, and
strongly denied by others, that this separation was the
result of an impulse towards religious reform on the
part of the Persian race. The claim to arbitrate between
these two parties, as far as their difference is grounded
in questions of scholarship, is here emphatically abjured.
But in all historic questions a religion must be its own
best witness, and in default of overwhelming external
evidence, it is enough to say that we most naturally
explain the change between the earliest and latest
form of the Indian faith if we suppose that when the
early hymns which compose the Veda were first sung—
though not when they were written down—the ancestors
of the Puritans of a later age dwelt still among their

Dr. Martin Haug, and generally accepted up to a recent period, is vehemently
opposed by M. James Darmesteter, an elegant writer and ripe scholar, whose
verdict on such a question it seems presumptuous to dispute. "Dans cette
prétendue revolution religieuse," he says, "il n'y a qu'un accident de langage,"
and he tries to explain away, in a dissertation, which is to my mind the only unsatisfactory passage in his brilliant work, "Ormazd et Ahriman," the facts
that the *devas* of India become the *divs* or devils of Persia, that the great deity
of India, Indra, becomes the demon Andra, and that the great *Ahura*, who is
Ormazd, is one of the Indian group Asura, in the Brahmanic period the official
name of demons. The latter fact, he thinks, loses all significance when we discover that at the Vedic period Asura was the most august name of the Divinity ;
a discovery which appears to me only to confirm, in its most rational
form, the theory against which he contends—*i.e.*, that the *evolution* of Indian
thought produced the *revolution* of Persian thought. This view surely depends
not on a few etymologies (though even these can be got rid of only by very
forced reasoning), but on the whole spirit of the Persian religion, deeply
stamped as it is with the character of reaction and protest, and moulded on
an ideal wholly antagonistic to that of India.

Pantheistic brethren, and that these early psalms held the germ of hostile creeds.

This view serves to render explicable the change which came over the spirit of the Indian faith. The early Aryans saw God in the sunny and starry sky, in the dawn, in the thunderstorm, in all the various manifestations of Light that revealed the world in its new wonderful beauty to the eyes of an infant race. Their Indian sons, mindful perhaps of their severance from the race which had discovered Ahriman as a sharer with Ormazd, turned from all the variety of the outward to the sense of oneness within as the interpreter of the Divine.[1] Indra, Ushas, Agni, what were they all but the varied hues that tinged and disguised the one white ray? What was the multiplicity of sense, the continually varying manifestation of the world revealed by eye or ear, but the veil of that great central Unity to which consciousness was the clue and of which it was interpreter? For man only reaches the idea of complete oneness when he says " I." Nothing in the lifeless world, so far as we come in contact with it on our earth, can be called truly one. Wherever we contemplate any external object as a unity we either see or imagine the principle of life. A stone has no unity;

---

[1] This is the central doctrine of the Upanishads, a collection of theologic or theosophic treatises of great antiquity " which close the canon of Vedic revelation " (" Philosophy of the Upanishads," A. E. Gough). It is by them, says Prof. Max Müller, that his love for Sanscrit literature was first kindled, and he has enabled all English readers to enjoy them in his own lucid English in the " Sacred Books of the East." He is not the first of his countrymen whom they have thus impressed. Schopenhauer, though making acquaintance with them only at third hand, was profoundly impressed by them. They had been, he said, the solace of his life, and would be of his death ; and he anticipated for the Sanscrit literature which they represented to his mind an influence not less profound than that of Greek at the revival of learning. I have given a few references to these volumes, always numbering them (the Indian division being so elaborate) merely by their position in Professor Müller's translation, and sometimes omitting a few words.

break it and the two halves are each as much one as
it was itself. Fire has no unity; a hundred candles
may be lighted from it and leave it undiminished. A
tree has a certain partial unity; but the typical unity,
that which gives meaning to every other, is only to be
found in the personal world. Apart from life oneness
is something imposed from without, like the oneness of
a constellation. There is no principle of affinity in
brick and slate and timber whereby these constitute
a house; they become a unity only in relation to the
aim of the architect. Nothing in all the outward world
is one as a man is one; but only in so far as any
object is the result of human purpose, or partakes
in the principle of life, can it be said to be a unity
in any sense. And when we would understand even
the lifeless world we are driven to conceptions which
belong to the realm of purpose and will. *Force*, the
elemental material of science, has no meaning to us
except in so far as we construe it by our own experience of muscular exertion; that is to say, of something
associated with all the attempts of the self to impress
the world around.[1] We find the many in the world
without only by finding the one in consciousness within,
and then the one within leads us to a One that is both
within and without, a Being who is at once the centre
and the ground of all personal being. The unity of
spirit, as we know it, is combined with a plurality.

---

[1] "Our notion of force is a generalisation of those muscular sensations
which we have when we are ourselves the producers of changes in outward
things. . . . The liberty we have to think of light, heat, sound, &c., as in
themselves different from our sensations of them is due to our possession of
other sensations by which to symbolize them—namely, those of mechanical
force. But if we endeavour to think of mechanical force itself as different from
our impression of it, there arises the unsurmountable difficulty that there is no
remaining species of impression to represent it. All other experiences being
represented to the mind in terms of this experience, this experience cannot be
represented in any terms but its own" (Herbert Spencer, "Psychology").

Consciousness reveals the One, but experience reveals a plurality of conscious beings. "La pluralité des consciences," says an acute thinker, "est un postulat que l'on peut considérer comme acquis à la science sans demonstration."[1] The most consistent sceptic does not doubt the existence of other men. He feels a unity within; he comes in contact with an assemblage of phenomena which suggest a similar unity without; he does not question this testimony. We do not realize how much of what we mean by Faith is involved in this acceptance unless we discern that it is a step towards a larger faith. Is there no central unity, only a succession of partial ephemeral unities? Surely all these partial selves are but fragments of a deeper self;—*the* one, of which all other ones are but varied and partial manifestations. Nor can the lesser self attain a true unity until it finds its place in the greater self, or rather these two achievements are one.[2] It is incomplete till it know its incompleteness, it is a prey to inward conflict till it find itself part of a larger whole.

---

[1] Paul Janet, "Problèmes du XIXᵉ Siècle," p. 313.

[2] "As one finds lost cattle by following their steps, thus one finds out everything if one has found out the Self" (Upanishads, ii. 86). . . . "He who dwells in the earth, whom the earth does not know, whose body the earth is, *he is thy Self*, the puller within" (ii. 128). "When the sun has set, and the moon has set, and the fire is gone out, and the sound hushed, what is then the light of man? . . . The Self indeed is his light" (ii. 163). . . . "The wise, who by meditation on his Self recognizes the Ancient who is difficult to see, who has entered into the dark, who dwells in the abyss, who is hidden in the cave as God, he indeed leaves joy and sorrow far behind" ("Secret of Death," in vol. ii.) . . . "That Self is hidden in all beings, and does not shine forth, but is seen by subtle seers" (*Ibid.*) . . . "The wise, when he knows that that by which he perceives all objects is the great omnipresent Self, grieves no more. He who knows this living soul as being the Self, always near the Lord of the past and future, henceforward fears no more" (*Ibid.*) . . . "As the arrow becomes one with the target, so shall a man become one with Brahman, . . . know him alone as the Self" (ii. 37). "To him who is conscious of the true Self within, all desires vanish even here on earth" (ii. 40). . . . "That Self is Agni (fire), it is Aditya (the sun), it is Kandramas (the moon)" (ii. 243).

The course of thought here suggested is essentially the same, whether it guide the thinker from the many human personalities to one Divine ground of all personality, or, as in the order of History, from the many Divine impersonations to the one Divine Being who is the ground of all that is.   For the Indian mind, indeed, the difference between gods and men was one of very little distinctness or importance.   The earlier gods were not denied, they were accepted as all manifestations of the One.   The discovery of the one in the many marks the glad awakening of a national genius to the consciousness of its true direction, the forward bound with which the traveller enters upon the path which, after long wanderings, he recognizes as that which leads him home.

The best interpreter of Hindu religion is nineteenth century science ; the scientific movement of our own day presents us with a type of that change by which the many gods of the Vedas were absorbed in God.   Our fathers studied what they called the imponderable agencies—light, heat, electricity, magnetism ; they dealt with them as ultimate forces of nature, separate individualities, the results of which might be registered and brought into orderly sequence, but which themselves formed ultimate objects of intellectual attention, and were regarded as resting-places of all analysis.   Then arose on the horizon the great idea of the correlation of force. Light, heat, electricity, were seen to differ only as varied manifestations of the first great unity which we know as force, the mystic agency which seemed to link the worlds of matter and of spirit, the tyrannous power which brings anthropomorphism into Science, and bids her import into the world of things the impulses and efforts of the personal world.

We have seen the wondrous stimulus which has come to all scientific thought with the dawn of this

unity, the strange charm which invested all the revelations of nature, from the time that nature was discerned to be One. To be shown a single actual being
as the explanation of a multitude of phenomena, to
recognize one permanent entity amid many shifting
forms, one element through all its various modifica-
tions—this is the fundamental craving of the human
intellect. In our day, as in Newton's day, Science has
exhibited on a grand scale that triumphant substitution
of the one for the many which at all times she is labour-
ing to achieve on some scale ; and the world has drunk
in her teaching with something like intoxication in its
delight. But that delight must be a feeble image of
what was felt by our forefathers when, some 2500 years
ago, they awoke up to discover that where they had
imagined themselves to see many gods they had merely
discerned the aspects, the different attributes, through
which God appears to man. It is impossible for us to
recover the sense of originality with which this idea
must have come upon the world for the first time. We
cannot divest ourselves of the peculiar message of
the Semitic race that God is one. But to our Indian
ancestors it was a discovery, just as the correlation of
force is a discovery. No traditions brought them the
message, " These many gods whom you adore are but
the different manifestations of the one Power, just as the
various hues of the rainbow mark successively the partial
obscurations of the one white ray ; " it was a revelation
to the children of the dawn. The prismatic hues of
the Outward melted, before their vision, into the pure
white ray of the Divine.

It is possible that a change in the circumstances
of the Indian tribes gave this inward change its expression in the development of a new symbolism.
In the centuries which elapse between the composition

of the Rig-Veda and any subsequent record they were
advancing farther into the peninsula of Hindustan, and
becoming more familiar with the Ocean, of which the
earlier mentions are slight. Several expressions in
their later philosophy would lead us to believe that the
spectacle of the rivers swallowed up in the sea, yet never
over-filling it, was to them an impressive sight, pregnant
with a symbolic meaning.[1] It presented to them a kind
of parable of the many and the One—the continual
change of the ideas of sense, the unchangeable calm of
the reality of consciousness, receiving all, yet still itself
unaffected by the abundant variety. The Ganges poured
its ceaseless floods into the Ocean, yet the Ocean never
overflowed its shore; the unpausing hurry of the river,
the unchanging fulness of the vast expanse in which it
was swallowed up, might well become the type of that
contrast between the vicissitude of the world of perception and the oneness felt by all who turned to the
inward world. But whether or not the changed circumstances of the Hindus gave them a new symbolism,
their thoughts on the Divine certainty took a new
channel; their attention was diverted from the religion
of its earlier activity, the discernment that God was
One was the discovery that He must be sought not in
the variety of nature, but within the soul of man.

Hitherto we have been only tracing the universal
thought of humanity in a particular example. In proportion as men believe in the spiritual world they tend
to give it a centre, whether they call its inhabitants
human or divine. But to regard God as the One is not
necessarily to regard Him as the All. If logic seem
to demand the inference, it is possible to disregard it

---

[1] *e.g.* Mahabharata, xii. 7971 *ff.*, pp. 249, 250:—" Just as all rivers when
they reach the ocean lose their individualities and their names, and the larger
rivers swallow up the smaller, so are beings absorbed."

as an invader when we are considering the Infinite.
Logic, we may believe, is a law of men's thought concerning objects of thought which can be expressed in
adequate nomenclature; a guide, therefore, which must
be regarded as fallacious when we deal with that concerning which all language is not only inadequate, but
to a certain extent misleading. Considerations such as
these enable us to make room for the Not-God beside
God—to regard Him as in some special sense the
One, and yet to believe the Universe of Being contains
that which is heterogeneous with Him. But to the more
logical and less moral Eastern mind this was impossible.
If He were the One, He must be the All. There could
be no discontinuity of Being between Him and any part
of Being. A man was an exclusive unity. Oneness
was in him combined with negation, he was this and
not that. But in God the unity was absolute. He was
all of Being. The seeming antagonism which separated
from Him any part of true existence was as fallacious
as some turn in a river by which it should seem to
flow away from the sea. "Thou," exclaims the Indian
seer, overwhelmed with the spectacle of the Divine in
the Universe—"Thou art youth, thou art maiden, thou
art woman, thou art man, thou as an old man totterest
along on thy staff. Thou art the dark blue bee, thou
art the green parrot with red eyes, thou art the thunder-
cloud, the seasons, the seas."[1] There is something
wonderfully expressive in this stammering hurry of
enumeration, this gathering up of the great All in
some hap-chosen specimens as they struck the keen,
eager fancy of one who, as much as Spinoza, might be
called a God-intoxicated man. He feels that all these
things conceal God as much as they reveal Him; we
must not look without for any manifestations of His

[1] Upanishads, ii. 249, 250.

presence. "There is no image of Him whose name is great Glory; no one perceives Him with the eye."[1] "He is the ruler of many who seem to act, but do not act; He makes the one seed manifold."[2] He is the hidden light, of whom all other light is but the shadow; "like the fire of the sun that is set in the Ocean,"[3] the suffused glow that lights up the world, but has no visible centre. Or again, He is symbolized by that fiery principle which converted all to its own essence, and which seems to have been contemplated also as the principle of growth so inseparably united with heat. But the difference in these varied manifestations of the one is only seeming; the identity is actual. All that seems to separate man from God belongs to the realm of illusion; in proportion as man approaches the True he recognizes his own being as embraced and inter-penetrated by the Divine, and sees that, so far as he truly *is*, he is one with God. "There is one eternal thinker, thinking non-eternal thoughts; He, though One, fulfils the desires of many. The wise who per-ceive Him within their Self, to them belongs eternal peace."[4] This, in truth, is the escape from all the per-turbation of our deceptive phenomenal existence—this is the secret of true wisdom. "In that vast Brahma wheel," the outward creation, "in which all things live and rest, the bird (the soul) flutters about so long as he thinks that the self in him is different from the mover. . . . But when that God is known all fetters fall off, all sufferings are destroyed."[5] The conflict is ended. Man is one with himself, and unsatisfied desire is at an end.

The intellectual attractions of Pantheism are equally strong at all times. It must always be a temptation to

[1] Upanishads, ii. 253.   [2] *Ibid.*, ii. 264.   [3] *Ibid.*, ii. 265.
[4] *Ibid.*, ii. 19.   [5] *Ibid.*, ii. 236, repeated, 243.

explain the universe of Being by a single principle; by setting all that exists on one level of claim, to make a clean sweep of all preliminary distinctions of a *right to be.* But as a doctrine satisfying to the moral nature, it will appear in very different aspects according as it is viewed in different states of society. For an inhabitant of London or Paris, familiar with the development of poverty and crime which our modern civilization forces on the attention of every one, the thought that God is *all* can surely never come as a gospel. Nor is it easy to imagine human beings so different from those we see around us as to delight in the thought that the Divine meant no more than the sum of all their own impulse and desire and all the circumstances which surrounded them. But perhaps this is partly due to the weakness of our imagination. Where nature is more genial and the needs of man are simpler and fewer, life is much less full of struggle, and there the circumstances of average humanity contain less to make it a mockery to regard the All as Divine.[1]   "As the sun, the eye of the world, is not contaminated by the external impurities seen by the eye, thus the one Self within all things is never contaminated by the suffering of the world, being Himself apart."[2]   To imagine the Divine Being contemplating unmoved "the sufferings of the world" would seem to transport into the Divine the worst attributes of humanity. But it depends partly on what the sufferings of the world are. And however we explain it, we must accept the fact that this belief in Pantheism came upon the early race as a great gospel for humanity. There was a sort

[1] " In India," says Max Müller, " the earth without much labour supplied all that was wanted, and the climate was such that life in the forest was not only easy but delightful. Several of the names given to the forest by the Aryans meant originally delight or bliss " (" Lectures on the Origin and Growth of Religions as illustrated by the Religions of India," 1882).

[2] Upanishads, ii. 19.

of rapture of repose in their belief that God was All, and to the Hindu repose was joy. After severance from the active Persian race, the delight in activity so marked in the earlier Scriptures seems to have gradually dried up. Perhaps a tropical climate opposed itself to all delight in activity. But though the world without might strengthen the delight in repose, this feeling had its source in the world within. It was the characteristic of a race that sought above all things the unity of the absolute, and turned from the various, the eventful, the multiform, as from the realm of illusion, the realm in which sojourn was inevitable, but in which it was impossible to find a home.

We can trace the association of this delight in repose —partly as cause and partly as effect, or rather perhaps in that deeper correlation which lies below the idea of causation—with all cosmic theory, and through cosmic theory on all moral aim. For the Indian mind there must be no event of transcendent importance in the history of the Universe. God is no Creator. The world is not a creation, but a growth. It has not been made, it commemorates no act of conscious will, no exertion of definitely directed power. Its origin is indistinct, a subject for vague surmise, for a confession of perplexity, for merely negative statement. The Hindu gazed backwards into the dim dawn of the Universe, and saw that " Being was not yet, nor Not-Being ; the atmosphere did not exist, nor the firmament above it. Where, then, was the world ? Where were the waters, the gulf which no plummet may sound ?[1] Death was not yet, nor therefore could there be immortality ; night and day " (their earthly types) " were indistinguishable." Only one belief was positive—the primal unity must have been there already.

---

[1] This hymn (Rigveda, x. 129), which has been frequently quoted, is given from M. Darmesteter's "Essais Orientaux," p. 205. He says that in the writer, " Pascal eût reconnu un frère, Spinoza lui eût tendu la main."

" A breath arose self-moved ; it was the One ; there was
nothing beside that One, nor above it.   All was darkness.   Enveloped in night, the Universe was but an
indistinct wave.   Whence came the ray which gave
shape to the world ? . . . Who knows ?   Who can say
whence issued this creation ?   The gods are younger ;
who, then, can declare its birth, or say whether it had a
Creator ?   He who from the height of the world surveys
the world, He knows ; or perhaps even He knows it
not." Nothing in the whole range of human speculation is
more sublimely consistent than this audacious agnosticism.
God is so far from being the Creator that He is not even
cognizant of the fact of Creation.   Sometimes Creation
and dissolution are represented as the breathing of God,
the coming forth and drawing back of His life in orderly
and harmonious exchange of expansion and contraction.
" When this God awakens, the universe accomplishes its
acts ; when He slumbers, plunged in a profound repose,
the world is dissolved." [1]   The differences of such views
are, from our point of view, unimportant ; their common
element—the negation of all Will in the origin of the
Universe—is that upon which the moral influence of
belief turns.   There is no stamp of Divine sympathy
upon work.   The world of incident lacks the one initial event which associated God in the activity of man.
No Indian teacher could ever say or feel, " My Father
worketh hitherto, and I work."   His aim was rather
to attain the eternal repose of the Divine—a repose not
alternating with and dependent on labour, as all repose
which is actually known by man, but something deeper—a
sort of sublime passivity, which knows no intermittence.

Creative impulse was no part of the Divine character,
and therefore work was no part of ideal humanity.
There was no Divine sanction on effort, no sacred sig-

1 " Institutes of Menu," i. 51, 52."

nificance in labour. It was associated with servitude, with social scorn and religious contempt. And then again history lost its importance, events had no Divine significance. "There is," says Professor Max Müller,[1] "no taste for history in India, still less for biography. Home life is shrouded in a veil which no one ventures to lift, while public life has no existence. On the other hand, fable and myth are marvellously busy in the East, and though Rammohun Roy has been dead only fifty years, several stories are told of him which have clearly a mythical character." Here we see the indifference to fact which is a result, indirect indeed, but not remote, of the belief that the One is the All. The realm of difference becomes insignificant, unworthy of careful attention. What matters accuracy in reference to the world of illusion? All event is unreal, myth has a deeper truth than fact. A transcript from experience can have none but unimportant truthfulness, but myth expresses wisdom. The truth of thought is so exclusively the Hindu ideal that it shuts out all care for accuracy of fact.

There is in all national morality something that illustrates that law by which the image of some bright object is impressed on the closed eye in reversed light and shade. The life of India reveals this Protestant tendency in more than one direction; the spirit of a true unity seems continually to bear witness against an exclusive and monotonous unity. "They who believe not in the identity of Being have fallen into a deep night, but they who believe only in its identity have fallen into one yet deeper. There is a recompense for those who believe in the identity of beings; there is another for those who believe in their difference."[2] This striking

---

[1] In an article, I think, in the *Contemporary Review*, March 1885.

[2] This passage is quoted by M. Adolphe Francke, in his very interesting "Études Orientales," 1861, as a quotation from the Veda, translated by B. St. Hilaire, but I have not been able to identify it.

passage is an instance of most rare union of insight
at once into a truth and into its opposite; the Indian
was apt to forget that "those who believe only the
identity of Being have fallen into a deep night;" what
we find for the most part is a protest against all
diversity. "The rivers in the sea do not know I am
this or that river;"[1] in like manner, man has as his
aim to escape all that is individual, to be "merged in
the true," *i.e.*, lost in an Ocean of Being wherein all
difference shall be swallowed up. "There is no bliss
in anything finite,"[2] and so it would seem there is no
reality in it. By a subtle development of this passive
spirit the idea of conflict is exchanged for the idea of
endurance; courage stiffens into asceticism. The contrast of good and evil, only dimly present at any stage of
this religion, wholly vanishes, and its place is taken by the
contrast of the real and the unreal. The world of sense
is seen as a fleeting vision; only what lies beyond it is
worthy of the attention of man. But the religion which
confuses God and man sets up lines of ineffaceable distinction between man and man. This harsh separateness
of the Hindu system of caste is not so much an exception
to this unifying tendency as a natural recoil from it.
Truth neglected in one direction must be exaggerated
in another, and a tendency which, carried to its logical
outcome, becomes destructive to society is always liable
to sudden and complete inversion. In the very first
glance at Indian literature we are struck by the confusion
between the human and divine worlds. We remember
with difficulty in any legend or myth which of the
personages are divine, which human; there is no clear
dividing line between the natural and supernatural

---

[1] Upanishads, i. 102.

[2] *Ibid.*, i. 123. The definition of the Infinite follows:—" When one hears and
sees nothing else" (when all sense of diversity is lost), "that is the Infinite."

sphere.   The divine combatant is revealed by his
superhuman strength, but awakens no surprise by his
supernatural nature.   It is a part of the same ideal that
there should be so ineffaceable a difference between the
Brahman and the Sudra.   The Divine oneness satisfied
the instinct which seeks unity, the human world was
given up to an opposite principle.   The whole system
of things in which we live is a mere fleeting phenomenon,
a ripple on the Ocean of Being, a rainbow in the eternal
light; within this system the Indian sought no unity;
that could only be discerned from a point beyond it.
The world of event was the world of illusion.   "If the
slayer think that he slays, if his victim think that he
is slain, they are both of them in error."[1]   The insignificance, the transitoriness of life suited well with the
hopeless division of the caste system.   The only thing
of value in it was the recognition of the Divine, and
the sacred caste set apart to bear witness to this was
naturally separated from all others by an impassable
chasm.

The caste system of Brahmanism is an emphatic assertion of Predestination in its most absolute form.   Birth
fixes the whole of life; to be born a priest, a warrior,
an artisan, a labourer, is to have marked out the whole
of fate and the bent of character.   The Sudra who sets
before himself the virtues of the Brahman commits deadly
sin, he disturbs the order of the universe.   The distinction of "the elect" and "the reprobate" lies at the base
of this system.   The lowest class is born and must
remain in sin; its members have no right to share in the
common rites of the superior castes; the Brahman is
even forbidden to accept their offerings.   If a Brahman
marry a Sudra "he sinks into the regions of torture;"

---

[1] Upanishads, ii. 11.   The passage has been versified by Mr. Muir in his
metrical translations from Sanscrit texts.

hell is the penalty for an unlawful condescension from the high to the low.[1] "The self-existent created the Sudra merely for the sake of the Brahman ; servitude is innate in him (the Sudra) ; who, then, can take it from him ?"[2] His whole duty is comprised in obedience to the higher class. He has no concern with religion ; the Brahman may *take* any of the Sudra's property if he need it for sacrifice, but must not *accept* it ;[3] if it be contributed to ritual observance, it must be involuntarily. The arrogance of the priestly caste is not left to take care of itself, but is ensured by a number of minute precepts, enjoining on men who live only to teach the meaning of holiness the mingled scorn of the Pharisee and the *Ancien Régime*—the hateful pride of righteousness combined with the vulgar pride of birth.[4] Scorn was needed for the defence of their pre-eminence ; it was the buttress of their virtue. "Better one's own duty performed ill than the duty of another performed well,"[5] is a sentence which occurs more than once in the sacred Indian code. In the sense in which we read the words there is a truth for all time. Better that a parent should perform the duties of a parent very imperfectly than that he or she should allow a child to govern. Better a very poor piece of handiwork than hands set to do the work of feet. But whenever we can say this we must feel duty rooted in the deep part of the nature. It must be either a claim resting on a broad human basis, like that of human kindred, or else on a deep inward vocation, like that of character. In the mere distinction of class the better mind of modern Europe sees nothing to be emphasized, nothing which natural endowments may not traverse. English aristocracy itself is a record of continuous infusion of a new element, it lives by that

---

[1] "Institutes of Menu," iii. 17.   [2] *Ibid.*, viii. 413, 414.
[3] *Ibid.*, viii. 417.   [4] *e.g., Ibid.*, ii. 119.   [5] *Ibid.*, x. 97.

very receptivity which Brahmanism abhors. Our Peerage is powerful because we open its doors to every form of capacity, because, in a word, it is not an Order. In India a member of the priestly caste was separate from a member of the servile caste by a chasm that could be bridged by no extremity of virtue, since the only possible virtue for the servile class was that spirit of docile submission, which, in attempting to quit this caste, he must lose. The Sudra who set before himself the virtues of the Brahman committed deadly sin, he disturbed the order of the universe—that order of human separateness which has succeeded to the Holy Order of Nature, and to which an equal loyalty was due.

We need no more emphatic testimony to the sacredness of the caste system in Indian feeling than the fact that India rejected Buddhism. What is Buddhism? It is, if we leave out its protest against the caste system, the completed development of all those impulses and instincts which we have endeavoured to set forth as characteristic of Indian thought.[1] It is the yearning for an escape from the bondage of desire carried out to a hope of escape from the trammels of existence. However we explain Nirvana[2]—whether or not we contrive to avoid, in interpreting it, the idea of absolute annihilation—still we must feel it a consummation of that negative ideal of life of which every utterance of the Indian is an expression. It is a gathering up of all the

---

[1] It is a striking testimony to this spirit that it is nowhere more evident than in this very Code of Menu, which contains so much that is directly hostile to it. The idea of Renunciation shines through the harshest assertion of privilege; *e.g.*, ii. 95, "Resignation of all pleasures is far better than attainment of them;" and there are several passages which equal the Christian Scriptures in the ideal of forbearance and forgiveness.

[2] "Le Nirvana," says Eugène Burnouf, the great authority on Buddhism, "est pour les Théistes l'absorption de la vie individuelle en Dieu, et pour les Athées l'absorption de cette vie individuelle dans le néant. Mais pour les uns et pour les autres le Nirvana c'est affranchissement suprême" ("Introduction à l'Histoire du Buddhisme Indien"). It is literally "blown-out-ness."

longing for rest, for silence, for escape from individual
limit into the desire to escape from all that we can
recognize as life. " Even in heavenly pleasures the
awakened finds no satisfaction, the disciple who is fully
awakened delights only in the destruction of all desires." [1]
Victory " breeds hatred, for the conquered is unhappy.
He who has given up victory is happy." [2]   " Those who
love nothing and hate nothing have no fetters." [3]   Everywhere the Desire is the *fetter*.   Freedom is found not in
enjoyment, but in renunciation.   The deliverance from
Self is the sole aim for the enlightened soul ; all else is
worthy of effort only in so far as it furthers this.   The
Indian ideal of negation is here at its height.   The life of
Çakya-Muni, the Indian prince who gives this ideal its
concrete illustration, sets forth this aim in its fullest accom-
plishment ; he leaves the joys of home, of marriage, of
paternity, to wander forth as a homeless mendicant ; he
has all this world can give, and he renounces all, trans-
lating into a splendid abdication the theory of surrender,
which, in its degree, must be the aim of each one who
knows the secret of blessedness.   His reward is to
teach suffering humanity the path of a true redemption—
the path to Nirvana.   However hard for a Western reader
to conceive that Heaven should mean the extinction from
which it seems to us hardly less natural to shrink than
from pain, yet we cannot but feel Nirvana the consummation of all those aspirations which we have endeavoured to
trace in following the development of Indian philosophy.
Buddhism is the essence of all that gives its moral interest
to Brahmanism.   Whence, then, was it treated by Brahmanism as its deadly foe ?   How comes it that, though
Indian in origin and in feeling, Buddhism has been

---

[1] Dhammapada, 187. Some part of this sacred book of the Buddhists is
believed to be the utterance of the Buddha himself.
[2] *Ibid.*, 201.   [3] *Ibid.*, 210.

driven from India to find its home among men of another race? There can be but one answer—its attack on the cherished caste system of India. In all else the two religions are at one. In the position of Çakya-Muni there was nothing original,[1] he was but one of those ascetics who had from immemorial time wandered homeless in India; his belief in transmigration, the basis of his gospel of Nirvana, was shared by him with other Indian teachers; the only novelty in his position was that he was a preacher, and by that fact alone an enemy to the caste system. " My law is a law of grace for all,"[2] he answered when taunted with the wretchedness of his converts. " Come unto me, all ye that are weary and heavy laden," seems to have been the animating spirit of his attitude towards all. In the Order founded by him, or, at all events, which grew up out of the crowd of disciples attracted by his preaching, the most wretched and despised slave could find a home, so that the aspirations nourished by the caste system were satisfied while all their limits were defied, the outcast found his place in an organic system, the human atom was the member of an Order. But this order was essentially a creation of spirit; the outward order was defied. " Is there," asks one of the lower caste, in a Buddhist legend[3]— " Is there between a Brahman and another man the difference of gold from stone? He has not issued from the ether or the wind, he has not burst forth from the

---

[1] " Il se présentait comme un de ces ascètes qui depuis les temps les plus anciens parcourent l'Inde en prêchant la morale, d'autant plus respectés de la société qu'ils affectent de la mépriser d'avantage " (" Introduction à l'Histoire du Buddhisme Indien," par Eugène Burnouf, 1844).

[2] *Ibid.*, p. 199.

[3] Given in Burnouf. The Tchandala (one of the lowest caste) has asked the daughter of a Brahman in marriage, and provokes an outburst of rage and hate from the Brahman, " Comment oses-tu demander l'union du plus noble avec l'être le plus vil?" The answer of the Tchandala has some passages curiously recalling the denunciations of the Pharisees by Christ.

earth, he is born of woman, as is the member of the caste
he most despises." It was the declaration of this truth,
and this alone, that made Buddhism a heresy.

In truth, no doctrine ever provokes a deadlier hatred
than that which opposes itself to the spirit of caste. It
thereby offends at once the low and the high impulses of
humanity. For the instincts which entrench themselves
within this rampart are not by any means altogether evil,
they are wrought up with the profoundly moral conviction
that " we are members one of another." The ideal of caste
is closely bound up with that organic character of virtue
which our own day, with its worship of equality, is but
too ready to overlook, but which can never be neglected
without a general lowering of all arduous ideals of
virtue. Nothing can be more elevating than the exposition of the duties of the warrior caste as given in the
Code of Menu, though it is streaked here and there with
strangely contrasting precepts :—" No one should in battle
slay enemies with concealed or poisoned weapons ;" [1]
" The warrior is bound to respect weakness, to pity even
cowardice ; " " That king is dead from whose kingdom
the people crying out are carried off by savages ; "
The chief duty of a warrior is the protection of the
people ; [2] " That king goes to hell who in exercise of his
sovereign power will not meekly bear reviling." [3] The
ascetic Brahman in like manner must bear a reproachful
spirit with patience, must speak reproachfully to no man ;
abused, he must answer mildly, he must be to all the
pattern of patience, high-mindedness, and spiritual devotion. The high castes are appointed to set forth the
excellence of their special virtues, they are to be to all
below them a luminous illustration of the meaning and
beauty of goodness. This is the aspect of caste to all

---

[1] " Institutes of Menu," vii. 90 ; *cf.* 91-93. [2] *Ibid.*, vii. 143, 144.
[3] *Ibid.*, viii. 313.

who find it attract the nobler part of their nature, an aspect without which it could not gain any permanent hold on the spirit of man. For nothing, we may be sure, that appeals wholly to the vulgar and self-centred elements in humanity keeps its hold on the human heart from generation to generation. The temptations that assail the mere self in each one of us are permanent only in their hostility to what is highest, in themselves is nothing enduring, they change their character from age to age, nay, from hour to hour. The institutions which human beings cherish and defend have pushed their roots into a part of the being below the limits of selfishness, though they may owe some nourishment also to this surface stratum of life. They could not obviously and irresistibly sway human desire if they had no connection with its vulgarest source, they could not retain their hold of a Nation, if this were all.

Of all the various forms taken by the spirit that identifies the one with the many, but not with the All, the family and the nation alone escape the baser temptations which creep in with the association of self. Hardly can it ever have happened in the whole course of the world's history that it might truly be said of a man's love for his country, " He loved not wisely but too well." In the literal sense of the words they cannot indeed be applied to any love; but even in that sense in which they are consecrated by the pathetic utterance of a jealous love suddenly revealed to itself as ignorant and erring, they have no place with reference to patriotism. A nation is indeed a limited being; it is conceivably possible to make the love of one the hate of more. But the love of the nation is the love of the neighbour. It is the love of all whom we have, in ordinary life, any power to help or hurt. It turns all beneficent effort into the same channel with knowledge and power, it leaves outside of interest those only whom interest would not profit. Such feeling is in its nature expansive. It finds within its scope the greatest possible variety; it can permit itself to grow rigid in no single attitude, it must look down, it must look up, it must accustom itself to the level gaze of equal right, to reverence for authority, to pity for weakness, to indignation against crime. All these things are found within the sacred enclosure of a Nation, all these feelings must be associated with the fervour of patriotism, and we may surely conclude that the character in which they have found their fullest exercise must be ready for all new attachment, must have become responsive to every claim and sensitive to every appeal. The love of the Nation is the love of humanity in germ. But nothing of this holds good of the class. Here the limit is the most conspicuous fact in the enclosure. The love of the Nation, we have said, is love of the neighbour; the love of the class is often scorn and hate of the neighbour. "He who declares the law to a servile man and instructs him in the mode of expiating sin sinks with that very man into hell."[1] Where could hatred breathe a deadlier spirit than in that declaration from the sacred Indian code? Here we see in ambush the fiercest spirit of persecution; here, long before the appearance of the Buddha, we come in contact with denunciation of all that was holy and beneficent and potent in the preaching of Buddha. It is as if the Indian worship of Unity had foreseen and denounced, as a fatal misconception, that spirit of unity which sought the redemption of all mankind. And with the hatred of baffled privilege and defeated arrogance there yet mingled, we may be sure, some element of the nobler feeling that comes in wherever men have learned to say "We" instead of "I," and to exchange

[1] "Institutes of Menu," iv. 81.

the narrowest forms of selfishness for something wider. There was the feeling that the break up of caste obligation "would cause the universe to shake,"[1] that Order must perish, if the limits of the high and low were confounded. And hence, though Buddhism was, in all but its neglect of the caste system, a mere carrying out of what is most characteristic of Indian thought, yet this one exception made it the object of deadly hostility to Brahmanism, and though the religion of a third of the human race, it is now the religion of a minority in India.

Buddhism is, in fact, no more than the purely spiritual half of Brahmanism, purified from that reactionary tendency which shows itself in the distinction of caste. It is the reassertion of the primal unity, against that element of rigid distinction which arose partly as a kind of guarantee to the practical side of human nature against the all-obliterating wave of the Infinite, partly as a protest against that ultimate antithesis of good and evil which is always the most dangerous foe of Pantheism. The condition of things in this world is a mere fleeting phenomenon, a ripple on the great Ocean of Being, a rainbow in eternal light. Within this cycle of fugitive phenomena no great distinction must be introduced dividing the actual from the conventional, the transient from the eternal, because that has been done once for all in recognizing the whole of life as transient and illusory. The substitution of virtues for virtue which marks the spirit of caste is the ally of the spirit of Pantheism. Virtue thus becomes something relative, temporary, earthly. The virtue of the warrior is one thing, that of the labourer another; the slave has no other virtue than docility and obedience. Goodness thus broken up and divided loses its distinctness as part of a great antithesis; there is no idea of a con-

---

[1] "Institutes of Menu," viii. 418.

flict of good and evil. And it is this idea of conflict which forms the stumbling-block to Pantheism.

The antagonist of this spirit of unity is not the belief in multiplicity, but the belief in dualism. It is not difficult for the many to be absorbed in the one; this process is a very natural one. That which resists it is the antithesis suggested by desire and fear, more especially by the desires and fears which belong to the realm of the conscience. All desire, it is true, is not moral; the larger part is not. But all desire is the material of morality, all suggests the antagonism of good and evil. The Indian clearly recognized this antagonism in all desire to the mystic Unity in which he found his life, and treated it consistently as a danger. The " pairs of opposites " are the object of continual warning in the " Divine lay "[1] which embodies the more dramatic form of Indian wisdom ; all wish and aversion are there treated as the opponents of truth. And so in a very important sense they are. To a Being of pure intellect Evil would be inconceivable. So far as man is purely intellectual he desires truth, but it would be a very forced and unnatural way of expressing this to say that he dreads error or ignorance. Ignorance is to him a mere nega-

---

[1] The Bhagavadgita, or " The Lord's Lay " (to give it the name chosen by its latest translator), is an episode in the Mahabharata, the Iliad of India, and has the special interest for an English reader of having been the medium in an English translation (1785) of awakening interest in Sanscrit literature. It is an address from the Divine Being to Arjuna, a warrior prince, who in the hour of battle shrinks back from the duty of slaughter and needs the Divine warning, impressing on him the insignificance and illusory nature of all event, before he can rouse himself to take his place as a *K'schatriyia* at the head of his battalions. It is an interesting and impressive illustration of the close connection between the caste system and Pantheism. A comparison between this lengthy discourse spoken on the field of battle and the gleaming Theophanies of Homer brings out strongly the undramatic character of Indian thought, drama melting into philosophy on the one hand, as philosophy melts into drama on the other. The warnings against the " pairs of opposites " occur constantly, *e.g.*, iv. 23. The work is translated in the " Sacred Books of the East." I have also consulted what appears an admirable translation by John Davies (1882).

tion, and just so far as his mind becomes wholly intellectual he loses the sense of any difference between
ignorance and error.   This is the explanation of the
fierce antagonism exhibited at all times, and so conspicuous in our day, between the love of truth and the love
of a truth.   " I cannot conceive," said a celebrated man
of science of our day, when he was speaking to a person
who expressed a *dislike* to his theories—" I cannot conceive feeling either like or dislike to any theory whatever."   Perhaps it was not literally true either of the
speaker or of any actual man, but it would be true of
any one who dwelt in the region of pure intellect.   Is a
theory true ? let us believe it.   Is it untrue ? let us leave
it alone.   There is no antagonism here.   If the hatred
of error appear side by side of the love of truth, then
assuredly we have entered on a moral region.   We
thus enter a territory where the right borders on the
wrong, not on one in which the True is the whole of
reality, and the False a mere vacuum.   And to a people
whose whole life was in the latter region, the spirit of
Desire was the one antagonist to be dreaded ; it was
opposed by a fierce asceticism, which strove boldly to
conquer by inverting this antithesis of hope and fear ; it
turned the earlier courage of conflict into the channel of
endurance, and strove to demonstrate, by exhibiting this
eager pursuit of what was hated, that desire and fear
were mere temporal accidents, interchangeable at will—
incidents of the temporary, the transitory, and therefore
misleading as guides to the Eternal.

Thus it was that the ideal of India, though it started
in the worship of the Light, seems to attain its development rather in the worship of the Night,[1] for thus surely

---

[1] "πλείστοις δὖντοῖς εἶναι λόγους περὶ τοῦ θανάτου," said Megasthenes,
the Greek who was sent on a mission to India (cir. 300), in describing the
Indians (Strabo, xv. 59).   Such a contrast to the Hellenic spirit would impress
a Greek.

we may most truly symbolize that mystic yearning which seeks the revelation of the Divine not in the daylight of reason, but in the pause of an entire silence and passivity throughout the whole being. Unity becomes conscious of itself, it quits the world of appearance, it enters into the background of reality behind appearances. We have cited a text from the earlier scriptures in which the disappearance of a constellation at the return of morning is mentioned with a kind of surprise.[1] The discovery that "Light can thus deceive" seems to have dawned on the mind of the Aryan with something of the sense of a mystery that is so finely expanded in the sonnet from which we take these words.[2] It would be altogether out of harmony with the fresh, outward simplicity of the Rig-Veda to make much of this single allusion to the revelation of darkness. And yet it seems impossible not to accept it as an unconscious prophecy of the course which later thought was to follow. The faith of India turned from the seen to the unseen ; if this hint of a sense of Light as the concealer was a mere accident, at all events it was an accidental touch which gives the clue to the labyrinth. A potent influence beckoned the Indian race away from the realm of the Outward, curtained off the invasion of eye and ear from a realm where the spirit might study the mysteries which lay in the depth of its own being. The world of event, of observation, faded and became remote, and the thinker was alone in the world of thought in which he found his home. Duty became almost a negation. The moral life was one of pure receptivity. All effort was needed for the one great work of man—to make a vacuum within for that mighty

---

[1] See back. p. 10.

[2] " Why do we then shun Death with restless strife?
If Light can thus deceive, wherefore not Life?"
    —*Sonnet by Blanco White.*

tide of God always surging up into every human heart
that was open to receive it. To this belief God was the
universal agent; man had but to cease from exertion, and
the Divine life would flood his own with its inexhaustible
wealth. "When a man sleeps here," says the mystic
teacher, "he becomes united with the True, he is gone to
his own Self."[1] The silence of sense is the revelation of
spirit; the outer eye must be closed before the inner eye
can be opened. "He, the highest Person, is awake in
us while we are asleep."[2] There is a curious fable many
times repeated in these sacred scriptures which would
seem to set in the strongest manner the supremacy of
the passive over the active principle in man. The senses
strive with breath for the pre-eminence, and are successively defeated; that is, we may suppose, the principle
in man which connects him with the outer world, which
fosters the exercise of will, which is associated with
desire, is a part of the lower order, of the deceptive unreal world. "A wise man should keep down speech and
mind."[3] He should make room for the evolution of the
primal unity by repressing all that is individual—all that
belongs to the world of the many, all that records the
separateness of individual being, with its hopes and
fears, its futile activities, its illusive centre of creative
influence. The need of Humanity was a deliverance
from all that was multiform, a simple recognition of that
mysterious ground of all being, so near the consciousness of every man that its least misleading name was
the Self.

It is not without a great effort, both of the imagination and the reason, that we come near enough to the
doctrine here set forth, either to agree or disagree with
it. It is apt to seem not merely erroneous, but mean-

---

[1] Upanishads, i. 98.   [2] Ibid., ii. 19.
[3] Ibid., ii. 13.

ingless. How can we cease from our own personality? What is the meaning of this teaching which would rob us of ourselves? We find it difficult to construe to imagination any concrete result of such exhortation, and turn from it impatiently, as from mere words; and yet the words meet us from very different quarters, and we are forced to believe in some common ideal, which appeals to the most various minds and the most remote ages. Fénelon and Madame Guyon repeat the lesson of the Indian mystic,[1] and again we find it in the raptures of Mohammedan piety. And there are phases in most human lives, if they pass beyond a merely child-like or outward experience, which light up the fervours of mystic piety with an illumination rendering them intelligible to many who could not use their dialect. No one, surely, ever looked back on some action that he recognized as wrong without feeling, " I have followed too much the devices and desires of my own heart." He has substituted the Individual for the Universal. Where Personality should have been quiescent, leaving place to Law, some gust of individual feeling has broken in, and disturbed the harmony of things. The great maxim of the moral life formulated by a philosophic teacher, " Act so that thy principle of action could become that of every moral agent," can never be translated into experience by any one desiring to leave the impress of his own individuality on the structure of circumstances. " Do unto all men as you would they should do unto you " may be so read as to encourage each man thus to impress his own individuality on the world; but it means, in fact, the same as Kant's maxim, it bids us invert the impulses of individuality, test them by their effects, see them in another mind.

---

[1] The reader of the Buddhist scriptures is constantly reminded of Thomas à Kempis.

He who has ever truly sought to put himself in the place of another has, unless he has merely identified himself with another, risen above the differences of human beings towards the common platform of Humanity. My enemy has wounded my feelings, mortified my vanity, injured my interests, and an opportunity has arisen where I might in some degree do unto him as he has done unto me; it is easy for every man to persuade himself at such a crisis that he is following the precept of Kant, if not of Christ. It may seem for the advantage of all that this man should be made to recognize what he has made me suffer; we may place ourselves so close to our own interests that they may seem the interests of Humanity. But when we look back on such a course after long years, we see that we have thus looked at the individual, where the object of our own view should have been the moral commonwealth of our kind. My enemy, it may be pleaded, is an individual as much as I am. Yes; but when I endeavour to respect his rights, to imagine his excuses, to consult his interests, I am driven perforce out of the confines of individuality into the realm of the human. I quit the enclosure of idiosyncrasy for the open space of common desires and fears. How can it be otherwise? I have no other clue to the desires I seek to gratify. Between us, as separate individuals, there is nothing but repulsion; to find our common gravitation I must turn to that which is a characteristic of catholic humanity.

The law of truth is here the same as the law of love. What is all party spirit, all fanaticism, all prejudice, but the intrusion of choice into the realm of passivity? "Surtout messieurs point de zèle," though the warning be spoken by worldly lips, is one constantly needed by the seeker after truth. Truth, as much as Right, if indeed they can be severed, demands the sacrifice of individual choice,[1] the silence of individual activity ; it demands that creation of a vacuum which we have discovered in the material world to afford one of the mightiest forces, and which we must learn in the same way to recognize as a power in the spiritual world. When Paul proclaimed with stammering and pleonastic eagerness which often broke down grammar and logic that man is justified by Faith, he saw what the Indian saw, that God is everywhere pressing around man like the atmosphere, that wherever man empties himself of his own choice, his own notions, his own opinion, God fills the vacuum with Himself. And over and over again, in the progress of the ages, this discovery has burst upon some human spirit as it did upon Paul's, and has given an equal energy and resonance to his call to his brethren to come and share his joy ;—for the joy and the message are one, the truth is in its very nature a truth for all.

1 The most interesting illustration of the truth here suggested is to my mind the word *heresy* (αἴρεσις). Its original meaning of choice or election remains as an unconscious protest, embedded in the very structure of language, against the tendency of man to impress his individuality on his belief, and bears witness to the deep principle which we can express only as an audacious paradox, that in some sense Free Will must often be regarded rather as an infirmity than a power.

CHAPTER II.

PERSIA AND THE RELIGION OF CONFLICT.

In reviewing life we often find our thoughts carried back to a time when we lived in close and satisfied union with some whose voices .now come faintly towards us across a wide interval, yet without being able to recognize any violent change of belief or feeling, either on their side or our own. We remember a sense of sympathy, of common ground, which seems strange to us now. We see in looking back that every step carried us farther apart, though we hardly know how to account for the divergence. Perhaps this may be the feeling of both sides. It sometimes happens that the mere growth of thought brings out the strongest antagonism between two who during long periods of their intellectual journey could travel almost hand in hand. But more often probably one party feels that this gradual growth in the other has brought about a reaction in his own mind, and opened his eyes to the presence in his own creed of assumptions between which he was forced to make a choice. For all belief, all thought, is a development ; words which we could have echoed with perfect sincerity when their latent tendency was hidden from us may become hateful falsehood by the mere opening of that vista. We are often taught by facts that the words in which logic has failed to discover a flaw are the very opposite of our deepest convictions ; we thus learn to regard Truth and even Error (which is indeed but a parasitic growth of Truth) not as a set of opinions, but as a living organism. We come to see that whenever this ceases to be the case with any belief, then it can be called neither truth nor error, but an empty formula, a withered husk, that can tell us nothing of the germ from which it has parted company, nay, that may often lead to utter misconception as to its very nature.

Such a process must be familiar in our own day to many persons. Probably there never was a time when it was not going on more or less, for the twilight of one form of thought is always blending with the dawn of another, and men are constantly discovering that they have confused the two. All reformers, probably, have begun by aspirations that they have discarded as the progress of their own thought and action have acted upon each other, and shown them what it was that they were really attacking, and what it was that they actually sought to embody in life and fact. The discovery which thus separates many between whom at one stage of their progress sympathy was apparently complete is an incident of the development of thought throughout all history. But it can never have been so striking as in that remote age when the young race first awoke to the nascent antagonism within itself of the most fundamentally antithetic religions; never again could a reformer recoil from any creed with the same energy of protest as he who first discerned that the progress was towards an obliteration of the distinction of good and evil.

The Persian, if we have rightly seized the clue of his thought, was the first to give to belief the distinct outline created by denial. He first confronted a *false religion.*[1] The faith of later India is an important modi-

---

[1] The neighbourhood of heresy is clearly impressed on the pages of the Zendavesta (now made accessible to all our countrymen in M. James Darme-

fication of the faith of the Veda. The faith of Persia
is manifestly a recoil from the ripened and developed
faith of the Veda; it is distinctly a Protestant religion. Doubt, we have seen, was familiar long before,
but with the division of the two races there arose for
the first time the idea of a *wrong belief.* The beliefs
thus contrasted are the most antithetic of all beliefs.
The dividing question of all thought is—In this universe
of life and sense and feeling have we to do with a unity
or with a dualism ? Is the familiar contrast of right and
wrong, good and bad, a misleading expression for the
mere fact of more and less, or does it express a fundamental truth ? This was the question in which the two
races found their division line. India saw at the root of
all existence a vast unity, disguised under the multiplicity
of Nature ; Persia saw a profound Duality, carrying on
the struggle of Conscience beyond the boundaries of the
phenomenal world. On the one hand, the Indian faith
discovered everywhere the unfolding of a single principle ;
it recognised no other antagonism throughout existence
than the distinction of that which seems and that which
is. On the other hand, the Persian faith took up the
position of that faculty in man which keeps its arduous
watch on the boundary of good and evil ; every step was
an approach to or progress from a deadly foe. In the
legendary history, the mythology, the moral standard, and
even in the actual history of Persia we see in its fullest
development the kind of belief and character which springs
from and which again results in the ideal of warfare,
of struggle, of the choice between good and evil, the life
of the Conscience, the constant appeal of Duty with its

steter's translation in the "Sacred Books of the East," vols. iv. and xxiii., to
which all the following references are made), *e.g.* :—" It is a sin worthy of many
stripes to teach one of the faithful a wrong creed " ("Sacred Books of the East,"
iv. 172). It is true that the date of this passage is uncertain, but it seems to me
in accordance with the spirit of the whole.

shadow of sin, the sharp and all-pervading antithesis of Right and Wrong.

The idea of conflict does indeed haunt all mythology; all the heroes of legendary lore triumph over some incarnation of malignant destructive power, or some guardian of hidden wealth. Even in India, the least prone of any nation to the idea, we have the legendary conflict of the Mahabharata side by side with the mythic conflict of Indra and Vritra. But when we turn to the Persian faith, this conflict expands to fill the whole space occupied by the history of this world. It arose in conflict, endures in conflict; it is thus to end. Legend and myth alike are absorbed by the idea of a continuous struggle pervading all existence, the antithesis of good and evil runs through all creation with an exact equivalence, so that the evil world represents no mere mutiny against the good,[1] but a hostile power, confronting it from without; it ceases to be the expression of human failure, it becomes an ideal of all that against which human effort is directed. The conflict between the powers of good and evil began with the creation, which was itself the result of their discovering each other; the material universe is a bastion placed in the empty space which is between the two principles. The work of creation is an exercise of rivalry between these powers; the fair and fruitful regions called into existence by Ormazd became object of a kind of inverted imitation on the part of Ahriman; each new exertion of the creative power of

---

[1] " Le védisme connaît des forces mauvaises, il ne connaît pas des forces méchantes. . . . Le mazdéism a précisé: son démon fait le mal pour le mal : sa méchanceté est 'désir de destruction' tout ce que créera Ormazd deviendra la mire de son effort, sa méchanceté est organisée par la bonté d'Ormazd " (" Ormazd et Ahriman, leur Origines et leur Histoire," par James Darmesteter, 1877, pp. 9, 10). See also p. 244. Where no other reference is given, this treatise is the justification for any statement given here which needs a historic reference.

the beneficent Deity becomes the occasion of a like
exertion on the part of his opponent ; so that we must
think of the worlds of good and evil as opposed in
symmetric equivalence throughout all existence. The
whole of life is seen through this medium of fierce
antagonism. As Ahriman is opposed in deadly hostility
to Ormazd in the opening of the great drama of the
world, so the most important event in the course of
history is his antagonism to Zoroaster, and the victories
of both the God and the Prophet are blended in common visions of apocalyptic splendour, preluded by those
images of horror which naturally characterize the last
outbreak of hostile power before it is swept away for
ever.

Zoroaster is the representative of Ormazd on earth,
an incarnation of righteous law, of moral purity, of the
spirit, that is, which in face of evil is one of unresting
conflict. Before his birth his mother has a vision of
fearful wild beasts approaching to attack him,[1] and is
only reassured by his voice addressing her in tones of
encouragement, the portent being fully justified by a life
of struggle crowned by victory at every point, but assailed
with fierce persistence by all the powers of evil. He is
the first inhabitant of the material universe who proclaimed the word by which the demon is to be overcome.[2]
He is the object of a double attack from Ahriman, first
as a deadly foe, second in the more dangerous character
of the Tempter. "Zoroaster,"[3] says Ahriman, "is the only
one who can banish me from this world ; he smites me
with the mystic word as with the lightning." Vainly in
Ahriman's effort at resistance does he aim at confounding

[1] "L'Avesta, Zoroastre et le Mazdeisme," par Abel Hovelacque, p. 142,
1880 :—"La voix de l'enfant lui-même vient la rassurer."
[2] Zendavesta, translated by Darmesteter, "Sacred Books of the East," vol.
xxiii. 201, 2.
[3] Ibid., 274, 5 ; the passage is here in paraphrase merely.

the Prophet by his own weapons, assailing him by mystic
enigmas which would seem to symbolize the doubts
infused by the spirit of negation, weapons that would
be most deadly against the seeker after truth.   Vain
are his subsequent overtures of peace.[1]   " Destroy not
my creation, O holy Zoroaster.   Renounce the law of
Ormazd, and thou shalt possess the sovereignty of the
world for a thousand years."   " Never," declares Zoroaster,
" will I renounce the holy law ; no, not though my body
and soul should be shattered and crushed in the struggle."
And his recital of the mystic word, the invocation which
is the weapon of Faith, drives Ahriman to the depths of
hell.   Zoroaster is the revealer of the Law, the human
expression (as Ormazd is the Divine expression) of the
revealing Light, or, from another point of view which
hardly is another, of the revealing word ; for language is
to thought as Light to the material universe ; and silence
and darkness are the same negation expressed by a different symbol.

The victory of the Prophet is succeeded by an apparently final defeat, and completed by a miraculous
revival which needs that blackness of disaster to enhance
its splendour.   He is not an immortal being.   The
legend of his death takes various forms, according as it
is regarded through a mythic or a legendary medium ; he
is the victim of some hostile force human or divine ; his
life closes as it opens, in storm ; the lightning flash,
which is the weapon of the Demon as well as the God,
reaches him at last, and he perishes.   But the storm
which is the death of Light is also its birth.   In many
forms the hero rises from the tomb.   The spirit which
survives defeat and turns it to gain is incarnate in
an avenger, generally the brother or son of the dead
hero ; himself, that is, in another form.   Or else the

<hr>

[1] Vendidad, 19, 1, 6, 7.   " Sacred Books of the East," vol. iv. p. 206.

same idea takes shape in an aspect familiar to us. We know how often an earlier mythology, throwing its confusing shadows on history, takes possession of some actual hero, and hides him in mystic seclusion, whence it foretells his glorious reappearance as the conqueror in a conflict which shall bring in the final triumph over all that is conceived as evil. Persian mythology knows many a kindred hero with Arthur and Barbarossa. The daily resurrection of the dawn, the yearly resurrection of the spring, the sudden outburst of light from the thundercloud, all combined to leave on the imagination and hope of the Persian an ideal of the final triumph of light, expressed in one form among many as the awakening of some warrior from what had seemed the sleep of death to a new and more glorious activity. The hero seemed dead; he was but wrapt in slumber. He is to appear, when least expected, as the triumphant destroyer of evil.

For in all these dreams of a hero wrapped in death-like sleep there lies hid in germ the conception of a saviour of the world. The revival is always to be something glorious and mysterious, something fitted to herald the dawn of a brighter day. But the faith in a renovated future—in a "restitution of all things"—suggests the prophecy of some divine hero who has no other office; it concentrates itself in a being who is affiliated by inheritance with the past, but who himself belongs to the future which he is to herald. In the Persian faith this saviour of the world is a son of Zoroaster not yet born, who is to bring in that age in which the desires of all hearts shall be fulfilled. The appearance of the Deliverer is preluded by a storm of all the ills of this life, such as is painted in the apocalyptic visions of the New Testament. The days are shortened, the trees and plants lose their fertility, the world is ravaged by wars, enough blood is shed to turn the mills. A terrible winter draws on, lasting three years, bringing such bitter cold, such storms, that man and beast shall perish and the earth become a desert. But the night, the winter, the storm, are the heralds of a reign of eternal unclouded Light. When the tempest has raged itself away Ahriman has disappeared. The conflict of the ages, intensified in this last hour of the world's history into a combat between all the powers of good and their antagonist, is ended in a victory so complete that it conceals its own greatness; the world of evil has vanished; the Earth is renovated for the spirits of just men made perfect, and the long night of the world gives place to an eternal day.

Here, then, Dualism bears witness to its own incompleteness. We see that the religion of conflict, if it is to be in truth a religion, must keep before itself the hope of victory. The primal unity, banished as an actual basis of the world in which we live, returns as an ultimate hope, Darkness is the invading shadow, Light is the enduring reality. The whole course of the world's history, in comparison with that glorious morrow of the resurrection, is but one long night. The race has greeted the daily returning light with daily hope, but the curtain of night has been lifted on deadly strife, on crime, on wretchedness of every kind, the light of common day is, as it were, polluted by the deeds in which it has appeared as an accomplice; and the naïve joy with which primitive man greeted the dawn of common day is transfigured into a mystic hope for the "mighty dawn" which is to herald a brighter day than that of this world.

The very symbolism which expresses two principles is an implicit assertion of the predominance of good.

The abyss of light was a reality, the abyss of darkness was a logical creation, a supposed antithesis below the earth to that Heaven of brightness above it, an infinite expansion of the darkness of the tomb. Darkness itself was not a logical creation, that was real and terrible enough, but it was the logical imagination which condensed and intensified it into a principle and gave it an equivalence to the opposite world of light. There was no need, in like manner, for the Persian to discover a Divine Ruler over all things ; that belief seems to have been as old as humanity; at all events, as the typical humanity of the Aryan race. But the antagonist of this Divine Ruler is a new creation ; and this is the special work of the Zoroastrian creed. It gave distinctness to the ideal of right by first conceiving of the world of wrong, and then by intensifying this world into a central individuality. But note how the eternal laws oppose themselves to a false completeness in this antagonism. Ormazd is a much more simple conception than Ahriman ; Ormazd is akin to Varuna, he is the all-Father of Aryan worship. Ahriman is a mythic personage moulded on a contrasted ideal and transformed by the neighbourhood of his divine antagonist. But the antagonism is, after all, incomplete. Ormazd is Light, Ahriman is Darkness ; Ormazd has discernment, foreknowledge, Ahriman is blind.[1] The equivalent antagonist of Ormazd should be the spirit of lies. But Ahriman is saved from that by being the spirit of ignorance. He is accurately the spiritualized ideal of darkness, for darkness does not deceive, it only hides. Thus science is for ever on the side of Goodness, and the victory is certain. The antagonism of Light and Darkness, even when it is endowed with an ideal completeness which nature does

---

[1] "Bundahis," ch. 2., translated by E. W. West, in "Sacred Books of the East," v. 5.

not supply, gives no accurate model for an antagonism of Truth and Falsehood. And the metaphysical development of the religion repeats this lesson of its origin. With the process of rationalizing reflection a primeval unity arises behind the primitive dualism; Time, or Destiny, is the source both of good and evil, of Ormazd and Ahriman. Then the allegory is forgotten, and the impersonation of Time [1] becomes a conscious being who craved for a son, and Ormazd was born to him as the result of his sacrifices. Ahriman was the son of his doubts. A mysterious being is thus revealed to us even beyond this impersonation to whom these sacrifices may be paid. In every direction we are reminded that all Dualism, where it is based on a moral order, is compelled at last to bear witness to Unity. That which is a unity shall remain. Division is a property of the transient, even though it be a characteristic of the whole stage of our being that is passed on this world.

But to look forward to victory is not to deny conflict. There is the widest possible gulf between the religion which allows that struggling is transient and that which urges that struggle is unreal. The spirit that denies Difference is separated by a whole world of feeling and belief from the spirit which hopes for an ultimate unity, " If the slayer think that he slays, if the slain think that he is slain, they are both of them mistaken," is the verdict of Indian wisdom on the conflict of life, but Persian wisdom sees strife as the great reality of all experience; strife in the world without, and not less in the inner world, in which India sought its type of Unity. India described God as the Self, but Persia saw in the Self not a Unity, but a Dualism. That strange

---

[1] The sect of Zervanites who referred the two principles to Zervan (*i.e.,* Time) became orthodox in Persia in the fifth century of the Christian era.

but yet familiar experience by which, at the very depth
of our own individual being, we are made sensible of
multiplicity, that mystery by which Self seems at once
to lose and to double its meaning, is the true clue
to the Persian religion. "I have plainly two souls,
O Cyrus," says a Persian soldier in the earliest specimen of the historic novel that has come down to us,
"for a single soul cannot be at once good and bad." [1]
The "Cyropædia" is a mere romance, but it was written
by a Greek who knew Persia, and these words may be
taken as gathering up the aspect of Persian feeling as it
revealed itself to the soldier-pupil of Socrates.   He was
awakened by the teaching of his master to an interest in
the moral life of those among whom he sojourned ; and
though he knew the nation only in its military aspect,
he here records that consciousness of struggle which,
if we may trust its most ancient scriptures, was the
dominant influence in its moral life.

It is not only belief which is different according to
the apprehension of evil ; the whole world of duty and
of desire is influenced by the difference.   The object of
yearning and hope, in the Indian ideal, is the life of
repose ; all moral aspirations turn towards quiescence
of will, and the giving up of that which marks individual personality.   The Persian blessedness is the exact
opposite of all this.   It is found in the life of strenuous
activity, of resolute exertion.   Persian religion is, if we
sum up its tendencies in a single word, the religion of
will,—the religion which seeks everywhere to impress
personality on the world of things, which sees the
Universe of Being as a field for the exercise of choice,
which discerns through all the varied colouring of life the
fundamental contrast of light and darkness.   We appre-
hend this faith most distinctly when we give a large place

---

[1] Xenophon, Cyropædia, vi. 1, 41.

to its element of protest. The injunctions to industry, the elaborate provisions for agriculture, the constant stimulus to exertion of every kind,[1] are most intelligible when we see in them a recoil from the faith which appeared to this active race a confusion of good and evil.

We might express the contrast of the two religions with a certain exaggeration, but with a real indication of what is characteristic in each belief, by saying that India turns towards the ideal of Death, Persia upholds in every varied form of its manifestations the worship of Life. India craves a surrender of all independent existence, Persia reiterates the sanction on all that is individual, vivid, personal. Life and Death are not here the rhythmic breathing of the Supreme God, but the varying victory of the good and evil powers respectively. A spirit of keen activity penetrates the whole world of duty, every faculty is to be kept at the highest point, all that opposes itself to energetic life is seen as a spiritual foe ; thus even protracted sleep is the work of the demon Busyaçta with its " long hands " holding men back from vigorous exertion.[2] All that is not good is an enemy of good. Death is to the righteous the entrance on eternal joy, yet Death itself is to this vivid, life-loving religion an object of horror. The double feeling thus aroused is brought out in the account of the pilgrimage of the faithful soul who has " come from the material world to the world of the spirit, from the decaying world into the undecaying."[3] Even in those raptures there is a tone of

1 " He who does not till the Earth of Zoroaster with the left arm and the right, to him thus saith the Earth, 'O man who doth not till the Earth of Zoroaster, ever shalt thou stand at the door of the stranger among those who beg for bread, and wait there for the refuse that is brought to thee'" (Zendavesta, Fargard, iii. ; "Sacred Books of the East," vol. iv. 29).

2 " Busyaçta . . . runs with long hands from the north region, saying 'Sleep, O man ! Sleep ye who lead a sinful life'" (Khordah-Avesta, Frag. 39 ; Bleeck's translation of Spiegel, ii. 139 ; see Darmesteter, p. 181, 2).

3 Zendavesta ; "Sacred Books of the East," xxiii. 314-318.

solemnity, of awe, in the reference to Death. "How didst
thou depart this life, thou holy man?" he is asked by
one who is gone before, with a profound glance backward to the homely pleasures of Earth that is full of
pathos. "How didst thou come from the abodes full
of cattle, and full of wishes and enjoyments of love?"
And Ormazd interposes to keep that reminiscence unspoken. "Ask him not—him who hast just gone the
dreary way, full of fear and distress, where the soul and
the body separate." It is the way on which man tastes
more bliss than all that is enjoyed in the life that is
ended: but there is a horror in the thought that it is
the way of Death. The body is no burden which it is
a release to lay down. There is a solemn shudder in
the thought of that divorce even in the blessedness of
Heaven.

For, in truth, the fulness of achievement, the strain
of tense endeavour, of unremitting activity, which
belongs to this ideal is exactly that which appears to
man inseparable from the life of this world. When we
contemplate an existence beyond the grave, we have to
imagine the pure life of spirit, a life remote from all
images of activity and exertion such as we most easily
conceive. The Persian religion, almost alone among
the religions of antiquity, made immortality a definite
and vivid hope by joining to it the belief in a human
Resurrection; yet even so it could not but pay the tribute
of this reverent awe to the separation of the spirit from
the associate and implements of its active days. No
other religion sets so deep a stamp of importance on the
activities of this life. When the great Persian host
gathered up its shattered strength for its last struggle
at Platæa after the departure of Xerxes, a banquet given
by the friendly Thebans brought Greek and Persian
side by side, and left on the page of the historian an

expressive utterance of this yearning after achievement.
"See'st thou this host?" asks the Persian noble, addressing
his Greek neighbour. "All shortly shall perish, and leave
but a few survivors from the vast multitude." "Surely,"
urges his neighbour, "thou shouldst communicate this
knowledge to the general of the army." "My friend,"
answers the Persian, with a flood of tears, "the effort
were in vain. This is the curse of life, with abundant
knowledge to accomplish nothing."[1] In that lament
we discern clearly the aim of the *historic* nation, we feel
ourselves among the people whose rise marks the start
of the narrative of civilized human life, as a single
sequence of connected events. When we turn from
India to Persia we have crossed the barrier that separates
the men who breathe philosophy from the men who make
history. On that side no chronology, no definiteness,
no narrative. On this everything is definite, everything
is expressed in terms of time and space, of before and
after, of event and circumstance. There the ideal is
resignation, silence, repose; here it is courage, speech,
activity. India, we have allowed ourselves to say, has
no history; we may say, with the same kind of one-sided
truth, that history begins only with the rise of Persia.
There must have been great events in the previous ages;
the rise and fall of great nations is impossible without
them. But the historian may ignore them all, till he
comes to the race that worshipped Ormazd and dreaded
Ahriman.

It is the fierce swoop of Persian invasion which
overcomes the mutual repulsion of the Hellenic States

1 ἐχθίστη δὲ ὀδύνη ἐστὶ τῶν ἐν ἀνθρώποισι αὐτὴ, πολλὰ φρονέοντα μηδενὸς κρατέειν (Herodotus, ix. 16). Grote, who quotes this passage, points out its antagonism to the Greek ideal. The way in which Herodotus mentions the name of his informant, and the fact that the latter was said to have told others what he told the historian, surely justify us in believing that we have here a genuine Persian utterance.

and welds Greece into a nation. Even for the history
of England,[1] says a thinker who has very little sympathy
with classic life, the battle of Marathon is more important
than that of Hastings.   Alone of the empires of Asia,
Persia must be recognised by the student of European
history.   Xerxes is an image almost as familiar to our
imagination as an English king ; his words have become
proverbial among us ; we feel him to belong to the
classical world.   He, almost as much as Homer, may be
called the author of Greek unity.   With his appearance
on European soil, all that in the most typical sense
we recognise as History takes it rise.   Before that
event we have isolated facts and vague surmise ; after
it History is consecutive, coherent, organic.   We might
almost say that no history is so historic as the tale of
Thermopylæ, of Salamis, of Platæa.   None other condenses into so narrow a space the destiny of States, the
lessons of national experience, the images of colossal
hopes, and not less colossal achievements.   It seems
a rehearsal, in its most condensed form, of the drama
of History, before the stage clears for its detailed representation.

The strong historic spirit of Persia is equally manifest also in that glow of legendary narrative which is
but the penumbra of history.   The scholar[2] to whose
industry Western Europe owes its knowledge of these
legends as a whole gives as a reason for their wealth
the extent of Persian conquest, the mingled vicissitude
and continuity of Persian dominion, and the magni-

---

[1] "The battle of Marathon, even as an event in English history, is more
important than the battle of Hastings.   If the issue of that day had been
different, the Britons and the Saxons might still have been wandering in the
woods " (" Dissertations and Discussions," J. S. Mill, ii. 283).

[2] M. Jules Mohl, whose French translation of the Shah-Nameh, "Livre des
Rois," enables the reader to enjoy these legends with all the effortless interest
with which he peruses contemporary fiction.   The references here are to the
first edition in folio.

ficence of the monuments by which it is recorded;
—all strong conservative influences no doubt, yet we
may perhaps regard as the strongest one not mentioned
in his enumeration, the spirit of a faith which in its
protest against the confusion of good and evil marked
all action with a stamp of praise or of blame. Narrative becomes vivid when events are regarded as
important. In India we cannot say that any event
is important. There is a great wealth of tradition
there; the epic which embodies it is the longest in the
world; but the interest that it has for the Western
reader lies in its being a repository of philosophic thought
rather than a narrative; the best-known portion of it is,
indeed, a striking testimony to that negative ideal which
is opposed to the historic spirit. In its assumption
that the temptation of the wise and good is to a profound resignation which would amount to civil suicide, it
takes the heart out of all history and even all legend; and
its protest against this temptation renders the testimony
only the stronger. Nothing can be more undramatic
than these Indian legends; they melt into vague thought,
glowing description; the events seem to fade as one
tries to grasp them. The legends of the Shah-Nameh,
on the other hand, are full of vivid dramatic interest,
of sharply contrasted character, of distinctly conceived
action, of elaborate plot and clearly marked design.
The only episode well known to the English reader—
the pathetic tale of Sohrab and Rustem [1]—is not, perhaps, a very typical specimen. The father and son who
encounter each other unconsciously in battle—the heroic
warrior who, with yearning in his heart for the father
known to him only by description, is prevented by
treachery from recognizing him when they meet on the

---

[1] "Cette histoire d'un père et d'un fils que ne se reconnaissent pas a fait le
tour du monde" (Mohl, Preface).

battlefield, and learns his name only in receiving from
him his death-blow—these touching images of heroic
disaster are not characteristic samples from the drama
of the conflict of Iran and Turan. They seem rather to
express a sort of unconscious protest against the religion
of conflict, to hint that the fierce blow may be given
ignorantly, and may perchance wound a beloved son.
This is the lesson of a large part of life, and the
animating principle of much that is most interesting in
history and drama. But it is not characteristic of a
keen eye for the struggle of virtue with crime to perceive distinctly the hardly less frequent struggle of virtue
with virtue. The ideal of the Shah-Nameh is utterly
unlike that of either classic or of chivalric romance. We
find here a curiously modern type of feeling; magnanimous forgiveness meets gigantic crime, generally to
fall as its victim, but always to bring out its meaning
by contrast with its extreme opposite. In no classical
epic, probably in no other epic whatever, does ingratitude
play so large a part. Zohak, the wicked king of the
Arabs, begins his career of superhuman wickedness by
yielding to the temptation of Ahriman and murdering his
father,[1] and the manifestation of pure evil shown in the
return of evil for good is repeated again and again
throughout the series of legends, together with the
manifestation of pure good shown in the return of good
for evil. Perhaps the most striking instance is in the
murder of Iridj,[2] the eponymous hero of the Iranian
race, by his two brothers, of whom Tur in like manner
represents the Turanian. Their antagonism typifies at
once the conflict between two races and two ideals; the
hero of the noble Persian race represents the ideal of
heroic purity, and his Turanian opponent is clothed in
all the darkest hues of moral evil. Nothing more truly

[1] Mohl, " Livre des Rois," i. 57–59.   [2] Ibid., 159.

Christian has ever been imagined in fiction than the demeanour of Iridj when the envy of his brothers is aroused by the fond affection of their father, who has enriched his beloved son with the noblest portion of his domain. " O my brothers," he responds to their insulting demand that he should surrender to them the crown of Iran (Persia), placed on his head by their father, "dear to me as my own soul, the power that breeds discord is undesired by me. I yield to you the diadem; let my rule and your hatred die together. I do not attack you, I would not afflict the heart of any human being." The soft answer does not turn away wrath; the generous sacrifice is made in vain. The wicked brothers requite the trust which brings him, in voluntary defencelessness, to face their power, with treacherous murder, and send his head to their father with a message of scorn. A special significance is attached to the battle which avenges his death, by a mysterious voice declaring that the combat about to open is one with Ahriman, "who is in his heart the enemy of the Creator." The ideal saint and the ideal fiend, embodied as they are in the type of the Iranian and the Turanian races, never were delineated in sharper contrast or with a fuller sense of their mutual dependence. The wickedness of Tur could not reach its height apart from the neighbourhood of magnanimous generosity; the pure and gentle Iridj would likewise lose his halo if the background of perfidious cruelty were withdrawn. We are kept throughout the legend on that boundary-line of good and evil, where each is seen in its sharpest distinctness against its opposite. And this one legend is typical of the whole.

This spirit is manifest in all Persian history and mythology for good and for evil. Its evil is seen, perhaps, in the hideous cruelty which stains the annals

E

of Persian rule, for it is a part of the belief that life is a conflict between virtue and crime, to infuse cruelty into all struggle. Its good is seen in a high ideal of truth and a profound reverence for labour. The religion of Persia has been called [1] " the revelation of the Word." We have seen that the Indian thought of God is that He is only to be expressed by "No, No." To the Persian, on the other hand, the word reveals as the light reveals, and the demon is vanquished by its utterance. Language is sacred, its perversion is a crime. With the sense of a great spiritual conflict—a struggle against invisible enemies—Deceit rises to an importance which it could never possess when contemplated as mere failure of accuracy. The non-historic nation could not care for such failure; facts are not sufficiently important to be buttressed with reverence. What is a distortion of experience but a mere additional illusion where all is illusory ? A Pantheistic religion can never admit of any steady condemnation of falsehood; all thought is divine, all is in some sense true. Of course in all societies the inconveniences of lies about matters of fact must be more or less recognized; but Truth will never be the ideal virtue where Falsehood is mere misstatement. Where one vast Unity lies at the root of all things, there is no room for any development of the antithesis which separates truth and falsehood. But the Persian race, inasmuch as it begins History, vindicates Truth. Falsehood is no longer mere inaccuracy, but an act of treason against the Divine Being.

The later development of the Persian religion impersonated this Divine claim. Mithra, the god whose fading radiance shone forth in the dawn of Christianity,[2]

---

[1] By Edgar Quinet, " Génie des Religions."

[2] " Mithra, ce dieu puissant qui un instant disputa au Christ l'empire du monde" (Darmesteter's " Ormazd and Ahriman," p. 21).

is an embodiment of the Divine sympathy with human faithfulness. " The ruffian who lies to Mithra brings death upon the whole country."[1] Mithra represents the idea of light as the witness to all contract, the guardian of open and fair feeling, the upholder of that in man which man can trust. No strength or agility makes up for the withdrawal of support from the God of Truth ; no skill can give a true aim to the weapons of the deceiver. "The spear that the foe of Mithra flings darts backward ; . . . even though his spear be truly aimed, it makes no wound."[2] Mithra upholds the columns of the lofty house, and makes its pillars solid ; he sets the battle a-going, and stands against armies in battle. . . . Sad is the abode, unprovided with children, where abide men who lie unto Mithra"[3] (who hears and avenges all lies). All power of discernment, all the sight of the eyes, the hearing of the ears, is from him ; he is the Revealer, the witness to all truth ; he takes sight from the eyes, hearing from the ears of those who have misused their sight and hearing to the confusion of another. Especially the connection of courage with truth is dwelt on with a lofty confidence. Mithra guards the life of the true man, blunts the darts and hinders the aim of the false man, supplies the lack or annuls the aid of all material weapons, according as the warrior has or has not kept his allegiance to the Revealer. He watches with a discriminating care over graduated claim ; " Mithra," or the contract, " is twenty-fold between two friends, fiftyfold between husband and wife, a hundredfold between father and son."[4] So far, perhaps, we may doubt the wisdom of a gradation which leaves least guarded the contract in which there is least affection ; but there is something very

[1] Zendavesta, "Sacred Books of the East," vol. xxiii. 120.
[2] *Ibid.*, 124. 5.   [3] *Ibid.*, pp. 126-129.   [4] *Ibid.*, 149, 150.

characteristic of this religion of distinctness in the view of human beings, however closely connected, as still separate individualities, facing each other as parties to a contract. And observe the sanction laid on the contract which after so many centuries we are still far from regarding with a worthy reverence. "Mithra is a thousandfold between nations;"—"a fair recognition of the *jus gentium*," says the brilliant scholar to whom we owe the translation here epitomized. This is a recognition of the duty of nation to nation which modern Europe has not yet succeeded in working out in its practical application. We must remember, too, in this connection, that the study of truth is not limited to our dealings with those who are loyal subjects of the truth. "Break not the contract which thou hast entered into with one of the faithful or the unfaithful, for *Mithra stands for both the faithful and the unfaithful.*"[1] Surely an unique expression of that sublime principle which all true religion should uphold, and which all forms of religion often practically deny, that Truth is no claim of an individual, but an act of loyalty to that which makes humanity one.

This ideal of truth is indeed discernible even in the narration which ascribes falsehood to Persian agents. "When a lie is to be told, let it be told,"[2] says Darius to his fellow-conspirators, when they are meditating the deceit by which they will win entrance to the apartments of the false Smerdis. How often in history would a soldier feel even such a momentary hesitation as the words imply in using deceit to overthrow an impostor? It may be objected that we are now criticising a narrative which is the mere work of Greek

---

[1] Zendavesta, "Sacred Books of the East," vol. xxiii. 120.

[2] Herodotus, iii. 72. The conclusion of the speech, it is true, is rather Greek than Persian in this respect; but the mere fact of an apology from any one in the position of Darius appears to suggest a conventional respect for truth.

imagination. But if Herodotus gives us a romance in his account of the overthrow of the false Smerdis by the seven conspirators, his fiction is almost as good evidence to the characters he describes as his facts are. For at least he knows what the Persians were, and his truthfulness as a dramatist is unquestionable, whatever his accuracy as a historian may be. And the most unassailable portion of his narrative corroborates this testimony ; it teaches us, at least, that something in the Persian atmosphere created an expectation of hearing the truth, in circumstances where most minds would be set to disbelieve. The invasion of Greece by Xerxes was surely an occasion for exceptional wariness of belief. There was every possible temptation to deceit on the part of the tiny nation confronted with the might of Asia ; and we should naturally have expected that their dangerous foe would be perpetually on the alert against every apparently friendly communication which might be the channel of hostile intent ; instead of which we find that Xerxes believed every word the Greeks said to him. He never seemed to have suspected that a Greek message could be anything but what it professed to be. In this confidence he hurries to the disaster of Salamis ;[1] and in his subsequent flight from Greece he still acts on Greek advice with absolute confidence. Falsehood must have been a more unnatural idea to him than to most rulers of an invading army. The Great King must have known plenty of instances of it, but some influence was at work on him which made

---

[1] Herodotus, viii. 75. This instance of credulity on the part of the Persian commanders appears the more striking because Sicinnus, the Greek who brings the message which was to lure them into the trap, does not claim reward or shelter. Ὁ μὲν ταῦτά σημήνας ἐκποδὼν ἀπηλλάσσετο. It would almost seem as if the historian intended to express surprise at their credulity in the next sentence (76):—Τοῖσι δὲ ὡς πιστὰ ἐγίνετο τὰ ἀγγελθέντα. Sicinnus returns quite fearlessly to Xerxes after the battle. See viii. 110, with the comments of Grote, v. 191, note.

him curiously unsuspicious. Truth was the assumption as to human intercourse, even where all experience must have supplied a warning against credulity.

The Persian reverence for industry is closely connected with the Persian reverence for truth. The two qualities belong to the same ideal. The Greek on the one hand, the Indian on the other, despises both. As Pantheism knows no error in falsehood, so it also discerns no danger in indolence. And then again, to the lively Greek falsehood is a mark of intellect, as indolence is of freedom. Persia sees both claims from what we may perhaps call a modern point of view. Agriculture is, in its sacred scriptures, surrounded with religious sanction. "When wheat is coming up, it is as though red-hot irons were turned in the throats of the demons." "Unhappy is the land that has long lain unsown, and wants a husbandman, as a fair maiden a husband;" the earth is to be to the husbandman "as a loving bride." The place "where the Earth feels most happy" is the place whereon "one of the faithful erects a house, with a priest within, with cattle, with wife, child, and good herds; where the cattle thrive, where the dog thrives, the wife and child and every blessing of life, where one of the faithful cultivates much corn, grass, and fruit, where he waters ground that is dry, or dries ground that is wet." [1] Perhaps we may find in the course of a nation's legendary history a more impressive testimony to its ideal than even in the injunctions of its sacred scriptures; and the testimony of the Shah-Nameh is not less emphatic on this point than that of the Zend-avesta. Djemschid, the ideal Persian king, institutes castes, as does the ideal Indian legislator; but note the difference. The labourers in the Persian epic render neither homage nor obedience to any one, although their

---

[1] Zendavesta, "Sacred Books of the East," vol. iv. pp. 22-30.

garments are mean and their work arduous. "They are free; they have no enemies, no quarrels. A wise man has said, "'Tis indolence which enslaves those who should be free.'"[1] No figure of prince or noble in these legends is more full of heroic significance than the blacksmith Gaveh, whose leathern apron set with gold and gems, increased by every successive Persian monarch, becomes the standard of Persia, and from whom the proudest are glad to claim descent.[2] It is this son of lowly toil who resists the tyrant Zohak and sets the glorious Feridun upon the throne. Zohak has permitted the demon Iblis to kiss his shoulders, and from each kiss has sprung a serpent, to whose hunger the miserable people over whom he has usurped dominion are compelled to furnish a tribute; for these creatures, true to their devilish origin, feed only on human brains. The two sons of the blacksmith have been seized as their prey, but his fierce indignation compels their restitution and initiates a revolt, in which the demon usurper perishes, and a member of the lawful dynasty is placed upon the throne. Honour to toil is secure with a people whose imagination associates labour and glory, and makes of the apron of toil the sacred standard of victory.

This spirit of reverence for work is equally manifest in the religion of Persia. The change of feeling from sympathy with repose to sympathy with activity, is shown in the fact that all the ideas of cosmogony seemed to have passed over from the region of growth to the region of art. India knows nothing of that which we mean by Creation. The universe is an egg, a germ in a fluid environment; it has *become;* it was not *made.* Whence came that germ of being is a point on which, as we have seen, not only the human but even the Divine Teacher is profoundly ignorant. God himself partakes in the uncertainty of man.　That of which He speaks is a Unity including all existence; it lies outside all Will, it precedes, and therefore baffles, all Thought.　None can possess any record of that primal dawn which initiated the whole of Being, for all are the product of that evolution which then took its start.　Gods and men alike are but the fruit of its later growth, and can preserve no independent view of a process commemorated in the very structure of their being; it is, then, in vain to seek to pass beyond its scope and decide on anything external to its operation.　We can but catch a glimpse of its later stages and chronicle some observations of a process of which we are as much the result as the spectator; and the form in which all suggestions exceeding this limit are cast is quite unhistorical.

Nothing can be more strongly contrasted with this audacious agnosticism than the Persian Genesis.[1]　The origin of this universe is related in terms much more definite than those of a great part of ordinary history. The whole conflict of good and evil which makes up the history of the universe is contained within a cycle of 12,000 years, that is to say, a gigantic year, of which every month is a millennium; and the same sharp distinctness which defines this period arranges its various stages; there are æonian seasons for this æonian year. The conception is definite, chronological, almost geographical.　The worlds of Ormazd and Ahriman are conceived as two vast regions, separated by an empty

---

[1] "Le rôle capitale d'Ormazd," says M. Hovelacque, "est celui du Dieu créateur. . . . Zoroastre, implorant d'Ormazd la révélation l'appelle a chaque instant de ce nom: *dâtare* ô créateur ! . . . . A plusieurs reprises, Ormazd lui-même se proclame créateur. . . . Azem . . . yo dadhwāō Ahurōmazdāō, 'moi qui suis le créateur Ahuramazda,' . . . Darius dit dans son inscription d'Alvend, Auramazda est un dieu puissant, qui a fait cette terre, qui a fait le ciel, qui a fait l'homme, qui a fait la satisfaction de l'homme.　Il répète cette formule dans les inscriptions de Persépolis, et Xerxes la repete après lui" ("L'Avesta, Zoroastre et le Mazdéisme," par Abel Hovelacque, 1880, p. 168-171).

space—an idealization of the sky and subterranean darkness, with the atmosphere as a sort of neutral space between them. Ormazd in his realm of light is conscious of the opposed darkness, but Ahriman has no corresponding knowledge, he suspects the presence of no mighty rival, and to all appearance thinks that his congenial darkness is the whole of being. But Ormazd, aware of the impending battle, makes his preparations; he calls into existence spiritual beings who are to be enlisted in the hosts of righteousness, and for the first great season of the secular year this spiritual creation exists alone. The second 3000 years begin with the emerging of Ahriman from his native darkness and his discovery of the Light. Filled with hatred and fierce wrath at the sight, he prepares for battle, but the first approach to his mighty rival changes his wrath to terror; he takes flight into the abyss, and calls into existence his army of demons, preparatory to the struggle which he is ready to undertake.[1] Ormazd meanwhile occupies this second season of the great year in his material creation, which is a sort of bastion placed in the empty space between the two principles—the face which the Divine world turns towards Evil—the outlying barrier of the light as it confronts the realm of darkness. Beyond this barrier the two great chiefs meet in preliminary conference, and the overtures of Ormazd being rejected, the battle begins, and the third season of the great year makes up the whole history of human kind. Throughout the whole nothing is dim or uncertain; the record is one of continuous activity. We are confronted at every stage with the result of vigorous, efficient will. In Indian life we see history itself melting into philosophy. In Persia it is the very opposite; religious philosophy takes the form of the most definite history. The universe takes

---

[1] See the Bundahis, "Sacred Books of the East," v. 7-10, 15.

shape before our eyes in the clear daylight of historic record, and for every stage of creation we have a definite date and an adequate explanatory motive.

The strong monarchic spirit of Persia is the natural result of such a faith as has been described. It is the tendency of all organized warfare to cultivate uncritical devotion to a single head. The religion of conflict was the religion of loyalty. We are reminded continually that "the Great King" was the name by which the deadliest enemies of Persia spoke of its ruler. There are kings in plenty in Indian tradition, but none of them emerges into this typical importance, as a link between the human and the Divine. The caste system is utterly opposed to all monarchic feeling; an elaborately organized aristocracy is incompatible with the dominion of an autocrat. In Persia, on the other hand, the distinction between the sovereign and the subject is one that leaves scant room for any other. The latest editor of Herodotus [1] notes an instructive instance of the want of Greek knowledge of Persian feeling in this respect; the messenger, in the drama of Æschylus, who brings the news of the colossal disaster, fails to announce the monarch's safety as his opening communication. [2] "The Persians," says Herodotus (viii. 99), with truer apprehension, "were overwhelmed with consternation when they heard of the disaster at Salamis, *not so much on account of the destruction of the fleet* as from their fears for the safety of Xerxes, . . . and their lamentations were kept up until the king put an end to them by his return." His return removed, it would seem, their deepest anxiety. To lose their king would be a

---

[1] Instead of representing the safety of the King as the first thought of the Persians, the messenger is on the stage for half a scene before the point is touched (Rawlinson's Herodotus, iv. pp. 336, 337, note).

[2] Æschylus, Persæ, 248, *seq.*

calamity more terrible than to lose all that vast host that had drained the strength of Asia. There was nothing rational in such a feeling; it was a part of their worship.

Loyalty cannot be incorporated with religion without profoundly modifying the whole spirit of both. Political feeling becomes a different thing when it is developed in such close proximity to religious feelings that it is subject to the contagion of all religious impulse. The cruelty which is naturally developed by the belief in a conflict between good and evil pervading all existence, finds an additional stimulus in the prostrate submission of a race at the feet of a monarch whose dominion is regarded as something almost divine. The earthly ruler who shares the claim of the heavenly to uncritical obedience, must develop a tendency towards ruthless tyranny, unless he be secured by some peculiar idiosyncrasy of gentleness or wisdom. Man shares in his own worship; the reluctance of his worshipper becomes an object not alone of human displeasure, but of indignation against impiety. The blackest crime narrated by Herodotus of Xerxes—his slaughter of four noble Lydian youths,[1] freely offered to his service, because their father, alarmed by a dream, asked for the restoration of one —would assume to the Great King, the reader feels, the aspect almost of a zeal for religion. The father who grudged his all to the sovereign was, in his view, worthy of the severest tortures that could lacerate a father's heart. This is no mere exhibition of human rage, it is justified to the tyrant by a confusion of the Divine claim with the claim of self. There are not wanting instances which prove the character of Xerxes to have been by no means one of universal barbarity where the sense of his own Divinity was not concerned, which exhibit even magnanimity in dealing with those

[1] Herodotus, vii. 27, 28, 38, 39.

who did not come within the circuit of his regal claim.
It is in contrast with what could be regarded as disloyalty that we see in him the cruelty of a fiend. And
cruelty in the strong, when it is watched without resistance or indignation, is sure to become cruelty in the
weak. Our moral standard is influenced far more by
those actions which we admire or condemn than by
those which we endeavour to imitate. A thousand
accidents decide what part of our neighbour's conduct
shall be the model of our own, but our ideal acts on us
at every moment, and influences our whole being in a
region far deeper than the conscious will. And thus
a religion which finds in a series of individual men a
special type and representative of God upon earth, tends
to make room in its moral ideal for the passions of hatred
and resentment, and to incorporate the zeal for what is
divine with the worst forms of cruelty and revenge.

This characteristic of Persian morals is brought out
by the Persian antagonism to the nation which has
most strongly influenced the intellectual development of
Europe. The narrative of the deliverance of Greece
shows the impression made by Persian barbarity on a
people comparatively humane, and the reader is taught
to shudder at the dominion of Persia as synonymous
with the triumph of all that is terrible and hateful; the
conflict not only of a lower with a higher form of civilization, but of a hideous despotism with an enlightened,
beneficent form of government and of society. We feel
as if the salvation of Greece had been the repulse of all
that was evil; we seem to see the combat of Ahriman
with Ormazd in flesh and blood. The Persian faith
seems to detach itself from the Persian nation, and to
exhibit its worshippers, from an external point of view,
as an embodiment of that evil principle in which it
taught men to believe. Doubtless it was so, in the

aspect which it showed itself to Greece. Persian victory would here have been the touch of paralysis on all that has been, to the intellectual development of Europe, the very spring of energy and fount of inspiration. It would have been slavery instead of freedom, torpor instead of genius, death instead of life.

But there was another race, equally well known to the modern world, to which Persian victory brought deliverance, and to whose faith that of the Persians seemed closely akin. The Jew felt that the Persian might join him in the worship of Jehovah, if only the Evil Principle were deposed from sharing the Heavenly throne. We seem to hear a protest against the dual Divinities of the Persian from that great Hebrew Prophet whose utterances we have been taught to confuse with those of Isaiah— " Thus saith the Lord thy Redeemer, I am the Lord that maketh all things, that stretcheth forth the heavens alone, that spreadeth abroad the earth by myself" [1]—the God who has had no hostile partner in creation, who has made both light and darkness—" who saith to the deep, Be dry, and I will dry up thy rivers ;" [2]—the God who destroys all separation at His will—" that saith of Cyrus, He is my shepherd, and shall perform all my pleasure ; even saying to Jerusalem, Thou shalt be built ; and to the temple, Thy foundation shall be laid." [3] The Great King is the shepherd of Israel ; to him is applied a title elsewhere only given to David and to the Son of David. He has, indeed, a more sacred title ; we might startle Christian ears by quoting the passage of Scripture which names him literally—he is the Christ, the Anointed, " whose right hand I have holden, to subdue nations before him ; to make the crooked places straight, to break in pieces the gates of brass, and cut in sunder the bars of iron." [4]

---

[1] Isa. xliv. 24.   [2] Isa. xliv. 27.
[3] Isa. xliv. 28.   [4] Isa. xlv. 1, 2.

To him shall be revealed the excellence of that which
has taken the aspect of the foe of all excellence—" I will
give thee the treasures of darkness, that thou mayest
know that I, which call thee by thy name, am the God
of Israel. I have surnamed thee, though thou hast not
known me. I am the Lord, and there is none else,"
no rival creator, no hostile ruler, no potent Ahriman.
Darkness is no foe of Light, only the shadow that gives
it meaning. " I form the light and create darkness. . . .
I the Lord do all these things."

The protest is there, and yet it is not emphatic, and it
is not finally victorious. The Persian dualism filtered
into the religion which here repudiates it, and emerges
in the religion which was born of Judaism, in a more
distinct form. Satan gradually expands to the limits
of Ahriman. The earlier books of the Old Testament
know nothing of him, his name does not occur, nor is
there any place for him in the scheme of thought they
portray. Jehovah is the one Supreme Ruler of all
things visible and invisible ; there are evil agencies (as
also in the Veda), but they are neither prominent nor in
our sense of the word diabolic ; they are all indistinct and,
we may say, excusable. An adversary provokes Hannah
to make her fret,[1] but her urgent importunity wins its
object and makes her the mother of Samuel ; a lying
spirit appears before the throne of Jehovah,[2] but it is to
carry out His purpose, in the destruction of Ahab ; finally
(for here the idea seems to have taken its full development as far as it was independent of Persian influence),
" *the* adversary" appears among the sons of God to
accuse a righteous man, but it is to bring forth that
righteousness sifted and purified ; and after the trials

---

[1] 1 Samuel i. 6.
[2] 1 Kings xxii. 21-23. *Cf.* Job i. 6-12. The similarity of the lying spirit
to the οὖλος ὄνειρος of Iliad ii. 8 has been often noticed.

which have separated the chaff from the wheat we hear
no more of Satan;[1] the human adversaries are rebuked,
but the accusing spirit is forgotten. Was he really an
evil spirit? Is not the sifting spirit a part of the
agency of Heaven? Judaism leaves the question un-
answered, or perhaps we may say that it suggests an
affirmative answer, though the spirit that sifts is too
near the spirit that doubts for it to give that answer
distinctly. The influence that questions what is good
is wonderfully close to the influence that purifies what
is partly evil. We should be struck by this in the
allusions of Christ if we could read the Bible with the
same unprejudiced mind as we read any other book.
" Simon, Simon, Satan hath desired to have you that
he may sift you as wheat."[2] An arrogant purpose in
a created being, but not in itself evil, nay, dangerous
only because it is a copy of that which is the prerogative
of the creator. Satan *desires* to sift the true Israel, but
the Lord achieves that sifting so that " not the least
grain falls upon the earth." His alone is the power, but
not His alone is the desire. It is shared by the one
in whom men have seen the principle of all evil. And
there is no doubt that that conception was developed
by the Hebrew contact with Persia. The later books
show a strong trace of this influence, while they exhibit
in a striking form that tendency by which the Tempter
stands so near the Redeemer that it almost seems as
if they may at some moment exchange parts. Jehovah
provokes David to number Israel in the original history,
but in the redaction made after the exile that part
is ascribed to " the adversary; " and the exchange is
a significant, though it seems a trifling, instance of the
tendency by which at last Satan is elevated into the
strong conspicuous position which he takes in the latest

[1] Job xlii. 1-3.   [2] Luke xxii. 31. *Cf.* Amos ix. 9.

expression of Jewish feeling in the Bible—the Book of Revelation. Here we are again on the battlefield of two principles. Evil is once more a mighty, for the present we may say even a victorious power, and its future defeat is not (for it cannot be) more distinct than it is in the religion of Persia. Here, then, we may say that the element which entered Judaism with Persian influence attains its fullest development; we have here an army of evil powers, a Prince of darkness, a mighty foe to the Divine ruler. To many persons it seems that we have all this in the teaching of Christ. They forget that He beheld Satan fall *from Heaven;* [1] that He applied the name to the most trusted of His followers; [2] that when His own homage was claimed for this evil being, He answered with no denunciation, [3] but with a calm assertion of the claim of the One. The teaching of His disciple has obscured His own, and there is a great deal of what we must call Christianity in which the belief in Ahriman is quite as real, and more active, than it was in the ancient creed of Persia. And so deep has this spirit put its roots into the faith of Christendom, that, now that it has fallen, a great vacuum seems left in our religion, and much of what is most essential to it is, there can be no doubt, explained away by those who still speak its language and call themselves by its name.

---

[1] Luke x. 18.
[2] Matt. xvi. 23, and parallel passages in the other synoptics.
[3] Matt. iv. 10, and parallel passages.

CHAPTER III.

GREECE, AND THE HARMONY OF OPPOSITES.

WE only half understand the principle of dualism when we contrast it with the principle of unity. The spirit that sees all events, all characters, all phenomena, as the development or symbol of a great conflict between two fundamental principles is not more antagonistic to the spirit which sees them all as the various expression of one, than each is to that which looks with an impartial interest on the whole play of natural impulse, and sees in the struggle of life's opposing forces the appropriate gymnastic for all that is most truly human, the battle that tests and develops all that is destined for rule. It is only on a superficial view that we could suppose this latter spirit an ally of either antagonist against its enemy. According to our point of view, it is either impartially hostile to both or impartially friendly to both. "Life," said the Indian, "is the seeming change in one unchangeable reality ; let us neglect what seems, and turn to what is." "Life," said the Persian, "is the actual conflict between two deadly foes ; let us take part with the good and oppose the evil." But these two forms of thought, embodied not merely in two creeds of the past, but in many kinds of speculation that belong to all time, are hardly more unlike each other than both are unlike one which we may call by very different names, and recognize under very different aspects, for it also belongs to all time and to all thought ; while

F

its typical expression remains also fixed for all time in the records of a nation's life, and that the nation which has most deeply influenced the intellectual development of our race. It is the ideal of the artist throughout all history, and it is the ideal, at a particular point in history, of the artist people; it moulds the poetry, the art, and the philosophy of Greece.

This spirit is sympathetic to all forms of thought, and also critical to them all. It does not turn from what *seems* to absorb itself in what *is*, as the Pantheism of India. It does not rank itself on the side of righteousness, and find its very life in a conflict with evil, as the dualism of Persia. It admits no great fundamental antithesis either of illusion and reality or of good and evil; and from some points of view the two hostile doctrines which severally accept these contrasts as the leading distinctions of the moral world, are nearer to each other than is either to the spirit that finds truth in a balance of opposites, and the aim of life in a harmony of its contending forces.

This is the ideal of genius. It is the perennial aspect that life bears to the Poet. It is the side of all human dealings which they turn towards the world of Art. To the race dowered with genius it was the national ideal, and all the records of what they have done and been are but various and not always obvious illustrations of this spirit of balance, of harmony, of rhythm. At times it takes a deeply moral aspect, and seems to anticipate the deepest lessons and the most urgent warnings of the Christian Scriptures. But this resemblance is misleading. The Greek dread of extravagance has a merely external similarity to the Christian dread of sin; in its most characteristic aspects, it is indeed antagonistic to earnest moral feeling, to all zeal for righteousness, to all hatred of iniquity. Genius is not immoral; probably in this respect its records would show favourably in comparison with the records of commonplace humanity. But it is utterly unmoral. It metes out its interest according to other laws than those which regulate the moral sympathies; it demands only the play of opposite forces and the balance of contending impulses, and wherever these are found, there is the soil for its roots and the atmosphere in which its blossoms may expand in all their beauty. Against such an ideal the conscience, in some sense, always embodies a latent protest. It is a protest only in the sense in which we may imagine youthful vigour to protest against that invitation to repose which is to renew all its springs. But the faculty which centres in the conscience, and the creative powers of genius, are hostile in this sense, that they must emerge into distinctness alternately. It is as with the light of the sun and moon; if we are to see them together, the light of one or both must be comparatively faint. Genius, however we reconcile that truth with others not less certain, implies always a certain moral impartiality; hence its dangers: hence also—if we would remember that the whole of our nature, and no part more than the conscience, needs repose—its deepest benefits alike to those who share it and those who only share its gifts.

Greece represents the moral ideal of genius, with all its wealth and all its peril. It shows us moral truth as we see the moon by daylight—faint, delicate, forgetable, secondary, yet never indistinct. Not that passion is faint, not that the moral sympathies are feeble, but that it is manifold, that they are balanced. There is fierce wrath, there is passionate love, but wherever we can distinguish the poet's feeling it sympathises with both. Greek life is penetrated with that spirit of balanced judgment, of elastic sympathy, which, allowing vehement utterance to all feeling, refuses decided predominance to any;—which tends to exhibit all conflict as gymnastic, all antagonism as the harmonious play of opposite emotions. Greek mythology, Greek legend, Greek history, are all full of the idea of a struggle, but we never find that any combatant can be regarded as a principle of evil. As compared with the Persian ideal, we find that we have exchanged a moral contrast of light and darkness for an artistic balance of light and shade. The idea of a primeval conflict, symbolized by the great phenomena of nature and typical of all that is most impressive in human history—this fruitful germ of myth and legend was the inheritance of the Aryan race, and nowhere do we find it more prolific than on the soil of Greece. But it never develops into any parable of the conflict of good and evil. Greek mythology knows of no Ahriman and Ormazd; Greek deities are as little like one of these beings as like the other. Whatever is evil is vague; the objects of antagonism partake rather the character of things than of persons. Perhaps we may say that the contrast of persons and things marks the nearest approach made by the Greek mind towards the contrast of good and evil. All heroic achievement impresses on brute matter the record of Will, banishing the hurtful, the monstrous, the foul; humanizing the confused material world; extending the empire of Spirit. The conflict repeats in a condensed form the work of primitive man; the hero must slay monsters, drain marshes, go through arduous toils in subduing the powers of nature, but his struggles never take the aspect of a great duel between equal or nearly equal foes, he knows no spiritual adversary. Hercules is a great hunter, a daring traveller; a beneficent helper; he is never a wrestler with any principle of evil. He and all those heroes of whom he is a typical example express the spirit of civilization overcoming the lower forces that

rise up against it, never the spirit of righteousness setting itself to overcome the spirit of iniquity. That is an
antithesis of which Greece knows nothing ; when mythology and philosophy come nearest to such a conception
we see most clearly how impossible it was to the Greek
mind. Its philosophy, when most occupied with moral
problems, scarcely takes cognizance of right and wrong ;
its mythology, when absorbed in the moral aspects of the
Invisible world, seems at times to recognize this antithesis
only to invert it, and to give to the claimants for human
worship the attributes and aspect of the Tempter.

Those who know something of the writings of Plato,
and still more those who only know his name, may be
inclined to dispute this description of the philosophy
that has sown the seed of so much of the world's
thought. The name and the writings of his great pupil,
if equally familiar, would be a much stronger cause for
protest, for all our ethical study takes its rise with
Aristotle. And nevertheless it remains true that moral
truth is discernible on Greek soil only as the moon is
discernible by day. The very fact which seems to
confute this is its strongest proof. Aristotle originates
ethical science, it takes its start with the thought that
ripened in the stormy autumn of Greek life. Plato never
recognized the life of the Conscience. He knows only
two antitheses—the pleasant in contrast to the painful,
the true in contrast to the false. His own disastrous
and disappointing experience as the guide of a ruler who
embodied his ideal—that of the philosopher on a throne
—may have shown him that clear vision does not always
imply right action ; and the dialogue of his melancholy
old age appears to bear some traces of the dislocating
shock of that discovery.[1] But from all his characteristic

---

[1] It must be confessed that this is denied by the writer who has made of Plato
almost an English classic. But Dr. Jowett's assertion (Plato, vol. iv. p. 7) that

utterance we should conclude that the supreme glory which centred in the idea of Truth gathered up into itself all excellence, and left nothing to be appropriated by that of Duty and Virtue. What we mean by true and what we mean by right were blended for him in one great ideal, which he called the good. This was to the man's nature as light to the eye, as air to the lungs; nothing was wanted but that it should be presented to its appropriate organ. If this were so, the word *ought* would be emptied of its meaning. It would be as impossible to see that an action was right without doing it, as it is to see that a doctrine is true without believing it. In the wider sense of morals in which the word indicates the impulses, the sympathies, the ultimate needs of humanity, no people have contributed more to its development than the countrymen of Plato. To those who have given us the very name of Ethical Science we are indebted for the larger part of all that makes the subject interesting and vivid. In the narrower sense, in which it traces the claim of Duty, we can only say that Greek thought beckons us into realms whence we see the mountain as the cloud.

Thus it is that, while Greek philosophy is non-moral, Greek mythology is non-theistic. To the Greek mind, in its most natural and characteristic attitude, the Divine

---

there is no reason "to imagine that this melancholy tone is attributable to disappointment at having failed to convert a Sicilian tyrant into a philosopher" is very surprising to me. If the melancholy tone and the disappointment both exist, can we help connecting them? And when Plato says, Ἆρ' οὖν, ὦ θαυμάσιε λελήθαμεν ἄνθρωποι πάντες . . . οἰόμενοι μὲν ἑκάστοτέ τι καλὸν ὁρᾶν πρᾶγμα γενόμενον καὶ θαυμαστὰ ἂν ἐργασάμενον (Leges, 686), and continues that this opinion often turns out a mistake, is it possible not to connect this mournful confession with the assertion in the "Republic," 473:—'Ἐὰν μή, ἢ οἱ φιλόσοφοι βασιλεύσωσιν ἐν ταῖς πόλεσιν ἢ οἱ βασιλῆς . . . φιλοσοφήσωσι . . . οὐκ ἔστι κακῶν παῦλα (and then, it appeared, there would be)? Was Plato not remembering, when he wrote the sentence in the Laws, that he *had* seen this noble thing, a Philosopher on the throne, from which he had hoped so greatly; and could anything have blurred his memory of that disappointment?

Being was out of sight. Greek feeling is not atheistic, it denies nothing that human instincts have ever asserted. But it hurries on to other realms, it never lingers before the Divine Throne. We hear in its deeper music the note of a profound reverence and faith, but it is not a characteristic note ; the most Greek of all Greek poems knows nothing of it. Greek mythology knows neither a truly Divine nor a truly Satanic being, but if we are to associate the Greek divinities with either, they come nearer to the last. The desire of Plato to banish poets from his Republic is justified by many passages in Homer ; the gods are, from a moral point of view, inferior to the objects of their capricious protection and dislike. "The Law of Mithra is fiftyfold between nations," says the Persian hymn ; but when the enemies of the Greeks have to be defeated, the daughter of Jove, the divine Athene,[1] takes the part of Ahriman, and provokes a Trojan to a treacherous breach of the truce just agreed on. The poet has opened a vista towards all that enhances the guilt of this treachery—the weariness of long warfare, the longing for home, the yearning for all the blessings of Peace—and then, with no sense of anything surprising or unnatural, passes on to tell how the Goddess of Wisdom bends her irresistible might to pour temptation into a Trojan heart and wing from a Trojan bow the arrow that shall rekindle the half-extinguished flames of war. It is a striking illustration of the truth that no religion can be consistently unmoral. It is not enough to say that Olympus reflects the inconsistencies and contradictions of human beings, it must be confessed in this case enormously to exaggerate them ; and we are reminded, as we contemplate such

---

[1] Il., iv. 93. seq. Note especially 104, τῷ δὲ φρένας ἄφρονι πεῖθεν, words which Milton might have translated to describe the influence of the serpent on Eve ; cf. iii. 2.

a picture, that man's conception of the Divine, if it is not to rise above the human world, must sink far below it. Wherever God is not regarded as the inspirer of all high and pure desires He takes the aspect of the Tempter; if no spirit of trust lift to Him the prayer, "Lead us not into temptation," then all temptation seems to come from Him. And thus the characteristically Greek spirit is irreligious, and was felt as such even by the deeper thinkers among the Greeks themselves. It knows of no spiritual foe to humanity, but any God may take the place of such a foe, and those promptings to evil which Christianity has associated with a single invisible personality are diffused throughout the whole realm of supernatural agency and suggestion. And if ever we come near the distinct conception of a principle of Evil, we shall find that we are equally near the very opposite idea—that where the Greek spirit most approaches the contemplation of an Ahriman or a Satan there also it comes nearest to the sense of a Redeemer. Not because the two mutually suggest each other—in all religions we find the Tempter and the Saviour become visible together—but because to the Greek the two were but different aspects of one reality. They seem to have passed over by the merest hair's-breadth of change from the sense of evil, which is characteristic of the spirit that strives with evil, to evil itself. Like some eagle hovering on poised wing above the summit of the Andes, they exchanged, as it were with a stroke of the wing, the slope that sends its waters to the east for that which sends its waters to the west, and confused in their lofty gaze the springs of mighty rivers, which increase their remoteness with every foot of progress, and find their issue in oceans that are thousands of miles apart.

The group of Greek divinities known to some English

readers under the somewhat misleading title of "The
Furies," and supposed to be called "The Gentle Ones"
only by a euphemism, affords us the most striking example of this elastic vibration between the ideas of good
and evil, bringing us nearer a religious sense of the
meaning of remorse and repentance than we find elsewhere, and nearer also to an identification of these
feelings with evil. The Eumenides belong to an older
system [1] than the joyous gods of Olympus, and might
seem, if we let fancy settle their affinities, to embody
the reminiscence of an earlier historic phase, when all
that is characteristically Greek was undeveloped. We
might, from some points of view, call them the Greek
equivalent of Ahriman. They are daughters of night ;
they enter into conflict with the God of Day, who shelters
from them the object of their pursuit, banishes them
from his temple with fierce invective, and forces them to
surrender their victim to his protection. They are hateful beings, embodiments of the curses of vengeance, of
the spirit that, in seeking to cure ill by ill, would make
it eternal ; and their struggle with Apollo is the nearest
approach to the Persian symbolism of a struggle of
light and darkness that we can discover through the
Greek mythology—the radiant Sun-god, in all his
majesty and beauty, on the one hand ; on the other,
these daughters of night, odious in aspect and pitiless
to the hunted being to whom he extends a merciful and
soothing care. We are reminded of Satan by them
more than by any other representation known to classic
thought ; sometimes even of the vulgar Satan with
horns and hoofs,[2] of Mephistopheles clamorous for his
prey, for they inspire horror by their mere aspect, and
their haunting presence is the worst torment they can

[1] Æschylus, " Eumen.," 162, 731, 778, 847.
[2] *Ibid.*, 46-59.

inflict on their victim. And Satan as he appears in the Old Testament—the accusing spirit—seems exactly that which they are intended to represent. They take the same place as he does when he appears among the sons of God to bear witness against Job. But Greek thought, unlike Jewish, gives them a permanent place in Heaven, and passing on light wing that boundary-line of good and evil which never had much significance for it, sees them as types not of the resentment and hatred which attend the footsteps of and perpetuate wrong, but as that witness of wrong within which is also the eternal witness of right. The Goddess of Wisdom appeases the wrath of the pitiless beings, and even induces them to take up their abode with those who have dared to shelter their victim from them; they remain as beneficent guardians on the domain they had entered as foes; and the Furies become the Gracious ones; the Accuser of the Brethren is reverenced as the Guardian of Law.[1]

The poet who first brought the Eumenides into the world of tragic representation himself conceived of them under this dual aspect, and it is from his verse that we may draw the most emphatic vindication of the right of the daughters of night to a place in the elect city. But the successor of Æschylus takes a further step, and obliterates altogether that aspect of horror which is predominant in the earlier poem. He even ventures to reconcile these awful beings with their Divine foe. Phœbus himself, in the verse of Sophocles, appears as their ally, and the God of Day refers his supplicant to

---

[1] Æschylus, "Eumen.," 881, seq. Is it not possible that the reason why modern associations with these deities belong so exclusively to their malignant aspect may be the failure of the dull Roman intelligence to grasp this antithesis? The mention both of Tacitus and Lucretius shows that they were to the Roman merely " the Furies; " and when Pausanius visited Athens about A.D. 170, he seems to have been surprised to have found nothing horrible in the representation of them.

the healing care of night. His oracle has promised
peace to the woe-worn Œdipus "when he shall come to
the seat of awful Divinities;" and when, in their sacred
grove of Colonos, he learns that he is in their territory,
a solemn pathos like that of music breathes through
the prayer in which he entreats them to "be not harsh
to Phœbus and to me."[1] It is as if the younger
poet had set himself to complete the harmony of opposites which the elder had begun; to show us these
dark beings, who had been welcomed, in the verse of
Æschylus, by the Goddess of Wisdom, but detested
and defied by the God of Day, as reconciled even to the
God who had confronted them as Ormazd confronts
Ahriman. The God of radiance, of beauty, of healing,
recognizes the claim of the Divinities who typify
remorse and punishment; he points the weary pilgrim
to their shrine as to a shelter from the stormy blast.
We seem to grasp some clue which leads us to a unity
below the antithesis of Light and Darkness, and all that
they symbolize; to hear some whisper of a music in
which the harshest discords are to find their place as
elements of a harmony as much richer and more varied
than all that could be without them as harmony itself is
richer than unison.

Here we have in its fullest blossom the spirit that
always insists on hearing the other side. Greek worship
makes a place for that which is most abhorrent to Greek
feeling. Greece lives in the world of Light; here is
its home; the Sun-god is the "chief of all the gods;"[2]
yet the daughters of night are honoured not only with
reverent fear, but with a sort of mystic rapture. There
is a marvellous depth of meaning in the invocation of
the blind Œdipus to the "*sweet* daughters of the ancient

---

[1] Sophocles, (Ed. Col., 86 91.
[2] Œd. Tyr., 660.

darkness." [1] His life has, since the discovery of his unconscious crime, been spent in their realm, and the dread summons, which he alone of any Greek hero is to hear with joy, cannot remove him from the light, which in that moment of horror he resolved to see no more. To the powers of darkness he then devoted himself, and now that, after many wanderings, he finds himself in their sacred grove, and learns the name of propitious omen by which the Athenians worship them, he knows his toils are past, he feels the stillness of a vast and sudden calm and a mysterious hope. The Avengers have become the Gentle Ones, their sacred grove is the refuge of the broken heart, the domain on which the indigent wanderer is to deal with a Prince on equal terms. And yet this complete change of view is the result of no sudden and wonderful revelation, of no rush upwards into a higher region. It is due less to the teaching of the moralist than to the instinct of the artist. It does not (as we see from the harsh vindictiveness of Œdipus to his son) imply any of that sense of the blessedness of forgiveness which we cannot help reading into every line. It is simply an expression of that swift elastic expansion of sympathy which moves naturally to an opposite pole—of that spirit of measure and balance, which refuses confinement to a single point of view, and desires to look at its object from every side. It has an element of profound morality. It is pregnant with deep lessons on the meaning of Conscience; it vindicates with noble earnestness the homage owed by the city to the spirit of righteous fear; it sees with keen insight into the play of moral forces, and accepts as a great fact the sense of guilt and the need

---

[1] ἴτ' ὦ γλυκεῖαι παῖδες ἀρχαίου Σκότου (Œd. Col., 106). Professor Jebb thinks that no other poet of the classical ages "ventures on this use of γλυκύς in addressing Deities."

of expiation. But it sees these as facts just like any other facts, not as affording a clue to the central principles of our being. The impartial Greek spirit looks at crime from various points of view ; it finds a good deal to say for deeds which bear a criminal aspect as well as against them. It discovers the truth not in any single view, but in the harmony of all.

No legend can be richer in august associations than that which Sophocles has here treated. Much that has called itself history has evidently been moulded upon the story of Œdipus ; it is the refraction of his destiny through the legendary lore of Persia and of Rome which has created the more picturesque and vivid incidents in the biographies of Cyrus and of Romulus. The moral element in the legend is indeed dropped in its historic adaptation ; but it is surely to this moral element that the story owes all its power, and we may take the historic echoes of the theme of Sophocles as a tribute even to that portion which they fail to repeat. To him it would appear as if the tale of the House of Labdacus had gathered up the problem of guilt and of disaster ;—of man as a unit, and man as the member of a group in which his individual will was submerged, and his responsibility lost in some more mysterious embodiment of purpose and volition. We see the development of this idea in the comparison already suggested. Orestes is in truth the slayer of a parent ; the deed may be excused, but not denied. Fate works through his will, using it as an instrument ; he is fully conscious of what he is doing in slaying Clytemnestra, and works out the curse on his house by his own deliberate and impassioned purpose. Hence individual choice runs in the same current with the will of Fate, and cannot be distinguished from it. But in the case of Œdipus, guilt, if it does exist, exists outside the will.

The Labdacids may collectively be stained with crime, but
Œdipus individually is innocent. Who could be more
free from bloodguiltiness than one who, as an infant,
was cast out by his parents to perish, who had killed
his father only when, as a stranger, he was attacked by
him with a superior force, and married his mother only
when she appeared to him as the unknown queen of a
city he had just delivered from a deadly pest? And
yet in some form we are made to feel that guilt is there.
It is not merely that the penalty of guilt falls on
Œdipus ; we feel him in his utmost prosperity under a
curse.   If the crime be not his, it is that of some ancestor with whom we must think of him as identified in a
closeness of union that makes his suffering for sin in
some sense just.   Œdipus accepts it as such ; he bows
before the decree which hurls him from his throne,
and executes the vengeance of Heaven on himself by
depriving himself for ever of its blessed light.   There
is no remonstrance, no indignation against the Gods, in
the first discovery of their dreadful appointment for him ;
the doom which hurls him from his throne to wander a
fugitive, deprived by his own hands of sight, and dependent on the charity of the indifferent, "asking little and
receiving less "—this doom is surely in some form the
indignation of the Gods against guilt.   It stands in
some relation, however obscure, to the idea of justice
—it is in some form an exhibition of the law that
suffering should follow sin.

   This is the lesson of Œdipus the king.   It illustrates
with the brilliant light and shade of genius the ideal
—which we may, speaking broadly, call that of the
old world—of "man the fragment."   It sets forth in
colossal simplicity the predominance of Fate, the futility
of individual resolution, showing us man as a leaf on
the surface of a river ; as a thread of gossamer wafted

onwards by the breeze; as an arrow directed to the target by the hand of a practised archer. The very efforts which are made by this feeble and incomplete being to escape his destiny become links in the chain by which it binds him. The idea is far more definitely developed than in the trilogy of Æschylus. There we see how Apollo may enjoin what the Erinnys may avenge; how the same deed can be, according to the different points of view, an act of pious homage to one parent or of crime towards the other; but we see this only as we must always recognize it in that legacy of impulse which is bequeathed by father to son in every age, and which our own generation has made a subject of special investigation and has discovered to be a mine of scientific result. It is indeed not very easy to determine how far the audience is meant to be in sympathy with the plea of Orestes against the deities who would avenge his mother's murder, but we cannot be intended to look either upon their declamations or his apology as wholly void, and it is possible for us to concede a certain validity to both. The predestination here is a predestination of *choice;* the ills are done, not merely suffered. But when we turn to the tale of Œdipus, we see divinely ordained Fate and human Will in a much more distinct antagonism. We cannot feel that he contributed of his own choice any link to that chain in which his family is bound. The Gods are responsible for his murder of his father in quite a different sense from that in which they are responsible for the murder of Clytemnestra. It is as if the younger poet had felt dissatisfied with the assertion of their predestination in the work of his predecessor, and had brought it out far more distinctly through the protest of an individual. Œdipus the king represents, we have said, man the Fragment;—the death of Œdipus (let it be permitted to give as a substitute for the ordinary title an indication of the true impression of the play) brings us in face of man the Individual. As Œdipus looks at his history through the vista of years, he sees his acts from what we may call a modern point of view. These so-called crimes were, after all, only misfortunes. They were "suffered rather than done;"[1] the murder which he is expiating has yet left him "pure before the law"[2]—a remarkable expression, identifying guilt and will to an extent that perhaps we are not meant by the poet always to remember. How can it be any fault of his that the Gods before his birth decreed that he should slay his father? Creon is more guilty in speaking of his deeds than he in doing them.[3] Even the single admission that the burden of hereditary misfortune has any connection with what may properly be called guilt is faint and hesitating.[4]

> "These ills were Heaven's decree,
>   Perchance indignant with our race of yore."

The whole tone is that of absolute and entire self-justification. Modern feeling takes part with it; from our point of view Œdipus at Colonos is wholly right, the judgment of his enemies is mere error. But this, if it be taken alone, is not the point of view intended for the spectators of the tragedy by its author, nor that of its great critic,[5] when he pointed out Œdipus as the typical figure for a tragic hero, because he was neither wholly guilty nor wholly innocent. We must, if we would be

---

[1] Œd. Col., 266, 7.

[2] νόμῳ δὲ καθαρός (Œd. Col., 548).

[3] Œd. Col., 986, 7.

[4] τάχ' ἄν τι μηνίουσιν εἰς γένος πάλαι (*Ibid.*, 965.)

[5] Arist., "Poetica," cxiii. 5 :—Ἔστι δὲ τοιοῦτος ὁ μήτε ἀρετῇ διαφέρων καὶ δικαιοσύνῃ, μήτε διὰ κακίαν καὶ μοχθηρίαν μεταβάλλων εἰς τὴν δυστυχίαν, ἀλλὰ δι' ἁμαρτίαν τινά, τῶν ἐν μεγάλῃ δόξῃ ὄντων . . . οἷον Οἰδίπους. From the numerous references to Œdipus in this treatise, it was evidently almost a type of the ideal tragedy.

in sympathy with the spirit of ancient life, accept the belief that ancestral is in some sense real guilt. We must teach ourselves to regard the dogma of original sin as a great historic influence, whatever we may think of it on theologic ground. The sense in which the individual is a fragment and the sense in which he is a unity must both be taken into account if we would reach the point of view from which Greek feeling confronted Fate and Guilt.

But the antithesis which we have been endeavouring to set forth is no mere contrast of the past. It is what we see and feel every day. We blame ourselves, it may be, in the eyes of others even with an excessive blame; we lose for the moment every thought of what was inevitable in our wrongdoings; we see nothing but their wrong. Then some one else speaks of them—it may be in the gentlest of accents, it is conceivable that it should even be in tones of excuse. Even then it will generally be found that something in the measure of individual responsibility taken by the person who is not responsible rouses protest in the one who is. When most repentant the wrongdoer will almost always discern in wrong some *element of the inevitable* that is invisible to every eye but his own. To be conscious of wrongdoing, in fact, is almost the same as to be conscious of this fragmentary life in which we feel that our acts are "suffered rather than done." It is quite true that this is not the whole of the consciousness of wrong—that where there is no other feeling than this the consciousness is of being wronged merely. But the greater part of the self-reproach which saddens memory is entangled with some such feeling as this. So far as we condemn ourselves, of course we must be conscious of our own individuality; the very idea of moral responsibility is based on that sense of *initial action* which we speak of as Free Will, and which we can describe only by saying that our actions began with ourselves, and cannot be regarded as the transformation of any previous form of energy. But though most men are conscious of this feeling, they hardly ever know it apart from its opposite. They too feel like Œdipus that action is passion. One who knew the whole of a man's past as he knows it himself would probably be unable to reproach him with his worst crimes. If the judge could have before him the whole legacy of the past to the present, as he has it in his own experience, he would seem always to hear the remonstrance to Creon,[1] " Dost thou with right condemn the unwilling deed ? " And what each one of us feels for himself the poet shows us for all mankind.

Hence the Greek idea of Fate is no definite limitation of human Will, but a mysterious warp to which Will is illogically conceived as the woof. Ancestral guilt is in some sense real guilt, and has therefore for those under its shadow become fate; but there must have been a time when it was guilt in the ordinary sense ; divine displeasure must have had a beginning. The legends which have given Fate its moral significance record some whisper at least of the eternal protest against the belief in Fate. The very desire to know the future is rooted in the belief that it lies with man to change the future. If Œdipus were inexorably fated to slay his father and marry his mother, why poison the fragment of life unstained by crime with any prevision of the inevitable? His attempt to escape the announced parricide implies a disbelief in the oracle which announces it as an absolute prediction. But, in fact, the legend of Œdipus is the strongest evidence for the absolute character of Oracles. The event predicted in this case has no root in any

---

[1] Œd. Col., 977.

permanent condition of things such as might be made the subject of warning, but must be called, if we are to describe it in the language appropriate to purpose, a mere accident. No foresight, short of an absolute power to read the future, will explain the prevision of a chance encounter between a king and a stranger, and its result in the death of the king and all his train. Only the absolute prediction implies that the future lies open to the seer just as the past lies open to the ken of an ordinary mortal, the trivial accident no less than the tragic achievement. Yet in that case the whole object of consulting the Oracle would be gone. We might fancy it some ironical sense of this futility in the Œdipus legend which made the Oracle cause its own fulfilment, the means taken to avert the dreaded event proving the means of bringing it to pass; but that cannot have been the intention of the poet; the contemptuous expression applied to the Oracle by both the unhappy pair came too near that dread discovery of its truth which drives Jocasta to the halter and her son-spouse to madness. In truth, it is impossible to say that the Oracle was consistently either believed or disbelieved. Sometimes it seems to have been regarded as that which must happen, and sometimes as that which might be prevented from happening. Greek love of liberty speaks in the Greek belief in Fate, blurring its limits and hiding its source, but never wholly conquering its influence. The two ideas are held together, and we must forget logic when we try to judge of their mutual relations.

This oscillation between the ideas of Will and Law is a striking indication of the bent of national sympathy. The Greek mind seems to demand a certain vagueness in all that claims authority, and to ascribe ultimate power with some hesitation; where it is granted with one hand it seems revoked with the other, as though the distrust of power, which made the name of tyrant hateful, swayed belief in Divine, as well as concession to human rule. Whether we say that Fate is the will of Zeus, that Fate is a deity superior to Zeus, or that Fate is some influence antithetic to all personal will, in any case we have something to explain away. "Not thou, dear child, but the Gods, are responsible for this,"[1] the gracious Priam consoles the guilty Helen, as he surveys the hosts her flight has brought to Troy for the destruction of his city. But the consistent application of this identification of Fate with the Divine will would necessitate the sacrifice of all that is most striking in Greek poetry. Jove feels the law of Fate as a king feels the laws of nature, and in many respects the true analogy seems with these laws; events may be "super-fatal," as we say supernatural.[2] Jove cannot decide on the fate of rival heroes without reference to some standard independent of his will,[3] and whatever the meaning of the balance in which he weighs these contrasted fates, it is something which interferes with the idea of his absolute power. Most of all, perhaps, does the recent origin of his power conflict with the idea of its absoluteness. Omnipotence must have no history. Ormazd confronts Ahriman from the beginning. But Jove is a temporal monarch, his origin is a subject of legend, he has passed through infancy, his dominion is characterized by the harshness incident to "new rule."[4] Surely a reign which has had a beginning shall have an end. The dread of such a contingency is easily raised within his own mind; he is terrified at learning that he

---

[1] Il. iii. 164 ; *cf.* her address to Hector, vi. 344.

[2] *Ibid.*, ii. 155 :—Ἔνθα κεν' Ἀργείοισιν ὑπέρμορα νόστος ἐτύχθη, unless Athene had taken vigorous measures.

[3] *Ibid.*, xxii. 209.

[4] Æsch., "Prometheus Vinctus," 34, 35.

is doomed, if he contract certain nuptials, to bear a son mightier than himself; he exhausts all his arts to wring from the representative of Foresight a fuller knowledge of his own destiny. The destiny of Jove! The very words express this Greek reluctance to contemplate steadily any form of absolute power, the Greek tendency to bring in continually some counterbalancing influence to all that is monarchic. Behind the throne of a God who is so far from being omnipotent that he is not omniscient, hovers a dim mysterious power, so vague that we may or may not give it a moral colouring as our sympathies incline, which we cannot bring into any definite relation with the will of any other being, Divine or human. As it is not entirely subordinate to the will of God, so it is not entirely supreme above the will of man, but it is a real agent, and cannot be confused with either.

This curious reluctance to conceive distinctly of any source of ultimate power is most interesting in its political aspect. The same feeling which hems in royalty with multiform restrictions on Olympus, banishes it in the city; the impatience of individual authority is common to the visible and invisible worlds. The dread of any overpowering personal predominance is the more striking because it is in a certain sense opposed to the genius of a vivid, dramatic people. But the peculiarities which most strike an observer as national characteristics are largely made up of precautions against national temptations; the strong tendency to differentiation which in Greece produced so many types of genius must have been a perpetual source of danger from the presence of strong individualities, and Greek feeling in every direction was strongly tinged by the consciousness of the need for a guard against this danger. How much the temptation impressed a teacher who sought to imbue the

lively Greek temperament with the doctrines of the
Gospel we may gather from the frequent use by St.
Paul, in addressing the Corinthians, of the term we
translate " to be puffed up;"[1] an expression which,
except in addressing the Greek Christians, is not used
in the New Testament. And we may set the explicit
warnings of Paul beside the implicit warning of another
Greek thinker who showed the Greek fear of being
" puffed up " as Paul's converts showed the cause for
that fear. Æschylus, the poet of the supernatural,
breaks through, for once, the cycle of prehistoric legend
on which he finds his appropriate ground, and speaks
to his fellow-citizens of events they themselves remembered, and in which they had taken part. But "the
Persians"[2] is no exception to the general Æschylean
strain ; awe and terror are excited here more than elsewhere, for the tale is of the deliverance of Greece, and
the colossal character of the disaster lifts it out of the
mere course of earthly circumstance and invests it with
the awful dignity of Divine intervention. In telling the
tale of Persian ruin the page is crowded with Persian
names—mostly, one would suppose, the invention of the
poet—but throughout the play which celebrates the Greek
valour that had just worked a miracle not a single Greek
is mentioned. Miltiades and Themistocles—names which
shine through the haze of 2000 years with undiminished
brilliancy—might be supposed with perfect dramatic pro-
priety to be heard at the barbaric court where lies the
scene of the drama. But their countryman never allows
himself to mention them ; he celebrates the triumph of
Athens, he will bring no individual into rivalry with the
city of Athene.

The poet here speaks as the genius of Greece. The

[1] φυσιόω, 1 Cor. iv. 6, 18, 19 ; v. 2, &c.
[2] Æsch., " Persæ," 249, *seq.*

orators of a later age [1] looked back with longing regret
to the patriotic modesty of the earlier heroes, when the
battles of Salamis or Marathon were cited as victories
of the Athenian people, the name of the general being
left for silent gratitude. The "jealousy of the gods" is
shared by the city, the unseen power admits no rivalry
from any seen power. It seems as if the poet felt that
for a mortal to be clothed in the dazzling radiance
which shone upon the day of Greek deliverance was
more than mortal could bear. History justifies such
mistrust ; the leaders of the victorious host should all
have fallen like the victor of Thermopylæ, if they were
to keep their fame untarnished. Miltiades, Themistocles,
Pausanias—all might have envied Leonidas. It would
not be easy throughout the whole range of modern
history to find such traitors as the two last, and the
inglorious death in prison of the victor of Marathon [2] is
a hardly less expressive lesson on the dangers of Greek
glory. If the banishment of Aristides shows us the
other side of this danger, and illustrates the grudging
impatience of superiority felt by the vulgar, yet the very
institution which gave effect to the popular jealousy
tends to show that in itself the feeling was but the base
alloy of a true national instinct, guarding a race dowered
with genius from the temptations incident to such a
nature, and counteracting them with a strong attraction
to all that belonged to the golden mean, such as to
our notions would seem alien from poetic genius and
philosophic originality.

The Greek hatred of monarchy is but another aspect

[1] Demosthenes (if the speech be really his), περὶ ξύνταξεως, 171, 20, οὐδεὶς
ὅστις ἂν εἴποι τὴν ἐν Σαλαμῖνι ναυμαχίαν Θεμιστοκλέους, ἀλλ Ἀθηναίων, οὐδὲ
τὴν ἐν Μαραθῶνι μάχην Μιλτιάδου ἀλλὰ τῆς πόλεως.

[2] Grote does not believe that Miltiades was put in prison : see his arguments,
iv. 496. The reader must choose between him and Plutarch. The hero's
death was in any case disgraceful.

of this feeling. It is only another side of the Greek dread of all arrogance and excess. To set up any one human being at so vast a height above his kind seemed to them a sort of impiety to the gods, as well as an insult to his fellow-men; above all, it was impiety to that true Divinity of Greek worship—the State. Reverence paid to a visible head robbed of its right that unseen Being whose presence made the many a corporate whole; it broke the unseen bond, it destroyed Liberty. The sense of a common relation to the unseen, except in so far as any one excellence is connected with all excellence, has nothing to do with what we mean by Liberty. But few distinctions are so important for a true understanding of History as that between Liberty in the classic and in the modern sense of the word. An Englishman, when he desires Liberty, thinks of it as the opportunity of individual development, the soil on which strongly marked character flourishes most vigorously. It is doubtful whether a Greek would have understood what this means, and still more whether he would have thought it desirable. Indeed, to some extent, we may say that the Greek love of liberty embodied the very opposite feeling to this. There never could have been a city less free than Sparta, according to our ideas; and evidently in making it the model of his Republic Plato was not even contemplating as a possibility the reproach that he was a foe to Liberty. He and his contemporaries meant by Liberty something which was compatible with any amount of despotic regulation of individual life. The ideal Republic of liberty-loving Greece would have been a despotism more intolerable to modern feeling than the most despotic kingdom of modern Europe.

It is hardly a stretch of words to say that Liberty was to the Greek the unseen bond which made a collection of men into a city. What made the name of a tyrant hateful was not that he was cruel or despotic, but that he destroyed this invisible bond; he, a mortal, took the place of an immortal. And hence the love of liberty necessarily involved the reverence for law, as no doubt with the best men it does always, but as with ordinary men it does not now. The Spartans who, by a deeply religious influence, were led to the court of the great King to offer up their own lives as a voluntary atonement for the murder of his heralds slain by their city in defiance of sacred law, refused indignantly to prostrate themselves before the mortal at whose command they were ready to die.[1] They had made a long and toilsome journey from their own beloved city to confront the King on his throne and suffer his will, but they would not bow down before him, "for it was not their way to worship men;" and the great King, impressed by the rare spectacle of fearless submission, dismissed them unharmed. Their journey from Sparta to Susa, and their return, express the Greek submission to law and resistance to personal claim. That resistance implies no recoil from tyranny as we understand the words; there never was a more detested tyranny than that which Sperthias and Bulis would have died to perpetuate. While equally ready to die at the Divine command, they would not renounce an opportunity of protest against the claim of a mortal to intercept even the mere symbol of that homage which was the claim of the State. The bond which made a multitude into a city, the many into one, must be something invisible. The seen monarch was an embodiment not only of impious arrogance, but we might say (if all our associations with the words were not too shallow) of vulgarity and bad taste. The supreme despot was barbaric, lawless, and in the

---

[1] Herodotus, vii. 134, *seq.*

stress of conflict weak. The supreme Law was an inspiring and unconquerable influence, at whose command or in whose defence men were ready to die, and whose claim they would rather die than transfer to a mortal.

Any association of monarchy which seems incompatible with this supremacy of the unseen is wholly superficial. The Homeric kings are not kings in any other sense than that they are the leaders of the armies, and when Ulysses says that the rule of one is necessary, he means only that the rank and file must wait for the word of command.[1] Monarchy was un-Greek, Asiatic, an institution associated with barbarism, and discredited by Asiatic defeat in the one respect in which lay its supposed strength. The great King leading the might of Asia was ruined by the onset of the populations of a few small towns; and thus in those few generations which contain all that is most brilliant of Greek poetry and art, monarchy was associated not merely with degrading bondage, but also with degrading failure. Never was the tyrant opposed to the city without suffering defeat; the associations of victory were all on the side of the State that owned an invisible bond. The conquest over the seen power is closely associated with a trust in the unseen; some divine influence appears when human power fails to give its weight and sanction to the resolute spirit of freedom. The victory of Greece over Persia is the victory of spirit over matter, of will over might. The Gods protect the man who spurns mere human dominion. An Unseen Power fights on the side of those who dare to defy all law-

---

[1] Il. ii. 204. It does not seem, when we attend to the context, a good opportunity for the remark (εἷς κοίρανος ἔστω), which is perhaps made more familiar by the quotation of Aristotle (Met., Bk. x.), and its actual reference somewhat disguised thereby.

less power, and the supreme influences of the world
above are in harmony with those who reject all bondage
here.

It is necessary to dwell on this thought, because the
miracle by which a few small towns scattered the might
of Asia has not been always worked wherever brave men
have been willing to die for their country. Nor, on the
other hand, has the rule of the monarch, throughout
modern history, been invariably associated with tyranny ;
the despotism from which modern nations have suffered
most is not that of an individual, but an order. The
conditions which prevailed in the ancient world during
the short period of the life of Greece, were such that both
her dread of individual pre-eminence and her confidence
in unseen power were justified and enforced by all that
is most striking in her history. Nowhere, not even in
Judæa, do we find a nation more distinctly marked by
Heaven for the part it has to play in the world's history.
What a scholar meant by history until quite lately was little
more than Greek history ; and surely he who knows the
history of Greece may with very little exaggeration be
said to know what History means. He sees, disentangled
from the confusing cross lights of modern life, and exhibited
on a scale which the eye can take in, what the meaning
is of a *national vocation.* It is not more true of Greece
than of England that a national vocation exists, but the
writer who should endeavour to bring out in the history of England any moral purpose, as he cannot
help bringing it out in the history of Greece, would be
continually tempted to falsify facts ; he would lose that
intellectual disinterestedness which is the first duty of
a historian, and would take up the irritating position of
the teacher who infuses his moral into his facts instead
of drawing it from them. But it is hardly possible to
narrate the history of Greece without assuming that it

has a lesson for the world. In merely setting forth the
facts of Greek history we must speak of the triumph of
the resolute few, the downfall of the barbaric armament,
the Nemesis of arrogance, the vindication of the spirit of
liberty. No one can write the history of Greece without
expanding the text, " He hath put down the mighty from
their seat, and hath exalted the humble and meek."
What the historian longs to discover in all history is
written in the tale of Salamis and Thermopylæ, so that
he who runs may read.

Yet the sentiment which we best express in the text
just quoted was, after all, so faintly moral that it
melts into a belief known as much through the protest
of Plato[1] as the continued assertion of Herodotus—the
belief in the envy of the Gods. The words suggest
fallacious analogies. They have not really any relation
to the assertion, " I, the Lord thy God, am a jealous
God." The Greek feeling is not a claim on the devotion
of man, but a grudge against the advancement of man ;
it is the jealousy not of a spouse, but of a rival. It
seems to reproduce on the field of the Divine the lowest
and most vulgar feelings of earth, and to associate the
idea of Divinity with the temptations of a paltry aristocracy, repressing a pushing *bourgeoisie.* The displeasure of the Gods is attracted not only by arrogance or
intemperance, but by a mere excess of prosperity ; they
wish to keep unmingled good fortune to themselves, as
a privilege of their order, and are resolute to shut out
mankind into the realm of vicissitude, far from all partici-

---

[1] Timæus, 29, ἀγαθῷ δὲ οὐδεὶς περὶ οὐδενὸς οὐδέποτε ἐγγίγνεται φθόνος. The
emphatic form of this protest reminds us that the belief it opposes was popular
as well as orthodox. I suppose Plato was thinking of the speech of Achilles to
Priam, Il. xxiv. 525, 6, but he may also have intended to confute many passages
in Herodotus. Timæus, in whose mouth the remark is placed, was a Pytha-
gorean philosopher, who has, says the Platonic Socrates " attained the summits
of philosophy."

pation in their own invulnerable bliss. The prosperous
man who fails to propitiate them by sacrifice of a cherished
possession is doomed by them to a fearful death;[1] it does
not appear that anything but the prosperity of Polycrates
was hateful to them ; he dies a victim to their grudge,
not to their justice. The sentiments thus attributed to
the Gods were indeed, as one of their own poets has
said,[2] shameful among ordinary men. But see how this
mobile national spirit crosses on light wing the watershed of good and ill, and melts the low into the high.
The envy of the Gods, from a slightly shifted point of
view, becomes their compassion. The feeling to which
we may give either of these names, on one side so ignoble,
has its justification and expression in all that is grandest
in Greek history, and makes that history come nearer
than any other to being an exhibition of the justice of
that power which rules the world.

The profound and hidden junction between piety
and pity—between a reverent awe for what is high,
a generous compassion for what is lowly—seems continually indicated by the expressions in which Herodotus clothes this belief. The shipwreck of Asia on
the rock of Greek freedom does not appear to a modern
reader an illustration of that theme; he is already too
familiar with the issue. But if we had been present at
the conflict and watched the result, we should have felt,
as Herodotus did, that God had rebuked the insolence
of the proud, and taken part with the weak. The wise
Persian who endeavours to turn Xerxes from the expedition that is to end in his ruin uses almost the same words
as we have cited from a Psalm,[3] and though, no doubt,
he is chiefly a creation of Greek imagination, he is none

---

[1] Herodotus, iii. 41 43, 125.
[2] See the Fragments of Xenophanes, ed. by Karsten; Fr. vii.
[3] Herodotus, vii. 10, 5 :—φιλέει γὰρ ὁ θεὸς τὰ ὑπερέχοντα πάντα κολούειν.

the less a figure of historic significance on the canvas of
Herodotus. He tells us how that great event looked
to those who were to pass on its influence to the modern
world, and such a representation must be allowed to
possess the highest kind of historic truth, even if from
the literal point of view it is mere fiction. And some
of the forms in which Herodotus expresses this feeling
must be allowed to have more than this kind of authen-
ticity. When he represents Greek envoys from the
army at Thermopylæ striving to encourage allies with
the reminder that [1] "the invader is not a God, but a man,
and that there never had been and never would be a man
who was not liable to misfortunes *greater in proportion
to his own greatness;*" when he paints a victorious general
dissuading the army from pursuit of the defeated host
with the reminder that [2] "we have not achieved this
victory by our own might, it is the work of Gods and
heroes who were jealous that one man should be king at
once over Greece and Asia"—the reader may doubt
whether these are the very expressions which were actually used as a matter of fact, but can hardly suppose
that the historian, in professing to cite words so memor-
able, so recent, and so public, would make use of any
very unlike those which were actually uttered. The
sense of the constant nearness of disappointment to hope,
of a hidden irony in the adjustment of anticipation and
effort to result, is not ordinarily or necessarily a moral
feeling; sometimes it is an immoral feeling. But, as we
have said of the Eumenides, it belongs to that frontier
region of human thought where a step sets us on a
different kingdom. It seems almost as if the same words,
with a different emphasis, might belong to either realm
—as if we might cross over with hardly any change
of a word from the envy of the Gods to the love of

[1] Herodotus, vii. 203.   [2] *Ibid.,* viii. 109.

the Father that chasteneth His children for their profit. Doubtless this is an illusion; when we have reached this belief we have quitted the hand of our guide. But the illusion is almost inevitable, and it is difficult to understand the true Greek feeling without entertaining it for a moment.

The feeling gives an epic unity to the great prose Iliad. A spectator, watching the mighty host passing the Hellespont,[1] wonders why Jove, in the likeness of a Persian, has led the whole race of men for the destruction of Greece; and the subsequent fall is prefaced and preluded by the presumption which these words reflected. It casts back shadows on the impetuous spirit of Xerxes; the tears which he explains by the transitoriness of all things earthly suggest a sense of inadequacy in any prize to justify such effort in beings so ephemeral. Some dim foreboding seems present of the illusory nature of the hopes on which such efforts are founded, a conviction, as in the words which follow, that, short as life is, it is too long for success, that the shadow of disappointment and failure darkens what is spared from the darkness of the grave. And this conviction is presented always with a sense of compassion; we feel the ills of humanity lamented, not those alone of an individual. "Short as our time here is," answers the Persian prince to the lament of Xerxes over the transitoriness of life, "there is no man who is so fortunate as not to have felt the wish for death, not once, but many times." [2] Is there not in these words a sense of compassion for the dumb multitudes whom the great King had just reviewed, who were driven

---

[1] Herodotus, vii. 56.

[2] *Ibid.*, vii. 45, 46 :—τεθνάναι βούλεσθαι μᾶλλον ἢ ζώειν. The speech curiously resembles Hamlet's "To be, or not to be," and is spoken by a Prince in somewhat similar circumstances.

on under the lash to a fate which was certain for
many of them, however the presumptuous hopes of their
monarch might be fulfilled ?   Such a feeling seems
always heard as a tremulous undertone through the
cheerful, light-hearted strain of the narrative, everywhere
we feel the sighs of suffering mingle with notes of
triumph ; we see the envy of the Gods melt into the
compassion of noble men.

At times we watch a higher transformation, we see
the envy of the Gods as a thin veil, covering the love of
God.   The dispensation which takes the aspect of Divine
envy to mortals might, it seems, from a higher point of
view, be discerned as the very opposite ; human vicissitude is the result of a Divine love anxious not to keep
but to share the true blessedness which comes in the
form of sorrow.   The fall of Crœsus changes a tyrant
to a philosopher.[1]   No contrast between different men
could be more striking than that between the vain-
glorious King and the philosophic exile ; he emerges from
that hour's anguish on the burning pyre a sage to whom
the great King may safely bequeath the onerous task of
admonishing his son, and who never betrays that trust.
His history is an eloquent sermon on the teaching of
adversity.   Christian interpretation, we have allowed,
infuses a foreign element into this teaching.   We misinterpret it when we see it under the shadow of the
Cross ; the only words we *can* use to replace the Greek
expressions are for us marked indelibly by the worship
of a suffering God ; and to the Greek the associations of
pity and pardon which they convey are wholly wanting.   Yet we hold a sure clue to the deepest feeling of
Greece when we point out that this misinterpretation is
almost inevitable.   " The quality of mercy," says Shakespeare, " is mightiest in the mighty."   " Zeus himself,"

---

[1] Herodotus, i. 86 ; *cf.* iii. 35.

says Sophocles, "hath mercy[1] for the sharer of his throne." We are not reminded that between the utterance of Sophocles and Shakespeare came the utterance of one who bade his hearers be merciful as their Father in Heaven was merciful; rather the resemblance is greatest where it could not possibly have been conscious. In both what moulds the thought is rather creative art than holy aspiration, yet we cannot sharply divide the two. The Venetian lady pleads for her friend as the Theban prince for himself; it is the insight of genius which gives a moral precept as an appeal of need. Probably it has happened only once in the world's history that mercy was enjoined on the heart and conscience by one who, in the hour of need, never sought it for himself. Man, for the most part, learns the excellence of the high by experiencing the needs of the low, and feels the beauty of tenderness first as the claim of weakness. And thus it is that the perfect artist cannot but preach virtue when all he desires is to paint the lot of ordinary humanity, with its burden of toil, and difficulty, and sorrow.

Among the artist people this is true of every great writer. The historian illustrates its force as well as the poet. We may almost say that on the soil of Greece the historian blossoms into the poet; poetry lies in his theme, a faithful transcript reproduces it on his page. We have seen how that sense of human vicissitude, disguised in a misleading garb as the "envy of the Gods," weaves in a continued strain of pathos into the narrative of Herodotus; we trace it with more difficulty in the work of his successor, yet perhaps the belief itself is more striking when it escapes as a half inconsistency in a dry neutral narrative than when it forms the central idea which gives the narrative epic

---

[1] Αἰδὼς, so translated by Prof. Jebb, Œd. Col., 1268, 9.

unity.   Not a single word is left us by Thucydides
to show that he believed in any power but that of
man ; his tone is in this respect curiously recent ; and
yet the shadow of some influence that seems to mock
at the hopes of man falls on his page, and the strange
dramatic contrast between men's hopes and their fortunes seems to intensify the narrative of facts into an
utterance of regret and a claim for compassion.   As
he describes the modest desire of Nicias "to leave to
posterity a name associated with no disaster to the city,"[1]
he suggests the terrible catastrophe by which the name
of Nicias is for ever associated with the greatest disaster
that Athens ever knew.   The description of the Athenian
Armada's start for Sicily glows with picturesque colouring ; the historian's dry tradesmanlike account of the
expense incurred in this, the most costly expedition
ever sent out from Athens, is mingled with a richness
of detail that seems almost to belong to the page of
romance.   We see the crowds hurrying from an emptied
city to the Piræus ; those who hastened to embrace sons
and brothers they were never to see again jostled by
idlers eager to behold a spectacle of splendour "exceeding belief;" the flashing gold and silver goblets catch
our eye as the libations are poured on the decks of the
noble fleet, gay with a wealth of adornment that attracts
the admiring gaze even of those from whom it bears
away their nearest and dearest.   We hear the clarion
note of the trumpet announce a solemn prayer which
goes up from the united army and from the attendant
crowds on the banks as from one man, and the musical
thunder of the Pæan, as it mingles with the rattle of
weighed anchors and the last bustle of the final start.[2]

---

[1] Νικίας μὲν βουλόμενος . . . τῷ μέλλοντι χρόνῳ καταλιπεῖν ὄνομα ὡς οὐδὲν
σφήλας τὴν πόλιν διεγένετο (Thucyd., vi. 1).

[2] Thucyd., vi. 30-32.

All that tells of pride and hope in that description reminds us that, of the joyous army then flushed with anticipations of victory, some few stragglers alone are to return to Athens with a ghastly tale of dead left unburied on a foreign soil, their corpses an object of envy to the wounded who cumbered the fugitives with helpless clinging, and made the inevitable flight seem heartless treachery. That impressive contrast on the page of Thucydides expresses a creed as well as an event. As we compare the triumphant but not un-reasonable hope with which the Sicilian expedition was decided on, with the unmatched disaster in which it issued, we feel that the jealous fate which shattered the pride of the Great King was to the Greek no partial Deity, but a supreme influence casting down all un-measured ambition, intervening to overthrow even reason-able when it was gigantic anticipation, and constantly bringing in unexpected hope to the vanquished, unexpected humiliation to the conqueror. It seemed the very same power which saved Athens from Persia and Syracuse from Athens. It was not the genius of Athens arising to repel her foes. It was the ultimate divine influence of the whole Hellenic world, the God of proportion, of measure, of balanced forces; the Divinity by whom all intemperance was abhorred and whose sway is repre-sented by the ceaseless vicissitude of human fortune, the chequered aspect of human life. When Athens is threatened by the might of Asia she rises; when her power appears to justify the aim at dominion within the Hellenic world she falls. There is no room on the soil of Greece for an "empire city;" the miniature Europe on which the struggles of history are repeated on a small scale, and with such vivid contrast of light and shade, does not allow any rehearsal of the part of Rome. The spirit of proportion, of limit, which animates Greek literature regulates Greek history; its ideal is that of equal and independent states, and those efforts which foreshadow empire initiate intestine strife and rapid national decay.

It is a striking illustration both of the richness and the balanced dualism of Greek life that the two historians who chronicled the brightness of its spring and the glowing decay of its autumn might have known each other.[1] If we imagine Froissart and Voltaire as contemporaries we bring home to our minds some shadow of the rich variety shown forth in the contrast between the historians of the Persian and Peloponnesian war. How wonderful is the adaptation between each of them and the subject he has made familiar to every student! There never was a narrator more perfectly adapted to the earlier tale than Herodotus. His genius seems ripened in the sunshine that flings its glow on his canvas; he tells of the glory of Greece, and Greek feeling moulds every line. All that is here set forth might be justified and illustrated from his page alone. Homer is not more fitly the singer of those legends than Herodotus a narrator of those events which alike worked to make Greece a unity. The reader who knows him, and him alone, is familiar with all that is most characteristic of Greek feeling and Greek life. All, we repeat, that is *most* characteristic. The cold scepticism of Thucydides has its own place; it is but one phase of the Greek desire to see the other side; it is such an example of Greek balance, Greek impartiality, as we find nowhere else. But if a reader desires to make acquaintance with Greek life in a single book, we should give him Herodotus. There he will find what is best

---

[1] Herodotus is said (on no good evidence) to have given a recitation of his History in 456 B.C. to an audience at Olympia, by which Thucydides, as a boy, was moved to tears. The legend measures chronological possibilities.

worth remembering in the history of Greece—what
stands out from the history known to students and takes
its place in the history known to all readers and to some
who can scarcely claim a place even among readers—
the history which has seasoned the world of allusion
and proverb, and glides into the mind almost apart from
its conscious effort. And there he finds too the fitting
spirit in which such history should be chronicled—the
unquestioning belief in the Invisible, the profound sense
of a national vocation, the light touches of delicate
humour and keen sarcasm without which this conception
would have lacked its true counterpoise and appropriate
relief. There he finds History written in the dialect in
which it reaches not only the student but the dreamer,
the idler, the lover of gossip, of anecdote, of moral
reflection. In that dialect it was fit that the world
should possess the history of the race which appeals
to it with the bewitching aspect of vast hope, immense
promise, and a vivid delight in freedom.

For the history of its decay another voice was needed,
a voice that reaches a different and a much smaller audience, but one which will never fail as long as men care
for literature. The prose life of Greece is set forth with
as much perfection as its poetry, and with, perhaps,
more of instruction and warning for modern Europe.
Indeed the extreme modernness of tone is what at first
most strikes the reader of Thucydides. The eighteenth
century seems to breathe in every page, especially if
memories of Herodotus be present to his mind. The
resemblance is not an accidental one. The history of
Greece after the Peloponnesian war continually suggests
the history of Europe after the Reformation. Europe
had its Catholic unity, as Greece had its Hellenic unity ;
and then Athens and Sparta represent much the same
entanglement of patriotism with an opposite principle,

bringing in cross lines of division that perplex the distinction of the city or the nation.　But the moving
forces that are in European history confused and indistinct show themselves in Greek history sharp and clear,
and make it the typical specimen of what we mean by
history.　Greece is modern Europe on a tiny scale, but
with all the intellectual forces of modern Europe on a
gigantic scale.　It presents that platform of culture above
barbarism which Europe, and that greater England which
forms a vast appendix to Europe, present in contrast to
the African and Asiatic populations; while in diminish-
ing the breadth of the platform no less than in increasing
its height it concentrates and intensifies the teaching of
history, and is indeed to all other history what the best
fiction is to biography.　The art is present in the very
course of events which it traces.

Thus as the struggle of Greece with Persia shows the
dynamic vitality developed by a nation's first self-con-
sciousness—the heat generated by a rush of union—
so the struggle of Athens with Sparta shows the para-
lyzing touch of party spirit on patriotism, the chill of
disintegration.　If there be any principle of corporate
union of which we may say broadly that it is evil, we
may say it of party spirit.　In all that binds there must
be some good; and since almost all that binds also
separates, there will be probably some evil also.　But
nowhere else is the gain so small, and the loss so
great.　Reversing the noble sentence of Antigone, the
political partizan may almost say, "I was not born to
share thy love, but hate."　On that soil all love withers
and all hate flourishes.　The love of country is the
love of the neighbour.　It sets us in kindly relationship with those of whom we know most, for whom
we can do most; it includes every variety of opinion,
of circumstance, of character; it contains within itself

lessons of tolerance and forbearance, and it becomes in
a healthy mind an expansive feeling, passing beyond its
own large boundaries, and ready to embrace the world.
It may no doubt pass into the hatred of the foreigner,
but as far as it does so it becomes an exceptional
influence, not concerning the life of every day. Irra-
tional dislike, if it must be felt at all, had better be felt
for those whom we rarely see, and have small power to
injure. When it is turned into the current of partizan
feeling it sets up a principle of division in every household and stirs hostility where the power to give pain is
at its highest. It is the parent of that "madness in the
brain" that comes from being "wroth with one we love."
Its bonds have no elasticity. The patriot is the possible
philanthropist. The partizan is as much cut off from
that possibility as is the mere egotist. For, however
numerous the sharers of his sympathies, those sympathies have nothing catholic in them;—party spirit is
that spirit of taste, of preference, which is strong enough
in every man, strengthened by a sense of duty. Friendship on such a basis is a house built on the sand, for
the ally may any day become the traitor. Enmity,
on the other hand, is a fortress on a rock, for the foe
can never become the trusted ally. It is the negative
principle of human intercourse, put in the place of the
positive.

These considerations refer to party spirit at all time
and in all places. Wherever it prevails it is a solvent
to friendship and natural affection, an antagonist to pity,
generosity, and justice. But it never again shows itself
in its naked repulsiveness as in the history of Greece.
For no modern life is quite so sensitive to party spirit
as was the city life of antiquity. It is hurtful to all
national feelings, but a nation is large enough to absorb
it and triumph over it. A city becomes its prey. Eng-

land has survived the rise and fall of many parties.
But when Greece was divided between oligarchic Sparta
and democratic Athens its life was rent asunder in the
strife.   It is true that Athens was a small city, and that
the adherents of Democracy were a large party.   But
the smallest city is less exclusive than the largest party.
A family, a tribe, a city, a nation—any natural group
whatever—is founded on something more allied to self-
sacrifice than the spirit of choice.   A party is a consecration of all those egotistic impulses which everywhere
adhere to the spirit of choice.   Thus the exchange of
patriotism for partizan feeling in Greece was a narrowing influence, even though it did exchange a number
of small groups for two large ones.   It was the more
narrowing because the groups it dissolved were small.
The disease attacked an organism unfitted to cope with
it.   Party spirit was more hostile to civic than it could
ever be to national life, because it met with nothing
strong enough to swallow it up.   And it is still more
to our purpose to note that Greece was disloyal to its
fundamental principle when it gave itself up to party
spirit.   It ceased to hold to the spirit of the balance, it
loosed its hold on what was in truth the rudder of its
political life.   Greek feeling, divorced from the harmony
of opposites, lost all vitality, all coherent moral standard.   Greek liveliness was then converted to hatred.
Party spirit is a deliberate refusal to hear the other side.
The Greek ideal could not admit such a refusal ; where
the last was victorious the first perished.   We may
record the completeness of the victory in the oath
taken, in some states, at the time of Aristotle,[1] by
the members of the oligarchy, "I swear to be eter-
nally hostile to the commonalty, and to do it all the

---

[1] καὶ τῷ δήμῳ κακόνους ἔσομαι καὶ βουλεύσω ὅ τι ἂν ἔχω κακον (Ar., Pol.,
v. 7, 19).

harm in my power *by my counsels.*" Hatred and treachery were thus incorporated in political life, and Greece, broken up into warring factions, ceased to be a nation.

"The universe," says one of the earliest thinkers of Greece, "is the harmony of the lyre and bow."[1] The order of nature, in its widest sense, Heracleitus thought, rests on the harmony of all that the lyre symbolizes, and all that the bow symbolizes — the union of the power that gives to life all its value with the power that destroys life. The harmony would lose all its richness with the withdrawal of its discords. "The hidden harmony is better than that which is manifest." "It is not well that man should choose his fate; his true good is resignation, not pleasure." Pleasure is the manifest, resignation the hidden, harmony; —the element of discord is lacking where man has his own will, and with it all the finest music of humanity. Even death and life join in the lesson of the indissoluble unity of opposites ; man chooses life which is truly death, and flees from death which is truly life. The union of antagonistic principles is the clue to all that man can achieve or know.

"It is not well that man should choose his fate."[2] One might fancy that sentence as an utterance from the cloister; it seems a strange expression from one of the joy-loving, art-loving Greek race. Yet, in truth, it is one of the most characteristic that have come to us in the Greek tongue. It represents a large part of what is most impressive in Greek literature. It would not be possible, probably, to gather so many illustrations of the

[1] These fragments are taken from the work of Ferdinand Lassalle, "Die Philosophie Heracleitos des Dunklen," with his interpretation.
[2] Ἀνθρώποις γίνεσθαι ὁκόσα θέλουσιν, οὐκ ἄμεινον (Lassalle's "Heracleitos," ii. 449).

belief in the blessings of adversity from any other historian as from Herodotus. The story of Crœsus at its
opening sets the keynote, and Polycrates supplies the
best-known illustration of the theme; but perhaps nothing
is so impressive as the decision of Solon, so offensive to
Crœsus, that the second place in human happiness is
to be given to the two Argive youths who drew their
mother to the temple of Juno in place of the oxen, and
after her prayer to the goddess to grant them that which
is best for man, fell asleep in the holy precincts, and
awoke no more.[1]   What! one is tempted to ask, is the
earthly doom of humanity one prolonged mistake?   Is
it better to quit this scene of existence as soon as it is
fully open?   The spirit which seems to answer " Yes "
is the spirit which most delights in all the beauty,
the pleasure, the joy of earth.   The power to see its
charm seems but the other side of the power to see its
emptiness.   " Man is the dream of a shade," says the
poet who has immortalized the games of Greece.[2]   The
sense of life's brightness and the sense of its vanity seem
to have attained their summit together.   We have all
known moments in which we could understand the con-
junction—moments in which the crash of dance music
or the brightness of a summer's day seemed to hold
some profound, unspeakable melancholy, a melancholy
lying at the very core of all that was its very opposite.
Such a feeling is found often in the poetry of Scott,
and lends it a peculiar Greek grace—a grace with us
somewhat allied to what is conventional, and not characteristic of the highest poetry of the modern age, which
demands a fuller grasp on the great realities of the
spiritual world.   For we come in contact with hardly

---

[1] Herodotus, i. 31.

[2] Pindar, Pyth., viii. :—σκιᾶς ὄναρ ἄνθρωπος. The line is imitated by
Sophocles.

anything that is original, in our sense of the word, in Greek poetry; we meet very little thought stamped with idiosyncrasies of a peculiar character. But we meet the ideas to which we are accustomed in their well-worn, half-obliterated banality, fresh from the mint of human thought. And thus that sentiment of the fleetingness in all things earthly, which with us, from its very depth and breadth, has become commonplace, touches the grandest poetry of antiquity.

For, in truth, all modern literature is more or less impregnated with the ideas of Greece, and we meet here at first hand what elsewhere we meet at second hand. We have literatures which know nothing of the classical world, but all to which we give the name of *literature* absorbs this influence from a thousand sources, however little it may reproduce its form. Shakespeare himself is but the most perfect blossom of the Renaissance culture which found its root in the buried treasures of Greece, and all that has attained any perennial hold on the literary mind of Europe has hitherto owed its power to this magic influence. Other kinds of excellence there may be where the Greek sense of balance and harmony is wanting—philosophic or scientific thought, theologic earnestness, historic truth;—and it may be that in some books of very deep value it is lacking. But we cannot say that, in any deep sense, the result is literary. In the world of art this is obvious. Dramatic power is inseparable from intellectual disinterestedness, and intellectual disinterestedness means a fine sense of the opposite forces that mould character. Art can live only in the leisure of a mind not occupied by any sense of the claim of the Right to continual emphasis and unvaried illustration. Wherever we meet dramatic power we meet this spirit; the temper of mind which throws itself with strenuous resolve into the part of a defender of right, an avenger of wrong, affords the dramatist some of his finest material, but is itself undramatic. We take up the Iliad with a sense of escape from all we long to forget, because it is a picture of vivid, stirring life, reflected in the still waters of a perfectly dramatic impartiality. Few recognize the source of this mingled vigour and repose, but it is felt by all. The Greek poet takes all his most pathetic, most inspiring images from the foes of Greece. The noblest utterance of patriotism and the purest picture of domestic love are both from the Trojan side; the Trojan King sets an example of chivalrous courtesy; even the effeminate Asiatic prince touches the reader by his candid confession under the rebuke of his heroic brother. The intercourse which takes place between the warrior chiefs in the intervals of battle has nothing fierce or hostile; it is the discourse of brave men who hope to kill each other, but who in the meantime have no difficulty in recognizing each other's nobility. This makes the Iliad not a national but a human epic. We have described this excellence in negative terms, but it is in the highest degree positive. It is the secret which gives brightness of colour and delicacy of form to every touch. Achilles—Hector—Helen—they live and move before us, because their images are un-blurred by any ruffling breeze, because a fine balance of sympathies keeps the poise even and avoids every disturbing jar. We see Greek impartiality at its highest if we turn from the Greek to the Persian epic. The poem which enshrines the legend associated with a belief in Ahriman and Ormazd is indeed full of interest. But it is an interest for the student. It is a picture of the strife of good and evil. The contrast between the Hellenic and the Persian epics strikingly brings out the character of the two religions which they express.

The Shah-Nameh is, for the most part, a series of struggles between heroes of noble virtue and monsters of wickedness, and between a people of light (Iran, the Persian race) and a people of darkness (Turan). Where a hero falls, it is through the temptation of Ahriman. Zohak, the serpent king who bears on his shoulders twin snakes sprung from a kiss of the Evil One, has yielded to impious seductions; promises of splendid dominion have led him to plunge into guilt, and the crimes of his monstrous double nature have earned an awful punishment; he is not to be speedily slain, but to die a death of agony. How unlike anything in the Iliad! Where Homer gives us fierce anger Firdusi gives us bitter hatred. Where Firdusi gives us a combat of saints and devils Homer gives us a struggle of hero with hero. The poem that opens Greek literature can never grow old, because it is committed to no temporary, no local emotion—it sets no stamp of condemnation on any actor of the drama; it claims sympathy, in turn, for all.

This we may say of the poem which stands on the threshold of Greek literature, and to which, to a certain extent, we may say that Greece owes its unity. And then, again, we may say it of that work of literary genius which, of all that has been bequeathed us by Greece, has least of the poetic spirit, and which most expresses the antagonism within the bosom of Greece. Few immortal works treating of a similar subject can be so unlike as the Iliad, and the history which Thucydides has left of the Peloponnesian war. The contrast of poetry and prose, of the spirit of simple childlike faith, and of cold wary scepticism, of glowing fancy, and of realistic effort after accurate narration—all these are brought to a climax when we set the two works together: they seem to belong to different worlds. And yet we cannot forget that they belong to the same race. We can hardly say that Thucydides and Homer have anything else in common, but they are alike impartial. It is equally impossible to discern any various colouring in the sympathies of the narrator according as he follows the fortunes of those with whom his interests were identified, and of those to whom they were opposed. The narration keeps its hard disinterested accuracy whether it sets before us the fate of Athenian or Spartan, as the poem keeps its glowing richness of colouring whether it paints the fortune of Trojan or Greek. This equality of interest cannot be more absolute in the one case than the other, but it is far more striking on the page of the historian than in the song of the bard. Homer relates no deed of the Greek army that may be set by the side of the taking of Melos as a specimen of ruthless barbarity ; and Thucydides, even in that part of the narrative which must be due to his fancy, shows not the faintest temptation to soften a line in the picture of his country's crime.[1] That the Athenians slew the adult males and enslaved the women and children of a State which had done nothing to incur their enmity, was a fact which the great Athenian writer must recognize ; but when he describes the pleadings on either side, which must in great measure be due to his own fancy, we might have looked for some indication of a wish to make out a case for his own countrymen, such as, assuredly, an English writer would betray in narrating the bombardment of Copenhagen or the fate of Drogheda. Assuredly we shall not find it. "It is hard indeed," the Melians concede, "to contend against your power and your fortune ; yet we lose not our faith in Divine aid, for we are innocent and confronted with the unrighteous." "We are quite easy as to that," reply the

[1] Thucyd., v. 89-105.

Athenians. " It is certainly a law for human beings that they should take who have the power, and we suppose this law holds good in the Divine world also." What reader would not suspect, in reading that dramatic fragment, that the sympathies of the writer were with the vanquished ? Perhaps in some sense they were, but not in any sense that made Thucydides less of an Athenian, not in any sense that shows itself in one word of condemnation when he comes to speak of the cruel fate of those whose trust in Divine aid was met with utter failure. He sympathized with the Melians only so far as he threw himself on to their side with dramatic disinterestedness of attention, only so far, we may say, as he was a true Greek.

The " grand impartiality "[1] of Thucydides is not only national, it is personal. For twenty years the great historian was an exile from his native city. He was a general in the war he has made known to all time, and it is evident that he was banished for the failure to relieve an important city which he mentions; but the two facts are both mentioned so slightly that the reader has to discover their connection himself. Though his chronological method is one of somewhat tiresome accuracy and precision, he tells us of his own exile out of its proper place, and in a mere parenthesis of his narrative. " I happened to be in exile for twenty years after my command at Amphipolis, and thus to have great advantages for ascertaining the facts from both sides," is all he tells us about it. The unfortunate command which led to this punishment is told with the same brief, disinterested lightness. There is not a word in the few lines referring to it which, if he had left out " the present writer," would have led us to think he was speaking of himself. A historian of Greek

<hr>

[1] Jowett's "Thucydides," vol. ii. p. 303, note 26.

literature has been so much impressed with this reserve, that he explains it by supposing it to be due to the consciousness of guilt. Thucydides "neither attempts to vindicate himself nor specifies the ground of his sentence,"[1] his critic thinks, because he had been more occupied in looking after his own property than in the interests of his country. The fact may have been so. There is nothing whatever in literary impartiality to secure political disinterestedness. But so temperate a reference to the incident, by one who might have given his own colouring to the narrative, does not look like consciousness of guilt; it may have covered such a feeling, but what it expresses is the reticence demanded by that fine sense of proportion, which gives the art of Greece its immortal predominance.

If history shows us the harmony of opposites, in Greek life, as a momentary and swiftly baffled aspiration, in philosophy and in literature we find it as a perennial spring, which no frost can seal and no drought exhaust. We may associate the Greek virtue—temperance—with the productions, not of genius, but of talent. To us it suggests the performance, not of virtue, but of respectable mediocrity. But the Greek saw in this idea the key to all that is finest in art, noblest in virtue, most desirable in experience. Genius, by the very fact that it often reaches, never craves extravagance. There is a profound meaning in the seemingly fantastic Greek speculations on the principle of number as the mystic root of orderly and developed Being. "The art of measurement," says Plato, "is that which would save the soul;"[2] and the pupil of Plato expanded that statement into the doctrine so well known, yet so little understood,

---

[1] "A Critical History of the Language and Literature of Ancient Greece," by William Mure of Caldwell, v. 40.

[2] Plato, Protagoras, 356.

of the golden mean. To the English mind, a kind of dulness clings round the notion. We have it sufficiently represented in our achievement; what we crave in our ideal is something different. For Greek thought the idea of the mean takes in the moral universe the place taken in the physical universe by that law which marks out the path of the planet; it is, in like manner, a diagonal, the result of warring forces. What draws the spirit one way was to them no more evil than what draws it another. Cowardice drags it downwards; rashness drives it away from its true centre. A wise manliness finds its orbit settled by the contest of these two conflicting forces, and revolves about its centre with an equal attraction and repulsion for both. All vivid feelings were legitimate; their harmony, their balance, was the only conscious need. The ideal of the Conscience belonged to the great foe of Greece. The Hellenic spirit welcomed *all* impulse, but impressed its own delicate distinctness on all, and joined the Pantheistic fervour of India to Persian definiteness, with a wealth of illustration and glow of feeling that belongs to it alone, among all the nations of the earth.

CHAPTER IV.

ROME AND THE REIGN OF LAW.

Greece contains so much more than the ideal common to it with Rome, that, in confining our gaze to the life of Greece, we do not see clearly the contrast between Ancient and Modern thought. The race that is dowered with genius can hardly exhibit limitations, even when subject to them; amid the rich blossoming of distinct and striking individualities, we discern with difficulty that a *person* was hardly regarded as what we mean by an individual. But the ideal of antique life is illustrated as much by Athenian thought as by Roman life, or is only less illustrated there because Greek thought is various in its abounding wealth and Roman life is meagre in its simplicity. All the grandeur of the classical world, Greek or Roman, depends on a sense of corporate unity, which appears to the modern intellect rather the goal of eminent goodness than the possible assumption of average practical life. We hardly reach with much effort that sense of the value of organic corporate life which the citizen of antiquity could not lose. Among us, it would require exalted virtue to make the tribe or the nation the starting-point of thought, as it must have been the starting-point of thought to an average Athenian or Roman. The object of conservation to him was a set of groups; the individual was a fraction of one or more of these groups, not an entity that could be considered in himself. The mere perception that a certain regulation tended to preserve these groups gave motive-power; there was no need of adding to it (what unquestionably would be needed in modern life) some argument to show that the thing thus preserved was valuable.

At the very moment at which these lines are written (1887) it is less necessary than it was a short time ago to dwell on the social weakness produced by modern individualism. Perhaps we now more need reminding of its strength. But this reminder points out the difference of the two ideals quite as forcibly. We cannot attain the antique unity of the Family. The attempt without this to merge individuality in the State tends to deprive us of both the ancient and the modern unity. When we make the effort we are hindered as much by our virtues as by our vices; we are neither good enough nor bad enough for the thing we are trying to do. At our best, we cannot so surrender our own rights; at our worst, we cannot so trample on those of others. For the unity of the State, based as it was on the unity of the Family, was preserved by the relegation of all the perplexities of modern civilization to a region with which the State refused to concern itself. The fact that a Greek or Roman saw all Liberty against a background of slavery is as important as the fact that he meant by Liberty no mere immunity from interference, but an actual share in a corporate unity which preceded and would survive him. Here are the strength and the weakness of the antique ideal side by side. The Greek or Roman was better than the modern Englishman, so far as he was vitally the member of a commonwealth. He was worse, so far as he was the member of a dominant caste. It was no proof of exalted virtue in him to merge his own interests in those of his country to an extent which would require exalted

virtue now ; but neither was indifference to the interests
not bound up in this great dominant claim a sign of
exceptional hardness of heart, as it would be with us.
The best among the ancients disregarded the ills of all
beyond a certain enclosure, as the ills of others are, in
our day, disregarded only by the pre-eminently selfish ;
but they aimed at the welfare of all within that enclosure,
as in our day only the unselfish aim at any welfare but
their own.

What we have said of the abundant and almost bewildering wealth of Greek ideas is eminently true of the
Greek from whom all philosophy takes its start ; amid
the tropical luxuriance of Plato's thought, conceptions
which he held in common with his countrymen are not
conspicuous. But it is striking to note in that delineation
of an ideal State, which is, perhaps, the fragment of ancient
thought most familiar to modern ears, how far away was
the Greek starting-point of moral speculation from ours.
Among moderns no one would set about answering the
question, What is goodness ? by discussing forms of
government. A modern writer might incidentally illustrate his idea of goodness by pointing out what form of
government the best men would seek to establish (and
even this most people would feel a matter of very
questionable relevance), but to start from this point
would be impossible. When Socrates is made to say
that it is simpler to investigate Righteousness in a State
rather than in an individual,[1] his hearers see as little
room for doubt, as if he had said that they could judge
better of a man's character by taking in the whole of his
life rather than a part of it. An Englishman does not
think the thing that Plato meant by the righteousness
of a State less important or real than Plato did. He sees
that in some States the various members of the com-

---

[1] Plato, Rep., 368, 9.

munity keep more or less to their true function, and in
others they fail to do so ; and he is aware that the difference is one of vital importance. But he would deny that
the quality which makes a nation into a harmonious community is the quality which makes a righteous man ; at
all events he would never begin by assuming this. And
in all the dialogue there is no hint that any Greek could
even see as a difficulty what most Englishmen would feel
an insuperable objection.

This shifting of the moral centre of gravity has
affected every department of our moral being. It is
recorded in change of desires, of aspirations, of tastes ;
it is discernible in the new associations of some words
relating to that part of our nature which we should have
thought permanent ; it tinges with colouring unknown
to antiquity names which denote the largest objects
of human desire. Even that in man which is least
changeable is not entirely unchanged from generation
to generation. *Liberty*, we should have thought, must
always have had the same meaning. But it has the same
meaning now and 2000 years ago, only in the sense
that two copies of the same outline differently coloured
form the same picture. At all times a man must dislike being prevented doing what he chooses to do ;
that is merely saying twice over that he chooses to do
it ; but while the moderns mean no more than this
by Liberty, the ancients included so much beside, that
the whole idea was different. An Englishman thinks
of Freedom as something that is to be a limit to government ; to a Greek or a Roman the aim of limiting
government in order to leave scope to Freedom would
have been like cutting off the roots to leave room for
the branches. Freedom was, in their view, mainly a
share in government. It might include other advantages, but they were insignificant compared to this ;

take it away, and it would have been difficult, from the ancient point of view, to see what remained. To be free was not so much a condition as a relation. Liberty, in the modern world, is a part of the democratic ideal; in ancient life it was incurably aristocratic. It was there, an unquestionable privilege of the few; it is here, the inalienable right of the many. Liberty that is not liberty for all is something that the modern world regards without sympathy, something that individuals may desire, as men may desire selfishly to possess any good, but that can never unite them in a common aspiration or close their ranks in a firm resistance. To the modern mind it is the rightful possession of the human race, and in any sense in which this is impossible, it is not the rightful possession of any one.

When we turn from human desire to human admiration, this change of feeling becomes yet more evident. We should more accurately represent to ourselves the earlier force of the word *virtue* if we associated it with the sense still in use in which we speak of the virtues of plants; it is that which makes a man efficient; manliness, valour, distinction, public spirit—that, in short, which tells in the citizen. We may almost say that the modern sense is the very opposite of this. What an ordinary Englishman means by virtue is that kind of excellence which does not tell in the citizen. No one, for instance, would speak of Nelson as a virtuous man, though he had all, and more than all, that a Roman meant by virtue. What speaks most of the change is the fact that virtue has even altered its sex; the Roman would have found it difficult to associate *virtus* with any possible feminine excellence; the Englishman rarely uses the word except with reference to women. When Cicero said of his daughter, "Her virtue is wonderful," [1] he

---

[1] "Cujus quidem virtus mirifica. Quo modo illa fert publicam cladem !

meant, " It is wonderful to see so much manly fortitude
in a woman," and accordingly his best translator has
here rendered the word *spirit.*   The woman had no place
in the civic world, any more than the slave had ; and
the civic world was the world of virtue.   Beyond it,
virtue became merely a negative thing ; the woman
could be a criminal as the slave might, and as a
mother she was capable of a vicarious lustre which the
slave could not share ; but the sphere of womanly goodness did not exist.   The world of duty was wholly
masculine.

In the case of Virtue, modern association has changed
manliness into womanliness ; in the case of Freedom, it
has changed manliness into humanliness.   It is men as
human beings who desire Freedom in England, France,
and Germany ; it was men as embodying the ideal of
manliness who desired it in Greece and Rome.   On
both sides we have an expression, more or less distinct,
of the great watershed which divides the moral life of
the ancients from ours.   Political duty for them *was*
duty.   Excellence which did not buttress the life of the
citizen was to their eyes almost invisible.   Freedom
which did not mean a life of government hardly counted
as freedom, and the life of government meant a life free
from the cares that are, on the modern view, the lot of
average humanity.

The change we are considering has affected the moral
world in its widest sense ; it extends to a region where
questions of right and wrong are out of sight ; it
speaks of a new attitude as much of taste as of conscience.   The word *Nature* to a Roman meant human
nature ; its most dignified associations were those of the

Quo modo domesticas tricas ! " (Cic., Ad Att., x. 8).   See the translation of this
passage in the " Life and Letters of Cicero," by the Rev. G. E. Jeans, p. 247.
Cf. Quæst. Tusc., ii. 18, " Appellata est ex viro virtus."

Senate and the forum; its whole scope of reference lay
in the desires and actions of men. To a countryman of
Wordsworth's the word suggests the shade of bird-haunted
thickets, the trackless breadth of moorland; it fills his
ears with the rustle of the wind in the trees or the wave
on the shingle, and sways his mind with the rhythm of
the seasons, the pulsation of yearly growth and decay.
Every image is for our generation associated with the
utterance of genius, as well as the investigations of
thinkers.   Poetry and science, foes as they appear,
have worked in harmony to enrich and illustrate the
world of beauty and orderly sequence that begins where
human effort ends.   We see this change very clearly
when we put side by side ancient and modern specimens
of identical feeling.   Socrates did not, for he could not,
care less for the country than Dr. Johnson did, but Dr.
Johnson was a man who could not be left alone with
his thoughts.   Many whose hearts were haunted by
something unbearable must have shared his clinging to
crowded streets, but probably no modern whose spirit
was as unclouded as that of Socrates would have cared
so little to visit that grassy bank within a few miles of the
Acropolis, where the waters of the Ilissus murmured
through the shade of the lofty plane-trees, and shrubs
framed the odorous nook with clustering blossoms,
shutting in the stroller into a paradise of sight, scent,
and sound.   So at least the Cockney of our day would
feel it, and so did Socrates for a moment, but apparently
for no longer.   He acquiesces in the scoff of his com-
panion, "You are really just like a tourist with your
guide."[1] "Trees and country places," he urges in apology,
"have nothing to teach a learner."   To the cultivated
inhabitant of Athens or Rome the country might be a
pleasing scene for music and lovemaking, or a prized

---

[1] ξεναγουμένῳ τινὶ καὶ οὐκ ἐπιχωρίῳ ἔοικας (Plato, Phædrus, 230).

source of wealth, but all that was an object of ordinary
and earnest aspiration was left behind in the towns.
The enjoyment of rural life belongs to the modern world,
where the unity is the nation, not the city ; where the
privacy of home has won itself a long tradition of reverence, where the passive side of life is associated with
honour and picturesqueness, and the city has fallen so
much into the background that a taste has arisen for
whatever is most unlike a town.

This local change thus gathers up and symbolizes the
moral change between the world of antiquity and of our
own day. What a Greek or Roman meant by a good man
was a good citizen.[1] A good man, in the modern conception, may possibly be a very indifferent citizen ; a good
citizen may certainly be an immoral man. Or rather
the very word citizen has ceased to be applicable, and
the difficulty of finding another with which to replace
it shows that the relation it expresses has changed its
importance. An English or French man may be in all
private relations just, truthful, and generous, and may
take very little interest in the welfare of his country.
It is a defect in him that he fails to do so, no doubt ;
still a man may have some good qualities and not all
good qualities. But how much more than this we
should mean if we were to speak of an Athenian as
indifferent to the welfare of Athens ! The difference
between him and a similar Englishman is twofold.
In one sense England is too large to be to an Englishman what Athens was to an Athenian ; in another
sense it is too small. It is not an entity that can be
associated with definite and familiar images, with ideas

---

[1] There is a passage in a letter of Cicero's to Lentulus, Ad Fam. ix. (quem
bonum civem semper habuisset, bonum virum esse pateretur), which may appear
a confutation of this statement. I believe that one who studies the whole letter
will find in it a fresh illustration of the view in the text, but it does also show
that Cicero was on the threshold of a different view.

all called up at once by the word *home.* It requires
some power of abstraction to take in.   And then, again,
it is only a part of that whole which a modern contemplates as making just the same sort of claim that
in the ancient world the city made upon the citizen.
The nation is a whole at once more vast and more
incomplete than was the city.   It loses unity both as
a combination of many classes and interests and also
as a fraction of humanity.   It refers to unities below
itself and a unity above ; and though it has a unity of
its own, and one of a majestic and enduring character,
still we feel that many causes may prevent good men
from entering into any conscious relation with this unity ;
they may fail to respond to the claim which it makes,
and yet be worthy of much respect.   But a Greek who
was indifferent to political duty had almost no other
duty to fall back upon ; a Roman had absolutely none.
Philosophy did present to a few spirits some such alternative among the nation of thinkers ; the Athenian could
find a country elsewhere than in the city which nestled
at the foot of the Acropolis.   But in the very mention
of such an alternative, we circumscribe the field of duty,
for average mankind, within the region that concerns the
relation of a man to the State of which he forms a part.

   We cannot follow this change on the supposition that
it is simply a matter of addition (if we regard the
duties that a sense of individuality has added to the
ancient standard as the most important element), or of
subtraction (if we think that of the political energy which
we have lost by the change.)   It is not arithmetic but
chemistry that gives us its type.   The whole of duty is
modified when we change the hierarchy of duty.   How
significant is the etymology of " prerogative," the section
that was asked first for its opinion !   There lies the
whole force of an ideal.   *Which do you consult first ?*

Everything else will be different. An Englishman is asked first whether he is a good son, a good father, a good husband; if he be all these, the fact that he is not a good citizen is viewed indulgently. A Greek was asked first whether he was a good citizen; if he must answer this in the negative, his filial, paternal, conjugal excellence went for nothing. What we demand first gives the keynote to duty; duties are not merely re-arranged, they are transformed by change of order. Those influences which gave the ancient State its sacred character cannot so expand their area as to take in humanity; their power and their limitations disappear together. The class, the nation, even the human race in its totality, are all unfitted to succeed the classical ideal of the State. There is no possible human group which we can contemplate as the Greek contemplated the city; no man can feel himself a part of the human race with the same definiteness of loyal reverence as an Athenian felt himself a son of Athens or a Roman of Rome. And yet the moment we fix our attention on some smaller group than the human race, we encumber ourselves with a problem almost as strange to the ancients as the differential calculus;—we want some code as to our demeanour to "them that are without." It is an essential part of this ancient ideal that only some human beings should have rights. The city was an exclusive unity in a sense in which no modern group is exclusive. We cannot look at the world or at the nation as the Greek looked at the city; his city had its slaves, his world had its foes; his virtue depended on both. Give the slave and the enemy rights and you need a new starting-point of moral thought.

Slavery has been a part of modern life for at least as long as it was of ancient life, and has been defended in modern, far more passionately than in ancient times.

But the whole movement of modern thought has been away from it. It has been defended by those who were interested in its preservation. In ancient times there was neither defence nor attack. When Plato drew up a constitution for an ideal State—a State so far removed from all actual experience that no mother among the governing class should know her own child—the only change he suggested in reference to slavery was that no Greek should enslave a Greek. And this mild measure of reform was so little original to his genius that it had already been put in practice by one of the Athenian generals in the great war drawing to its conclusion at the supposed date of the Dialogue.[1] Plato only conceived it possible to imagine, in his ideal city, such a modification of slavery as a countryman had already carried out amid all the difficulties of actual warfare. Perhaps no other passage shows us so forcibly how deeply slavery had sent its roots into the heart of all ancient thought. The experience of the teacher, we should have thought, would have been no less suggestive than that of the soldier; the life of Socrates himself might surely have shown that it was possible for a man to lead the life of a freeman with hardly any recourse to the labour of a slave. But it was not so. Greek was not, in the ideal Greek city, to enslave Greek; the men who shared each other's language and religion were not to strip each other of all that made life worth having; but this was all. And it is evident, from the whole history of the time, that to men reared in the atmosphere of slavery, this was much.

The men who felt so differently about slavery would feel differently about much beside. It would form the

---

[1] Plato, Rep., 469 ; *cf.* Xenoph., Hellen., i. 6, 14. Callicratidas, the Spartan admiral, who refused to sell Greek prisoners into slavery, succeeded Lysander, B.C. 406.

mould of all subordination and supply the associations of all power. It would fix the position of those who were not slaves in name, but who were, almost as much as slaves, cut off from the life which a Greek regarded as alone worth living. The whole artizan class was attracted, as it were, by the neighbourhood of slavery into an atmosphere of degradation. Labour was servile ; its associations all carried the mind towards a life of bondage. " There is nothing disgraceful in work," says Hesiod,[1] but the words are rather a protest against Greek feeling than an expression of it. The hatred of labour was stamped on the very structure of language ; Greek denotes labour and pain by the same word. All work rendered political life impossible, and there was no interest in any other. The union of professional and political life is a discovery of the modern world; it belongs to representative government. What we mean by the Franchise was a boon that a Greek would have despised. Once every three or four years to take part in nominating the legislators of the land would have been to his imagination a very paltry advance towards the life of a Freeman. We come nearer his point of view in regarding all Greek citizens as members of Parliament, as, in fact, they were. Englishmen feel it very flat to lose this keen interest when once they have shared it, but they do not connect the loss with any ideas or disgrace. They know that a man may lead a refined, liberal life—the life of a gentleman in the best sense of the word—without taking any part in the work of legislation. But the loss of this interest deprived a

[1] " Works and Days," 300. *Cf.* Plato, Charmides, 163, for a curiously vivid illustration of Greek recoil from this praise of industry :— ἔμαθον γὰρ παρ' Ἡσιόδου (says Critias) ὅς ἔφη ἔργον δ' οὐδὲν ὄνειδος· οἴει οὖν αὐτόν, . . . εἰ τὰ τοιαῦτα οὐδενὶ ἂν ὄνειδος φάναι εἶναι σκυτοτομοῦντι, &c. Critias thinks that Hesiod could not possibly have had such work as the shoemaker's in his mind when he said work was not disgraceful.

Greek of all that was worth having. The associations of slave labour took the heart out of all work. And a man obliged to work for his living could even less have taken part in the ancient than the modern Parliamentary councils, the former not being arranged, like the latter, with a view to professional life. Hence the life of a Freeman stopped where industry, as we understand the word, began. On the one hand there was the life of politics, on the other that of slavery, and there was no other difference between human beings which could approach in importance that between these two lives.

Hence the division between the rich and the poor was, in a political point of view, greater in the ancient city than in the modern State. No difference between two inhabitants of Athens or Sparta, it is true, can have equalled the differences that separate an inhabitant of Park Lane from the inhabitants of some back street, as far as all outward circumstances go. But the development of industrial and commercial life on the one hand, and on the other that of representative government, have changed all the associations of labour. A Duke's son in England engages in employment that an Athenian would have thought disgraceful for any freeman ; while those who would hardly have ranked with freemen, if we take in all the associations of the word, assist in the nomination of the governors. We must empty in imagination the chasm which has thus been filled up, if we would understand the ancient contempt for labour. It is the foremost thinkers of Greece, who formulate in its hardest distinctness, the scorn for the artizan class which means virtual slavery. The artizans, Plato tells us, must be taught that they differ from the true freemen of a city as wood differs from gold.[1] " The artizan,"

---

[1] Plato, Rep., 415. This passage is curiously like the description of castes in the " Institutes of Menu," but it is also unlike, for Socrates says :—ἔστι δ' ὅτε ἐκ χρυσοῦ γεννηθείη ἂν ἀργυροῦν. But the guardians were to judge of this.

says Aristotle, "only partakes of virtue as far as he partakes of slavery."[1] They both felt that civil life, in the true sense of the word, must be something exceptional. It would be a gain that the artizan class should be reduced to slavery, inasmuch as the free labourers seemed a specimen of that chaotic condition which showed what all society would be if a share in freedom ceased to mean a share in government. The slave stood closer to civil life than the artizan, since he belonged to a governing family, and in some sense, therefore, must be considered more of a participant in the blessing of freedom. For those who, by the decrees of nature, were shut out from taking a share in government the next best thing was to be fully and entirely its objects.

We cannot too often remind ourselves of the difference between the sanction of reluctant practical acquiescence and that of incorporation in an ideal. When Disraeli called the rich and the poor the two nations, he pointed to a blot on our civilization which all reformers desire to remove. But when Socrates is made by Plato to use the same language about the "two States," he refers to a division which his ideal was to exaggerate and petrify.[2] People who know Plato only by repute are apt to imagine that the regulations as to women and children, which are all that they know about his "Republic," apply to the bulk of his citizens. This seems to have been the belief even of so diligent a student of Plato as Sir T. More, when he gave his version of Plato's romance and enriched our language with a word which commemorates the yearning for an ideal State.

---

[1] Ar., Pol., i. 13, 13 :—καὶ τοσοῦτον ἐπιβάλλει (sc. ὁ δοῦλος) ἀρετῆς ὅσον περ καὶ δουλείας.

[2] Plato, Rep., 422, 3 :—δύο μέν, κἂν ὁτιοῦν ᾖ, &c. He thought he was going to get rid of this duality, but his pupil has all readers with him when he says, ἐν μιᾷ γὰρ πόλει δύο πόλεις ἀναγκαῖον εἶναι (Ar., Pol., ii. 5, p. 1254, a, 24).

It is a natural mistake, and one which a hasty perusal
of the " Republic" does not remove. The truth is, that
Plato took so very little interest in average citizens that
we may almost forget their existence when we are considering his political ideas. The bulk of his commonwealth must, like any other, have been made up of
those employed in the hard, prosaic work of life ; and,
as he himself reminds us, every single class among his
artizans and mechanics must have outnumbered the
class of the guardians many times over. And yet when
Socrates seems to be speaking of the citizens, we find
that he always means the rulers—the aristocracy, as we
should best name them if we wanted to keep in mind
their relative proportion to the rest. The habit of
mind engendered by slavery made it easy for him to
ignore average mankind to an extent that a modern
finds it impossible to follow. The artizans, the agriculturists, the mechanics, who would make up the average
body of citizens, are in the " Republic" absorbed into
that vast atmosphere of slavery which encircles the life
of the city with a bulk far exceeding its own. To all
intents and purposes they are slaves. They have no
share in the government ; they are simple objects of rule
to the guardians, whose necessities they are obliged
to supply, and whose decisions they have no power of
influencing. The guardians are self-denying beings,
devoted to the welfare of the State ; and in our modern
sense they may be regarded as less free than any other
class, for all those oppressive regulations which Plato
had adapted from the discipline of Lycurgus apply to
them alone. The rest of the citizens are to be treated,
we must presume, like commonplace mortals, but we
hear almost nothing about them. They stand side by
side with the true citizens as aliens do, and thus constitute a sort of rival State, which had little interest for the

philosophic thinker, but in which the modern politician finds the main object of his care. This moral insignificance, to a mind like Plato's, of the whole artizan class, measures for us the contagion of slavery far more effectively than any severe regulations for the repression of this class. No cleft is so deep as that between beings who are and are not worth the effort of discipline.

Greece gathers up the ideal of the past and the future. It was impossible that such a nation should be other than short-lived. Of that brilliant blossoming-time of early life and thought, as perhaps of the blossoming-time of all that is most precious in human development, we may say, if we measure it by the lifetime of nations, that it was—

> " Momentary as a sound,
>   Swift as a shadow, short as any dream ;
>   Brief as the lightning in the collied night
>   That, in a spleen, unfolds both heaven and earth,
>   And ere a man hath power to say ' Behold ! '
>   The jaws of darkness do devour it up.
>   So quick bright things come to confusion."

Two long lives, indeed, would include the whole of that period of " bright things " which has left the trace of its lustre so deeply impressed on the thought and imagination of all subsequent ages that we are apt to forget how transitory it was as an actual fact. Ancient life was not constituted for any " balance of power." Its genius led irresistibly to a view of national relations in which every member was either master or slave, and the life of a nation organized on an ideal other than this was necessarily brief. Indeed, it is just this element of equality which explains the fugitiveness of Greek life ; it was the amount of divergent impulse within itself that prevented any stable unity, and left it a prey to attack from without. The whole life of Greece must be regarded

K

as a sort of prophetic rehearsal of modern Europe, before the stage was cleared for that drama of history which forms a consecutive whole.

The ideal city in the classic essay of Greek political genius embodies the hard and narrow exclusiveness which belonged to ancient politics. But this exclusive unity is very imperfectly exhibited in the life of Greece. A rich genius, on the one hand, brings out individual life into compromising predominance ; on the other, a strong national tendency confuses the unity of the city by suggesting the unity of the race. We have endeavoured to measure the tendency towards individual distinctness by showing how fierce a jealousy watched over every personality that seemed to draw the eye away from the supreme oneness of the State ; we have sought to shadow forth the prophetic element which was embodied in the life of the artist people, and which awakened that fine repulsion by which genius is warned to turn aside from the solicitations of something tempting and premature. But we see the tendency more clearly than the checks on it. Greece foreshadowed both the individual and the international life that belong to the modern world. Greek political life is troubled by its own wealth ; it seems to have realized the saying of Montaigne—" Malheur à celui qui est en avance de son siècle ! " It anticipates in its tiny area the life of Europe, and shows the swift decay that follows so often on premature development. The state of antiquity must be either hammer or anvil. But Greece, with its system of varied and equivalent interests and its common ideas and beliefs, presented the same kind of unity and the same kind of diversity that modern Europe exhibits on a larger scale, while yet it occupied only the moral stage of a race totally unequipped for relations with foreigners. The cities of Greece, like the nations of Europe, were the occupants of a common platform, from which they looked down on the barbarian world, and within which each member felt himself bound to his fellows by the close and indestructible ties of a common race; but, unlike the nations of modern Europe, they had no standard for the mutual relations of such members. Europe has had little enough at any time, it is true; but Dante's dream of a Holy Roman Empire throws a thin, pure ray across the dust of the ages, and that sense of human brotherhood which formed the vital influence of the eighteenth century, begins to dawn before it is quite extinct. We have always been struggling towards some ideal of a brotherhood of nations. The ancient world, if it caught sight of such an ideal for a moment, had to struggle away from it.

It is in the power contrasted with Greece, as the oak is contrasted with the blossom of a day, that we find this ideal of inequality and exclusiveness which makes up the moral code of antiquity, worked out consistently and logically. The master and slave view of human life colours not only the individual relations, but the national ideal of the Roman. Here are no Athens and Sparta; here is no community of kindred States among which rivalry is possible, and from which a prophetic genius might conceivably fashion forth some such expansion of development as modern Europe. Here in that civilization, under the shadow of which we must look for the origin of ours, the belief that some men exist for the sake of others is worked out in its hardest distinctness. Rome is to rule the world, and Romans alone are truly free. Greece, with its wealth of relations, hesitated between the unity of the city and of the nation, and, belonging to that ancient life in which there was no other unity, it perished in the struggle. Rome, in its meagre and monotonous development, is free from all such perplexity; it accepts consistently and logically the aristocratic theory on which ancient society is based, and carries out the ideal of the old world in all its naked impressiveness. It is here, then, that we must seek the true moral bearing of a view of life which depends in the last resort upon slavery. Greece shows us this, but show us so much else, that in Greek life we do not see it distinctly. Rome shows us this, and shows us little else. As we turn from the variety, the dramatic effectiveness, the light and shade, the strong individuality of Greek history, to the monotonous onward march of that in which it is swallowed up, we cannot but feel that here the life of antiquity reaches its maturity. The hesitation of a rich ideal is past, and the leading shoot, as it were, is allowed a free development. The individual and the nation are alike crushed, and the unity of the city is recognized as the only basis of right.

Both those influences, which at once enrich and disturb the course of Greek development, are wanting to Rome. She would never have become the mistress of the world if there had been an ancient Italy in the same sense as there was an ancient Greece. And then, again, Rome has no personal interest; the Roman character is monotonous, prosaic, intellectually commonplace, wanting in vividness and individuality. All the interest of Roman history lies in its victims; the only striking figure it shows us, till we reach the threshold of the modern world, is that of Rome's heroic foe, shattered in the attempt to save his country from being pulverized beneath her tread. The blank of character brings out the greatness of destiny. The valour of Romans explains insufficiently the sway of Rome; its success suggests some supernatural influence seconding their patriotism by a hostile demeanour to every foe and neutralizing alike the power of genius and of numbers,

when they combined against the elect city. Hannibal
was brought to seek peace by being taught to distrust
the fortune of his race,[1] "seeing how she sports with
us as with children;" but Cæsar could encourage his
soldiers in their hour of despondency[2] by urging them
to trust in his fortune no less than in his prowess, and
the dagger of the assassin could not confute a trust commemorated in the establishment of the Empire.   The
Fortune of Hannibal shows us the fitful gleam accorded
to the adversary of Rome, as the Fortune of Cæsar
shows us the steady blaze shed on its representative.
The historian who reviewed the progress of Rome from
its summit discovered in it a harmony of the colossal
and the minute which bore witness to the all-inclusive
character of the supernatural power to which it was due.
The genius of Rome seemed to Plutarch to watch over
the smallest events with unfaltering vigilance and over
the greatest with unimpaired power.[3]   By him the death
of Alexander and the cackling of geese in the Capitol
were equally regarded as links in the mighty chain.
In his eyes the premature close of the greatest earthly
career was not more distinctly foreordained with a view
to the protection of the State which that career might
have overshadowed, than was the hiss of frightened fowl,
preserving the city from enemies more numerous but
less formidable.   Rome is, in fact, the heir of Alexander,[4]
succeeding to his influence, his fame, and, above all,
his Fortune.   This brilliant personality condenses and
prefigures the part that Rome is to play in the world's

---

[1] In his address to Scipio before Zama (Polybius, Excerpt xv. 1).
[2] Cæsar, "De Bello Gallico," i. 40 ; Plutarch, "De Fortunâ Romanorum," 6.
[3] See his treatise, "De Fortunâ Romanorum," *passim*. Virtue and Fortune
contest the authorship of Roman greatness ; the speech of Fortune only is preserved, and was therefore, one imagines, the best. For the geese in the Capitol,
c. 12 ; for the death of Alexander, c. 13.
[4] Plutarch, "De Alexandri Magni Fortunâ aut Virtute."

history, and the antithesis of the conquering State and the conquering hero is not confused by any striking heroic figure within the State itself. The throne is left empty for supernatural power by the failure of any natural claimant.

In truth, it is first with the rise of Rome that the History of Europe may be said to begin. The history of Greece is one of the most interesting chapters in the biography of our race; the history of Rome, so far as that is possible to a series of very important events, would be allowed by most readers to be one of the least interesting. Yet the arid, prosaic narrative is a part of history in a sense that the vivid drama is not. It would be possible to know the outward development of the modern world thoroughly, and not to know that Greece had existed. Philosophy and Literature bear its record in the very structure of their growth, but History, as a connected sequence of events, finds no point of juncture between the life of Greece and that of our own day. It blossomed into a sudden wealth of life and beauty, withered as suddenly, and dropping a hundred seeds into the bosom of all art and all thought, passed away, leaving no heir in the life of nations. Rome, on the other hand, lived its hard, narrow, prosaic life as a member of the genealogy of modern Europe. History is inexplicable if it omit her life; we shall never find ourselves at home in France or Germany, or even in England, unless we know Rome. And we may say, therefore, that the idea of a philosophy of history first emerges in the allegoric conception of a Fortune of Rome. The expression sounds exaggerated, but it is almost copied from the Greek historian, who tells us that he began his history from the assured predominance of Rome because this is the very start of all he understands by History. Before that time he could discern only a desultory narrative of unconnected events ;

after it History assumes[1] "an entire and perfect body," to which the Empire State has supplied a heart.   All events take a new meaning in their relation to the goal which then appears for the first time.   Other nations have "had their day and ceased to be;" they are episodes in the biography of the race.   But Rome, when she has ceased to exist as a ruling power, remains as an ancestral reminiscence; she bequeathed to the world the mould of Government and the framework of a Church. The connection of such a State with divine influence is visible from the first; a mysterious power seemed to hover over the small spot of earth hemmed in by so great a multitude of enemies, and to explain its triumph over all.

Hence we may say of Roman rule that it is, in an important, though a narrow, sense, a preparation for monotheism.   It is not, as in Greece, where Mythology seems to provide some sort of rival to Law, a fount of picturesque imagery, of various and fanciful legend; it is reticent, prosaic, sombre, affording little food to the imagination, and no point of crystallization of allegory and mystic thought.   But it tends from the first towards unity. Its abundant abstractions, evidently mere epithets of the supreme power of which Rome appeared the incarnate expression, reveal its true meaning, and, prosaic as they are, yet prepare a place for the One.   In almost all moral aspects we may say that Rome was a sort of antitype of the God made known by Christ.   But a large element of awe of the Unseen is non-moral.   Not only in that just law which Roman dominion was always defying even while it spread its area, but even in that very dominion in the establishment of which there was no attempt at justice, and sometimes the most flagrant injustice, there yet was a training for submission, a

---

[1] σωματοειδῆ συμβαίνει γίνεσθαι τὴν ἱστορίαν (Polybius, i. 3).

discipline in acceptance of the inevitable, which develops capacities needed, and only fully exercised, in
the acknowledgment of the One Invisible Ruler. The
power of Rome was not elevating in any spiritual sense ;
it was a hard, crushing despotism. But even a hard
crushing despotism is more tolerable when it is strong
and steady. Tyranny is usually a fitful thing ; we hardly
recognize how much easier it is to bear when it is perfectly stable. There was something in the very completeness of Roman conquests that, to a certain extent,
softened the evil of conquest. If Freedom be the first
blessing of a State, surely the second is subordination
to a conqueror who rules the world. The subject thus
escapes the cruelty springing from fear—that is, the
larger part of all cruelty.

The progress of a conquering nation to the rule of the
world, the gradual attraction to itself of all power, the
evolution, as it were, of the central idea of history—all
this supplied the rule of Rome with potent and subtle
allies, captivating to the imagination, enthralling to the
intellect, even of those whose national life it crushed.
The desire for unity is so deep in the human heart that
even in what is arduous and trying, the sense of a plan,
a meaning, brings with it a wonderful alleviation. It
cannot, indeed, overcome the intensity of vivid individual
desire ; it cannot allay the fever of anguish or melt the
ice of a hard despair. But in all ordinary human trials
it will be found that there is a wonderful influence in
the contemplation of a large enduring reality, the sense
of a link with the past and the future, the neighbourhood
of what is impressive and permanent. It may exist
where there is no love, no justice, no moral nobility,
and yet it has its own steady, persistent claim ; it overcomes weak resistance, and there is more weak than
strong resistance in the world.

The rule of Rome was rarely moral; it was sometimes profoundly immoral. Nevertheless its irresistible
onward march roused a profound feeling of resignation
when once it obtained any submission at all. That
State of which the assured predominance was the central
fact in the world's history might claim from its subjects an obedience in which there was nothing base.
" The Carthaginians at the moment of their fall perished
from the earth, but the Greeks look on at their own
calamities,"[1] exclaims a Greek, with a sense of envy, it
would appear, for the victim of Rome whose fate was
that of more absolute ruin. Yet when he speaks of the
conqueror of Greece as the favourite of Providence, the
expression is neither a mere flight of rhetoric nor a
piece of abject flattery, but a simple summing up in a
few words of the impression made by the records he
had set himself to interpret. The Fortune of Rome
was for Polybius no partial goddess, though she had
set her inexorable decree against his own country, but
a being in whose predominance there was a claim to
allegiance swallowing up even the claim of patriotism ;
the State was marked by indications of Divine care so
definite and overwhelming, that the duty of submission to
its sway was a part of the duty of submission to Heaven.

Hence it arises that to the children of Rome there
seems to have been in the very idea of dominion that
same kind of fascination which ordinarily belongs only
to the sense of its exercise. Occupying the summit of
an elaborately fortified position, not only secured from
invasion by the eager hope kindled in the circle immediately below, but strengthened by the organization
which kept up within the citadel itself the principle
of unreserved subjection and irresponsible control, they

---

[1] Polybius, Excerpt xxxviii. 1a. See an excellent article in the *Quarterly Review*, vol. cxlviii.

were trained by every influence of education and association to join perfect liberty with dominion as part of the
same ideal.   Every aspiration to escape bondage found
itself, by the necessity of things, aiming at dominion.
Independence was assumed to be an exceptional condition of humanity, and by that very fact was invariably
associated with rule.   While to us the question is always,
Why should such a one be deprived of the right of
control over his own acts ? to them it was rather, Why
should he be endowed with it ?   The absolute submission which every one owed the State he also either
owed or claimed as a member of that group which was
the unit of political organization.   He was thus taught
from his earliest hour to regard irresponsible control as
natural.   He was led by all the potent and subtle influences of law to submit to or to exercise this dominion
without criticism or scruple.   Irresponsible authority,
unreserved obedience, were the two poles of domestic,
no less than of political, relation.   The "Son under
Power" was, against his father, no less defenceless than
the slave.   No age, almost no dignity, ended his subjection ; he might be a father himself, he might fill the
highest offices of the State—he none the less held life,
liberty, and fortune at the pleasure of another.   History
describes to us few and dubious exercises of these paternal
rights, but what may be done has always some relation
to what is done.   The relation of the most indulgent
father to the most independent son must have been influenced by the fact that if the parental authority had
been exercised to the detriment of the son's life or liberty
the law would not have stepped in to abridge it.   We
see this influence of legal right in the only part of
English law which contemplates (or did contemplate till
very lately) the exercise of control over mature and
blameless human beings—the position of married women.

This is a fair but inadequate illustration of the effect of the Roman *patria potestas.* The English law takes cognizance of offences within the relation of dependence; the Roman law did not recognize right on the one side, or duty on the other. The plea which has more than once been set up for an English female offender, that she could not refuse to obey the orders of her husband, has been felt by every one, even where it was not overruled, to be wholly out of harmony with the spirit of our legal system. But when a Roman officer [1] was accused in the Senate of the heaviest crime of which it could take cognizance—organizing Civil War— Tiberius, not speaking with authority as Emperor, but pleading as an anxious and careful vindicator of the laws, seems to have carried the Senate with him in his decision that "a son *cannot* decline the command of his father." He was speaking at a time when the whole system of which this paternal authority was the keystone had admitted a foreign element, when there was another spirit in the world, and the whole fabric of Roman greatness was about to enter on its period of decay. Yet even then it appeared to a conservative that disloyalty to the State, great as was the crime, had no possible alternative in disobedience to the Father. "There are hardly any other men," says the Roman jurist,[2] "who have such power over their sons as we have." It was a natural result that no other State had such power over its subjects as Rome.

How large and lofty was the Roman ideal of Obedience, compared with that temporary or degrading submission which is all that the word suggests to the average mind of our own day, is seen in the noble

---

[1] Marcus, son of the Piso who was accused of poisoning Germanicus. See Tac., Ann., iii. 17.

[2] Gaius, "Corp. Jur. Rom. Ante-Just.," § 55.

words of Cicero, when he speaks of the incomplete virtue—what we should call Duty—as typified by the obedience of the soldier, a loyal but difficult obedience, and contrasts it with that moral rightness which is higher than duty, when a man is made aware of a claim that unites kindred with authority, and meets it with the obedience of a son.[1] Perhaps there is no passage in classical literature that comes so near the spirit of Christianity; yet it is no more than the perfection of that sense of membership which was the starting-point of political life in antiquity, and which Rome first disentangled from all admixture and brought out in its naked simplicity. In the life of Rome was fulfilled the command with promise made to the chosen people ; she taught the honour of the Father, and the days of her children were long in the land. In truth, union of the command with the promise is no exceptional grant to a favoured race, but a permanent law of human society. The generations of man are thus " bound each to each in natural piety ; " the nation has the foundations of a religion. It is rooted in the order that is permanent.

And while this central claim for an unlimited subjection—the power of the Father—gave Roman dominion its keynote, we have not less to remark the political wisdom, perhaps never absent from this high standard of domestic obedience, which taught Romans to secure their dominion by setting off every added shade of liberty against a background of subjection, and thus rousing a vivid appreciation for every grant by bringing it into a close proximity to vain desire. Unbuttressed by concessions, privilege would be short-lived ; the many excluded would not quietly confront the view included if these two parties stood face to face. If a system of

[1] Cicero, Quæst. Tusc., ii. 22.

privilege is to be durable, the harshness of contrast
must be broken, the transition from power to weakness
must be made to seem natural by being gradual; a
neutral zone must intervene between the privileged and
unprivileged, keeping up hope in the last body, and
assigning a set of defenders to the first.   The disfran-
chised world was not homogeneous; the compromise it
exhibited between entire independence and entire subjection it also repeated within its own limits, and carried
out in a graduated approach to the position of aspiration
and envy.   A dawn of Roman right preceded its full
concession, and Rome had always a band of subjects
who were in that most favourable position for loyalty
—in sight of coveted advantages only just beyond their
reach.   Perhaps in enumerating all that was tangible
in these advantages we hardly exhaust the attractions
of Roman citizenship.   There is a kind of satisfaction
in association with a favoured race which escapes the
analysis of Logic ;—which may be connected with
the instinct in our nature that turns in weariness from
the transitoriness of things to whatever presents any
show of permanence, and takes the mind into the far
past and the distant future.   Nor must we leave out
of sight the alloy of mere vulgar feeling, which gave
the compound no small share of its firmness and
strength.   As we watch the invasion of this platform
of privilege by the excluded class, the successive devices
by which the defenders endeavoured to render their
concessions meaningless, and the strange transformation by which the sons of the victorious assailants are
found among the most resolute defenders of the coveted
vantage-ground, we are forced to realize that in the idea
of privilege there is something which objects of desire,
in themselves far more excellent, cannot rival.   We see
that in the evolution of national life what is desirable

is always at first confused with what is exceptional, and we thus learn to accept as an inevitable phase of social development, that husk of ungenerous denial which guards the kernel of almost all righteous claim.

When we cross the chasm which formed the most characteristic division of the old world we realize the full power of this exclusive ideal, and its darkest influences. Another people, distinguished by no mark of complexion, dress, or cultivation, were separated from the children of Rome, among whom they dwelt, by the barrier of legal helplessness. We underrate the importance of slavery in the ancient world when we replace in imagination our domestic servants by slaves. The free-born Roman had no monopoly of cultivation. Few pursuits which in our day absorb and reward the attention of the professional class were unrepresented in the slave-gang of a wealthy Roman. A writer who has made the subject his study has given his opinion, borne out to some extent by the low price of books at Rome, that what the press performs for modern life was effected for the ancient world by slavery.[1] What a world of thought, feeling, hope, and fear, shut out from all large interests of life, is implied in the fact that it is possible to suppose the slaves under the Empire as active in diffusing literature as the printing-press ! The friend and fellow-worker of the cultured thinker of antiquity was the specimen of a class that had no rights.[2] We need no harrowing pictures to make us believe in the forlorn condition of a people legally defenceless ; such a condition is painted for us by the tone of allusion to cruelties in men who were not otherwise cruel. The philosophic historian records,[3] with

---

[1] See a note in Merivale's "Roman Empire," vi. 233.
[2] Tiro, Cicero's freedman, is believed to have edited his letters.
[3] Tac., Ann., xiv. 42–45. Their only crime was their failure to prevent the

apparent sympathy, the arguments by which the massacre of four hundred innocent slaves was justified in the Roman Senate, as a measure of expediency, about the same time that Seneca was reminding his correspondent, with an eloquence doubtless meant for posterity, that "he whom thou callest slave is sprung from the same race as thyself." The most humane, perhaps, of all classic writers expresses a certain sympathy with an example of heartless cruelty that will to many readers appear more odious—the crucifixion of a poor Sicilian shepherd who had, at a time when the use of weapons was forbidden to slaves, rid the country of the ravages of a fierce boar.[1] What Tacitus and Cicero could record without protest must have been possible to every Roman. The cruelties they sanctioned with their sympathy were not the excesses of bad men, but the illustrations of an ideal.

The structure of Roman dominion rests on a fusion of the loyal obedience of the son and the hopeless subjection of the slave. The legal system which graduated and defended civic right shows the skilful blending of both which made them work to a common end. A sense of separateness, unsoftened by any admixture of that sense of a common humanity present to some degree in almost all modern feeling, is exhibited to us in slavery; and it is vain to deny that here Rome and the whole antique world, but Rome in a special sense, had a simplicity of strength lacking to all modern government. We may almost say that

murder of their master by one of their number. The indignation of the populace at this barbarity almost occasioned an *émeute*.

[1] Cicero, "In Verrem," v. 3. At least, he says that some will think this hard, but he declares himself "maluisse Domitium (the prætor) crudelem in animadvertendo quam in prætermittendo dissolutum videri." He preferred that a public benefactor should be rewarded with the cross, rather than that a slave should, at a critical moment, be trusted with a hunting-spear. I know of no other passage which so vividly illustrates what is hateful in slavery.

Rome drew from slavery the strength that any modern
Government would gain if its poor suddenly became
satisfied.   True, the slave sometimes made Rome feel
that he was not satisfied.   But the insurrection of a
Spartacus did hardly as much to diminish the power
of government as the discontent of the least discontented
peasantry of the modern world does.   It was, while it
lasted, a terror and a danger.   But an insurrection does
not sap the strength of the nation if it does not in any
degree enlist the sympathy of the upper class.   Spartacus,
in any modern State, would have had sympathizing ad-
mirers in the Senate.   We can hardly conceive that it
never entered into the heart of a Roman to hesitate in
his desire for the defeat of the slaves.   Probably the
only result of their approach to success was to weld the
structure they attacked into a closer unity.   Not a single
arm was paralyzed by the doubt whether the blow was
just.   We might be favoured by Nature with abundant
harvests, and by Fortune with prosperous trade ; all
legislative concession might be made to the lower
class, all but the inevitable privileges of the higher
abolished—and still we should not have reached that
position of convenient and secure independence which
the Romans gained by being steeled against pity.   Perfect justice in poor and rich alike would be needed
before we should reach the disentanglement from all our
difficulties that they gained by perfect injustice, by a
repudiation of all those feelings and ideas on which
justice is founded.

The contrast of Rome and Greece is, in this respect,
almost as instructive as the contrast of Rome and England.   Both the precept of the Platonic Socrates and
the example of Callicratidas show us that when one
Greek enslaved another there must have been a latent
doubt as to the right, than which nothing can be

more numbing to vigorous action. The double vision which hovered before the mental eye makes a sure aim impossible. May we smite our enemies fearlessly? What is meant by *we ?* The second question prevents all clear answer to the first. Englishmen engaged in strife with Africans or Asiatics know something of the feeling which the Greeks had only just begun to feel in strife with each other. But they had begun to feel it; and its disturbing influence is shown in the distraction and desultoriness of Greek history. This hesitation between the unity of the city and that of the nation made a place for that which opposes all true unity, the centrifugal impulse of Party. A nation under this impulse is on the path to a swift decay. But in Rome there was something stronger than party spirit. The civil wars passed away, and left the whole world embraced in an organism to which Rome supplied a heart. And the good and evil of human nature both contributed so much to the unity of this organism that we can hardly say which formed its strength.

This double element is discernible in the characteristic bequest of Rome to the world. Roman Law is the sole product of Roman thought that bears any stamp of originality. The artist people have left their records in work that has taken its place as the perennial model of humanity as to form; with Rome the idea of Law, as separate from laws, may be almost said to begin. Yet the Roman law, in its narrowest sense, the civil law of Rome, was a consecration of all that is narrow and exclusive; it embodied the spirit that is willing to inhabit a paradise "haunted by shrieks of far-off misery;" it was an elaboration of the ideal of privilege. This forms no part of the Roman law known to modern Europe; it withered away, while Roman law in its wider sense— the prætorian law, by which justice was administered to

L.

the subjects of Rome—grew to its maturity. The latter
was the nurse of a liberal justice, the mould of a high
morality, the philosophic teacher of political wisdom and
guardian of national life. It supplied to all the countries
beneath Roman rule a pattern of righteous dealing between the governors and governed—a pattern, indeed,
which its administrators neglected and ignored, but which
none the less remained as a rebuke to their injustice,
and a goal of all true efforts to carry out the ideal
dominion of Rome. And it included within its impartial
embrace the whole civilized world. An Athenian obeyed
a law that many Greeks regarded as a thing external to
any loyalty of theirs. The law of the Roman had all
the universality of a law of nature, and perhaps we
should never have had the latter expression if there had
not existed a State which possessed a realm so wide and
a sway so irresistible, that its laws gained the association
of natural powers, and thus passed into their type.

Hence the moral legacy of Rome to the world is
that of submission to law. Translated into intellectual
language, this becomes the central principle of physical
science; and little as the Romans cared for physical
science, it is in the first great poem written in their
tongue that we see this central conception first steadily
grasped and consistently retained. Nothing can be more
characteristic of the Roman spirit than the poem of
Lucretius, and nothing, surely, that was written more
than 2000 years ago is so full of the ideas and beliefs of
modern thought. It is unscientific in this sense, that it
shows a fundamental misconception of the right *method*
of science; it assumes, in common with the whole of
antiquity, that reason and not experience is to supply,
as well as to sift and arrange, the data of physical
theory; and it betrays an indifference to detail which
vividly illustrates the result of this false view. But so

pregnant is the thought which forms its nucleus that, perhaps, the mistaken notions with which it is associated only bring out its importance the more forcibly ; for the scope and force of a truth come out vividly in its power to swallow up, as it were, the mistakes which cluster round it. The poem is the first manifesto of that school of thought which we know as Positivism, the belief that the investigation of nature begins with the renunciation of those spiritual conceptions which lead man on to the search for truth, and appear to his infant mind as the appointed guide throughout the journey. The analysis of the mental evolution of the race into epochs characterized by the successive dominance of the three ideas of Will, of Cause, and of Force, and thence named the Theologic, Meta-physic, and Positive stage of thought, has been hailed as one of the widest generalizations ever won to science. But it is present in germ in a poem by a thinker who had no more idea of the experimental method which we almost identify with science itself than he had of using the micro-scope. Yet he was the herald of scientific principle ; and though no man of science ever consulted his work as an authority for a single fact or law, yet all may turn to it for the statement of principles and the expression of feelings which give to science its light and its atmosphere. The " cosmic emotion " of our latest thought is there in its fulness ; and of all who have found a religion in the contemplation of nature, none ever was a more fervent and devout worshipper than the poet of whom we can hardly say that he knew a single one of its laws.

What Lucretius felt in nature was the spirit of law, of which Rome was the embodiment. He did not, in-deed, consciously recognize what we could call law in nature ; what he did recognize there, was, if we look at it from our point of view, a mere privation of law. But to him Chance was (almost the contrary of what it is to us) the negation of the arbitrary element, of which all Will was the expression. To an Englishman the type of orderly action is Will, and Chance is a mere negation of Will; but to the Roman, Will was the disorderly interrupting agency, Chance was that general tendency of things which makes for order, if only it be not interfered with by the irregular impulse of human passions. Just as Fortune had brought out of the atomic life of separate cities the vast structure of the Roman dominion, so Chance had from the rain of atoms evolved the stately fabric of the Universe and the elaborate life of civil society. The process of evolution between this beginning and the Roman Empire was imperilled only by the desultory impulses of individual desire and aversion; and Lucretius lived in the days when this individual agency was assuming large and turbulent proportions, when the passions of a Marius and a Sulla seemed to threaten the very existence of the one State of the world. His early life was passed amid the terrors of sedition and the horrors of civil bloodshed. In childhood he may have trembled at the days of slaughter which followed the return of Marius; in boyhood he must have shuddered at the months of assassination which followed the return of Sulla; the conspiracy of Catiline renewed these memories in his ripe manhood; and his life closed amid the turmoil which associated itself with the name of Clodius and the tremors of the coming civil war. He lived when the dread of individuality, which animated so much of ancient life, was justified by ebullitions of terrible hatred, deadly revenge, reckless ambition; when it would seem as if the first necessity of a State was to get rid of its great men. To him Will was the destructive, not the constructive, agency. He saw in nature an escape from its dominion, and when he eagerly explained away all

purpose in the Universe, he was, little as we can sym-
pathize with the feeling, making room for that orderly
impulse of law so deeply rooted in his mind that, like
the atmosphere, it rushed in to fill every vacancy, and
seemed present, wherever the agency of man was withdrawn. The object of his poem is well marked in a few
lines [1] where he describes the effect of watching a review
from a distance, and after painting the tumult, the glitter,
and the movement of the mighty legions, ends with the
touch of quiet :—

> " Yet sees the traveller from the mountain's height
> The hurrying crowds as some still speck of light."

It was his object to contemplate the hurrying crowds of
life from that remote height where their distracted movement was reduced to rest and their vehement tumult was
still.

Hence the tone of delight in which the poet set forth
a scheme of life which, though it must be accepted if it
be certain, could never, we should have thought, be an
object of any higher feeling than despairing resignation.
No divine hope could be too great for the burst of apocalyptic joy with which Lucretius brings this scheme forward. The new Jerusalem descending out of Heaven
is hardly hymned with more mystic rapture than the
emptied world from which all divinities have been
banished—the world which in the opinion of the singer
was then first delivered from the shadow of human
jealousy and malignancy, falsely projected upon the
heavens. The power and the weakness of the poem
are strikingly illustrated by its effect on its most illus-
trious reader of modern times. It was a favourite study
with Frederick the Great, and was recommended by him

[1] Lucretius, "De Rerum Natura," ii. 323 332. In what follows I am much
indebted to M. Martha's study of this poem.

to a bereaved friend as a manual of consolation. Yet when he turned to it in his own troubles, he discovered it to teach only that evil was necessary and remedies were futile.[1] The great general was probably far nearer the intellectual position of the Roman poet than is any reader of our day; he too had been delivered from an oppressive bondage, associated with a religion powerless to elevate and purify, potent only to narrow and harden the soul. He must have come much nearer to the rapture of escape, as from a galling prison, expressed in this Pagan psalm, than almost any Christian who has ever read the poem. And yet even he found it potent only for the ills of his neighbour; it broke down as a remedy for his own. The Pagan King, the friend of Voltaire, was too Christian for the consolations of Lucretius. He felt as a Pagan of our day :—

> " Je souffre, il est trop tard ; le monde s'est fait vieux.
> Une immense espérance a traversé la terre
> Malgré nous vers le ciel il faut tourner les yeux ; "

or, at all events, it was no gospel to him in the hour of defeat to be told that there was no Heaven which could meet glances either of hope or of dread.

A modern, whether he be Christian or Pagan, brings to this poem the inheritance of all that reverence for personal life which has been developed through Christianity. The immense hope of the world has passed into his soul, if not as a belief, then as an irremovable contrast to every other belief; it has fixed the cravings of his heart even when it has not touched a single conviction of his mind. The infinite future it has opened to every soul has remained as a yearning when it has vanished as an

---

[1] " C'est un palliatif pour les maladies de l'ame," he wrote to D'Alembert on the death of Mlle. de Lespinasse. " Je n'y ai trouvé que la necessité du mal et l'inutilité du remède," he answered D'Argens, under the discouragement of defeat in the Seven Years' War.

expectation ; nothing can close that vista ; and the hope of Heaven, that has thrilled many a heart cold beneath the sod, survives in other forms in those who scoff at it as folly or argue against it as delusion.   It is hard for us to put ourselves in the place of men who had neither the hope itself nor any of the visions or regrets into which it is transformed—men to whom the world of the citizen, with its finite claims, filled the horizon of interest and became the nurse of all desire.   And perhaps it is specially difficult to realise this in the poem of Lucretius, because its tone is in many ways so modern.   The subject—the physical scheme of the Universe—is the great interest of our day, and the way in which Lucretius regards it constantly reminds us of the very fashion of the hour.   But this resemblance is, to a great extent, misleading.   The poet has all the indifference of a Roman to physical science, in itself.   His purpose is wholly negative ; all his concern is to banish that idea of Divine agency which we should represent to our minds far more clearly as a system of interference than of government ; and far from bringing him into harmony with our modern ideas, this aim prevented his keeping abreast with the foremost physical speculation of his own day.   We find him both anticipating and rejecting the ideas that have been ratified by Science, and it is hard to say whether we may learn most from his latent Darwinism, or from his scorn of the idea that is associated with the great name of Newton, and which was in some dim fashion manifest to his contemporaries.

Men make their way up the mountain of truth, as up every other mountain, by a perpetual zig-zag.   The progress of Science is the result of oscillation between opposites ; it has turned alternately to the organic and the mechanical view of nature, alternatives perhaps brought home more clearly to the imagination when con-

trasted as personal and impersonal. We see them most
sharply contrasted in the great scientific battle of our day.
Many of us were taught in our childhood that the reason
why a horse and an ass, for instance, were as like each
other as they are, was the will of the Creator. This
can hardly be called a scientific theory; it was rather
accepted by scientific men as the boundary of science;
but it was so accepted within living memory by the
scientific world. Then came the doctrine familiar under
the name of Natural Selection, and we were all taught
that the reason why a horse and an ass were alike was
their descent from a common ancestor; and the reason
they were different was that small hereditary variations
had proved useful in the struggle for life. Now this
latest triumph of science marks its swing towards the
impersonable view of nature. Nothing can be more
unlike the action of human will than the production
of these small variations, useless for the most part,
and the wasteful destruction of the greater part of what
is produced. Accordingly we find that Lucretius here
speaks the language of modern science. Accident, he
says, originated all kinds of varieties of structure (that
he made them great instead of small has nothing to
do with the argument), and those only were preserved which were fitted to the condition of things in
which they found themselves.[1] The exposition must
be discerned, whenever any one can look at it without
prejudice, as an unquestionable anticipation of the great
scientific theory of our day. But now go back two centuries nearer to Lucretius, to the widest generalization,
perhaps, that science has ever achieved—the discovery of
gravitation. This was a swing to the other side, a turn

---

[1] Lucretius, " De Rerum Natura," v. 837, 77.   I once showed the passage to
Mr. Darwin, but the dialect was too unscientific for him, and I do not think he
recognized it as the anticipation of his own views.

in the zig-zag that brings the traveller very near the
idea of personal action. We can hardly enunciate the law
without using words that belong to the personal world.
" The most perfect vacuum," says a modern writer,[1]
" may be truly said to be full of this influence," which,
though so subtle, so impalpable, that it needs the utmost
efforts of genius to demonstrate its existence and its
laws, " is yet a necessary concomitant of matter." Now
here, surely, we are on the borders of the *spiritual* world.
Imagine yourself hearing, for the first time, that at midnight, when the whole bulk of earth shut off the sun's
light and heat, its gravitation was still acting on every
particle of matter in the dark hemisphere, and whirling
it through space, and you would feel as if what was
described must be supernatural Will. And it is evident that this resemblance to personal agency impelled
Lucretius to scorn that dim vision of the law of gravitation which was present to his contemporaries ; it is
ridiculed by him as an absurd fiction, ascribing the " love
of a centre "[2] to entities of which the chief thing he
wanted to say was, that they felt no love. His passionate desire to expunge from nature all relation, all
resemblance even, to human agency, to sweep it clear,
as it were, of every organic tendency, would have made
our modern science appear to him almost as full of impersonations as ancient mythology. We are startled to
find the anticipator of the origin of species by natural
selection rejecting the theory of the four elements ; a
theory which, already preached by one whom he calls
" the holiest of men,"[3] lasted till it was absorbed into

[1] The Bishop of Carlisle, in the *Nineteenth Century Review*, December 1886.

[2] " Haud igitur possunt tali ratione teneri
Res in concilio medii cuppedine victae."
—De Rerum Natura, i. 1081, 2.

See the whole argument against gravitation from 1052.

[3] *i.e.*, Empedocles : *Ibid.*, i. 712 733.

the chemistry of the eighteenth century, and laid the basis of the idea of chemical action. It is set aside in favour of the most childish, the most meagre scheme of the age, simply because it was the most inhuman. The perpetual rain of atoms rushing downwards through void space was surely the most reduced apparatus a philosopher could concede to his scheme of the Universe. But it was this rigid parsimony which was the attraction of his scheme to a mind seeking, above all things, the impersonal. We see the anthropomorphism of our scientific ideas when we contrast them with his; we are forced to realise that it is not less in the world without than the world within that we have grown more personal. He would have found no repose in a world composed of our molecules, with their attractions and repulsions; ridiculous figments, as it would have seemed to him, of love and hatred. His atoms were as unlike as possible to persons, and that was all he asked of them. This meagre simplicity was exactly what his spirit craved. It was the ideal of the one State of the world. All special tendency found its analogue in that individual feeling which Rome set itself to crush, and which, when it could not crush, it feared. Sulla and Marius embodied the individual agency on its darker side, while the dagger of Brutus was, as it were, already sharpening to express the defiance of Rome to their noblest successor. Rome enforced a barren uniformity, and this was the idea carried out by the Roman poet.

The poem of Lucretius is an expression, in a prosaic and protestant form, of that idea of a Holy Order which we have seen, at its highest pitch, in the speculations of Indian theosophy. His reader is often reminded of these speculations. He finds the same yearning for a deep repose, the same consciousness of a possible deliverance from all the restlessness of life, in a surrender to nature.

Lucretius did not deny the existence of the Gods ; he rather saw in them the models for man.   They live apart from all desire and fear, in a profound repose. Man too might reach their repose if he would enter into their vision of reality, if he would cease from those impulses of ambition, of avarice, of revenge, which are the invaders of human life, not its legitimate rulers ; if he would recognize the realm of law, which is to him a prison when he endeavours to escape from it, but when he accepts its restraints, the most blessed home.   The Indian ideal of Resignation pervades the whole poem ; Nature stretches her compassionate arms towards the feverish sons of man, and woos them to repose on that calm bosom that knows not love or hate—knows only what to the Roman took the aspect of Law.   But we have passed from the East to the West, and man needs Resignation, not to live, but to die.   Life is finite ; man has to accept its limits.   The nation that has left its memorials in the long straight roads that led to the city, the aqueducts that brought it water, the triumphal arch that spoke its glories, had no hope of a Hereafter.   That was associated with terror and dread.   Rome had no mysteries.   The Roman poet rebukes the desire of life beyond the grave, as the Indian would have rebuked it if he could ever have imagined it to exist.   But the desire offended the Roman not only because it expressed that arrogance of individualism which to both races was equally abhorrent, but because it embodied a yearning after the Infinite, which, while it was the very breath of life to the Indian, was the seed of all disorder to the definite positive spirit of the prosaic Roman race.

The ideal of Lucretius is the indifference of Natural Law to human desire.   He has a few passages of exquisite pathos, passages which foreshadow the tender human sympathies of Gray, the pure, delicate, natural

sympathics of Wordsworth.   Nothing in poetry is more
full of a subdued, hidden pity than the lines in which
he describes the wanderings of the cow whose calf has
fallen at the altars of superstition.[1]   Nothing is more
full of a deep sense of human love and its frail tenure
than the description which the English reader knows in
the beautiful but still inferior imitation by Gray:[2]—

> " For thee no more the cheerful hearth shall burn,
>   And busy housewife ply her evening care,
>   No children run to lisp their sire's return,
>   And climb his knees the envied kiss to share."

But these passages cannot be called characteristic of
Lucretius ; or, at least, they are characteristic only as
the rare gleams when a finer self seems to break through
the habitual self.   They are not the utterance of his continuous thought.   His habitual theme is the dominance
of Law, and this interpolation of pity almost interrupts
it ; it is a modulation into a key which must be quitted
before the original theme can be taken up.

When we turn to Virgil we find that the interpolation
has become the theme.   The feeling that touched the
earlier poem with streaks of tender irrelevance expands
to colour the whole.   Virgil sings the growth of Rome,
as Lucretius the formation of the Universe; there is a
kindred nature in the theme, but the note of triumphant
dominion in the Roman has dropped into a note of sad
submission in the Italian.   All the interest of Roman
history, we have said, lies in its victims.   Virgil gives
that interest its supreme expression.   He, the dispos-
sessed Italian, with the longing for his Mantuan home

---

[1] Lucretius, " De Rerum Natura," ii. 352–366.

[2] "Jam jam non domus accipiet te læta, neque uxor
      Optima, nec dulces occurrent oscula nati
      Præripere, et tacita pectus dulcedine tangent."
                                        —Ib. iii. 894.

always in his heart, and yet with a deep acquiescence in that Imperial rule which implies a world of
such mournful exiles as himself, was marked out alike by
Fate and Nature as the poet of Resignation. This is
the clue to his mystic charm; this explains his strange
legendary position as the herald of a faith of which
he never heard, and in which he would probably have
taken a merely literary interest if he had heard of
it. The ideal of obedience, of surrender, is the seed
of all that has made him immortal.[1] In his resolute
avoidance of originality he stands alone among the great
poets of the world. No other name known to succeeding generations belongs to an avowed, unvarying imitator; Virgil's commentators supply us with the Greek
original of almost every important passage; it is as
if Goethe had piqued himself on having produced
perfect German adaptations from Corneille and Racine.
The literature of Greece filled the whole horizon of the
intellectual world for the conquerors of Greece; to
adapt, to embody, to imitate, was, they thought, the only
possible intellectual aim for themselves. The Roman
took towards Greek literature the kind of attitude which
English faith has taken towards that of Judæa; originality would have been regarded as equally an error in
both cases. The very word by which the Church has
designated false doctrine expresses the Roman dread
of originality; a heresy is a "choice." The spirit of
orthodoxy discourages originality. Ultimately, perhaps,
it will not be found that the ages of orthodoxy have been
those deficient in originality; but, for good and for ill

---

[1] " Una salus victis nullam sperare salutem."—Æn. ii. 354.

This line, which gives the Æneid its keynote, might well have been taken as
a motto by the subject of Rome. Note also the deep religious feeling which
makes Anchises at first refuse to leave Troy :—

" Me si coelicolae voluissent ducere vitam ;
Has mihi servassent sedes."—Ib. ii. 641 642.

alike, the fact is, that wherever orthodoxy exists, all thought stamped with individual impulse is at a certain disadvantage.   And the fact that Roman writers found their orthodox model in Greek literature explains what might almost be called the servile element in Virgil ; his intellectual submission to Greece explains and illustrates the spirit that brought a world into subjection to the dominion of Rome.

We see in Lucretius the rapture with which the idea of Law—the influence that moulds and penetrates all Roman thought—is hailed when contrasted with images of disorderly impulse and caprice ; we discern the spirit of science in that first energy of distinctness and of narrow limitation which is given by protest against the spirit of superstition.   In Virgil this reverence for order is even deeper, but it is less logical.   It is deeper, for it demands that continuity with the past which surely is a test of a true order.   It accepts history as a witness for man's nature no less trustworthy than science ; it cherishes the fragment of truth hidden in the legendary lore of the past, and never rejects any fiction that may prove a husk of the smallest fact or a vehicle of the vaguest truth. And, at the time, it welcomes with an eager homage the great idea, to some extent inconsistent with the other, of Natural Law.[1]   There is no care for an exact harmony between these two divergent tendencies, only a fearless reverence for both, and a dim feeling of some underlying reality deeper than either.   A vague Pantheism harmonizes the world of mythology and the world of science, and enables the poet to tread in the footsteps of Lucretius,

[1] Compare, for instance, Geo. i. 60–62 :—

> " Continuo has leges æternaque fœdera certis
> Imposuit *Natura* locis, quo tempore primum
> Deucalion vacuum lapides jactavit in orbem."

These lines are exactly divided by a complete change in the point of view.

and yet to remain a constant and reverent visitor in the
domain that Lucretius hated. The poet who best interprets him to the English reader is Wordsworth. Nature
draws from both the Italian and the English poet the
solemn delight of confronting—

> " A presence that disturbs me with the joy
> Of elevated thoughts ; a sense sublime
> Of something far more deeply interfused,
> Whose dwelling is the light of setting suns,
> And the round ocean and the living air,
> And the blue sky, and in the mind of man :
> A motion and a spirit, that impels
> All thinking things, all objects of all thought,
> And rolls through all things." [1]

In these noble lines we have no more than a full and
fluent expression of a feeling that meets us more than
once in brief and broken hints from the earlier poet.
The intervening 2000 years, the birth and death of
nations, the development of a new faith—all these leave
the religion of nature substantially unaffected ; it is more
diffuse in Wordsworth than in Virgil, but that is all.

On the one hand this feeling melts into sympathy
with the old mythology, on the other it passes into
admiration for the orderly sequences of nature ; so that
the two feelings which in the mind of Lucretius, as in
that of so many a religious thinker of our day, seem
hopelessly opposed, were harmonized by Virgil's vague
Pantheism, harmonized more fully than is possible to
any one who looks back from our present position, and,
watching the conflict of Religion and Science through so
many centuries, sees the argument of each side tested
by the keen acid of hostile criticism. Thus Virgil has

---

[1] Wordsworth, "Tintern Abbey." The quoted lines are almost a translation of the address of Anchises to Æneas (Æn. vi. 724–729), but perhaps Wordsworth was not thinking of Virgil when he wrote it.

far more sympathy with the scientific spirit than Wordsworth; there is in him no touch of scorn such as that
uttered in Wordsworth's " Poet's Epitaph " :—

> " Physician art thou ?—one, all eyes,
> Philosopher ! a fingering slave,
> One that would peep and botanize
> Upon his mother's grave ? "

To Virgil there would be nothing jarring in the juxta-
position of any possible interest in nature and any
possible human sorrow; the harmony of Natural Law
was to him the fitting theme of the bard, partly because
individual human sorrow was a slighter thing to the
ancients than to us, but partly also because the laws
of nature were something deeper. Thus the lay which
excites enthusiastic admiration from weary, storm-tossed
guests contains the explanation of—

> " The various labours of the wandering moon,
> And whence proceed the eclipses of the sun ;
> The original of men and beasts, and whence
> The rains arise, and fires their warmth dispense,
> And fixed and erring stars dispose their influence ;
> What shakes the solid earth, what cause delays
> The summer nights and shortens winter days." [1]

The feeling which here binds the poet to Lucretius
separates him from Wordsworth; it is as unlike any
modern poet to find in Natural Science the material
of Poetry as it is unlike Homer. The choice of such
a subject marks the dawn of scientific thought and the
twilight of classical poetry. But Virgil's yearnings after
science were not stronger than his love of the legendary
past; his devout sense of the Divine Presence that
animated Nature did not conflict with a sort of belief in
the Gods of Greece, nor, on the other hand, with a deep

---

[1] Æneid, i. 746, Dryden's translation.

reverence for the natural laws that seemed to his fore-runner an effective and welcome substitute for the presence of anything that had been thought Divine.

For he stood at that point in History in which the idea of a universal dominion gathered up into itself the philosophy, mythology, and science of the world. The idea of Law in nature, which to his fore-runner was mainly a negation of personal will in nature, was to him the real presence of a spirit of order, penetrating the whole of nature, and infusing its own impulse into all life. It is the spirit which sets everything in its place and brings the " perpetual edict " of a Catholic rule to regulate the varied sphere of human achievement. This, we may say, is the ideal of the Universal Empire, as it passed into the ideal of the Universal Church ; and so far as the Roman Empire became universal, it was because, to some extent, it did embody this principle, upholding Law against individual tyranny. This, at least, was the aspect under which such spirits as those of Virgil were able to submit themselves to its dominion. That central influence which makes nature one, that great idea which in our day has dawned upon the world as the correlation of force—the idea, that is, of an energy underlying all phenomena, identical under various forms—this idea, translated into the political world, finds its best symbol in such an empire as that of Rome, as it represented itself to its best men. And the mind of the great Italian poet reflects this ideal both in the natural and the human world. Nature is a stern ruler, relaxing no severity of claim in pity to human weakness ; man must serve her by arduous, unvarying toil, carrying on a perpetual warfare (as it seems to him) against some hostile power which seeks to withhold from him the produce of the soil, and from which he is designed to wrest it by vigorous struggle. But this arduous

M

struggle is, in truth, the task appointed by a beneficent
ruler, and in this seeming strife man is truly engaged
with a "most just" being, who requites all trust with
rich payment.[1]   The steadiness, the law-abiding spirit
of nature haunts Virgil's mind with an image of repose
deeper than the sense of arduous toil which also belongs
to it.   The two are sometimes illogically combined, but
they have an actual harmony.   Virgil is in this the true
exponent of his nation.   The Latin language first contains
the word by which we express fortitude in toil; *industry*
was an expression unknown to the Greek tongue, and
where it seems indicated in Greek phrase the eulogium
is almost an apology.   The race which first awakens to
the majesty of law also first sets forth the dignity of
toil; the two ideas are correlative; in the verse of Virgil
we find both set to music.

The same combination of submission to a severe
lawgiver and loyalty to a steadfast law is found in his
philosophy of life.   The power that decides on the
destiny of nations is also stern and ruthless; often it
seems cruel.   Virtue and piety win no obvious reward;
the sympathy of the poet takes one course, and the
decision of Providence another.   There is no writer who
more than Virgil enlarges on the text, "God moves in
a mysterious way."   Trust in a lying Greek brings on
the ruin of Troy, and no God interposes to avenge the
treachery which has requited compassionate aid with
ruin.   Dido suffers for taking pity on Æneas, as Priam
for taking pity on Sino, and the hospitality of Latinus
involves his country in the miseries of war.   As long as
we look to the merits and the fate of individuals, all
is confusion; we see nothing but injustice and wanton
cruelty.   But from the moment when the ghost of
Hector[2] appears, in all the horror of the fall of Troy, to

---

[1] Georg., ii. 459.   [2] Æneid, ii. 270.

announce the rising of a new city whose foundations were
to be eternal, the glory of Rome closes every vista, and
supplies a purpose for all that was bewildering and a justification of all that is harsh. We see no loving Father,
not even a just judge, as far as individual fate is concerned.
But we do see a single ruler, a single plan, a single goal ;
we see in the distance the great idea of a central interest
and historic purpose in life, enough to give dignity and
strength to resignation, if not enough to give life to hope.

And if the ways of God are stern and, except by
reference to a distant future, inexplicable, the characteristic quality of ideal man is a tender compassion,
embracing all that is weak, all that is sad, all even that
is repulsive. This is the dominant impression of the
Æneid. The fall of Troy, narrated by a survivor of the
royal family, prefigures, in all its incidents of pathos and
horror, the fate of that city whose Queen hears the tale ;
it flings its lurid light on the long train of victims
to the great Power whose rise is yet announced with
religious reverence, as, in a special sense, the agent of
the Divine Will. Dido and Turnus, the Carthaginian
Queen and the Italian Prince, gather up the claims of
all the vast world that was to be crushed by Rome, and
embody all that sympathy with the vanquished and
unhappy which we feel latent in every line. Many a
minor touch fills in the music with its own subtle variations ; we are taught to feel for the hunted deer[1] that
flies to die at the feet of the mistress who has tended
him, the generous steed that shares the ardour of the
fierce Mezentius[2] and alone attracts his affections ; even

---

[1] " Saucius at quadrupes nota intra tecta refugit
   Successitque gemens stabulis, questuque cruentus
   Atque imploranti similis tectum omne replebat."
                                        —Æneid, vii. 500 502.

[2] " Haud dejectus equum duci jubet. Hoc decus illi
   Hoc solamen erat."—Ibid., x. 858-859.

for the monster Polyphemus,[1] followed by the flock whose
devotion forms his sole consolation, and the picture of
whose attachment to him brings images of gentleness
into what is most savage.   Much of all this may be
found in Homer, but the change of tone from Homer
is made the more striking by the similarity of their
material, and in proportion as the reader appreciates the
song of each he feels the chasm which divides them.
Nothing can be more unlike the cheerful bustle of the
earlier singer than the plaintive pathos of his imitator.
As we read the Iliad we think of Hector, of Achilles, of
Priam.   As we read the Æneid we think of Virgil.   We
feel always in the poetry of Virgil just that neighbourhood of a suffering human soul that it is refreshing to
miss in the poetry of Homer.   A mist of unshed tears
seems to haunt the stream of his genius.   Sorrow, and
endurance, and patience weave themselves into the very
web of his verse.   He gives a voice to the unhappy, the
vanquished; in touching the inmost heart with a sense
of pity, he lightens the burden of humanity by reminding
us that we bear it in common.

Here we have an explanation of the fact that Virgil
has become a legendary precursor of Christianity.   In
choosing him as his guide through the mysteries of the
unseen world, Dante was not giving him a totally new
position, but expanding many a hint in the previous
history of his fame.[2]   It appears a strange destiny which

---

[1] " Monstrum horrendum, informe, ingens, cui lumen ademptum.

      *   *   *   *   *   *

Lanigeræ comitantur oves ; ea sola voluptas
Solamenque mali."—*Æneid*, iii. 658-661.

The word *solamen*, twice applied to an animal, and in each case expressing
the feeling with which it was regarded by a fierce and cruel nature, seems to me
to open a vista of wonderful tenderness and pity, quite unlike anything else in
ancient literature.

[2] As, for instance, the fact that Constantine read Virgil's Fourth Eclogue at
the Council of Nice, and the legend that St. Paul came to weep at his tomb.

has transformed the careful revivalist of a past religion
into the prophet of one that was in the future ; but, in
fact, these two things are closely connected; it is his
reverence towards the past which forms his affinity with
Christianity. The idea of this affinity is true in so deep
a sense that the falsehood in its legendary translation
may be called unimportant. He has translated the
blessing on the poor into sympathy with the vanquished ; he has made failure pathetic, and lifted resignation into the region of heroic endeavour. We have
compared Virgil with Wordsworth, and it may be said
that the poem, where Wordsworth has clothed the idea
of Christian resignation in a classic dialect, is no more
than the expansion of a few words from the Æneid.
Laodamia, the wife whose love calls back her husband
across the barrier of death, says in many words only
what Creusa, the wife whose love causes her herself to
pass that barrier, says in a few :—" Why this immo-
derate grief, beloved spouse ? It is the will of God." [1]
Not the will of one without whom no sparrow falls
to the ground, in whose eyes our hairs are all num-
bered. Such a will, if we can for a moment discern it,
craves our embrace rather than our resignation. The
fate that tore Creusa from passionate devotion was the
will of one who was not loving, not exactly just, certainly
not careful to apportion the sufferings to the needs of
each one. But it was a will fixed on a design including
a vast benefit to the human race—the incorporation of
the civilized world in a single system of law and order,
the establishment of a single rule that was to give peace
to a storm-tossed world. And for such an aim it was
worth while to suffer and to perish ; the sacrifice would
be made by any one who could realize that gain of which
it was the price.

[1] Æneid, ii. 775, 6.

The end was worth the means, on the whole. But
in that end there is no compensation for the sufferers.
Rather the sufferers do but shadow forth as individuals
what nations must endure under the stern dominion
which the Gods prepared. The pangs of Dido prefigure
and embody the pangs of Carthage : the Queen perishes,
as her city is to perish ; and the very words in which
the Trojans, entreating her shelter, deprecate the idea of
hostile intentions toward her people, seem to reflect upon
the barbarous policy to be carried out against her city
by the descendants of those to whom she gives a generous shelter.[1] The dominion towards which the whole
action of the story moves on was one of crushing
severity, and this thought seems never out of the mind
of the poet, who treats it as an ordinance of Heaven.
Nevertheless he contemplates the stately structure with
awe that is not servile ; he feels it to belong to that order
of colossal events which must be explained by Divine
purpose, and in that light submission takes the aspect of
a religious duty. The craving of his soul is for repose.
His storm-tossed spirit poured its yearnings into the
wail of his wandering hero, and he uttered as aspirations
after the unbuilt Rome that desire for the staple Empire
which, after the long earthquake of the civil wars, he
imagined and desired with passionate need as the very
presentation and embodiment of the City of God. There
is a passage in the Æneid that bears the comparison it
invites with one of the most striking parts of the Old
Testament. When the servant of Elisha, terrified at the
crowd of hostile Syrians, turns to his master for comfort,
he is answered by the prayer that his eyes may be opened,
and by the sight of the chariots of fire that form the

---

[1] " Non nos aut ferro Libyces populare Penates
   Venimus, aut raptas ad littora vertere prædas."
                                   —Æneid, i. 526.

invisible guards of the Holy City.[1] The revelation to
Æneas by his Divine mother of the invisible host come
not to guard but to destroy the city of doom would
be felt not less full of significance and poetry if we
could make the comparison fairly. True, the vision of
Elisha is full of triumph, and that of Æneas has the
aspect of despair. But at the core of that despair lies
a hope capable of infinite expansion. The gods have
indeed deserted Troy ; "Let them that are in Judæa flee
unto the mountains" is the warning prefigured no less
clearly than the vision of Elisha is recalled. But the fall
of Troy no less than the fall of Jerusalem precedes a
mystic resurrection ; from its ashes shall arise a city
not unworthy, in the imagination of Virgil, to be set
beside all that is loftiest in human achievement. The
severity of Heaven, interpreted by Divine Love, must
be at all times an idea full of hope and consolation. But
many influences when Virgil wrote prepared the mind of
humanity to receive this idea with a peculiar welcome.
He saw glimmering in the future a mystic vision of
Peace ;[2] his heart was stirred by yearnings after a blessed
unity of all life and all nature, and found this unity for
the first time suggested by the world without. Human
history embodied the idea of purpose, and Will suggests
even when it does not express Love. The mere wide-
reaching habit of submission to central power, the stately

---

[1] II. Kings vi. 17. Compare *Æneid*, ii. 601, ff. :—
    " Non tibi Tyndaridis facies invisa Lacænæ
    Culpatusve Paris ; divum inclementia, divum,
    Has evertit opes, sternitque a culmine Trojam,
    Aspice, namque omnem, quæ nunc obducta tuenti
    Mortales hebetat visus tibi, et humida circum
    Caligit, nubem eripiam."

[2] " Magnus ab integro sæclorum nascitur ordo
    Jam nova progenies cœlo demittitur alto.
    Jam redit et Virgo, redeunt Saturnia regna."
                                        —Ec. iv.

and growing fabric of universal Law, claimed a sort of reverence that passed into religion.   Whether the dying request of the poet to destroy his poem was due in any measure to some dim prophetic anticipations of the verdict of History on the Empire, whether some flash of the inspiration of genius revealed to him the fugitive and injurious character of that dominion his Jove had pronounced eternal, we cannot say.   He was fastidious, aspiring, exacting in his ideal ; his poem had not received its last touches ; perhaps that was all.   But if the other feeling had come in, it would have thrown a strange light on his relations to his own time, and to that which was to succeed him.

When, therefore, Virgil hails the foundation of the Empire with a record of the legendary past full of mere fiction, and yet containing a prophecy of its eternity, we must not look upon him as a courtly sycophant inaugurating the new art of flattery by a prostitution of genius.   Virgil, belonging by blood and bound by sympathy to the conquered Italian race, while culture and friendship attached him to the court of Augustus, was fitted to express both a true loyalty for a ruler of Rome, and a deep sympathy for its subjects and victims. The two feelings seem inharmonious, and in this nineteenth century after Christ perhaps they are so.   We look back upon a long course of struggle between the rulers and the ruled, and discern that no earthly power is the rightful claimant of uncritical submission from mature human beings.   We see that the great unity which Virgil welcomed was, in the long course of things,

---

[1] " His ego nec metas rerum nec tempora pono ;
     Imperium sine fine dedi.

          *   *   *   *   *   *

     Nascetur pulchra Trojanus origine Cæsar
     Imperium oceano, famam qui terminet astris."
                              —Æneid, i. 278- 287.

the foe of Liberty without being the friend of Peace.
While we cannot but recognize the sway of Rome as
an important and indispensable stage in the evolution of
European civilization—as divine in the sense that that
whole evolution is divine—we see also that the antagonism
of barbaric invasion was divine in just the same sense,
and brought its own contribution to the life of modern
Europe. And this would have been to Virgil like saying
that good and evil were both divine. He saw a great
unity impressed on all life ; and though he felt a keen and
almost oppressive sympathy with the life that was crushed,
still he never faltered in the conviction that loyalty was
due to this unity, and that the sacrifice was made for an
adequate object. And then to recognize that this unity
was to be broken up, that, so far as it was to endure, it
was to pass into the realm of the Invisible, and that even
as a Church it was again to become an object of attack
from the healthy national life, and of repulsion to the true
individual conscience—this was impossible to any one
who hailed the Empire. It was not impossible to hate
and oppose it, but to see as much of its Divine purpose
as Virgil did, and also to see that it was to be swept
away, was a discernment only possible to the reverted
gaze of History. To anticipate the verdict of History
on his own time would not help a man of genius to
express and explain it. Doubtless the verdict of History
will contain all that is true in his expression. But
Virgil could not have told us what the Roman Empire
was if he saw what it was to become. We are not
meant to judge any stage of life from the point of view
of our successors. Looking back, we see good everywhere, and evil everywhere. If the men of the time
had seen this, life would be even more desultory, more
purposeless, than it is.

We gain a clue to the whole meaning of the change

that was coming over the world, and to Virgil's part in
producing and responding to it, when we note the place
that woman takes in the Æneid. The Iliad is a story
of *men.* Women take a large part in it, as in all
vivid dramas of life. But they are mere subordinates
—the pictures of Andromache, of Helen, beautiful as
they are, occupy the background of interest ; they are
mere accessories to the male actors. Helen, though
she ought to be the principal person of the drama, is
a faint, delicate sketch, and for the greater part of the
poem we are inclined to forget her altogether. But
when we turn to the Æneid the whole action depends
on female influence. Its most impressive figure is the
Carthaginian queen; its central Deity is the Divine mother.
The worship of the Virgin seems in the greater part of
the poem just trembling into life; it is one of the many
respects in which Virgil may be considered in a double
sense the poet of Rome. The image of motherly love,
glimmering through the storms of life with a continual
reminder of Divine care, and a continual claim on human
submission, more prefigures that element in Christian
faith which was welcomed by the world with the most
urgent sense of need, than any of the loftiest utterances
of Greek religion. Homer knows nothing of it; the
tragedians only hint at it ; the mysteries may have
cherished it, but it attains its first literary expression
in Virgil ; and nothing surely distinguishes more clearly
the purity of his character and refinement of his genius
than the transformation of the ignoble temptress of the
Iliad into that ideal of almost omnipotent power shown
forth in beneficent tenderness, which Christendom for so
many ages accepted as its guiding star.[1]

---

[1] Any one who will read carefully the last part of Æneid ii. from 589 will discover the suggestion of a " Holy Family "—the Divine Mother, the child with
the nimbus, and the mystic Star. See note at end of volume.

The worship of the Divine mother links in wondrous harmony the worlds that lie beneath and above humanity. In the mother's love some ocean seems to break through the shallow vessel which holds ordinary love, as though the Infinite came welling through the limitations of individual human nature ; what exalted virtue hardly produces in any other relation, the mere conditions of physiology seem to ensure between the mother and child. Here we seem to have reached a law wider than humanity ; here we come down to the primal rock of sentient nature, and discern the elements of morality that are older than man. It needs the barest hint of permission to justify worship, where such an ideal passes into the Divine world. Out of a few scanty mentions in the Gospels, some of them apparently conveying a distinct warning against the tendency which fed upon them, Christendom made itself a goddess, and transformed its yearnings after what Goethe calls " the eternal womanliness " into the legend of a Virgin Mother. The subjects of Rome welcomed a mother in the Heavens ; on earth they knew only a hard master, and the Divine Father had associations that shut out love. The transformation of the goddess of lawless self-pleasing love into the goddess of a maternal compassionate love, forms the clue to the power of Virgil over the ages that were to come ; it shows us the imitator of Homer as the teacher of Dante ; the transformation of the classical into the Christian ideal of life. The elevation of woman is the symbol of all that is most vital in that change ; the new meaning given to the passive side of life comes out in the new honour paid to the passive sex, and the elevation of that sex into the Divine world.

When Virgil wrote, the virtues even of the slave were emerging into a development which Christianity was shortly to recognize and adopt. Obedience to steady systematic power, whether the power be in its own nature good or evil, does bring out some valuable qualities which nothing else can develop, and the list of Christian martyrs records the stored-up force of generations of patient, resolute endurance. The death in the amphitheatre that witnessed to the faith of Christ, witnessed also to power bequeathed by men who had no faith to enlighten their last moments with visions of an opening Heaven. The victim of Roman cruelty, whose only protest was the cry, " I am a citizen of Rome,"[1] died in a spirit that prepared his successors in calamity to triumph in their citizenship of the Heavenly City; for the sense of some dim justice accessible in the name of the City has a real, though a remote, relation to the love and power manifest in the death of Christ. Not only so; the spirit of fortitude thus developed spread beyond the limits of those ideas by which it was nourished. When we read of female slaves enduring the extremity of torture rather than betray the unhappy mistress they could not save,[2] or finding strength to end life under the very hands of the tormentors lest the exquisite anguish should wring from half-conscious lips denunciations of those who were, as the historian reminds us, not bound to the sufferer by blood, and hardly by acquaintance,[3] we feel that the new consecration of suffering and of weakness, the message of the Cross, was realized by those who had never heard it. Rome, the tyrant of the world, taught the lesson of Christ; under its stern and often cruel rule was learnt the power of submission; and that power was ready, when adopted by a new faith, to renew the world.

---

[1] Cic., " In Verrem," v. 62.   [2] Tac., Annals, xiv. 60.

[3] Epicharis, a freedwoman, in the conspiracy of Piso. " At illam non verbera, non ignes, non ira eo acrius torquentium ne a feminâ spernerentur, percivêre quin objecta denegaret " (*Ibid.*, xv. 57). It is one of the few passages in which the historian shows a certain sympathy with the victim.

CHAPTER V.

THE law of human progress is a complex one. Change makes itself manifest at first, mainly as loss. A negative succeeds a positive stage, and it is only after long patience that we find the new life develop into some reminiscence of the old. The perfection of manhood contains the perfection of childhood, but boyhood seems often a mere breaking away from all that is pure and beautiful in the earlier stage. Youth is negative, critical; the trust of the child reappears only in the trust of maturity. The caterpillar has far more life than the chrysalis, and if our knowledge stopped with that stage of growth we should believe that growth was death. The three conditions which we may here discover as distinct stages in an upward progress are dimly visible in history. The change of moral ideal from ancient to modern life may be roughly described as a substitution of the aims of the individual for those of the citizen, a transference of hope and fear from corporate to personal achievement. The transition takes place by the same law of development as that which transforms the zoophyte into the animal ; it is a change from a lower to a higher form of life ; the gain is immense and obvious. In our own day the deadliest war and the worst explosion of crime alike bear witness, that ordinary men now recognize a relation among human beings as such, of which the best men of antiquity had no conception.

Nevertheless, when we compare our sense of union with theirs, we shall often see the loss more clearly than the gain, even after eighteen centuries of growth. Perhaps the wider union can never be recognized as the narrower was ; perhaps the large ideal must always appear vacillating and imperfect, when it is compared with the small.

Much more shall we feel this if we return to the period that intervenes between the ancient and modern world ; to that age which we may, according to our point of view, call the death of the city, or the birth of the nation. In the dark winter that intervenes between the autumn and the spring, the instincts which measured the vital strength of antiquity had much less scope than they have now. The nation is not the dominant interest that the city was, but still in modern life, as in ancient life, men have felt themselves part of a whole. Only in the epoch of transition was there no bond from man to man, except that which united one man to all men. Men have never been so isolated since then. Christianity has always been a strong binding influence, if also a strong dividing influence ; but at its dawn there was in the whole world no binding influence except that which included the whole world. For while the union of the city or of the nation is a vital reality, that agglomeration which makes up an Empire is strong by means of negation only ; it lives on the crushed lives of the races that are submitted to it; and the moment they awaken to energetic self-assertion it must perish. It marks a complete blank of national life. The dominion of Roman imperialism was indeed the occasion of a new sense of individual life, a sudden and yet permanent illumination of those relations which bind man to man. But the bond which unites one man to all men is a weak thing if it stand alone. The sense of human kindred, if it know no gradation, is powerless to overcome the repulsions of self-interest or aversion, and to weld separate individuals into a whole that can withstand shocks from without. Even in the best men of that time (who, indeed, may be reckoned among the best men of any time) we do still discern, that meagreness of moral life, that poverty of organic relation which in other representatives of the age comes out in every utterance, and which is stamped upon the history of this period in characters that none may ignore.

For the history of the first three centuries of our era is inexplicable without a constant recollection of this moral poverty. The rule of the bad Roman Emperors is remembered as a type of cruel and oppressive tyranny, even by persons who have no equally definite ideas of any other. Perhaps the dominion of a Nero was not really so oppressive to the body of the people as that of many less celebrated tyrants; but still we have to account for the strange paralysis that lay on the minds of those distinguished men who *did* suffer and could have resisted. Other tyrants have been supported either by the spell of genius or the authority of hereditary claim. Genius in the first century after Christ seemed extinct, and inherited authority was an idea associated with barbarism and opposed to all the glorious memories of the past.[1] The tyrants of the Roman Empire, the most widespread tyranny the world has ever known, were as devoid of energetic character and resolute will as of the prestige of tradition. They had as little legitimate claim as Napoleon, and as little genius as the Bourbons. Yet as we read how they were obeyed, we feel as if they must have possessed something which all modern tyrants have lacked. Brave and guiltless men, when their death was decreed by the Emperor, heard in vain the appeal of what would seem the irresistible voice

---

[1] " Urbem Romam a principio reges habuere. Libertatem et consulatum L. Brutus instituit."—Tac., Ann., i. 1.

of common sense to make use of the common sympathy
and the common danger;[1] they submitted to the doom
in resisting which they would have found thousands of
comrades; they even inflicted it with their own hands
at the imperial order. The history of the Roman
Empire is as much a problem as a narrative. Why
should a General who had enlarged the boundaries of
Roman dominion fall on his spear at the command of
Nero?[2] Why should the virtuous sages he sent to the
scaffold bow to his will as to something divine?[3] The
answer is as certain as it is instructive. Because on the
side of the oppressor was an ideal of corporate unity, and
on the side of the victim was nothing but himself. The
traditional loyalty to the State had been transferred to
a succession of parvenus, and the filial obedience rendered
by the citizen of the Republic was succeeded by the
servile obedience rendered by the subject of the Empire.
The Emperor had no true strength, but there was no
other strength than his. While his victims were mere
individuals, in him was incarnate the ideal of the past;
he represented the dead Commonwealth; and noble
spirits, like the faithful hound, keep a long watch beside
a corpse.

The power of resisting tyranny lies in the sense of
some organic union between its victims. The common
suffering of individuals does not of itself make them
into a unity. If they feel that nothing is injured but
themselves, they may indeed resist what is intolerable;

---

[1] As Rubellius Plautus, who incurred the jealousy of Nero, and was its
unresisting victim, A. D. 62. See Tac., Ann., xiv. 58, 59; *cf.* appeal to Piso, xv.
59; and the lament of the historian, xvi. 16.

[2] Corbulo, the conqueror of the Parthians, thus killed himself, A. D. 67.

[3] See Seneca, "De Tranquillitate Animi," xiv. 3, for a striking instance of
this adulation in the case of Canus Julius, whom Seneca calls one of the greatest
of men, and who thanked Caligula for sending him to the scaffold. The most
striking case of ignoble submission is mentioned by the same writer, as shown
to the same prince by a Roman knight named Pastor ("De Irá.," ii. 33).

but exactly in proportion as they are good and generous, they will be slow to disturb, for the sake of any concern personal to themselves, the advantages produced by any kind of settled order. An injury, if it be not a wrong, is always more gladly endured than resisted by a noble nature ; it is the generous flame of indignation alone which can fuse the varied elements of individual suffering into the unity that makes a multitude formidable. And thus no number of individuals will possess a common strength, if they are united only by impulses that slacken in the heart of every man in proportion as he is un-selfish. When men have arisen in successful revolt, they have felt something more than that tyranny was painful ; they have been united by the sense that the tyrant had abused a sacred trust, that he could be called to account for the charge of a sacred deposit. They have represented some corporate unity ; they have felt themselves bound together by a common race or a common faith. When there is no binding influence on the side of the victims but that common wish for life and case which is felt by every man, while on the side of the oppressor there is even the ghost of a great idea, the one will be strong, and the many almost powerless.

Hence that ideal of resignation, which we have seen in Virgil as the moral bequest of Roman dominion, came under the Empire to gather to itself all the moral energy of the nation, and men were strong only in the virtues of the slave. As we look at the outward history of the time, we can remember only what is equally true, that they were weak in his vices. We cannot in any other period bring forward, either on so large or on so small a scale, illustrations of a general servility. We need it to explain the submission of a world ; we discern it also in the minutest habits of polite society. No other

N

period has possessed an important and influential class of men who had once occupied the position of menials, and having exhibited the abjectness of slavery as shown in the cringing dependent, revealed its other side in the insolence of the upstart, and the cruelty that is bred of inherited fear. A slave utters the loftiest aspirations of that age; its freedmen show forth its warnings. The business of life was servility; those must have succeeded best who had known its lowest depths. Thus the spirit that made the Empire possible was exercised and developed in all social intercourse; and politeness showed itself in a series of attentions not unlike those of the upper servants of a luxurious household to a pampered master (only that in our age some of them would be to the taste of hardly any one). A sort of inverted subservience seems to have found satisfaction in attentions void of all other object than the manifestation of servility; those men who made the world tremble showed most clearly the tastes engendered by slavery. "Tremble before the slave when he bursts his fetters, not before the freeman," says Schiller,[1] and the lesson has never been better illustrated than by the society of the Roman Empire. The distinction between the freedman and the freeman was one the Roman of that age could never forget; it is one he has left recorded in deeds and words which convey its meaning to all time.[2]

---

[1] "Vor dem Sklaven, wenn er die Kette bricht,
Vor dem freien Menschen erzittert nicht."
—Schiller, " Die Worte des Glaubens."

[2] The writers who seem to me to bring out most forcibly the tendencies of a servile society, reinforced from the ranks of slaves, are Martial and Seneca, chiefly the former. I should not think so many begging-letters were contained in any other book belonging to literature as in his epigrams; they are a testimony o universal habits of mendicancy, which make his gross flattery of Domitian (*e.g.,* i. 17, 28) a comparative trifle. But perhaps the most striking single llustration of this servile spirit, as it was encouraged by Stoicism, is the flattery of Nero in the opening of the Pharsalia, i. 33–66. If all the miseries

How deeply rooted was this spirit of servility is shown by its hold on the intellect of the age. Genius has never stooped so low as in the abasement of men of letters before Nero and Domitian. Perhaps they will, in all ages, be apt to be found on the side of submission; students are generally timid in the face of revolutionary change. They are apt to feel that the din of civil tumult interrupts things more precious than it can ever establish; and men trained in the atmosphere of study and meditation find it easier to die than to resist. "If all are grateful to him whose overruling power secures untroubled repose," says Seneca,[1] "the man whose leisure is occupied with profound and fertile meditation will surely, considering to whom he owes this priceless treasure, be ready to exclaim, in the words of Virgil's shepherd, 'O Melibœus, a god has given us this repose!'" the god being Nero. Nor did he grudge his life as the price of it, when the claim was made by the god of his ignoble idolatry. No far-reaching, deep-rooted national life made a background and shelter for the separate individualities which had formerly owed all their vigour and beauty to such a support. Whatever survived of the belief in that national life ranked itself on the side of submission to Nero; whatever suggested resistance belonged to the mere unit. The commonplace secular world was useful only as a husk to preserve the little kernel of Philosophy; it had no sacredness of its own. The only important duty of the Prince was to keep things quiet, in order that the Philosopher might think and write in peace. If that was all that could be accomplished by the best of princes, it is not surprising that Nero was not felt to be the worst.

of the civil wars were the necessary price to pay for the blessing of Nero's rule, says the nephew of Seneca, they were well worth while. The first three books of the *Pharsalia* were published in A.D. 62.

[1] Epist. 73; *cf.* Virgil, *l.c.* l.

Men know little of the meaning of a true Resignation when they imagine it to be the foe of manly activity, of heroic aspiration. No heroic achievement is possible without it ; nothing great was ever done but by one who knew how to endure; in all achievement lies the latent heat of renunciation. But a true resignation implies a worthy allegiance ; it implies some organic unity for the sake of which all that pertains to the Self may be resigned. The dying Socrates preaches such a resignation when he refuses to quit the prison from which escape is easy, and declares that the laws of his country sound in his ears like some strange music deafening him to the appeal of his eager disciple,[1] and bidding him rather endure the worst that can be inflicted, than resist the claim whose validity he feels more deeply than any other certainty. But the dying Corbulo, falling on his sword at the command of Nero, preaches the very opposite lesson ; he warns all who follow his history against the slavish spirit that prepared a world of victims, and set a monster on the throne. He shows not the heroism that can lay down life for a noble cause, but the weariness and despair that found it easier to die than to resist any authority clothed with an appearance of legitimate claim ; he measures the vacuum of hope and fear that remained even for a brave and successful soldier, when the Commonwealth had ceased to exist.

The meagreness and poverty of the private life of antiquity is best seen in the life of which this private side was richest. Cicero is known to us much as we know the hero of a modern biography; we have his intimate letters, as well as his public utterances, and know his private opinions almost as well as the facts of

---

[1] ταῦτα . . . ἐγὼ δοκῶ ἀκούειν, ὥσπερ οἱ κορυβαντιῶντες τῶν αὐλῶν δοκοῦ-
σιν ἀκούειν, καὶ ἐν ἐμοὶ αὕτη ἡ ἠχὴ τούτων τῶν λόγων βομβεῖ καὶ ποιεῖ μὴ
δύνασθαι τῶν ἄλλων ἀκούειν (Plato, Crito., 54).

his history. In him we come near enough to the life of a Roman gentleman, in order to see the strange gaps which it exhibits as compared with any life among the cultured classes in modern times. Perhaps the most striking change, from this point of view, is the entire lack of what we mean by a sense of honour. We must descend to an uneducated stratum of society before we reach the bluntness of feeling which seems to have characterized the best society of Rome. When a letter not addressed to himself falls into the hands of Cicero, and he wishes to know what is inside it, it seems to be the most natural thing in the world to break the seal and peruse its contents. The only approach to an apology is his request to the husband of the writer, to whom he mentions the fact, never to let her know what he has done.[1] An impertinent footman in London would be more embarrassed by the confession than was the finest gentleman of Rome.

The same moral poverty is discernible in a coldness and coarseness of his private relations in other ways. The reader comes with a strange shock on the story of his second marriage ; it would be impossible for any equally affectionate modern, to have divorced a wife who had been in tender relations with him for thirty years, and immediately married a young heiress. He was evidently the most warm-hearted and considerate of kinsmen ; yet his father's death is huddled into a letter of commissions with a brevity which in an intimate communication an Englishman would feel jarring in the

[1] See Cic., Ad Att., v. 11. The letter he opened was one from Pilia, the wife of Atticus, perhaps referring to the conjugal troubles of his brother, Quintus, who was married to Atticus's sister. "Accepi fasciculum in quo erat epistola Piliae, abstuli, aperui, legi," is his straightforward account of the matter. Another time he tells Atticus that he had advised his nephew always to open and read any letter to his (the young man's) father—"Si quid forte sit quod opus sit sciri" (Ad Att., vi. 3).

announcement of almost any death among kindred; and the betrothal of his beloved Tullia is mentioned with just the same apparent carelessness. It is hardly possible to doubt that Cicero was an excellent son; it is certain that he was an excellent father; but private relation was evidently a slighter thing to him than it is to an average man in modern England or France. Certainly the lack of delicacy was not personal; there never was a nature more adapted than that of Cicero for all the fine shades of feeling by which intercourse is kept pure and easy. But he belonged to a race that had no moral attention for any private relation, inasmuch as it took no interest in any individual claim. Everything individual was, as it were, considered in a hurry; the important business of life summoned thought away to other realms, and the group of sentiments and impulses which make up the moral standard of refinement and culture were as little dreamt of among the refined and cultivated classes of Rome as in modern Europe among those crushed by penury, and dulled by arduous and unremitting toil. In his life we see the difference between a private life enriched by a long tradition of moral interest, and one which is a mere parenthesis in the life of the citizen.

But the interests of the citizen came to an end. This bare and meagre life became the only one. And men were thus driven back for the first time on the meaning of the word *Self.* There were only two objects of attention in the whole world which could be regarded as a unity. The first was that vast Empire which enfolded in its rigid embrace so various a group of races that it might well seem to include all humanity; the second was the soul of man. Nothing came between that could be called *One.* Athens, Sparta, Thebes—all that gathered up the glorious memories of the past; Gaul, Britain, Spain—all then known of that which pre-

figured the development of the future, were alike mere
fragments of the Empire; none could form the focus of
any inspiring hope; any attempt to discover such was
associated with disappointment. As for the Empire
itself, it was far too vast and too various to exercise in
any practical sense the political capacities and energies
bequeathed from days when the life of the City was a
reality. That stately, satisfying life had passed away,
leaving no successor. There was for the subject of the
Empire a sense of repose, of security, which the citizen
of antiquity had never known; but that which had made
life worth living was gone utterly. What could occupy
the void left by such a bereavement? Only that which
was a unity in even a deeper sense than the City had
ever been; that which is the very type of oneness; that
which each man means when he says " I." There we
reach not only *a* unity, but *the* Unity. It may be
thought that it is in so special a sense *the* Unity that
there could have been no period of history at which
men made the discovery that it was so, but we think
thus only when we fail in historic imagination. The
correlation of our moral being is no less complex than
that of our physical organism, and here also we shall
find loss and gain hand in hand. "When the seeds in
our fruits become atrophied," says Darwin, "the fruit
itself gains largely in size and quality." In the evolution of our modern life this process has been inverted,
and when we return to the rich civil life of antiquity,
we find that, as compared with our own, it had a similar
price. Nothing is so hostile to the spiritual life, at any
time, as the political; nothing so entirely calls away
attention from the problems of the inward world as
the responsibilities of the statesman; and we might
call every citizen of antiquity in some sense a statesman. We must exaggerate all political interest, we must

enormously diminish all other interest, before we can
appreciate the absorbing power of the life of the State
on a citizen of Athens.   Thus only shall we understand
the immense fund of intellectual energy released and
craving exercise when the Old World came to an end ;
thus only enter into the meaning of those emphatic platitudes, as they seem to us, which meet us in the more
earnest writings of this time.   Platitudes to the reader
of the nineteenth century, to the writer of the first or
second they are original and striking thoughts.   If we
could imagine ourselves entering upon moral questions
of which we found no hint in the New Testament, we
should put ourselves in the position of those writers
who at this time began to investigate a world of reflection, of emotion, of intellectual interest, on which Plato
had hardly touched.   It was in very truth to them the
entrance on a new world.

The citizen of Athens or Rome had felt himself to
derive all his worth from his relation to an invisible
being which preceded, and would survive, him—the
State.   The life that he most prized was a life that he
believed immortal, and it was his participation in this
which gave value to his own.   The subject of the
Roman Empire could cherish no such belief.   He stood
in no relation to any city, for Rome had ceased to be a
city—she was a world.   He was no longer a portion
of any other life ; he felt, for the first time, that he
must be himself a whole.   He could not any longer say
We with any fulness of meaning ; he began to realize
what it is that each man means when he says *I.*   As
the fruit withered, the seed detached itself.   It is not
that this was a time of vigorous individuality ; quite
the reverse.   There was less individuality during the
two centuries to which these remarks chiefly apply[1] in

---

[1] *i.e.,* from the death of Virgil, 19 B.C., to the death of Marcus Aurelius,

the whole civilized world than there was during the life of Greece, within a region about as large as Wales. But as men missed the exceptional endowment, they learned to prize that universal quality of which it is no more than the conspicuous exhibition. Everywhere the exceptional was changing to the universal. The proud privilege of Roman citizenship was vulgarized by the intrusion of a mob; even the distinction of bond and free, though not in the slightest degree weakened in practice, was beginning to be felt, by the foremost thinkers of the day, out of harmony with the true ideal of humanity. The idea of the State—that which is essentially limited, that which, according to the conditions of ancient life, was connected with something exceptional, inasmuch as it could not include in its organic framework every human being who came under its sway—this idea was giving way to the most expansive, the most widely inclusive that is known to abstract thought, the idea of Nature.

A man had felt himself called on to live as a citizen; he was now bidden to live according to Nature. The injunction is little more than an epitaph on the ideal of ancient life, and when it has been repeated in the modern world, it has lost half its meaning. From the most concrete object of human loyalty the men of that day turned towards the most abstract. The city was indeed an invisible reality, but those outward images with which it was associated were small and definite almost beyond what a modern can bring himself to realize.[1] Nature, on the other hand, is the vaguest idea, perhaps, that we associate with a single word. It is strange to reflect that about two thou-

---

180 A.D. The half-century which saw the invasion of Xerxes, 500 450 B.C., has a far greater wealth of character and genius.

[1] The minute range of impressive associations is vividly brought home to the reader by the whole of the Œdipus at Colonus. One constantly imagines distances ten times as great as the reality.

sand years after the belief of Life according to Nature came to men as a gospel, John Stuart Mill devoted an Essay, left behind as the expression of his latest thought, to ask— What is Nature ? How could the Roman Stoics have felt it any gain to live according to something of which Mill, looking back on many centuries of other people's study of it, and his own long life of studying their opinions, declared that he did not know what it was ? Because the word came to them as the symbol of a sudden expansion of moral aim which was best expressed by the vaguest of names. It started them on a new path ; it carried them far away from that which, they clearly saw, should be left behind. It came with the irresistible charm of a new inspiration to men cumbered and shackled by the ruins of the old ; it left the old barriers out of sight, and men for the hour asked no more. To inhabit the city of Zeus [1] instead of the city of Cecrops seemed a wonderful expansion given to all possibilities on which the heart of man could dwell ; and in their recoil from what was narrow, the men of that day failed to discern that in removing the limitations of their ideal home they deprived it of all form. They escaped from the river to the ocean, and forgot that the change would leave them without guidance till they learned to guide themselves by the stars.

The breeze of their own high aims, to a certain extent, served to direct them. The words of all thinkers in the age we speak of were full of a lofty humanity. The extreme Radicals of our own day do not go beyond them in their recognition of the truth, ignored or denied by heroic Greece, that the sacred thing in man is his humanity. But, indeed, that belief is so entirely a commonplace of our day, that the only difference between

---

[1] Ἐκεῖνος μέν φησι πόλι φίλη κέκροπος· σὺ δὲ οὐκ ἐρεῖς ὦ πόλι φίλη Διός ;— Marcus Aurelius Antoninus, iv. 23.

the highest Tory and the broadest Radical is as to the
fitness of their respective schemes for bringing this
fundamental truth into practice. "When you have
come to my age, my dear," said Sir Walter Scott to
his daughter, who had spoken of something as "vulgar"
which he thought undeserving of contempt, "you will
thank God that everything which is supremely precious
is common." He was essentially a Tory; his genius
was quickened and stirred by all that was exceptional;
the pomp of chivalry kindled his imagination, a tawdry
imitation of it ruined his life; yet that gentle rebuke to
his child expresses the deepest part of his ideal; to the
very core of his being he felt, and rejoiced to feel, that
all which is supremely precious is common. There is
the ideal of the modern world; in the ages of classic
antiquity the best of men had just as little sympathy
with it as the worst had.

If we judge by men's words, we should say that in
the first century of our era, the latter standard was in
its fullest maturity substituted for the earlier. If we
judge by their deeds, we should say that the new day
had not yet begun to dawn. Seneca preaches a morality
that our own time has not surpassed; and he may have
been a listener to that debate in the Senate which decided
on the slaughter of 400 innocent slaves.[1] But we must
not think that words without deeds are necessarily
empty of all meaning. The birth of the Enthusiasm of
Humanity is a great epoch in the moral life of man,
even though we must date it by words only. That
enthusiasm seemed in some sense a greater thing then
than it does now. The very fact that people did not

---

[1] But that debate shows also that the feeling of the minority was growing
stronger. "Nemo unus contra ire ausus est," says the Historian, after giving
the arguments for severity, "ita dissonae voces respondebant, numerum . . .
ac plurimorum indubitam innocentiam miserantium" (Ann., xiv. 45). This
was A.D. 60.

act upon it kept it from perilous shocks. We have seen, after eighteen centuries of the ideal, what it cannot do ; to the Roman Stoics it seemed omnipotent. It may be said, that to us, as to them, its true powers are untried ; but it has at all events been in the modern world a standard of life steadily advancing in claim, influencing always what men wish to seem, and sometimes, therefore, what they wish to be. Eighteen hundred years ago nothing was known of the difficulties of philanthropy ; the idea was unfamiliar, the attempt to carry it out was unheard of. It was possible to think that the attempt would unite the human race with a firmer cohesion than that which bound the Roman oligarchy of the past, that it would bring into a unity such as that of Rome all that claimed the name of man.

The fact that an old ideal is perishing must always be a stronger, or at least a more obvious, moral influence than the fact that a new one is coming into life. A death is more impressive than a birth. We always see what we are losing more clearly than what we are gaining ; we never, indeed, see what we have possessed so clearly as in the moment of losing it. Hence we find impressed on these first centuries of our era—the age between the secure establishment of the Empire and that of Christianity—a set of feelings and beliefs that we best sum up in describing it as the Age of Death. The words may be taken quite literally. All life seems at that time to have been coloured by an anticipation of its end. Why, the reader asks continually, this new sense of impressiveness in Death ? How can it be more significant to one generation than to another, that man is snatched away from all work and interest, often before he has come to any full discernment of their purport, almost always before he is ready to depart ? The sense of

hurry in life must be almost coeval with humanity;
wherever men have lived they must have found Death
as much the interruption as the close of Life. Why at
this time do we come upon the sort of occupation of
mind about Death which usually occurs only on the
discovery of a new truth, which would, if it were possible, suggest that it was new in the world ? Because
in an important sense Death was new. It had been for
the first time in history recognized as an influence in the
career of nations. The citizen of the old world shared
in the perennial life of a commonwealth, and had no ear
for those lessons of mortality which did not touch the
deeper life. The subjects of the Empire had learnt that
the perennial life was not eternal. The new scope given
to the fact of mortality brought in this new impressiveness to the close of human life. Nothing is so impressive as Death itself, and therefore, for those who live in
the full blaze of literary expression, nothing is so trite
as reflections about Death. But to the men of the first
and second centuries these reflections came like a new
revelation. An Englishman looking back on the vicissi-
tudes of the seventeen centuries which separate us from
the thinkers of that time is not more struck than they
were with the fact that a State can perish—is not so
much struck with it. All the variety of illustration inaccessible to them which we possess of that truth does not
equal in impressiveness the mere fact itself, when it was
recognized for the first time.[1]

[1] See the well-known letter of Servius Sulpicius on the death of Tullia, from
which Cicero declares himself to have derived much consolation, Ep. ad
Diversos (Ernesti), iv. 5 :—" Post me erat Ægina, ante Megara : dextra Piræus
. . . quæ oppida quodam tempore florentissima fuerunt." The English reader
knows the passage in " Childe Harold "—

> " The Roman saw these tombs in his own age,
> The sepulchres of cities, which excite
> Sad wonder, and his yet surviving page
> The moral lesson bears, drawn from such pilgrimage."

The influence of the idea was curiously strong in opposite directions. We have to describe it in language of candid paradox; death seems never to have been feared so much, or so little. It was accepted with an acquiescence in ordinary times unknown, except in association with some lofty and inspiring cause, and it was even voluntarily sought to a degree that is probably unique in the world's history. At the same time, it was dreaded as it had never been in the heroic days of antiquity, and men of genius were ready to commit any baseness to escape it. The dread was strong enough to lead the poet of the civil wars to denounce his mother,[1] the preacher of fine Stoic morality to connive at the murder of the Emperor's mother, yet it collapsed the moment it might have inspired vigorous action. Death occupied men's minds with a sway which could change in a moment from terror to fascination; the General who fell on his sword at the Emperor's command was probably ready, unless he was unlike the other great men of the time, to have saved his life at the expense of that of his own kindred. Although something had gone out of the world which made life worth living, that did not give men courage to face Death in resolute resistance; on the contrary, there is no age when it seems to have been so abjectly feared.

It is but another way of saying that Death had obtained a new hold on men's minds to add that the problem of a life beyond Death had begun to take new significance. It is easy not to think of Death, but who an think of Death and not ask whether it be the end of desire and fear, or a great crisis in the development of all desires and fears? Thus the general disintegration and decay which made Death an object of attention

---

[1] See the account of Lucan's treachery in the conspiracy of Piso (Tac., Ann., xv. 56), and of Seneca's acquiescence in Agrippina's murder (Ann., xiv. 7).

quickened the yearnings after immortality into new vividness. We see them pierce the husk of worldly frivolity;[1] we find them in the vivid recognition given to the hopes cherished by those races with which Rome was now for the first time coming into contact, and to whom belonged the world of the future. Death was, the Romans discovered, regarded by the mystic priests of the Gauls as " an incident in a long life,"[2] and the poet who was afterwards to attempt to buy his life at so hideous a price records their confidence with a sigh of envy. Why, it may be asked, should the successor of Virgil envy the Druids a faith which Virgil was to confirm in Dante? The expression we have quoted explains it—an incident in a long *life*. Some dim survival in a mysterious underworld was the ancestral belief of the race. Virgil had indeed deepened and illumined the picture drawn by Homer with gleams of a purer radiance and shadows of more sombre significance, but had left it still a mere epilogue to the life of this world. We see in this longing mention of the Druidic belief how the world was beginning to thirst for something beyond this, how men were yearning for a future that should not merely reflect in pallid memories the life of earth, but should carry on all that had begun here into new development, and fill out the hopes and aspirations of earth with achievement. That burst of enthusiasm with which Lucan records this possible vista into the life beyond the grave, measures for us the longings shadowed forth indeed in the Æneid, but brought into distinctness, it seems, only by contact with the race whose whole life lay in the future. " Happy

---

[1] Several times in the most frivolous writer, I should think, who ever used the Latin tongue. See Martial, Ep. v. 34, a pretty little poem on the death of a child, and ix. 21 ; x. 101. I do not mean that we see here more than the dawn of a conventional Heaven, but it is not less.

[2] Lucan, Pharsalia, i. 442, *seq.*

are they in their delusion," sighs Lucan ; and it is a characteristic expression ; he could not conceive of their belief as truth, yet yearned to share it as a mere dream.

To nobler spirits it seemed more than a dream.   Shut out from the life of the State, to which there was no definite term, men were awakening to the discovery that the individual life contained some principle of growth for which the State provided no scope, that within the heart of man lay emotions and desires which were an enormous over-provision for any call that this world was to make on them, and that if man's existence were an intelligible whole, it could not end with the threescore years and ten of his sojourn here.   We mis-understand the hope of immortality when we look upon it as a mere anticipation.   It is rather an actual dis-cernment of some principle of growth disproportionate to its environment, and suggesting a different scheme of existence from the outward one.   The prospect of Immortality was, in the ages of classical antiquity, a dim and not specially attractive anticipation, detached from all experience interesting to the hearts of men. It became, in the age of which we speak, a belief necessary to render life in this world harmonious and explicable, an indispensable refuge for the need of per-manence formerly satisfied by the life of the Common-wealth, an answer to the craving now first made con-scious of its own infinite scope, and satisfied only by Eternity.

The thinker in whom these new ideas find their most characteristic expression is the Stoic Emperor, Marcus Aurelius Antoninus.   His *"Journal intime"* is, in some ways, a deeper revelation of an individual soul than almost any other book that ever was written.   We have here the outpourings of one whom we might almost call the first hermit.   He was not a hermit; he lived a family life as well as that of a soldier and monarch—his was a career of varied activity and constant companionship—but nothing of this reaches the reader; we never breathe the atmosphere of the camp or the court; we find ourselves overhearing, for the first time, the communings of a human spirit with itself. It is this which M. Renan must mean when he says of the book, " C'est le livre le plus purement humain qu'il y ait." Those who take it up with that introduction will be apt to lay it down with disappointment. It is not human in the sense that it makes any approach towards the various, many-sided utterance which belongs to any complete human character; it contains no trace of subtle observation; we are never reminded of the writers to whom we turn for mottoes; we never come to a thought that makes us stop to say, " There is the man who knew mankind." Except so far as we are now and then reminded that a court must have the same dangers in all ages, we find nothing in it that bears on the concrete difficulties and temptations of particular bodies of men or of individuals. But it is human in this sense, that it opens to us those depths in a human soul which belong to humanity as such; not to the second century or to the nineteenth century, not to the Italian or English race, not to the king or the slave, but to a human soul at all times and in all places, wherever it is made conscious of its own personality, wherever it is led to retire into its own depths, and realize that which remains to a man apart from all circumstance. This spiritual attitude is not characteristic of the most important periods of history; a great man's own personality is not there an object of supreme interest to himself. It is characteristic of an Age of Death, and is most completely exhibited in one, who even in that age of disintegration must have been the loneliest of men.

o

All monarchs must be solitary in some sense, but a monarch in modern Europe is a member of a select society ; he is one of a band of equals. The Emperor of Rome was alone in the world. We see in a Caligula or a Tiberius the moral insanity which results from such unnatural isolation ; in Marcus Aurelius that influence is traceable in a freezing loneliness, a sense of almost despair, softened into resignation. He was as lonely in literary communion as in the intercourse of society and the commerce of daily life ; he did not know the Psalms, and there was then nothing else at all like his Meditations. In some ways he is curiously modern, and to the modern reader this tells as a disadvantage. He was the first to come in sight of certain ideas that the modern world has dwelt on and returned upon until they have become commonplace, and we turn from many of his most original reflections as tedious, because they spring from a seed that has been eminently fertile. The writer whom he oftenest recalls is Pascal. A deep mournfulness, a sense of transitoriness and futility in all things earthly, an utter detachment from all interest in the fleeting pageant, seems set to exactly the same key in the thoughts of the Frenchman and the Roman ; we should hardly discover the difference if, as we turned the leaf, the one book were exchanged for the other. "Comme tout disparait en un instant ! dans le monde les personnes, et dans la durée les souvenirs ! comment des objets si frivoles, si décousus pourraient ils occuper notre intelligence et notre raison." That is not Pascal, but Marcus Aurelius speaking through a French translation ; and he returns to the thought again and again with a persistence which reminds us that it was an original one to him. " Serait-ce la vaine opinion des hommes qui t'agite ? alors regarde l'oubli rapide de toutes les choses, l'abîme du temps pris dans les deux sens" (*i.e.*, the boundless past and the boundless future), " et l'exiguité du lieu où la renommée se renferme." It is exactly the feeling of Pascal, but it has a typical impressiveness which Pascal lacks. There speaks the man who has touched the limits of all earthly desire. Is there any one, since the line of his successors came to an end, of whom we may say, as we can of him, that it was impossible for him to frame a wish for any earthly gain? Kings in the modern world have not been shut out from ambition; they have seen a height above them. But the master of the Roman world had touched the summit of earth, and if he found it joyless, there was no refuge but in the world within.

What Marcus Aurelius felt was the unique and profound disappointment of the Philosopher on a throne. Plato at Syracuse may, perhaps, have known something of the feeling; he must have discovered how little the approach there made towards his own ideal—that kings should become philosophers, or philosophers kings— had done for the happiness of mankind. But with the Emperor that dream was realized more fully than it had been realized under the influence of the greatest of Philosophers on one of the most virtuous of Statesmen. Plato might discover some shadow of an explanation of Dion's grievous failure in the baleful inheritance of despotic rule; but for an Antonine there was no such refuge from the oppressive discovery that the Philosopher on a throne could do but little to make his subjects wise and good, or even happy.[1] To him the whole of life must have been coloured and shaped by disap-

---

[1] See Wordsworth's poem on Dion:—

" And what pure homage *then* did wait
On Dion's virtues, while the lunar beam
Of Plato's genius, from its lofty sphere,
Fell round him in the grove of Academe,

pointment, and his sense of its transitoriness is even a deeper feeling than that of its futility. "Reflect often on thy last hour," is the burden of the Meditations. Life is a vapour, a smoke, a winter torrent; the interval between the shortest and the longest life is comparable to that between the disappearance of two grains of incense flung into the altar-fire.[1] Life hurries to its close; its futilities are soon to be hushed in the silence of the tomb: why make ado about anything so ephemeral? Is there no Life that more truly deserves the name?

This question is not answered by Marcus Aurelius, otherwise than with dim yearnings, repressed by pious resignation. "How is it," he writes at a time apparently not long before his death, "that the Gods, who have arranged all things well, and lovingly for mortals, have in this one respect overlooked their interest, that men, even excellent men, who have entered into frequent communion with them, through devout ministrations—when once they have died quit existence altogether, and are utterly extinguished? If, indeed, this is so, be assured that the Gods would have arranged it otherwise, if that had been right. For it would have been possible if it had been right."[2] It is instructive in this respect to compare him with a shallower and more cheerful writer,

Softening their inbred dignity austere.

  * * * * * *

Mourn hills and groves of Attica! and mourn
Ilissus, bending o'er thy classic urn!
Mourn, and lament for him whose spirit dreads
Your once sweet memory, studious walks and shades'!"

No history is more tragic than that commemorated in these noble lines. Dion was surely the noblest pupil of Plato, and the attempt to establish a righteous government at Syracuse, in which he incurred the hatred of those whose welfare was his supreme aim, and fell a victim to their wrath, must have seemed to his master almost like a great experiment exhibiting the futility of his loftiest hopes.

[1] M. Antoninus, x. 31 ; iv. 15 ; v. 23.
[2] M. Antoninus, xii. 5 :—Εἰ γὰρ δίκαιον ἦν, ἦν ἂν καὶ δυνατόν.

who belongs to the past as he does to the future. To
Plutarch the fact that it was right became a witness that
it was possible. The mere spectacle of Life shut off
from a hereafter was self-refuting; so deep down in his
heart was the conception of Divine purpose, that the contemplation of high aims, far-reaching hopes, became to
him the pledge of a future large enough to contain them;
and the narrow limits of this life shrivelled away under
the mere view of all that this life held of capacity and
aspiration. "If God," he says, "make so much of creatures in whom there is nothing permanent, He is like
women who sow the seeds of plants within the soil
enclosed in an oyster-shell."[1] In that quaint metaphor
is conveyed perhaps almost all that the intellect can
decipher of the heart's confidence in a larger future
for the aspirations of instincts cramped in this earthly
life, and seeking a deeper soil. It seems strange that
Plutarch should have felt these hopes—Plutarch, the
reviewer of the past—and that Marcus, whose heart
throbbed with the life of the future, should be without
them. But perhaps, as Plutarch studied the lives of
the great men of the past and vividly realized their
influence, he felt that they had *not* quitted existence
altogether, that God was not the God of the dead, but
of the living.[2] Surely there is nothing more pathetic in
literature than the words in which the Emperor silences
his yearning for the faith of the Historian, and feeling
all the emptiness and poverty of life far more keenly,
yet teaches himself to acquiesce in its narrow limits,
since they were imposed by God.

Two ideas upheld him in this dreary and joyless

[1] Plutarch, "De his qui sero a Numine puniantur," c. 17.

[2] It is interesting to remember that one of those to whom Marcus records
his obligations was the grandson of Plutarch—Sextus of Chæronea. See the
pleasing character of him, M. Antoninus, i. 9.

resignation—the sense of an Order of Nature, and the sense of a constant invisible companionship. The second was the nearest his heart, but both were near. It is a deeply rooted thought in him that all sin is schism, that we are called upon to be one with the order in which we live, and one in an organic sense, "a member, not merely a portion ; " [1] and the idea of an organic whole,[2] a unity of Law, in which the human member may co-operate, and in which we may learn to regard disastrous events as parts of an orderly system, no less than the rose in summer and the harvest in autumn,[3] is latent in all his thought. He paints with all the associations of horror familiar to a soldier the wretched condition of the severed limb,[4] and reminds himself of the possibility that each one of us may enter on this condition at any moment—that we may choose, each one for himself, that separateness which is death for every being that is made to be part of a larger whole. In the constant disappoint-ment provided for regal beneficence by the neighbour-hood of ingratitude, stupidity, and treachery,[5] the thought of the vast order in which an inhabitant of the Roman world could, for the first time, recognize himself as a fellow-citizen of all men, seems to have been a perpetual source of religious thankfulness to him ; he returns again and again to the thought of this great Order in which he finds a place,[6] and seems, from the mere spectacle of its vastness and its unity, to derive some tranquilizing power, which we should imagine the ex-clusive result of being consciously in subjection to a

---

[1] M. Antoninus, vii. 13. [2] *Ibid.*, iii. 11 ; iv. 29 ; v. 8.
[3] *Ibid.*, iv. 44. [4] *Ibid.*, viii. 34.
[5] ἐκ τοιούτου βίου ἀπέρχομαι, ἐν ᾧ αὐτοὶ οἱ κοιν ενοί, ἱπὲρ ὧν τὰ τοσαῦτα ἠγωνισάμην, ηὐξάμην, ἐφρόντισα, αὐτοὶ ἐκεῖνοι ἐθέλουσί με ἱπάγειν (x. 36). Perhaps he was thinking of his son.
[6] *e.g.*, iii. 11:—τὸν ἄνθρωπον, πολίτην ὄντα πόλεως; τῆς ἀνωτάτης ἧς αἱ λοιπαὶ πόλεις ὥσπερ οἰκίαι εἰσίν.

loving Will. Of that belief we can scarcely say that we find a trace in him; he seems to know neither a Father in heaven nor a brother on earth; but the Order of Nature, in its new and unexplored impressiveness, filled all that vacuum, and almost satisfied him with its realm of majestic Law.

It is not inconsistent to speak of its *new* impressiveness, although when Antoninus lived this idea was set forth in a poem rather older for him than "Paradise Lost" is for us.[1] It was new if we measure it by the life of an idea, and remember that we are speaking of ideas as they are felt apart from genius. We have seen, in Lucretius, the rise of a reverence for Nature that may be called modern, the sense of a calm permanent sway, contrasted with that "fitful fever" of personal dominion which raged so furiously in the lifetime of the poet; contrasted, too, when a high enough standpoint was taken, and the course of the ages was unrolled before the eye of the observer, with the steady but temporary rule of the cities of the past. We have seen in Virgil how the rise of the Empire harmonized this idea with that of political dominion, which originally seemed its ineffaceable contrast. The progress of national life, it seemed, was towards a unity that almost lost itself in the Unity of Nature; the Laws of Imperial Rome, so far as they approached their ideal, *were* the laws of Nature. If we consider the majestic system of Roman Law, and trace its connection with all the thought and life of Europe, we shall see nothing surprising in the approximation. All the philosophy of Rome, such as it was, was poured into its law. Perhaps without Roman Law we might never have known the expression, "a law of nature." Whether we should be any poorer for the

---

[1] The poem of Lucretius was published about 57 B.C. Marcus Aurelius died 180 A.D.

loss is another question ; some may think that the meaning of Law would be clearer if the same word were not used to express orders of sequence which impose themselves and cannot be broken, and claims which may, but ought not to be, rejected. All positive law is indeed in some sense a protest against the belief that the whole moral world is included within the realm of Nature, inasmuch as it is of its very essence to assume that man can know the right and do the wrong. Nevertheless when for the first time a single law regulated the known world, the two conceptions of Law and Nature almost coalesced in their close approach. The subordination of the whole known world to a single ruler and a single law gave a certain religious significance to the idea of Nature ; the outward world seemed to combine in a single majestic order, a fit object for the reverence and the submission of the most religious of mankind. " The world is a polity, for men have the same law,"[1] is one of the many sentences which remind us of the expansion now taken by the very word *law*, at the same time that the words are true in their narrowest sense. Under the Antonines there was only one law in the world. The Roman Law, with its long vista into the past, with its magnificent embrace for all the nationalities of the known world, seemed to the men of the new age a stately bridge between the realm of Morals and of Nature, a bridge which the pilgrim might cross in either direction, finding himself on both sides within the same realm of order, and among inhabitants who, if they occasionally used a different dialect, sought to express by it the same desires, the same fears, and the same convictions.

But this religion of Nature was not the deepest feeling in this Pascal of the second century ; his spirit finds the deepest satisfaction in a belief not entirely in harmony

----

[1] M. Antoninus, iv. 4.

with it, though both were real to him. We have seen
that his yearnings after an Eternal life were unable to
transform themselves into hopes, but they found another
refuge in the conviction of a permanent relation to an
Eternal Being—a truth, indeed, which, when it is fully
apprehended, is seen to be inseparable from the hope he
could not attain. Men approach a great truth by different paths, and fail to discern the common goal towards
which they are led. Marcus Aurelius saw something
in man which virtually implies his immortality, though
he could not follow out its teaching. He seems to have
been much impressed by the belief of the wisest man of
antiquity in special supernatural guardianship; and in
his own age all privilege naturally melted into universal
endowment. It had seemed natural that to Socrates a
special guide should be appointed, but now men were
ready to acknowledge that the best gifts of Heaven were
least special; the "divine sign"[1] with which Socrates
was familiar was recognized as the voice of an indwelling
spirit given as a comrade and guide to every son of man.
The change from the Dæmon of Socrates to the Dæmon
of Marcus Aurelius gathers up the whole moral evolution
of the ages; we interpret best the meaning of the earlier
and the later epoch when we remember that in the first
it was the wisest of men who believed that a peculiar
guidance was vouchsafed him by God; and in the
second this guidance was felt as no special endowment
of wisdom or virtue, but an inheritance of commonplace
humanity.

For, indeed, it was the great distinctive characteristic
of this time that the exceptional became the universal.
This was the very meaning of the new sense of Huma-

---

[1] It is rather misleading to speak of the dæmon of Socrates, as he always
alludes to it in this impersonal form. The dæmon of Marcus is always
personal, *e.g.*, viii. 13; iii. 5, &c.

nity that was come into the world. The spirit of antiquity is one of the narrowest aristocracy. There was
no more of a liberal spirit in great men than in the
insignificant vulgar ; the association of all excellence with
what is exceptional was just as strong in the noblest as
in the basest of the sons of Greece and Rome. The
citizen who was to-day a man, to-morrow a chattel, kept
before the mind of every human being the standard of
privilege. No one could ask why this man should have
some good thing lacked by his neighbour without ques-
tioning the foundation and structure of society ; for what
good could be greater or more absolutely limited than
Freedom ? That recognition of a Divine voice, therefore,
which seems to have had much influence in the condemnation of Socrates, as the introducer of new gods,[1] was
not in him or his contemporaries an expansive influence.
There was nothing strange, to Socrates, in believing
that a Divine influence should be real and exceptional.
But the lapse of six hundred years brought men to a
different view of the Divine education of humanity ;
the insignificant nature of that which does not belong
to all was the characteristic moral discovery (so we
may call it) of the day ; it was held with the passionate
fervour and the inevitable exaggeration that belongs to
new truth. And none could feel this truth with more
depth and fervour of conviction than the lonely Emperor,
he who found in the exceptional position he occupied
no satisfaction, no immunity from sorrow and care—
only added causes of both, added difficulties, added
vexations. " Even in a palace life may be lived well ! "
The man who wrote those words on a page intended
for no eye but his own was one to feel vividly, that if
God gave guidance to any one, then it must be the
inheritance of every son of man.

---

[1] Plato, Apol. of Socrates, 24. *Cf.* Xenophon, Memorabilia, i. 1.

We are accustomed to speak of the so-called Athanasian creed as a mass of absurd contradictions. The
assertion that there are three persons in one God, it is
supposed, is one that can convey no meaning to any
mind anxious to find appropriate meaning in all words.
And yet it must be felt by all who have been accustomed
to look within, who have in any form accepted the idea
of an unseen world, that something very like this in-
credible description of God is true of man. No one can
feel that anything within himself is sacred if he believe
only in himself, and probably there are moments in the
life of almost all when it has been felt that each one, if
he stand alone, is incomplete; that what we need to
give us fulness of personality is union with another.
We know the meaning of Self for the first time when
we know the meaning of another than Self; each is a
fragment till he cease to be a mere unit. And this is
felt here and there by many an ordinary man with regard
to a companionship which is not human. In entire
solitude he becomes sensible of the presence of that
which may be best described as an ideal Self; some close
neighbourhood makes itself discernible through remonstrance for what he is, or seems to hover above his will
with some pattern of that which he feels himself called
upon to become. The sense of rightness is something
deeper, more authoritative, than anything can be that is
wholly contained within his own personality. Conscience,
that "knowledge with another," which awakes at the
approach of evil, is but one aspect of this unseen companionship; it is felt in regions where the dividing-line
of right and wrong is hardly discernible. It is to those,
who have ever known it, the central reality of the moral
life; nevertheless it is easily ignored, and there is much
experience besides that of wrongdoing in which it is
hidden. The whole life of the outward conceals this

unseen companionship, and most of all that satisfying
life of the outward, in which a man enters into relation
with the State.   It is most known probably to the lonely ;
to the loneliest of men it took the aspect of an influence
so subtle, so penetrating, that it was impossible to describe
without falling into contradiction.[1] Sometimes on his page
it appears as the protector, sometimes as the protected ; it
is a being that at once commands and obeys, both guards
man and is guarded by him.   It is nearer to him than
any other human being is, but it is distinct from himself,
and may be an object of reverence to a man who feels
himself utterly poor and feeble.   It belongs to such an
order as is commemorated in the Mysteries—something
intimate, mysterious, and separate from the rest of
nature, to the whole of which it is infinitely to be
preferred.   It is strange, when we read the passages
in which Marcus Aurelius speaks of it, to think of him
as a persecutor of the Christians, for the thought of a
mediator between God and man comes out as distinctly
in his Meditations as in any Christian writings.   He is
a preacher of the doctrine of the Holy Ghost.[2]

This newly discerned sacredness in individual life was
no privilege of the good and the pure-minded ; it could
not be forfeited by the worst of criminals.   The doom
which the State inflicted on its enemy was no longer to
be regarded as the mere rejection of something vile, but
as a concession to the necessities of the criminal himself.
The State could not take the life of the worst of her
sons, even for the good of all the rest, if it were not
also good for him.   " Thy soul "—Seneca addresses an
imaginary criminal—" is incurable ; it has woven itself a
warp and woof of crime.   Sin has become its own motive.

---

[1] Compare, for instance, ii. 17 :— . . . τηρεῖν τὸν ἔνδον δαίμονα ἀνύβριστον,
καὶ ἀσινῆ, with such passages as iii. 5 ; v. 27.

[2] See also Epictetus, Diss. ab Arr., i. 14, and elsewhere.

All we can do for thee is to give thee that which for thee is the sole good—death."[1] It is the claim of the individual which is considered here, even when the individual is a public enemy. How completely is the ideal of antiquity left behind ! The city could not have allowed that anything was sacred in an individual life when it was a question of asserting her majesty against a traitor. The criminal was a mere invader ; his welfare was no more to be considered than that of a wolf in the fold ; all that was sacred lay in that which he was doing his best to destroy. But as we read these words of Seneca we feel that a change has in this respect come over the world. The State exists in order to guard something which may conceivably survive it. The integral unity of moral thought was new. The city had demanded loyalty in word and deed, but men now became conscious of belonging to one whose demand included the hidden things of the heart. " God enters into our inmost thoughts ; nay, he never departs from them."[2] No individual endowment was needed to confer a priceless value on every human soul ; each was the work of one whose care for his workmanship was but faintly typified by the affectionate brooding of the artist over his work ;[3] every man was sacred, for every man was the work of God.

Men's aspirations contain an inverted history of their lives ; whatever has been missed from earth is projected on to the Heavens. The age of slavery was the age when all that men desire and hope was gathered up in the one word Freedom. It was a word which had always expressed " our being's end and aim " more fully and definitely than that aim has ever been expressed by

[1] Seneca, De Irâ., i. 16, 3.   [2] Seneca, Epist., 83.
[3] This idea of the Artist as the type of God is found more than once in the dissertations of Epictetus ; e.g., Diss. ab Arr., i. 6.

the word Happiness.   Even now it is not possible to
differ so much about what constitutes Freedom as about
what constitutes Happiness, though when every one is
more or less free the idea of Freedom is always vague.
But to the Greek and Roman the meaning of Freedom
was kept definite by the neighbourhood of its opposite ;
with us the criminal does not so clearly exhibit its
absence as with them the slave.   There is no distinction
in the modern world so definite and so universal as the
distinction between liberty and bondage in antiquity.
Freedom occupied the desires of mankind, through the
ages of the classical world, as no equally definite object
has ever occupied them since then, and when the
classical world came to an end its ideal was only intensified in being spiritualized.   When the City perished,
the deep and vivid yearnings it had nourished could not
develop into that desire for constitutional government
and uncorrupt representation, which the men of that day
would have needed the spirit of prophecy even to conceive, and which would have seemed to them a very
poor thing if they could have conceived it.   It took
a richer field—it turned from the world without, where
all was wintry and full of decay, to that inner life
which men had for the first time leisure to observe, and
which in comparison seemed to burgeon with the promise
of spring.

   An age which exhibited on a gigantic scale the vices
of slavery in men just delivered from slavery was one
fitted to bring out by contrast, as never before or since,
the meaning of inward liberty.   When the Stoic poet declares, "Our one need is Freedom, but not such freedom
as belongs to any enfranchised slave whom the ceremony
of manumissión has elevated to the rank of a Roman
citizen,"[1] he is alluding to an event of daily occurrence.

---

[1] Persius, Sat., v. 73–80 (paraphrased).

When he adds, " No mere ceremony can change a menial
to a true Freeman ; there are other masters than those
from whom the prætor's rod sets free,"[1] he was preaching
a truth that none of his readers could ignore.   One who
desires to realize what that slavery was from which the
prætor's rod did set free should turn to the records of
a Roman trial, and read of men and women given up
to tortures which seem to have roused much less remonstrance from the best of men than do the pangs of animals in our day ; and remember that this was not as a
penalty for anything they had done (their innocence was
admitted by all), but as a supposed security for the
truth of the evidence thus wrung from them.   But from
such records, also, we may learn what the true Freedom
was, which man can neither give nor take away ; the
martyrs of loyalty, we have seen, teach that lesson no
less than the martyrs of faith.   By their endurance and
their virtue men must have been reminded that the freedom which was the object of such passionate and reason-
able desire, was not the only freedom.   To those who
for the first time confronted the other it seemed not to
be the true Freedom.   The great chasm which separated
the human world into persons and things shrank to
nothing when compared with that abyss which separated
those who realized the freedom of the spirit, and those
in bondage to low desires.   The bondage of the freedman
taught the lesson no less decidedly, and, of course, far
more frequently, than the spiritual emancipation of the
slave.   The crowds pressing across the boundary that
separated bond and free exhibited in every variety of
distinctness the temper of bondage ; the demeanour of
the freedmen taught the spectator that " Avarice and
Luxury enforce a harder toil than the most severe master,

---

[1] Persius, Sat., v. 90, 130.   " An dominum ignoras, nisi quem vindicta
relaxat," seems the central idea, often obscured by his oddity.

and add to it the distraction of their own discord. The
load imposed by Ambition, the continual restraints and
fears which belong to the dominion of Superstition, alike
declare to us that the true enfranchisement we need is
within."[1]   But it was by an enfranchised slave that the
lesson was formulated for all time.   Here and there, at
many a Roman trial, some spectator must have felt that
such a thing might be ; but when Stoicism gained a voice
in a Phrygian bondsman, the message took a resonance
that preserved it for the ears of posterity.

There is something very impressive in the fact that
the best representative of this new morality was an
Emperor, and the next best was a slave.   It tells forcibly
for the wide-reaching influence of the new spirit of personality which was coming upon the world, that we
should find it hard to decide which of two men occupying
the extremes of society was its typical exponent.   On
the whole, that position must be assigned to Marcus
Aurelius.   But the most typical is not necessarily the
most original expression ; we may find all the ideas of
the Emperor on the page of his predecessor,[2] from whom,
indeed, he sometimes cites them.   His Meditations are
far more coloured by the feelings, desires, and aspirations
of an individual mind than the record of the teaching
of Epictetus ; but the presentment of a religion (so we
must regard their common belief) which has lifted the
speaker himself above the degradation and sufferings of
bondage must in some respects stand alone.

In turning from the writings of the Emperor to those
of the slave, it is striking to find that profound sad-
ness has given way to a bright and steadfast cheerful-
ness.   Partly we have to remember that Marcus Aurelius
wrote for himself, and Epictetus addressed disciples ; but

---

[1] Persius, Sat., v. 131-157, 180-188 (paraphrased).
[2] By about a century.

the difference is no mere accident of method. The sense of pettiness, of worthlessness in life, which oppressed the ruler of the Roman world had no place in the thoughts of the slave. He too felt life a sojourn in a strange land,[1] but the sense of exile was lost in the sense of freedom. This was the keynote of all his thought; to this he returns with a somewhat monotonous recurrence; but the reader can never forget that what he preached with his lips he taught by his life. Freedom, in the outward world the associate of the spirit that refuses to submit, he recognized in the world within as inseparable from the spirit that refuses to rebel.[2] It is not more separate from Law in one region than in the other; the citizen had accepted Law as the basis of Liberty; the philosopher could do no more.[3] But in the inward realm in which he learned to find a home, the law which gives perfect freedom is that of renunciation; the great achievement is to withdraw all energy from that spirit of preference which would impress the idiosyncrasies of the Self on the world of Nature; to bestow this energy rather on a recognition of Law producing that receptive attitude by which character receives its stamp.[4] His own life was a demonstration of such possibility. His emancipation could have been no crisis in his spiritual career;[5] he was as free when a master could kill or torture his body as when he knew no master, for the emancipation from the tyrants of the soul was in him complete. The saying of Socrates, "Anytus and Meletus can kill me, but cannot hurt me,"[6] is the constant text of his dis-

---

[1] Life, he says (Enchiridion, 5), should be like the saunter near port of a passenger who has landed for an hour or two.

[2] Ep., Diss. ab Arr., ii. 4.   [3] Ibid., ii. 11.   [4] Ibid., i. 12.

[5] Ibid., ii. 23, 24, where he almost repeats the passage in Persius quoted above, and shows how much more impressive the thought is when expressed more simply.

[6] Ibid., ii. 2, 5.

course; in those words Socrates had proclaimed the freedom of the slave. " Let us be imitators of Socrates, who sang pæans in his dungeon," [1] was in him no mere sermonizing; it was the exhortation of one who knew that what he exhorted was possible. He had taken his start from that complete surrender which he was urging on his disciples ; he had been detached by the decree of Fate from all those possessions from which the soul should always be detached by a sense of their insignificance ; he had been shut off from the realm of the indifferent by circumstance, and had thus no choice but to find his good elsewhere, if he were to find any good at all.

Epictetus was thus set apart by the discipline of life to proclaim what we may call the inverted Freedom of the invisible. His experience of bondage exhibited to him the true character of bondage—he saw its limitations, he saw that within the man which it could not touch. Or, rather, he enormously exaggerated that within the man which it could not touch.[2] He and his spiritual brethren represent a phase, in regard to the Will, very similar to that which we find in Plato with regard to the intellect. They saw the faculty on which they bent their attentive gaze enlarged through the mists of dawning thought. Epictetus believed in the omnipotence of Will, as Plato in the omnipotence of Knowledge ; perhaps it was the only way in which the scope of either faculty could be adequately discerned by him whose mission it was to impress its meaning upon the world. We see that Moral Freedom is, as it has been called,[3] the freedom

---

[1] Ep., Diss. ab Arr., ii. 6.

[2] See especially ii. 23, where he seems to take the power to close the eyes as a typical specimen of the relation of Will over Sense. We may, he seems to think, in like manner shut off all impression from without, if we will but make the resolve to do so.

[3] By Professor Clerk Maxwell.

of a bird in its cage; that what a man can *be* depends, to a certain extent, on what he can *do*. We cannot but allow that some part of Character is the inevitable result of Circumstance. And yet, as we listen to the teaching of Epictetus, we may feel his truth the deeper one; we may recognize its limitations as belonging to a temporary order of things in comparison with that to which he leads us. We may believe that what strikes us as exaggeration after seventeen hundred years of an individual morality was, in the first freshness of that new life, a literal possibility—a moral miracle, worked by the preacher of a new Faith.

The contrast between persons and things forms the whole subject-matter of the philosophy of Epictetus. There is in it no wealth of thought, no varied paths of wide-reaching investigation, only a single idea repeated again and again. Good and evil, he says, are both to be sought in the realm of choice; the involuntary and the indifferent begin together.[1] The clue to a true order in our moral being, he felt, is a right understanding of the contrasted worlds of the *necessary* and the *voluntary*. The necessary world is the outward world; the world where accident reigns, where many are stronger than one, and this world, properly understood, must be regarded as the realm of indifference.[2] External events are important only so far as they afford the material for disciplining the will, and bringing out the distinctness of that personal element which can recognize itself only in this struggle. In this region there is no true good or evil. Here, according to the point of view, we may say that everything is good, or that nothing is good.

---

[1] Ποῦ τὸ ἀγαθόν; Ἐν προαιρέσει. Ποῦ τὸ κακὸν; Ἐν προαιρέσει. Ποῦ τὸ οὐδέτερον; Ἐν τοῖς ἀπροαιρέτοις (Epicteti, Diss. ab Arr., ii. 16). This is the kernel of almost all he has to say.

[2] External things should be to us no more than *tessera* with which we play at dice (Diss. Arr., ii. 5).

In the realm of the Voluntary, on the other hand, every step we take is towards good or evil. Not what happens to a man, but what he chooses, is the proper object of desire or of fear. If his will has no part in any event, that event is a pure object of indifference.

The work of Philosophy, therefore, is to effect a complete inversion of the ordinary view of these two regions. We are like stags,[1] terrified by feathers and driven into snares. We seek to escape fancied evil in the realm of Necessity, and fly into real evil in the realm of the Voluntary. We choose crime to escape exile or death, though in exile or death there is nothing evil, and crime is the greatest of evils. We mistake the material of Virtue for the source of Vice. We turn away blindly from the very threshold of Liberty. What is Liberty? Life in accordance with desire. Men strive to gain this universal object by bending things to their wishes, and they strive in vain. The world is so made that it cannot be remoulded upon the tastes and fancies of men; as long as men persist in this effort they are in bondage, they are subjected to the rule of hard masters, forcing them to actions in which their will has no part. From the fear of death, or from the desire of luxury, they are subjected to a necessity which constrains the Will, that one rightful ruler, that sole legitimate cause. If they would remould desire to fit the world they would find themselves secure upon the territory of Freedom. The will is not the lord of the outer world. When exerted here, it constantly finds itself a slave, and not a ruler. But let it turn to its own domain and it finds itself at once supreme. Though it is not possible to bring facts into accordance with individual desire, it is possible so to remould desire that it shall never conflict with fact. He who has learnt to

[1] Diss. Arr., ii. ch. 1, 8.

desire nothing that he may not choose has entered into the region of perfect Freedom.

At the root of this idea of the contrasted worlds of servitude and of freedom lies a deep religious reverence for the Order of Nature, such as we have seen, on its intellectual side, in the poem of Lucretius.[1] The outer world is the world of necessity; it is the unchangeable world. But also it is the world which, if we rightly understand it, we shall not wish to change.[2] No exponent of modern Science confronts the world of existing reality with a more absolute conviction that in a knowledge of its laws lies a sure deliverance from all the ills of life. Epictetus knew nothing of the powers with which modern Science has equipped the will of man in its dealings with the external world; but his confidence in the power of Truth to bring the mind to a condition in which any modification of outward things should appear a matter of absolute indifference, gave it quite as high a place as the modern view—perhaps higher. The powers of Science, as revealed to our time, have done almost all that magic had ever promised; before its influence even the limitations of time and space seem to disappear. But the weak and helpless creature, as Epictetus imagined him, in face of the unchangeable, was more invincible among the terrors of the outward world than the inhabitant of a world renovated by Science, himself undisciplined by Truth. The ideal Stoic could not transform those dangers; but none can transform them all, and he did not need to transform any. To Epictetus all the dangers and necessities of the material universe were but as the discomforts of the palestra,[3] leading up to

---

[1] It is interesting to remark that in the marginal annotations with which Bentley has enriched a copy of Epictetus now in the British Museum, the only comparison is with Lucretius.

[2] Diss. ab Arr., ii. ch. 2.   [3] *Ibid.*, i. ch. 24.

the disciplined strength which was to equip the victor for the contest of a nobler Olympia. He loves to surround the trials and struggles of life with associations of dignity and charm borrowed from the Greek games—associations very difficult for a modern reader to appreciate, even with all the aid afforded by St. Paul. These majestic and venerable institutions, the concentrated reminiscence and type of the dignity, the beauty, the grandeur, dear to the pride of Greece, appeared to the Phrygian slave but as a parable symbolizing that which God had intended the whole outward world to be to man, and the actions of other men to be to each individual. To the meanest slave the circumstances amid which he was placed were an Olympia, where Divine spectators looked on at the struggle, and applauded the conquest which nothing could prevent but the choice of the combatant. He had but to *will* in order to quit that short contest a triumphant conqueror. No outward impediment could affect the result, for the victory lay within a region to which outward influences could not penetrate. They brought the mere apparatus for preparing him for the contest ; for that contest itself nothing was necessary but his choice.

But the choice itself was one needing that discipline which comes from the knowledge of Law. To Epictetus the fact that man's will should be a disorderly, unscientific influence seemed a part of that strange dislocation which it is the business of Philosophy to set right. While the outward world is under the influence of some fixed law, so that we know, for instance, the weight of anything, not by holding it in our hands and consulting our sensations, but by weighing it in scales, how is it, he asks, that in the most important matter of all, the preferences and desires of men, we can form no judgment, but can only watch in each individual case the varying, accidental response of chance preference, as if in every case of contested weight we could only ask the opinion of a bystander whether a particular object were light or heavy ?   Perhaps we might gather up all of value that Epictetus has to teach when we say that he regarded it as the business of Philosophy to set up a standard of weight for the moral world.[1]   The moral world is no more subject to chance than the material world; indeed, in the view of Epictetus, for whom chance had a real meaning, it was far less so.   A pound weight is a pound weight in the hand of a child or a man, however different the sensations caused by it.   So in this Stoic philosophy motives have their absolute value, whether they appeal to the mind of a Socrates or of some base courtier of Nero.   Socrates knows that it is better to die than to be false to the highest that is discerned as truth ; the cowardly sycophant thinks that death is worse ; but the intrinsic merit of the alternatives remains the same in either case.   The scale is not altered when it is overlooked.   The Order of Nature is beyond the reach of our choice ; we have only to conform ourselves to it, or to suffer the consequences.

We may say, in an important sense, that Epictetus was the first to preach this truth.   Of course, no one can have ever taught his fellows anything of real moral value without assuming it ; but it is not so impressive anywhere else as in the teaching of the enfranchised slave.   Epictetus had known all that men dread—blows, ill-usage, tyranny, hard labour, need—and he proclaimed that these were not evils.   Who else had such a platform for making that declaration ?   Who else had, as he expresses it forcibly, so entirely turned round the

[1] Here again he closely approaches Persius, who uses even this very comparison of moral and physical weight (v. 100), and sets off, by his far-fetched quaintness, the homeliness and simplicity of his successor.

masks by which mankind are terrified, and seen whether there was anything really terrible behind them ? Of the words of such as him we may say, indeed, as one Italian poet[1] said of another, " Egli dice cose, e voi parole." He showed forth the perfect freedom that is bound up with the ideal of perfect resignation as it can only be truly shown forth in the achievement of a life and character.

Marcus Aurelius and Epictetus exhibit the strength of this new morality. The Emperor, in a journal meant for his own eye alone, shows the meaning of the new doctrine of Personality—the sudden energy set free for introspection, the sacredness transferred from national to individual life. The slave, in his didactic utterances, presents rather that aspect in which the new ideal joins the old. He speaks as the heir of an inheritance hitherto inadequately though deeply prized, of an estate rich in unsuspected mineral wealth, a possession coveted by all, in ignorance of its actual advantages. Freedom had been the yearning of all hearts, and although none had known the true Freedom to be that of the inward life, yet the aspiration after the outer Freedom had kept alive the inner. This, which from his platform of servitude he proclaimed to be the only true Freedom, he also declared to be the right of all. Heroic Greece and triumphant Rome had looked on Freedom as the privilege of the few ; by the Phrygian slave it was preached as the inalienable inheritance of every son of man.

When we ponder the difference between the new and old meaning of Freedom, we may be tempted to consider it a mere accident that the name is the same. But we blind ourselves to the meaning of History if we yield to this temptation. Inheritance, in the world of the Invisible, is secure ; no man can acquire that which he

---

[1] Berni, of Michael Angelo.

does not in some form bequeath. The thoughts of one generation, it has been well said,[1] form the feelings of its successor. The fathers would not always recognize their legacy in the wealth of the sons. The heroes of the past might have disclaimed all parentage in the conception of Freedom that glowed in the heart of Epictetus; but they would have erred; he gave their aspirations the only form possible to them in that bereavement of civil life which they could not have conceived possible. His ideal was the fruit of a different soil and a different atmosphere from theirs, but it sprang from the seed they had sown.

How, then, it may be asked, can we speak of this as an age of general servility? What more can protect an age from servility than that the idea of Freedom should enter the realm of the Invisible, that man should learn to recognize his true Freedom? If this was the commonplace of the age—if we find it on the page of rhetoricians no less than on that of men who set it forth in their lives—how could it be that the moral life of man, as far as it is associated with manly aim, seems then to have touched its nadir? We have given the answer to this question, but we must often repeat it. Men in this age were mere units. They awoke to perceive two great ideas—the sacredness of Personality, and the oneness of the race. But between these two ideas there was no combining element. The sense of human brotherhood knew no concentration; nowhere throughout the world of human relation could it find a focus. And our moral life depends on gradation; what we owe equally to all mankind we shall be slow to recognize as the claim of any one to whom we do not give it gladly. A Marcus Aurelius or an Epictetus will no doubt be

---

[1] By Mr. Joseph Jacobs, in an article on "The God of Israel," in the *Nineteenth Century* for September 1878.

ready to give every human being the rights of a brother; the average man will rather let the rights of a brother sink to the admitted claims of every human being, and act only from selfishness or preference.

The expansion of the City to include the race was to the men of that time a great idea. Earnest thinkers were never tired of speaking of man as a part of the universe; it was one of their stock themes, that as in the great ages of antiquity each one had felt himself the member of a State, so now he was to feel himself a part of that great whole, in which was included not only all human society, but all the system of things which we know by the name of Nature. He was to transfer his loyalty from Athens or Rome to the Order of Nature, and to find exercise for all the sentiments which had formerly been known as patriotism, in the fact of membership in a great system of law which included the human world and the world which was not human. They were even fond of illustrating this idea by the comparison with a living organism which St. Paul has made so familiar to Christendom; the criminal, they felt, was the schismatic; his condition comparable to that of the hand or foot which said to the rest of the body, "I have no need of thee." Nevertheless it is true that they were the strongest opponents of this idea, so far as it is a vital, practical reality. They spoke much of man's relation to the universe, they returned again and again to his position of membership in a society of Gods and men,[1] but they made this a mere phrase, because they recognized no other membership but this.

If a man's relationship to Humanity be his only membership, it is a mere name. A human brotherhood,

---

[1] The seeker after righteousness is to be constantly reminding himself, ὅτι μέλος εἰμὶ τοῦ ἐκ τῶν λογικῶν συστήματος. If he change μέλος to μέρος, he " does not love men from his heart " (M. Antoninus, vii. 13).

made up of mere individuals, is a rope of sand. When a man has been moulded under the idea of an organic corporate life, gradually developing from the duties of a son to the responsibilities of a citizen, he is ready to carry on the sense of kindred to a wider whole. When this preliminary training is wanting, the unity of the human race becomes a mere name, except so far as pre-eminent goodness overleaps the mighty chasm between the large thing and the small.

It is a hard thing to love the neighbour as the self, but it is not impossible to make life a continual approach towards this ideal. We have only to accept the teaching of circumstance—to *see* no pain we do not strive to mitigate—and we are set on a path that leads us hourly nearer to our goal ; we shall never pass by on the other side when need makes its appeal, and thus the foreigner will become the neighbour, and we shall pass the limit in the very attempt to reach it. Or, rather, we shall discern that the limit belongs only to the outward, and that, in truth, the love of the neighbour is the love of the needy. But the injunction to act as a member of humanity supplies no beginning. Its effect, rather, is negative. I am a member of humanity : why, then, should my neighbour make any special claim upon me ? My kinship is with the human race : why should my family be specially dear ? If we *begin* our moral progress with a recognition of the bonds which unite us with all men, we annihilate those which unite us with any. Moral theory, on this basis, has no relation to life ; the world of thought becomes its proper sphere ; the world of action is a mere realm of indifference, a region given up to disaster, a piece of waste ground, where chance may take its course, and which we must make different throughout, before any truly moral action is possible.

This combination of lofty theory and ignoble life is

shown most distinctly in the philosopher Seneca. It
would be very easy to read from the pulpit, as a sermon,
a collection of extracts from his writings, and it might
be made a sermon deeply moving to the most earnest
Christian congregation. Perhaps we could not succeed in
this attempt with any other writer who either never heard,
or never cared to hear, the name of Christ.[1] No biography more earnestly preaches the lesson of that little
understood warning—" If ye know these things, happy
are ye if ye do them." That knowledge may be actually
a barrier to action, and words no less earnest than noble
prove a screen for ignoble deeds, is a lesson taught by
many a preacher, but by none so forcibly as by one who
flattered the living and libelled the dead Claudius, and
apologized for the matricide of Nero. Still, the knowledge that words like his were sterile for all action should
never lead us to charge them with hypocrisy ; when
Seneca spoke of the God in every man, of the peace
which fortune neither gives nor takes away, he was
doubtless using expressions that corresponded to his
true feeling, for the moment. He mistook a kind of
moral taste which has, in fact, little more than an
æsthetic value, for that dynamic impulse which tells on
action. Or at least he only recognized the difference
by fleeting glimpses which never stirred his heart with
remorse or shame, as they would have done had he
ever compared the standard enforced by his preaching
and that suggested by his life.

But we do not need the spectacle of a moral teacher
apologizing for hideous crime in order to teach us the
weakness of a merely individual morality. We see that
weakness in the noblest specimens of Stoicism. " We

---

[1] A series of letters, purporting to be addressed by Seneca to St. Paul, is
still extant, and though plainly a mere fiction, is not without interest as indicating the associations naturally suggested by his teaching.

must leave the sins of other people alone," says Marcus Aurelius. The ruler who accepted that axiom was in some respects a worse Emperor than Nero. What an illustration of its influence is afforded by the fact that he was the father of Commodus![1] It was not for want of the very noblest ideal of an individual morality ever held by man that the Stoic Emperor left his throne to a monster. And this ideal was the concentration, in a beautiful soul, of aims that were characteristic of an age. None more than the men of that time have said fine and true things of the organic connection of man with man; they were fond of speaking of individuals as leaves of a plant sharing a common life. But the actual tendency of their teaching was rather to reduce men to the mere contiguity of pebbles on the sea-shore. The hand or foot need not, in the Stoic view, participate in the disease of the body. It need only feel its own ills. On its best side we see this belief as a disintegrating, pulverizing influence—an influence that could be accepted by the best men only at a period of the world's history in which the universal need and tendency was towards a deep and long repose.

When the union with Humanity is the only union, corporate responsibility is lost. The idea of Duty becomes narrowly individual; there is no standard which forms a moral union for the group. Men can never say, " We ought." There is no place for indignation in the world. When we see how often indignation is futile, when we realize the narrow limits within which man can judge his fellow, we are often tempted to believe that Duty should never be recognized except in the sphere

---

[1] Epictetus has some even more offensive assertions of a similar character, *e.g.*, i. 18 :—μὴ θαύμαζε τὸ κάλλος τῆς γυναικὸς, καὶ τῷ μοιχῷ οὐ χαλεπαίνεις, a sentence which it is painfully interesting to compare with the toleration of Marcus for the vices of Faustina. But Epictetus was not sinning against his special vocation as a ruler.

which each man encloses when he says " I."   The Age
of Death is a forcible refutation of that belief.   If any
one think that it is enough for each individual himself
to refrain from wrong actions, himself to press forward
to every noble aim, rigidly excluding from his endeavours
any judgment of others, no period of history could be
presented to him more full of instruction than the first
few centuries of our era.   He will see in the teaching
of Marcus Aurelius and Epictetus, and even in some
parts of Seneca, a standard of goodness that was not
surpassed in some directions by any moral teaching, and
that was at the same time perfectly sterile for any result
of which History can take account.   The philosophers of
this age taught and sincerely believed a large part of
all that the teaching of Christ sets before man, a much
larger part than can be claimed as the practical exhibition of Christianity at any stage of its development ; and
the result of their teaching was to make sycophants
and cowards.   Theirs was a mutilated ideal ; not incomplete only in the sense that an ideal is the product
of fallible human aspirations and on every side capable of
expansion, but in the sense that on one side it has cut
itself off from expansion.   It was not growth arrested
at an immature stage, but an organism that had
deprived itself of the means of growth.   It considered man out of his natural condition, man as he
is cut off from the bonds of human society, detached
from all ties of family and country, isolated as in some
spiritual Juan Fernandez.   It regarded as a whole that
being of which it is one of the most important facts to
remember that he is part of a larger whole ; and thus
omitted from its content his most important relations,
and the most organic necessities of his being.

CHAPTER VI.

THE JEW AT ALEXANDRIA.

THAT age which closes the history of the old world we have called the Age of Death; the title seems justified by the exhibition of its strongest interests and its habitual tendencies. But the death of one phase of life was the birth of another. The Roman Empire, in truth, might in some sense be called rather the beginning of modern than the end of ancient history. From some points of view, we may regard it as a presentation of that ideal Unity to which the civilization of the modern world seems continually to aspire; it shows us the nations of Europe bound in a corporate union which they have never actually possessed, but towards which their whole history seems an indistinct and baffled progress. We understand the Middle Ages best, when we keep as a clue to their history the yearning in the great mind which may be taken as the representative of mediæval Faith after a corporate union of which the Pope should be the heart, and the Emperor the head. Dante feels the "Holy Roman Empire"[1] a sacred ideal. He, the truest son of Italy, wrote his treatise on Monarchy to celebrate the arrival of a German Emperor in Italy. That the book is "an epitaph instead of a prophecy" detracts nothing from its significance. It is an epitaph which implies a legacy; the aspirations which it embodies prefigure a large part of the struggles of modern Europe,

---

[1] See the valuable and interesting work with this title by Mr. Bryce, a little volume which seems to me to contain the kernel of mediæval history.

perhaps even of the struggles of the future. The organization after which Dante yearned gave Europe a certain imperfect but actual Unity until a new dividing-line separated Protestant from Catholic ; it even lingered on as an empty shade up to the cockcrow of the Revolution. That Holy Roman Empire, which was neither Holy, nor Roman, nor an Empire, and yet perished only yesterday, was the representative of a great idea ; we may say of it, as Cicero of Cato : " The influence of the dead was undying."[1] Its influence is traceable in the work of a thinker whom his followers regard as the typical representative of modern thought. Comte, too, dreams of a Holy Empire, and sees in the future some kind of reflex of that national union of which Roman law was the bond and expression. The Frenchman and the Italian, wide as the poles asunder, agree in a belief that a common civilization implies a common faith, that Europe shall at last find its soul.

The aspiration of Dante and of Comte was in some sense the possession of those whose moral life we have been endeavouring to follow. The Roman Stoics and their contemporaries inhabited a united Europe, they lived under a single law (perhaps the wisest the world has ever known), and in its new expansion, including all that they meant by *the world*, they felt a new meaning given to law, a new faith to the heart of man. The world without always gives, in some sense, a model to the world within, and the world had never before been a Unity ; nor, indeed, has it ever since been a Unity in the same sense. The struggles of cities fill the record of the ancient world ; the struggles of nations fill the record of the modern ; between them intervenes a time in which the scene of all previous and subsequent conflicts was filled by one vast political organism, confronting all

[1] " Etiam mortui valuit auctoritas."

opposition as mere revolt. Hence all endeavour in the realm of thought took this ideal of Unity as its goal. As one dominion bound all the various races of the known world into a single kingdom, acknowledging a single head, so one aim was predominant in speculation ; intellectual effort was bent to harmonize all existent varieties of thought, to find in all something to assent to, something to accept. As Greece, Africa, the East, had each become a province of the Roman Empire, so Hellenic, Alexandrian, Oriental speculation must all become a part of the true faith. Everything that had ever been declared with earnestness must in some sense be true.

This new sense of the oneness of truth beneath the variety of opinions must have been wonderfully quickened by the mere fact that cultivation came, at the time of which we speak, to include a knowledge of more languages than one. When we compare any modern thinker with Plato, we perceive that the most profound philosopher of antiquity, or rather of any time, is in some respects at a disadvantage in comparison with an ordinary person who knows that his own language is but one of many actual forms of speech. Plato could not shake off the belief that to understand a word is to discover the nature of a thing ; the mistake is impossible for any modern. It was hardly possible for a subject of the Roman Empire ; acquaintance with even two languages sufficiently confutes the error that language is a photograph of existence. The Roman could not but know that Latin *was* language in just the same sense that Greek was. He must sometimes have suspected (as Plato never did) that language is an imperfect vehicle of thought, and that incomplete or even misleading expression need not be erroneous statement.[1] As we study the faded metaphor,

---

[1] For instance, when Anthony wrote of ζηλοτυπία to Cicero (see the letter

the illogical associations, the misleading suggestions, embodied in the history of words, we feel that a portion
of the search for truth consists in disentangling what a
writer means from what he is obliged to say. When
once men were taught this lesson of language, a new
light fell on religion.   Mythology was assimilated to
this linguistic variety.   While there was one language
and many barbaric dialects, men never realized that truth
might be subject to variety of expression, or conversely,
that varied expression might point to a single truth.   Of
course, the Greek had always known that barbarians
could make themselves mutually intelligible ; but it was
impossible for him ever really to believe that any other
language stood in the same relation to thought as his own
did.   When once a barbaric language enshrined the law
by which the world was governed, the exclusive race was
forced to recognize that it was a fragment of the human
race.   We might almost say, that all which divided man
from man became transparent to that underlying reality
in which man was bound to man, when once it was discerned that beneath the variety of languages lay hid the
Unity of Thought.

The exponent of this new feeling of Catholic sympathy
with all human imagination and thought was also the
enthusiastic student of the heroic past.   The new aim
of discovering unity beneath divergence occupies a proportion of Plutarch's space quite equal to that study of
the great figures of the antique world to which he owes
his fame.   He saw beneath the antagonistic aspect of
various creeds a single aspiration after the Divine, the
one ray of Divine light tinged by the varied colouring

enclosed to Atticus in Epist. ad Att., x. 8), each must have felt that there was
a feeling—jealousy—for which the Latin language provided no name, and for
which one was needed.   Cicero's frequent recourse to scraps of Greek must
have been a continual reminder of this new idea to himself and his corre-
spondents.

of human imagination;[1] and the refracted rays, he felt, might be recombined; the many was but a transparent disguise for the one. The Gods, he urges, are not different in different places, they differ only as the names for the sun in different languages. The races which could not understand each other's names for the sun all see the same sun. Osiris and Bacchus are not different beings any more than the sun which shines in Egypt is different from the sun which shines in Greece.[2] And then, further, Bacchus, Osiris, and all their kindred are but varying aspects of the one Invisible God, who shall become the Guide and King of men when they are delivered from the prison of the body and migrate into the distant land where He reigns alone.[3] While men are yet bound in the chains of material surroundings (he felt) they can discern Him only under these various aspects; they must express the great truths which they dimly perceive as to His nature under the guise of fragmentary metaphor, which becomes mythology. Those who take Bacchus for wine and Vulcan for flame, he says, make the same mistake as those who confuse the oar with the pilot, or the loom with the weaver; and those err also who see in nature so many separate agencies, and do not discern that all are at bottom but various aspects of one great primal unity.[4] The various allegories by which men have accounted for the fictitious histories that have sprung up concerning these separate beings are singly erroneous, but in their totality they are true. The fragment is a fiction, the totality is a truth. Typho is not the principle of darkness, of dryness, or of barrenness; he is generally the hurtful principle in Nature; every specialization of this truth is good as its illustration, and becomes false only when it is taken as complete in itself.

---

[1] See Plutarch, De Iside et Osiride, c. 20.

[2] *Ibid.*, c. 67.   [3] *Ibid.*, c. 78.   [4] *Ibid.*, c. 65.

The discernment that all the diversities which separate human beings, are less important than that underlying unity which forms their bond, came home to the men of that time as a religious truth. Mahomet did not believe more emphatically that God was one than did the thinkers of the first two centuries of our era that Man was one. It was recognized that what was common to the slave and the emperor was more important than what was special for each, and it is hardly possible for us who see this as a truism to realize what it was to those who hailed it as a great moral discovery. The preciousness of man as man was felt more strongly in this earliest age of the modern world than it was felt again before the eighteenth century. It was opposed by the spirit of chivalry, by mediæval religion, and then again by the spirit of the Renaissance; each of these laid stress on something exceptional; that recognition of the *common* as the uniting element was a prophecy of all that is most advanced in modern democracy. Under this new light the lesson of the Greek took a new meaning. He had shown forth the exceptional elements of human life—its beauty, its genius, its loftiest virtue; his language enshrined all that was most precious in merely human thought; his hands had fashioned all that was most ideal in the representation of human beauty. But under the new view of human oneness all this became a "promise and potency" of human life itself. The work of Phidias, of Homer, of Sophocles, became a tribute to the dignity of *Man*. All that was conspicuous in the man of exceptional gifts became a measure of the value of that common humanity which dwarfed its eminence. Thus the Greek sense of humanity took a new meaning. It gained, as the fragmentary expression of a truth it had imperfectly contained, a depth and pregnancy that it had lacked as a whole in itself.

As the name of *man* became more precious than the name of Greek, so even beyond that broad humanity was discerned a deeper unity, and Humanity was seen to contain a seed of something greater than itself. As the human element had lain hidden within the Greek element, so the Divine element had lain hidden within the human element. The oneness latent beneath the divergence of Greek and Barbarian was seen as a guide to a deeper oneness; the larger whole, which had replaced the smaller whole, became in its turn a fragment, and craved its completion. This is the rhythm of all thought. The one—the many—and then again the one, deeper and wider than before, till we reach that Unity which is the foundation of all others. God and Man were seen to be one in a new sense; it was felt vaguely that all which was most precious in human relation was a clue to and symbol of the relation by which Man was bound to God. It was confusedly discerned that we must ascend to a level higher than humanity before we can understand the laws of human relation; that the idea of Man in relation to something beyond himself gains a luminous intelligibility for ever absent from those speculations as to his nature and development in which he is treated as a whole. It had been the truth of the ancient world that he was a fragment of the State, and as the states of the ancient world perished individuality took a new meaning. But by the same movement of thought, a new relation came in to replace the old; the Eternal succeeded the perennial; Man ceased to think of himself as a member of the State, and discerned his position as a son of God.

This was felt vaguely by all who entered into the deeper currents of thought. But the Jew had known this always, so far as he was true to his own special message; and in this age he was taught to recognize it

afresh by discovering its harmony with all that had
appeared its most striking opposite. The great Antithesis of all human thought is that of Judaism and
Hellenism. It is hardly possible for us to conceive
of another moral and intellectual contrast so striking,
so complete, so exhaustive of all the tendencies that
belong to human endeavour and interest. When we
have entered into the depth of Hebrew thought, have
felt its thrill of awe at the ineffable Name suggested
by all creation, and least inadequately associated with
that declaration " I am ; "—and then, returning from
that plunge into an abyss, have soared to a height from
which we may overlook the wide, varied, contrast-full
extent of Hellenic life and thought, we seem to have
left no region of human interest unvisited. Fresh from
Hebrew awe of God, and Hellenic interest in Man—
from the Hebrew sense of Righteousness and Iniquity
—the Hellenic sympathy with varied impulse and
elasticity of moral view—we have touched the extremes
of all moral life, and seem to have confronted the
blankest contradiction which can set human thoughts on
paths of hopeless divergence.

The Greek, with his harmony of opposites, his swift
inversion of sympathy, his delight in varied thought, his
elastic expansiveness of comprehension, had declared in
brilliant and enduring poetry and art that man is various ;
he saw everywhere the human even when he sought
the Divine. He enthroned Humanity in Heaven, and
saw there, not the pure white ray, but the rainbow into
which that ray was refracted by his prismatic genius.
The very opposite of all this describes the faith of the
Jew. In his abhorrence of all worship of the Visible,
his profound loyalty to the Unseen, he never ceased to
uphold his conviction that God is one, and more and
more came to feel that the true Man was the son of God.

The antagonism of the two races was unabated. Perhaps it was increased. Their mutual opportunities of intercourse revealed to each the depths of their divergence. The worship of the Formless, the Unseen, presented itself to the classic mind as mere Pantheism, or degrading superstition. The worshipper of the outward Unity recoiled from the worshipper of the inward as from a mere opponent to the Gods. Almost all references to the Jews in Greek or Latin seem to ignore their faith. The Jews,[1] says a Greek historian, had been taught that God was merely " what we call Heaven and the universe and the nature of things." The Roman satirist declares that they " pray to the clouds and the power of Heaven."[2] The Roman historian describes them as " given over to superstition, but disinclined to religion."[3] They, who saw God everywhere, seemed to see Him nowhere. They did see Him nowhere in the sense that he was *there* and not here. The Roman General in the sacred shrine, where he found no image, and where he must have deemed himself confronted with a vacuum as much of faith as of imagination,[4] is a type of the mind formed on Greek culture, in presence of a profound faith rooted in a depth to which he could not penetrate ; as, in like manner, the Jewish Apostle, at the centre of Greek art, indignant at the shapes of beauty on every side, which he deemed objects of idolatry, is a

---

[1] Strabo, xvi. 2.

[2] " Nil præter nubes, et cœli numen adorant " (Juvenal. xiv. 95).

[3] " Gens superstitioni obnoxia, religionibus adversa " (Tacitus, Hist., v. 13).

[4] Pompey did in fact order the sanctuary to be purified and the sacrifices continued, but respect for the religion of the conquered was a part of Roman policy, and we may take the impression given in these citations as including that which he was the means of bringing to Rome. For the contempt and hatred with which the Jews were regarded by the Romans see Cic. Pro Flacco, 28, and Tac. Hist. v. 4. Profana illic omnia quæ apud nos sacra : rursum concessa apud illis quæ nobis incesta ; a mere calumny, vividly expressing the detestation which gave it birth.

type of the mind formed by Hebrew faith in presence of
that Greek worship of the beautiful which he could not
comprehend. We should think of Paul at Athens, side
by side with Pompey in the Holy of Holies, as showing
forth respectively the illusions which beset the worshipper of the Unseen and the lover of the Beautiful
when they attempt to judge each other. Paul thought
that the citizens of Athens were superstitious—they who
probably had the least superstition of any men then on the
face of the earth. Pompey, or at all events those who
took their impressions through the medium of his conquest, thought that nation to be irreligious whose very
existence was grounded on an acknowledgment of the
One Invisible ground of Heaven and Earth, and all that
in them is. Athens superstitious and Jerusalem irreligious ! The fact that such things were said is a warning for the critics of all time.

But the time was come when the thinker of each race
was to learn that the lesson of his own nation was incomplete when standing alone. The testimony of Israel
to the Divine Unity mirrored itself in that humanity
which his Scriptures declared to be moulded in the image
of God, and which the spirit of the age discovered to
lie at the root of all divergences of national character.
And in the same way, though not by any means to the
same degree, the lesson of the Greek was mirrored back
on the lore of the Jew. He was beginning to read,
even into his Scriptures, the belief that the Divine nature
enfolds in its own oneness the variety of Man.[1] He saw
that Unity was not uniformity, that God reveals Himself
in many ways to His creatures, that all the wealth of contrast discernible in His work must be first within His own
nature ; he felt dimly that there might be many persons

---

[1] In the Septuagint version of the Old Testament, the Theophanies reveal
not the Supreme Himself, but some inferior manifestation of His will.

in one God. But his sense of the Divine oneness was not lost in this sense of the Divine multiformity ; rather it was intensified. Man was at once Many and One, and God must be more full of contrast and more entirely One than His creature was. It is no fanciful view of the varied and seething thought of this age to say that in its combination of many elements in a single civilization was prepared and prefigured the belief in the Trinity. Men saw that that was true of human nature which, in the view of Man's relation to God then dawning upon the world, they were to express in dogmas concerning the Divine. At that point in the world's history, it was felt, as never before, that the human race was at once many and one. Before that time there had been a certain ideal unity, typified on one side by the Greek, on the other by the Jew, towards which all that called itself Man was supposed to be in some sense aspiring ; but the Barbarian was not really one with the Greek, nor the Gentile with the Jew. Between each race and the outer world there was a vast chasm which no aspirations could bridge. Plato felt the imperfect *logical* character of the division of Greeks and barbarians ; it was, he said, as if cranes should divide the whole animal world into cranes and not-cranes ;[1] but morally he felt its influence, and his countrymen probably never saw any flaw in it at all. To the Jew at Alexandria both Greek exclusiveness and Jewish exclusiveness were revealed to some extent in their true character. He was forced to see that the specially Jewish lesson entirely, and the special Greek lesson to a great extent, was lost when the Greek or the Jew refused to be a member of Humanity. They had each, in their different languages, borne witness to the oneness of humanity, and when the whole outward structure of society proclaimed that humanity was one, a

[1] Plato, *Politicus,* 263.

new meaning was reflected back on their own teaching, a new force was given to their own words.

To those who look back on this phase in the evolution of moral life from a stage of much fuller development, it may appear that this trinity of earth, soon to be mirrored in the Trinity of Heaven, was a mere accident. It cannot be said that the stream of Christian thought is complete when it is enriched by the tributaries of Greece, of Judæa, and of Rome; it has yet to accept the deep waters of Teutonic influence, the element on which the very life of modern Europe depends. But, in truth, this human trinity is independent of a particular historic phase; it is an expression of a law of thought repeated again and again in the most various quarters. It has never again been expressed with the same colossal impressiveness and deep pregnant force of expansion which it found, when the nation which declared the Divine Unity stood face to face with the nation which illustrated and enfolded the human variety, under the harsh dominion and the wise law of that nation whose call was to the Mediatorship of all nations. But it is more or less expressed in the history of all thought so far as any moral evolution can be discerned there. The collision of opposites—the presence of a Mediator—this is the universal rhythm of human development. And that theological dogma which finds the Divine Father, the Eternal Son, and the Holy Spirit to constitute "not three Gods, but One God," does but translate this rhythmic human law into that Divine expression which every moral law requires if it is to be felt an enduring reality. The trinity of the Athanasian Creed is the expression of human development, as it was exhibited to the eyes of the world, when the two races who severally have done most for the spiritual and intellectual development of mankind, met under the rule of that race

who has done most for its government. It would probably not be possible at any other crisis of history to
point out three nations thus related to each other; but
their relation expresses the law of history; it has been
felt again and again in individual development and recognized in philosophy, and the age in which it was seen, as
it were, in its naked simplicity, will always be felt in
some sense the key to the history of the human race.

The typical representative of this new sense of a
Unity underlying all difference is Philo, the Alexandrian
Jew.[1] On the soil of Alexandria it had become impossible for the son of Israel to perpetuate the exclusiveness either of his own race or of the race by whose
culture his mind had been formed. Escaping from the
narrow horizon of both, he saw their several histories as
each a chapter in the history of humanity, but in one
the typical chapter—the clue to all the volume. He felt,
as only the select few of his countrymen had ever felt
before, that the message of his nation was a message to
the human race. " In thy seed shall all the families of
the earth be blessed," was a promise that came home to
him with new meaning; he saw all that had separated
his countrymen from the Gentiles as a promise of their
beneficent union with the Gentiles. An intimate knowledge of all that is most precious in Gentile lore prepared
him to discover its readiness to enrich and to be enriched
by a yet higher lore; to feel that its most characteristic
lessons were incomplete until they were combined with
the doctrine of which they might on a narrow view
appear almost the denial, and that they first found their
deepest meaning when they met their antithetic belief.
He shows us how close may be the relation of convic-

1 Philo takes the same place with regard to Judaism that Plutarch does with
regard to Hellenism. They each represent the spirit that prizes the traditions
of a race, and awakens to a unity in which it is a mere fragment.

tions separated by the fiercest intellectual opposition, and how men, who seem to meet in blank antagonism, may but illustrate, complete, and expand each other's thought.

It was not by any endowment of exceptional genius that a Jew, steeped in the religious conviction of his race, welcomed and assimilated the convictions diametrically opposed to it, discerned the nearness of the most fundamental opposites, and blended the lesson of those who would have had nothing for each other but indifference or denunciation. His was no soaring spirit, ready to spring to heights from which the great outlines of the moral world take a new aspect ; he was but an attentive traveller along its highway, studious of all that was revealed to the eye of average power. What he saw, all could see who would look around with any earnest care; the lesson he taught was one that all could learn. If he, first of those whose recorded thought has reached the modern world, saw that the Greek and the Hebrew corresponded each to each, as the human corresponded to the Divine, it must have been because the time was come for all to see this. The Hebrew Scriptures revealed the only true Being, the Invisible One, lying beyond and behind all phenomena. Greek literature revealed Man, the various, the diverse, the divergent, the being who found his very meaning in conflict. When Philo lived, these two revelations converged ; it needed no penetrating gaze to pursue their paths to a common goal, only a patient attention to the external circumstances of the world. Greece and Judæa bowed beneath a single law. The teacher of Righteousness, the lover of Beauty, were taught their oneness in their common relation to a government which brought both into a single framework, and forced them to feel some kind of mutual relation.

Philo brought to this great truth, not the distinctness of genius, but the confusion of ordinary prejudice ; on his page we find prefigured the theological confusion which has always obscured the meaning of inspiration to the eyes of mankind. He saw that Greek and Hebrew wisdom were ready to unite ; but he blurred that truth by mistaking antithesis for resemblance, and insisting that a harmony was a unison.[1] He turned the convergence into a union in which the distinctness was lost in one sense, and yet in another exaggerated. The Old Testament, he urges continually, does not mean what it says ; its actual meaning is a kernel within a husk, which many have taken for the fruit, and either thus fed on the husks, or else trampled under foot the precious grain. At Alexandria probably he knew most of the last, and is always trying to prepare his readers to bear Greek raillery. It is very easy, he tells those Greeks who must have sharpened their wits on the Septuagint,[2] to make merry with the sacred writings, if we regard them as a narrative of *events*. But the wise man does not regard Hebrew history as a record of event. The history, which merely informs a careless reader that the serpent tempted Eve, and that she tempted Adam, teaches the seeker after truth that Pleasure, the tempter, appeals first to sense, and sense to mind.[3] In narrating the destruction of the

---

[1] See, e.g., Quis Rerum Divinarum Hæres, Mangey, vol. iv. 92-94, where he seems to suppose that the harmony of opposites taught by Heracleitus was plagiarized from the Pentateuch, being suggested apparently by so simple a passage as Genesis xv. 10 :—"Ελληνες τὸν μέγαν καὶ ἀοίδιμον παρ᾽ αὐτοῖς Ἡράκλειτον, κεφάλαιον τῆς αὐτοῦ προστησάμενον φιλοσοφίας, αὐχεῖν ὡς ἐφ᾽ εὑρέσει καινῇ ; παλαιὸν γὰρ εὕρεμα Μωσέως ἐστί. This citation, and most of those which follow, are from the Erlangen edition of Mangey's Philo, in four vols., 1785 92.

[2] ὦ καταγέλαστοι καὶ λίαν εὐχερεῖς, he answers an imaginary objection, Ibid., p. 36. He seems to have been irritated by very minute and pedantic criticism, if that to which he here replies be a fair specimen.

[3] De Mundi Opificio, Mangey, i. 112 114. Cf. Leg. Allegor., ii., passim, same vol.

old world by a flood, it really sets forth the awful calamity of permission to sin, of that oneness of impulse
from which the *distraction* of wrong is removed,[1] and the
whole nature is turned to evil, when the moral order is,
as it were, submerged beneath instincts from which God
has withdrawn His protest; and even from the Heavens
above the destroying influence pours down to meet the
rising tide below.   Nor is it only in the vast events of
History that this mystic wisdom is discernible; we can
learn from the minutest details, as from the grandest outlines of the sacred record, some principle of the divine
teaching of humanity.   When we read in the account
of the mysterious sacrifice of Abraham, " The birds he
did not divide," [2] we may learn, if we truly receive what
is there conveyed to us, the great lesson of unity of
mind, the bird being an emblem of that spiritual principle in every man which makes him one.   The Hebrew
writings take the form of narrative, because that is the
only form in which the deepest truths can be presented
to man; but those truths are not to be conceived of
under the time-relations of history; they are the expressions, necessarily imperfect, and to the superficial reader
misleading, of that which is eternal.   It is not that these
things might not have happened—Philo takes so very
little interest in that question that it is not always easy to
say which way he answered it—*but that which happened
is not their meaning for us.*[3]   We have to seek out that
meaning as ore in a mine, not take it ready made as

---

[1] De Confessione Linguarum, Mangey, iii. 327 :—Τοῦ παθήματος τοῦτο (*i.e.,*
permission to sin) ὁ μέγας ἀναγραφεις παρὰ τῷ νεμοθέτῃ κατακλυσμός ἐστι.

[2] Quis Rerum, &c., Mangey, iv. 100, 102.

[3] Sometimes he must have regarded the narrative as literally false ; he says
this definitely of the sacrifice of Isaac.   Τότε γὰρ καὶ τὸν ἀγαπητὸν υἱὸν
ἱερούργησει, οὐχὶ ἄνθρωπον. οὐ γὰρ τεκνόκτονος ὁ σοφὸς (De Migratione
Abrahami, Mangey, iii. 474). But he says elsewhere things quite inconsistent with this, and I suppose he never really made up his own mind on
the point.

coins from the Mint. We have, in a certain sense, to be fellow-workers with the writer; we hardly need less mental activity to decipher than he to compose his narrative. It is true only to those who can thus decipher it.

Philo is here the ancestor of an important section of the Church, lasting from its first existence to our own day. Perhaps none is more fundamentally hostile to the spirit of Science. When the seeker after Truth, asking, " What happened at a particular time ? " or " What was meant by a particular writer ? " is answered, " This and this is the lesson we are meant to learn from the words you are striving to interpret," he feels that a serious investigation is transformed into a game of cross-questions. Nothing can be more unsatisfactory, from the scientific point of view, than a mode of exegesis which insists that a seeming narrative is an actual sermon ; which forbids us to compare dates, when the history is elaborately chronological ; which treats as impiety the analysis of numbers, when our text is full of statistics ; which ignores a historic aim elaborately insisted on, and thrusts in a homiletic aim nowhere hinted at. This view of Inspiration puts a moral premium on an intellectual attitude in which the ignorance of fact is deliberately cultivated. It represents, therefore, all that the scientific mind abhors. Nevertheless, we shall not understand history unless we are prepared to make a certain place in our intellectual sympathy for those who have cherished it in the past. God speaks through the deeds of men no less than through their words ; history is the Divine language. It is indeed a language hard to understand, easy to misinterpret ; we shall never discover in its sentences that exact and accurate justice after which human law is continually but vainly aspiring ; we shall sometimes be forced to read there verdicts which seem to outrage the very conception of Divine law. Yet still we must recognize that the purpose of Heaven lies hid in the events of the past, we may, here and there, be enabled to discover that purpose. Perhaps the superstitious reverence for the letter of Scripture which we are fast outgrowing was the withering husk to a seed of truth—the belief that principles applicable to all history are applicable to one history in a special sense.[1] As the seventh day was hallowed to the Lord in order that all days might be recognized as holy, so the elect race was set apart as the ideal Son of God, in order that all races might be recognized as actual sons of God. The inner meaning of the Jewish history once deciphered, a " Rosetta stone " was set up for all the hieroglyphics of human history, however remote from that of Israel. In carrying out this principle, in seeking for the symbolism of fact, Philo betrays a more than ordinary lack of the historic sense ; it is the characteristic error of the theologian that he hurries on to the principle, before making sure of the event, and blames carefulness concerning accuracy of fact as indifference to the principle which facts involve. But this is an error of very different importance at different periods in the development of thought. In hurrying on to the symbolic meaning of a story before deciding whether it was true or false, Philo was not opposing any obvious principle, as he would have been in a generation familiarized with a long course of historical investigation and with the accuracy that is bred of physical science. He may, indeed, have read one or two histories whose authors sought for accuracy as much as do the great historians of our own day, but that aim was wholly alien

---

[1] " The history of Israel," it was once said to me, in answer to a question regarding the Divine mission of the Jewish race, " is the type of an individual history in a sense that no other history is." I have never known any one who more prized that history than the speaker—Thomas Erskine of Linlathen.

to the spirit of his time on the whole. He was not defying, as his theological successors have defied, the universally accepted tests of his intellectual world. In another
respect also he may be favourably compared with them
—he never set up a date, or a geographical boundary, at
which inspiration ceased; it was the condition of all direct
influence from God to man, at all times. He speaks of
it quite simply from his own experience.[1] Man under
this influence hears a voice which is not his own, and
feels that his personality becomes in a special sense
what the very word *person* would seem to witness that it
is always in some sense, a channel through which comes
an utterance he accepts, but does not originate. The
subjective element of inspiration was in his view common
to humanity. As history was the language of God, so
the ear to hear it might be opened in every son of man.

The lesson appointed for that multitude of races
brought into unity as subjects of the Roman Empire
may be described, on one side, as the transformation
of the part into the whole. Man as an individual had
been a fragment, and was, in the age we have reached,
discovered to be a Unity. But the lesson is quite as
true in an inverted form; what the Jew at Alexandria
had to learn was, that human history became intelligible
when the former Unity was treated as a fragment; that,
for Jew and Greek alike, love for the nation led to the
discernment that the nation was a mere fragment of
humanity. The antithesis of Hellenic and Hebrew
thought was felt as a convergence pointing to a fundamental unity. From Judæa came that vision of the Divine
in which the Human was on one side transfigured with
its glory; on the other, seen in black shadow against
that dazzling radiance. On that ground was no other
interest in the history of Man but his relation to God;
the creature and Creator stood face to face; this one anti-

[1] De Migratione Abrahami, c. 7.

R

thesis filled the world of thought. What could be more
unlike Greek love of variety, Greek feeling of dramatic
sympathy with all impulse, and the bright, fearless irre-
verence which marked the Greek attitude towards the
supernatural? But an impartial inexorable dominion over
each brought them into relation with each other. The
monotonous receptivity of Rome, attentive, unsympa-
thizing, yet in a certain sense respectful, full of recognition for all that could make out for itself the claim
of tradition, ready to give space and legitimacy to
everything that would own Roman authority in the
political sphere, supplied all opposites with a plan of
mediation. That impartial wide-reaching Law came in
as the harmonizing element, beneficent to all, recognized as the power "through whom we enjoy very
great quietness,"[1] felt as a refuge even from the tyranny
of those who administered it, and a protector even from
the enormities that were perpetrated in its name.

The place of Rome, at that stage of the world, would
be more intelligible to modern Christendom if it were
less familiar. Who could peruse, for the first time,
those four accounts of the great tragedy of the world's
history which we know too well as a narrative to understand as a fact, without seeing that the victory of
fanaticism was the defeat of Rome? "He that delivered
me unto thee hath the greater sin." How expressive of
the influence of Roman law is it that from the moment
of hearing those words Pilate sought to release his
captive! He recognized his vocation at that strange
excuse for his failure in fulfilling it; he felt that the
Roman governor was called on to teach the peoples
committed to his charge the common element of Law.
"We have a law, and by this law he ought to die;" he
was not to ignore this Jewish law, if this particular Jew

---

[1] Acts xxiv. 2. The address is to an individual Governor, but might have
been made general.

was liable to its infliction. It was no part of his com-mission to revise the law of the Jew, but where appeal was made to the law of the Roman, there he was called on to give that judgment which was applicable to humanity. He was to take cognizance of all that was peculiar in Law, but he was never to leave hold of what was universal. When the cry of the rabble, " If thou let this man go thou art not Cæsar's friend," overcame the loyalty of the Judge, an example was set up for all time of that obliteration of the justice of Rome by the weakness or vice of Romans, which doubtless was the most familiar aspect of its legal system to its subjects ; but in that concession the Roman law had no part ; it was defied, not distorted. And we see, in the specu-lations of Philo's contemporary, Paul, how deep into the heart of the sons of Israel sank that new conception of Law as something universal, which it was the mission of Roman law to bring home to the heart of the nations. " The law was our pedagogue to bring us to Christ," is no more than a statement of a single aspect of that character in Law which Roman law most perfectly realized and embodied. It was the Mediator of the Nations ; and whether or not Philo was consciously remembering it when he wrote of the Logos, certainly it was an actual influence on his thoughts.

None could be better prepared for a true apprehension of the meaning of law than a son of Israel. The deep and passionate devotion of Jews to the oppressive system of precepts which they had inherited from the past per-plexed even the Romans. A people who allowed their enemy to prepare on the Sabbath the ruin of their city unhindered by them, rather than violate the command which only on the narrowest literalism could seem to prohibit their defence of their native land,[1] had learned

---

[1] It is said that the Jews allowed their city to be taken by the General of

at least what it was to escape from the "unchartered freedom" of individual desire into the repose of obedience, had come to feel this obedience the very object of life. In this strange fanaticism for a code to which most would think it much to yield a reluctant obedience, they learned the stability, the strength, the oneness that is given a people who keep a law—almost any law. Even if it be unreasonable and fantastic, it still impresses on the Many the unity of a single ideal ; and the Jew in face of the Roman—suffering any torture rather than violate the Mosaic commands,[1] watching in passivity the approaches of the hated invader, rather than clutch on the Sabbath the sword after which his hands must have always yearned—formed a magnificent tribute to the irresistible attraction of that which was but the casket and framework of Duty. As far as we know, this fanaticism impressed the Roman with mere contempt ; and the feeling was mutual, except so far as on the other side it was diluted with fear. Nevertheless the fanaticism of the Jew was a preparation for that citizenship of Rome against which it was also, in its external aspect, the strongest barrier. The law was his pedagogue to bring him, not only to Christ, but to Rome.

Ptolemy Soter, 320 B.C., rather than pollute its sanctity by any attempt at self-defence ; and Josephus cites the reproach of a historian (hardly known elsewhere), that "they submitted to be under a hard master by reason of their unseasonable superstition." There is some doubt whether they would have resisted in any case, and Josephus is anxious to defend them from the imputation (as he seems to consider it) of this rigorous adherence to the letter of the law (see "Antiquities of the Jews," xii. i. 1). There is no doubt as to their abstinence; from action during the siege under Pompey, when they allowed the Roman engineers to carry on their siege-works unmolested on the Sabbath (*Ibid.*, xiv. 4, 2, 3); and Dio Cassius (xxxvii. 16) says that without this abstinence the Temple would never have been taken. A century earlier, at the outbreak of the Maccabean revolt, they let themselves be slaughtered like sheep rather than draw the sword on the sacred day. We see from the allusions in Juvenal and Horace how much impression their observance of the day made on the Romans.

[1] See Josephus contra Apion, ii. 33. The whole book is an important testimony to the influence of the Mosaic legislation.

Hence it was that at this time the sense of a Mediator filled the world of thought. Philo finds in the history of Israel a continual type of a Divine Being, intermediate between God and man, an ambassador to man from God, a suppliant to God from man,[1] partaking in the character of both, and thus a bond between the two extremes of Being. The ideal Israel, the ideal Man, is in truth such a mediator; he is[2] indeed an embodiment and incarnation of Divine Law. "God our Saviour extends His all-healing medicine to His suppliants through the just man."[3] Man thus rises, by a perfect harmony with God's will, into a position above humanity. The just man is the ideal Law. We see here the side on which Philo approaches Rome. "Abraham went as the Lord commanded him," he says, "means the same thing as when it is said by Philosophers 'to follow Nature.' . . . The words of God are the actions of the wise man," and the *Word* of God is the Law of Nature.[4] Abraham was the ideal Stoic. The Jewish sense of a Mediator melts into the Roman sense of Law. It is a personal conception on this side of the barrier, on that an impersonal; but essentially the two conceptions are one.

The significance of this single Roman creation was brought out by the very barrenness and poverty of the Roman character. It had no other qualifications for its task than legal impartiality. Of itself Roman feeling[5] merely echoed and emphasized with its own

---

[1] *e.g.*, Quis Rerum Divinarum Hæres, Mangey, iv. 90.

[2] νόμος αὐτὸς ὤν, καὶ θέσμος ἄγραφος (De Abrah., last sentence).

[3] *Ibid.*, 22. The wise take God for their teacher ; the less perfect take the wise man (Quis Rerum Divinarum Hæres, 5).

[4] De Mig. Ab., c. 23.

[5] Lucan (Pharsalia, i. 52, 3) seems to me well to bring out true Roman feeling :—

"Omnibus hostes
Reddite nos populis, civile avertite bellum "—

" Make us the foes of all, so *we* be one."

hardness the exclusiveness of Greece.   It was avowedly
second hand ; it judged everything by a Greek standard ;
it met the deep spiritual intuition of the Jew with the
protest of Greek idealism, intensified by its own superstition, and narrowed by its own hardness.   There was
no touch of original genius in the Roman ; his work was
to organize, to   arrange, to   combine—never to create.
The Roman poet sings no heroic deeds, warms into life
no dim legend, creates no character, bids no memory
glow with the brilliancy of dramatic power.   His theme
is the Nature of Things ; his genius is devoted to the
subject least stimulating to genius of any that has ever
been set to the music of noble verse.   Yet the result
is imperishable, because here the positive genius of
Rome finds its true work, the lawgiver of the nations
interprets the law of the universe.   No matter that its
interpretation is childish if we look at it in the light
of full scientific development ; its errors are only in detail,
the spirit of law is there.

The spirit of reverence *for things that are* was deeper
than the deadly hatred that separated Rome and Judæa.
That spirit was, in truth, akin to the deep religious
genius which those who felt it could not comprehend.
It prepared the way for a reverence of the Divine Lawgiver, and for all the moral influence which invaded the
world with the Jewish belief in a Divine Law.   But the
whole tendency of the classic world was towards the
impersonal character of Law.   Although the lawgiver
formed an imposing figure in the legendary history both
of Greece and Rome, the deeper feeling of the ancient
world towards Law outside of Palestine is expressed in
the line of Sophocles—

" None knoweth the fountain of Eternal Law."

Within the Hebrew horizon this was exactly the knowledge which belonged of right to every true Son of Man. It is the change from the idea of Law to that of a Lawgiver which constitutes the transition from Rome to Judæa. All Law was for the Jew the Will of a Holy God ; and the Holy Man was this Law set forth in action and endurance. For Divine Will lay at the root of all being ; it was a Divine command which had called into existence all that meets eye and ear and touch, and by a Divine decision, therefore, every change in their order must be regulated. The object of worship to the Jew was not a Zeus, son of Time, not a vague principle of oneness to which the word *He* should be inapplicable, but the Maker of Heaven and Earth, and all that in them is. God was the *Creator*. He who made Man, and made all that surrounds him, was able to enter into relations with the being that His hands had fashioned ; He who had created could also guide and judge.

Deeply penetrating, widely reaching, was the influence that poured upon the world through this Hebrew belief in Creation. We may to some extent measure the positive effect of this belief by the extent of change in the moral aspect of the world taking place at its eclipse. We see before our eyes, in our own day, the converse of that great moral revolution which came upon the world when the Greek learned from the Jew to believe in a Creator. Centuries must pass before the inherited influence of that belief can wear out in the hearts of men ; but already we may discern that the intellectual abandonment of a conviction rooted in the moral structure of our race, tells to some extent on all debatable moral ground. But modern Europe has been moulded by a long inheritance of belief in Divine Will : it cannot, when it throws off that belief, return to the position of those to whom the conception of a personal Creator was unknown. The Will

of God—familiar as the words are to us—is a conception wholly wanting to classic antiquity. There was will
enough in the superhuman beings who hovered above
the world of mortal effort with benign or hostile influence,
but it was not the source of Destiny, only an eddy on its
stream ; it brought the mind into no contact with Origin.
Human Will takes a new meaning when men believe in
Divine Will ; when it is recognized that all that we see
and touch takes its source in the decision of a Divine
Mind, it loses much of that meaning with the belief. Man
is for ever being made in the image of God, and the
generation which regards the Divine Being rather as a
spectator or a product than as author and director of
the development of the Universe, cannot regard it as
the business of Man to control and shape the world of
humanity ; a strong impulse becomes a command Man
dare not disobey ; an indication of general tendency
claims all the loyalty, all the resignation, that was formerly given to an expression of Divine purpose. The
fatalism which has in our time invaded the world of
politics in a conspicuous form is latent everywhere,
and forces on the attention of all who look below the
surface of life the lesson that all Man's endeavours are
affected by his belief or disbelief of the world in which
he finds himself being the work of God.

When the Jew first taught the world this belief, its
influence was seen more clearly than it ever could be
seen again. However certain it may appear to the
logical intellect that that which is meant by *virtue* can
have no place in the Divine nature, some instinct deeper
than logic craves and discovers a Divine type of all
human excellence ; and all that Man seeks to be, he
must see in God, as long as he sees God at all.

We may say, with not more exaggeration than on
such a subject we need for distinctness, that human will

was first conceived of with fulness of meaning when
Divine will first shone upon the world in that belief.
The conception of a Divine Creator gave the active
powers of humanity a new glory, and also a new responsibility. The shadow of scorn passed from industry ; the
toil of the slave gained a Divine type. This shadow had
never reached the soil of Judæa. "My Father worketh
hitherto, and I work," said a Jew contemporary with
Philo, and the words gather up the life of Israel.
Labour, Philo tells us more than once, is the root of
every other excellence.[1] That scorn for toil which is
bred of slavery never could utterly pervert a son of
Israel. The corrupt Roman might scoff at his reverence
for the Sabbath as a varnish of superstition over sloth,[2]
but the truth was, that to revere the Sabbath was to
revere labour. No one can find rest who avoids toil.
"Six days shalt thou labour, and do all that thou hast
to do," is a part of the command that bade the Jew do
no manner of work on the seventh day. If observance
of that law was exaggerated into superstition when the
Jew watched, in his Sabbatic repose, the advance of the
Roman siege-works rather than draw his sword on the
day of rest, what stored-up force of patience and will is
not expressed in that act of obedience ! And who can
doubt that the energy for toil as much as for combat was
reinforced by that rhythmic abstinence ? Philo only
translated the law of the Sabbath into the language
of ethics when he declared that "labour was the root
of every other excellence." He brought the wisdom of
the Jew into a form in which it could be intelligible to
the Greek. It never would be acceptable to the Greek.

---

[1] πάντα οὖν ὁρᾷς τὰ ἀγαθὰ ἐκ πόνου καθάπερ ἐκ μιᾶς ῥίζης ἐκπεφυκότα.
De Sac. Abelis et Caini, see also De Posteritate Caini, 46. Philo's feeling for
the Sabbath is vividly expressed in the treatise " De Mundi Opificis."

[2] Juvenal, Sat., xiv. 105.

The city life, so dear to his heart, was inextricably entangled with slavery, and slavery out of Judæa made the command, " Six days shalt thou labour," unnecessary and hateful.   But a race which looked around on the earth and sky, and felt at every throb of joyous life that God was the maker of man, could never put hand to the plough or spade without some dim sense of partnership in the Divine work.   Labour was Divine, and therefore it was in the deepest sense of the word truly human.

Then, too, on the other side, this importance . given to the conception of Human Will came in to solve the very problem which the conception of Divine Will had evolved.   If God made the world, why is it full of evil ? It can be only because Man has re-made it.   God saw it, and it was very good.   Man must have refused the position of a creature and chosen to be an independent Creator.   This is not so much the doctrine of the Jew as that which the Gentile learnt from the fusion of their several creeds.   We indeed find it in our Bible, but we might take it away and leave no hiatus ; in many respects the Book of Genesis would be more coherent if we could withdraw from it that account " of Man's first disobedience," which we too much remember in its extended form on the page of Milton when we read it on that which has been attributed to Moses.   To the question, as it presents itself to a logical mind—" Being the work of God, why is man no better that he is ? " the Hebrew has no answer.   He does not really attempt to answer it.   He finds that the consciousness of this relation of Creature and Creator sets right all the difficulty he needs to have solved ; that so far as Man remembers himself to be the work of God, so far as he refrains from seeking to make a God which shall be his work, these difficulties vanish away, and that is enough for him.

To the Jewish mind the only evil was Sin. And Sin is schism—the cutting off the member from the organism, the substitution of the Many for the One. So far all are agreed who believe in anything that may be called sin ; the only difference is as to that Oneness which claims man's loyalty. Is it the nation, the family, the caste, or is it a still deeper Unity, which includes all other, and which man knows as God ? Between this Unity and that which each man means when he says I, there is a profound and hidden connection. The Indian creed, we have seen, confused the two ; the division line between the human and the Divine was indistinct. The Indian name of the Divine is the Self. It is a wonderful illustration of the nearness of opposites that in Hebrew thought the name for that which hides the Divine is the Self.[1] That which to the Indian reveals God conceals Him from the Jew ; the telescope hinders vision when it is not needed. God was so close to the human soul that the Self was a veil between it and Him. "If any yearning come upon thee, O soul, to inherit the Divine possessions, quit not only thy country—that is, the body—thy kindred—that is, sense —and thy father's house—that is, speech " (all of which are symbolized in the migration of Abraham), " but put off thyself, and depart out of thyself."[2] It is the Indian feeling, renewed and revivified by a sense of that distinctness of God and Man, which comes with the development of the life of the Conscience and the belief in

---

[1] Philo says that it is only in *remembering* the nothingness of self that we can remember the greatness of God. It seems to me that he would have expressed his meaning better if he had said it is only in *forgetting*, &c. Surely to remember the nothingness of anything is to forget it. De Sac. Ab. et Caini, Mangey, ii. 96-98.

[2] Quis Rerum Divinarum Hæres, Mangey's Philo, iv. 32 :—σεαυτὴν ἀπόδραθι, καὶ ἔκστηθι σεαυτῆς καθάπερ οἱ κορυβαντιῶντες, &c. Perhaps in these words Philo was remembering the last words of Socrates in the "Crito," quoted above, p. 196.

creation. God is the only true Being; the Creature is
for ever distinguished from the Creator, the Being whose
centre lies within from the Being whose centre lies
without. Self for the Jew was that independent claim,
that rejection of the attitude of a creature, in which
the Creator becomes invisible. The lesson of the Jew
is blurred for Christian ears by extreme familiarity, and
perhaps it may come home to us more forcibly from
Alexandria than from Jerusalem. We have become
accustomed to the ideal of Self-denial in the withered
form which any ideal must take that is adopted con-
ventionally as part of a creed; we have lost the full
import of those words, " If any man will come after
me, let him deny himself." It is not, " This and that
pleasant thing must be put away ; " it is, " The self-
assertion of the Creature is the denial of the Creator."
Man is the work of God ; his whole vocation lies in the
understanding of this relation to his Creator; he stands
face to face with a great Unity, before which no pro-
portionate recognition of the Self is possible ; its imperious claim must be met by a denial before it can enter
into that which is its true and abiding life. Here is
the eternal paradox, insoluble to logic, incontrovertible
to every soul that has felt its import. Man cannot
discern God till he has denied Self; but it will be
found, also, in the deepest sense, that he cannot discern
Self till he has acknowledged God. For none can know
anything till he knows something else ; and we first
know the Self when we know that which is to every
man the eternal Other of the human soul.

It is just because Man and God, in the Jewish conception, stand opposite to each other as Creature and
Creator (instead of both being equally creatures in one
sense, and both equally creators in another), that the
Jew felt himself near God in a sense the Greek never

could share. " Thou wilt have a desire *to the work of thine own hands.*" That confidence breathes through every line of the Jewish Scriptures, and its reflection on the page of Philo is much stronger than any ray from Greek wisdom which reaches his broad mirror. " We have the uncreated, the eternal Father, *who hears the silent and sees the hidden,*" he makes Joseph say to his brethren when reassuring them after their father's death ; and this sense of *the Father* can never, to the Jewish mind, be swallowed up in the idea of the King. God is more awful than the most awful earthly monarch, but no earthly monarch would permit that boldness of remonstrance which the Hebrew Scriptures give as the utterance of His trusted servant. No parts of the Old Testament seem to have laid more hold on Philo's imagination than those which record the appeals of Abraham and of Moses to a Divine Righteousness with which Divine appointment appeared inconsistent. " Shall not the judge of all the earth do right ? " seems to gather up for him the fearless confidence which mingled with boundless awe of the Creator.[1] Philo, the ambassador to Caligula, vividly realized the contrast between that bond which united the Jew to his unseen Lord and that which kept a nation of slaves trembling at the foot of their tyrant. The son of Israel was more akin to the unseen Unity, could use a greater freedom in that intercourse, than the Roman with the Emperor of Rome. Philo seems to return to this sense of confidence and boldness with a sort of relief, feeling vividly that the earthly Lord was not in any sense the image of the heavenly Lord ; that the least inadequate type of His absolute dominion was the Fatherly dominion, in

[1] ταῦτα γάρ (*i.e.*, the complaints of Moses, as Numb. xi. 11, Exod. v. 22, &c.) . . . ἴδοισεν ἄν τις καὶ πρὸς ἕνα τῶν ἐν μέρει βασιλέων εἰπεῖν (Quis Rerum Divinarum Hæres, Mangey's Philo, iv. 11).

which, at its best, dominion was less prominent than love.

All such types were inadequate ; the relation between Creator and Creature was one too deep, too intimate, to be fully expressed even by this close bond ; all that was most organic in human relation was but its shadow. The well-known words of Andromache to Hector seem to haunt him as its least inadequate expression. The wise man finds this world an exile, but he may say, " Lord, Thou art to me fatherland, kindred, and paternal hearth."[1] And, indeed, the relation of sex lies very near all his views of the relation of God and man. The distinction of the passive and the active, suggested by the two halves of humanity, is ideally complete in the relation of humanity to That which lies above it. Israel was the spouse of the Lord ; the ideal Humanity needed the Divine for its counterpart, as a bride her bridegroom. And thus the religion of the Jew held in germ all that elevation of woman which is most characteristic of modern, and most unlike classic thought. The race which realized the true oneness between God and man, realized for the first time the true oneness between man and woman. Modern scholarship indeed looks with scorn on the view which sees a hidden allegory in the little love-poem included in the Hebrew Scriptures ; but this mystic interpretation is no more than a refraction, through the mists of an exclusive worship, of that deep sense of the infinite in human passion, which, though it be constantly the rival of all sense of the Divine, is yet intimately akin to a sense of the antithesis of the Divine and human. The Song of Solomon may bear witness to its intelligent readers far more distinctly than to those who put an unreal meaning into every

---

[1] Quis Rerum Divinarum Hæres, Mangey's Philo, iv. p. 14 :—σύ μοι, δέσποτα, η πατρίς, &c.

word, that the feeling which prostrates man before God has a deep and hidden connection with that in which man and woman find, each in each, the completion and explanation of their being. The tenderest love known to human beings takes a fresh dimension when it is felt as an illustration and type of the Faith in that which engulfs and overshadows them—beyond, beneath, above, in every way transcending human vision and explaining it.

Humanity becomes a different thing when it is thus regarded as the spouse of the Divine. The fierce Hebrew was the first to recognize Humility as the characteristic human attitude; it was impossible for him ever to forget that Presence in face of which no other attitude seemed tolerable to him. "The meek shall inherit the earth" is (we often forget) a quotation from a psalm. If Greek dread of arrogance, Greek reverence for proportion, has left us many expressions outwardly resembling that text, the resemblance is merely outward. The envy of the Gods is widely remote from that Divine jealousy which guards the command, "Thou shalt not make to thyself any graven image;" they have almost nothing in common. Greek religion grew out of the self-assertion of Man; it knew nothing of the antithesis of Creator and Creature. God and Man to the Greek were not even contrasted as the perfect and imperfect, for Olympus repeats and exaggerates all the sins of earth. A God was merely an intensified, not a purified Man. This, at least, was true of the characteristically Greek element in Greek religion; and if by its side was what we may, in contrast with it, call a Jewish element—if the religion of the Mysteries[1] held the seed of a conception

---

[1] See, for this affinity to the Mysteries, De Gigantibus, 12. Μωϋσῆς . . . εἰς τὸν γνόφον, τον ἀειδῆ χῶρον εἰσελθών, . . . γίνεται οὐ μόνον μύστης ἀλλὰ καὶ ἱεροφάντης ὀργίων.

of the Divine less remote from Hebrew awe—yet still, on the whole, the Hebrew ideal was altogether opposite to one which in all its most vivid manifestations was a glorification of humanity—humanity with all its contrasts, all its diversities, all its sins. " The nothingness of the Creature " is an idea inconceivable to a Greek. Man was himself a Creator. All that most interested the Greek mind was created by man. The very name of *poet*, signifying creator, has passed into our language, indicating that which we feel the immortal work of the most exalted human intellect; and while attention is concentrated on the poet and the artist, the contrast of Creator and Creature grows dim. And then, too—for the Greek God was in some sense a creature—the Divine beings had their genealogy, their parentage; there had been a time when *they were not*. All the vicissitude that made a human being interesting applied to Zeus; there was nothing in him to oppose the idea of a Self. But to the Hebrew the property of God was to go out of Self. He was the *giver of Existence*. He, the absolute Being, sought always to bestow that which could be given of true Being. He calls into existence the things that are not. He is known to Man as a perpetual Becoming; Nature is a ceaseless stream from the " I am." The idea of Self is wholly alien from such a Being; he is known in the action which, if we are to describe it in the language of human analogy, is a perpetual quitting of Self. God has thus for ever set the pattern for Man. He denies Himself in a mysterious but deeply important sense when He bids this varied Creation arise in which Man may find objects of worship and forget the Creator; and the claim on Man, " Go thou and do likewise," is enforced by His example no less than by His authority. The Creation is in a certain sense an act of Self-denial in God; His

Creature is called on to copy when he seeks to obey his Maker.

For that which divides man from God divides man also from man. Self is the separating, the isolating influence; we must deny *ourselves* to become one with our kind no less than with our Creator. The word gathers up the whole problem of Morality; it seems at times the most positive reality in the world, at times a mere negation. How vivid is the sympathy, how profound the compassion, how active the benevolence, which has to confess itself overmastered by this tremendous gravitation! Only some centrifugal influence can measure that central pull; only he who best loves his neighbours knows that he does not love them as *himself.* Yet there are points of view from which this intense reality—the most real thing in the experience of many—is seen as a mere limit. All physical experience brings us back to this limit; but the impulses which quicken and elevate our being reveal to us that Self is only an aspect of our life; we *are* members one of another; we have not to bring about that membership. In all those moments which reveal to us our true being we feel that the *We* is a reality as much as the *I*, in some sense as much deeper as it is a wider reality, and at such moments we are aware that we touch on the solution of all morality, that we need no more, in order to satisfy the utmost claim of Duty, than to understand the sense in which the *We* swallows up the *I.* The Hebrew reached this solution in his vision of an *I* which is the ground and basis of all that we shadow forth when we say *We*—a Unity which is the measure of our multiplicity, an absolute Being from whom our derived Being takes all its meaning. He is One in the sense in which there is no other One, and in sharing his oneness we are united with each other. Self—the limit,

S

the separating influence—is that which divides us from Man as well as from God.

It is first on the page of Philo that we come upon the idea of Selfishness. We search in vain through all the ethical wealth of Greece for any germ of belief which could develop into such a sentiment ; we should have vainly endeavoured, probably, to make the feeling which condemns it intelligible to the thinkers who have made the Greek tongue a casket of imperishable moral treasures. The very word by which Philo describes it is almost unknown to classical Greek.[1] Self-love would be to the Hellenic imagination a mere accompaniment of consciousness, or, so far as it partook of any moral quality at all, it would be an element in virtue. " Know thyself," is the watchword of Hellenic wisdom, as " Deny thyself" is of Hebrew faith ; the goal of thought for the Greek was for the Jew a point of departure. All that affiliates itself with Greek teaching enforces reverence for the Self; only the Jew discerned the peril that lay close to the prize, and reminded himself, and all whom his voice could reach, that " Man should not regard the world as an appendage to himself, but himself as an appendage to the world."[2] In that strangely temperate injunction we have the note of a new morality. It breathes a spirit which apart from Judaism belongs wholly to the modern world. Selfishness is a word of yesterday. When first the thought dawned upon the world it was expressed by the same word which it bears on

---

[1] It is characteristic of Plutarch's latent sympathy with the vein of thought we have been tracing that we find φιλαυτία also in his writings. The passage in which Plato comes nearest the idea is in the Leges, 731, 732, τὸ δὲ ἀληθείᾳ γε πάντων ἁμαρτημάτων διὰ τὴν σφόδρα ἑαυτοῦ φιλίαν αἴτιον ἑκάστῳ γίγνεται ἑκάστοτε. Any one who studies the awkward involved passage of which this is the kernel, and compares it with that given in the text, will see clearly how Plato was groping after a new idea, while Philo was expressing one which he held in common with the modern world.

[2] Quod Deus Sit Immut., 4.

the page of Philo;[1] our Saxon compound belongs to Protestant England. Its need was felt with that post-Reformation morality which corresponded to the right of private judgment and justification by Faith. It expresses the moral dangers incident to the complete development of modern individuality; it lay beyond all the abundant wealth of Shakespearian thought; the word does not occur on his page. When he comes nearest it, he sees it as *Ambition;* if we seek for a Shakespearian parallel to the warning of Philo, we may find it best in the warning of Wolsey to Cromwell. The Jew devoid of genius saw farther into the moral world in the dawn of modern thought than did in its full noon the greatest genius that England has ever produced. The Hebrew vision of God threw a gleam on the whole history of Man, and lit up its moral development with a meaning which was borrowed from a higher sphere.

It is the rise into a dimension above morality which has made the Jew the moral lawgiver of our race. The most exclusive, the most un-Catholic of nations has given modern life not only its belief but its moral standard. The influence is visible in those to whom it is most obnoxious; to this day the dialect of men who deem it an obsolete error to connect humanity with aught beyond itself is stamped indelibly with the ideas and beliefs of those who felt all its value to lie in such a connection; the protest against Scriptural teaching, which is the form in which many in our day know most of the Scriptures, records their

---

1 The oldest author who used this rare English word seems to be Holinshed, in his account of the reign of Henry II., published 1577 :—"Here we see Phil-autie, or Self-love, which rageth in men so preposterouslie" (mark the appropriateness of this adverb, *which puts last that which should be first*) "that even naturall affection and dutie [are] quite forgotten." It was used as late as 1648 by the Rev. Joseph Beaumont, Professor of Divinity at Cambridge, in his "Psyche," an allegorical religious poem published in that year, some parts of which may have given suggestions to Milton for his "Paradise Regained."

influence in inverted outlines, ready to be restored to their original form when mirrored in a sympathetic mind. Hebrew thought has given its bias to all moral speculation, not because the Hebrew mind was itself specially interested in moral questions, but because it sprang at its initial movement to a point above them, and came upon them from a higher view. And for ever afterwards Man is reminded, in all speculations on his destiny and character, how imperfect is that attention that sets up limits around its object, and in how deep a sense " the half exceeds the whole." The Jew bears witness to the human race that Man is but the half of that which Humanity implies and involves; and that unless we look beyond the boundaries of its history and the limits of its nature we shall find its deepest problems unintelligible.

CHAPTER VII.

THE PROBLEM OF EVIL.

THOSE thinkers who have imagined themselves to sim-
plify the problems of life by explaining Virtue as a means
of Pleasure, have surely too readily taken for granted
that people are any more agreed as to what Pleasure is
than they are as to what Virtue is. If you mean by
pleasure *the end of pain*, you do indeed point out by the
word a goal of common human desire, indeed the goal
of common sentient desire; but if you accept a neutral
starting-point, if you refuse at starting to presuppose
suffering, you open just as many controversies in asking,
" What is Pleasure ? " as in asking, " What is Virtue ? "
" Are not the aims of the intellect higher than the aims
of the heart ? " asks the great Francis Bacon : his hum-
blest reader may answer with a confident negative.
Most persons desire love, many persons desire power,
some desire knowledge, but you cannot say that the
wish for any one of these things is absolutely universal.
If we want general consent, we must ask not what men
desire, but what they fear. He who thinks that the
aims of the intellect take precedence of the aims of the
heart, and he who thinks that the aims of the heart take
precedence of the aims of the intellect, both escape from
a fire with equal eagerness; and the travellers whom
no possible intelligence could inspire with a common
hope feel, on the verge of a precipice, a common fear.
It needs only the intensifying of physical pain to anguish,

or else the prolongation of it to monotonous pressure on the whole of life, to make every one recognize that there is a negative wish stronger for the moment than any positive desire ; that while Pleasure is a vague word, meaning something different for every individual, the word Pain points to something more definite, more simple, than any other that is familiar to men.

The problem of evil is inadequately conceived whenever men forget this dislocation of antithesis between good and evil. To the heart of the everyday man, roughing it in the world, it is not the existence of what is evil, but its apparent victory, that is oppressive and bewildering. It is indeed impossible for the logical intellect to reconcile the existence of God and evil, apart from any question as to proportion. But let no one think, if a problem be insoluble, that its manner of statement is unimportant. What men need is not to have this question answered, but to have it rightly asked. The whole moral grouping of mankind will be found to depend on those answers which may quite truly be described as a mere translation of it into various dialects. It is not the scientific instinct in Man, alone or chiefly, which seeks to penetrate the origin of the system in which he finds himself. Men are led to ask *how* the world arose by the lurking desire to know *why* it is as it is ; and the answers arrange themselves according to the antagonism of two impulses often combined, yet always divergent; that in which the *why* predominates, and that which conceives every statement in mere time relations, and is satisfied with knowing the sequence of events, without seeking to understand their aim. The whole antithesis known to our generation as that of Religion and Science is involved here. On the one hand the why gives a keynote to theory, and the narrative of Man's origin takes its start with a Fall. Things once

were good and fair, but there was a descent, variously
explained, but always conceived in terms of will and aim.
But men discern that the explanation which would account for evil really implies evil. Adam fell because
the serpent tempted him ; but why did God admit the
serpent into Eden ? The difficulty is moved a very
little way farther back. Logic pursues it. Thought is
wearied, and reverts from Why to How. Is not what
we call Evil the mere stimulus to effort, without which
Man could never have existed ? Is not failure of
balance the reminiscence in the human world of that
" origin of species by natural selection," which means,
when we put it into non-scientific language, that dispro-
portion between need and the means of its satisfaction
which fills so large a part of life with suffering and
struggle ? The ascent of Man states the facts of life
in one way, the fall of Man another ; there is no more
explanation in the one case than in the other. But
the two answers gather up the contrasts between two
moral worlds, and when we contemplate them we stand
at the parting of the ways, and see where travellers
turn to the right and the left to meet no more.

What hypothesis men take up as to the beginning of
things depends on what they want explained in things,
not on any superior logical cogency on either hand.
Logic begins to work after the choice is made. Experience is impartial in the matter. We are every day
familiarized with the two forms of production which
have become the models of the origin of the universe.
We are familiar with growth, and we are familiar with
works of art. We sit under the shade of a lofty oak,
and we know that it came from an acorn, such as it
drops at our feet. We say that the oak *was* once an
acorn, and we mean something definite by the words,
though it would be possible to find fault with them.

The processes of Nature are constantly reminding us of a change by which the simple becomes the manifold; and when we try to account for the origin of Nature, the processes of Nature itself may be thought to provide us with the most plausible analogy. But we watch the building of a house more consciously than the growth of a tree; and Will is a cause of which we know more than of any other. It is, indeed, the only cause which, in the true sense of the word, we can be said to *know*. A man who feels within him that *which originates*—who is conscious of *something which begins* in his own nature—will recognize in this, whatever he call it, the true analogy to the origin of all things. If Will be a word of any significance—if we feel that it is a cause in a more complete and typical sense than anything else is a cause—then, with whatever intellectual obstacles, we shall believe that God created the world. We may feel that the account in Genesis belongs to mythology, the account in modern scientific works to history; we may look to the latter for all in what we call Creation that can be narrated, all that belongs to the relations of time. But we shall feel that in a deep sense the assertion, " In the beginning God created the heavens and the earth," even when connected with any amount of erroneous illustration, still remains as an expression of the deepest truth which, on this subject, it is possible for us to attain.

This divergence is seen clearly by all logical thinkers, whether they consider the belief in Creation important truth or important error. The two sides might not accept even the description of their issue in the same words, but both would allow it to be extra-logical. One who holds that this world was created sees that his belief is a moral one. He does not mean that every one who believes it is good, and every one who disbelieves it is bad; he means that it is a belief which depends on some difference in the moral structure, and that those who have it will use the words good and bad in a different sense from those who have it not. A man who holds Evolution to be an adequate and exhaustive account of the origin of this world, would not, perhaps, be so ready to concede that his was a moral belief, because from his point of view what is moral is opposed to what is immoral, rather than to what is intellectual ; he supposes a moral belief to be the belief of a good man, and hardly anybody would accept what he would describe as the belief of a bad man. But he would concede, or indeed urge, that those who accepted and those who rejected this belief in Creation had different views of most important subjects ; and this is all we mean in calling it a moral belief.

These views are indeed so different that it is difficult to say that they are dissimilar. They are incomparable, they stand out of relation to each other ; those who hold them are mutually unintelligible, and all the worst confusion of the world has come from their tendency to translate each other's assertions into their own dialect. We might say, roughly, that growth excludes the idea of Evil, and Will suggests it. Whenever we contemplate growth we see no evil but disease. Whenever we contemplate Will our thought touches the world of Evil at every moment. God made the world ; why, then, is the world no better than it is? The man who thinks that the doctrine of Evolution tells us all there is to know about the world can hardly understand this question enough to dissent from the answers to it. The world is, according to his view, growing better every day ; its existence is a continual approach towards the better. To him the better takes the place of the good, and there are no two ideas more irreconcilable.

This primal antithesis has various aspects for different stages of the world's history. Our generation knows it as the antithesis of Religion and Science; when we trace it back in History we may discover it as the antagonism of the Jew and the Greek.   Our children, perhaps, will see it under some aspect so different that they will find it hard to associate it with either of these earlier forms; but through all runs this recurrent divergence of How and Why, of Growth and Will, of the spirit that is satisfied with the order of time-relations, and one that seeks a deeper order, disturbing to the very idea of before and after, because it tends to use those words in a different sense.   Perhaps it is a part of the dislocation of our nature that the antithesis should have been recorded in controversy; it may be that what we need to harmonize all our thought is the discernment that the Why concerns one part of our being, and the How another.   The world, it is true, cannot have been created twice; when we are considering its origin as a question of time we must take our choice between different hypotheses; no possible view can bring the account in the Book of Genesis into one framework with the " Origin of Species."   But may not the translation of a belief in initiative Will into time-relations be the error on one side, while the description of Growth as exhausting the whole question is the error on the other ?   One who aims at following the history of moral thought cannot do less than approach the question, or more than suggest it.

Art, even more than Science, leads away from the Eternal.   There is a deep mysterious connection between all that belongs to the region of the painter and the poet and that which is transient—that which is vanishing away.   The artist people less than any other is inclined to quit the conditions of before and after.   For the Greek the supreme Artist was himself the product of something that in modern language we may term evolution.   He needed accounting for as much as the world did.

The governor of the world is a son of Time. They who have bequeathed to the world all the human work that it has most loved, and the name by which the Creator is identified with the Poet in all modern languages, could neither conceive of what a Jew meant by Creation, nor see in it the difficulties which the Jew sought by moments to explain. For the Greek there was neither an evil world to be accounted for, nor a Holy Will to cause it ; the creation was not bad ; the Creator was not what the Jew meant by good. The History of Greece is a brief and concentrated tragedy, and its art is proportionately rich in tragic elements. The great figures of the Athenian stage pass before us in solemn procession as we think of life's deepest sorrows. Œdipus, Antigone, Electra, rise before the mind's eye to confute the notion that grief in the Greek world threw no shadow on Art ; but then this very shadow is indispensable to Art ; and that it should give rise, in the feeling of the Artist, to anything of the nature of perplexity is impossible. And, further, God is not good any more than the world is bad. Perhaps we may say it would even more misrepresent Greek thought to speak of a good Creator than of a bad Creation. The Greek awarded a prize to those creations which he felt so typical of the Creation as to keep the name for them ; he meant by a good Creator a good poet. That Creation in which Sophocles had borne the prize from Æschylus and Euripides from Sophocles, that work which was *good* according as it was rich in harmony, and therefore in a certain contrast, must give a type of Creation in which the idea of Holiness was inaccessible. The Creator could be good only in the sense in which Æschylus was a good poet, and from this point of view the evil in his work was one of its most important elements.

The problem which was non-existent for the Greek

was practically solved for the Jew. No nation is more remote from what we have come to call Pessimism than Israel. It is true that no literature presents specimens of a more profound melancholy than the Hebrew Scriptures. But what the Jew in his most despairing moment laments is, that man has chosen evil rather than good. He never feels that good is not there to choose. " O Lord, how excellent are Thy works ; in wisdom hast Thou made them all," is the deepest utterance of his faith ; and when he has added, " An unwise man doth not well understand this," he has made his utmost concession to the opposite feeling. He could pour forth the acknowledgment from a heart overflowing with reverent delight, because, in the first place, the works of God never included for man his own errors and imperfections, or anything that resulted from them ; and, in the second place, God was still more intelligibly and practically the Redeemer than even the Creator. The assertion " I am the Lord thy God, who brought thee up out of the land of Egypt," stands as the permanent aspect of the Divine Unity to the chosen race ; and the deliverance from Egypt foreshadows more than a deliverance from Babylon, from Syria, from Rome ; it is the first word of a promise, whose full scope the Jew needed the education of the ages to take in, and which he sees, as he dimly discerns it, to be for ever beyond the reach of all but a continually expanding grasp. From a logical point of view this celestial hope should have left the previous condition from which deliverance was promised under a black shadow. Redemption should have darkened Creation, but it never did so ; between Creation and Redemption, both the work of God, the Fall of Man lay in shadow sufficiently deep to bring out their brightness and conceal its own outline. The Jew never exactly knew what he meant by the Fall of Man ;

his accents, when he speaks of it, are always hesitating; he returns to it afresh, in oblivion that he has dealt with it before; he forgets whether, after all, it be the fall of *Man* he is speaking of, and his Adam becomes an angel.[1] But still he meant something by it, and something that was adequate to explain all he wanted. He felt that the will of God was good and the will of Man was evil continually, and that was enough for him. His God had called Man's spirit into being, and was its rightful Lord. He also had redeemed it from its evil, and was its Saviour. Man's own rebellion supplied the intellectual link between these ideas, and the Jew needed no other.

Neither for the Jew nor the Greek apart, therefore, was the problem of Evil a haunting perplexity; in different ways each answered or avoided it. But effects which result from neither of two substances in any possible condition apart, may be inseparable from the union of the two. The fusion of Greek and Jewish thought produced an effervescence in which this problem became one of the most seething elements in human thought. For it was in this fusion that the Gentile world contemplated for the first time the idea of Almighty Will at the world's origin. We cannot imagine power so great that the change to unlimited power tells as a question of degree. When the Creator is Almighty instead of Mighty the whole conception is altered. The fundamental divergence of Jewish and Greek feeling in this respect is disguised by their likeness. They both know

---

[1] It is evident, from Gen. iv. 3-12, that Cain and Abel do not start as the members of a fallen race, but that something in the conduct of each is the ground of their difference. " If thou doest well, shalt thou not be accepted? And if thou doest not well, sin lieth at the door," could not be interpreted, except by the advocate of a theological system, as an address to one who inherits a legacy of guilt. Note especially ver. 12, " The ground shall not *henceforth* yield to thee her fruit; " hitherto, then, it has done so. See also Gen. vi. 2, and the Book of Enoch.

of a Creation, but the two ideas are only confused by being seen in the same line. The Hebrew Creator looks on His work, and behold it is very good. The Greek Creator looks on his work, and knows that he has made it, "as far as possible, the fairest and best, out of things which were not good."[1] "Out of things which were not good; there is no getting behind that. He was hampered by pre-existing conditions, and has done the best he could under the circumstances. It is the Origin of Species by natural selection from a different point of view, and under a different dialect. It has no real connection with the first chapters of Genesis.

When the attempt is made to bring the two into one framework, that which for each separately was a narrative becomes a problem for both. "Whence, under a Holy and Omnipotent Creator, come the things that are not good?" The new dignity of Creation implied a new attention given to the dark side of the world. Evil emerged into a distinctness for the thinker,[2] which has led historians into imagining it as occupying an exceptional proportion in the life of ordinary men. Students of this age have explained its tendency to sombre feeling and speculation by supposing it to be one of special disaster. The period on which we have been dwelling would not suggest such predominance of misfortune to an impartial observer, any more than our own time does. The world is so constituted that we may find peculiar suffering, if we look for it, in any time; but the age of the Antonines has always been reckoned one of the

---

[1] τὸ δὲ ᾗ δυνατὸν ὡς κάλλιστα ἄριστα τε ἐξ οὐχ οὕτως ἐχόντων (Plato, Timæus, 53).

[2] See Gfrörer, "Urchristenthum," vol. i., a work of which much that follows is a transcript. He says of these times that they "gehörten zu den traurigsten, welche die Weltgeschichte kennt." This he means of the time of Philo, *i.e.*, about the time of Christ. I cannot but think that there must have been much more cause for suffering at an earlier period.

halcyon epochs in the stormy voyage of History; and if it does not exactly coincide with that of which we speak,[1] the same conditions were common to both. The happiness of the world under the Antonines cannot be wholly explained by the character of its rulers. It is impossible to remember what war is, to imagine what it was, and to suppose that when it ceased the nations were not better off. Experience does not require us to believe in anything so improbable; it is not in lives crushed with misery that we shall find much perplexity as to the existence of suffering; such perplexity rarely, indeed, exists except in the minds of those whom the world would call prosperous. But amid great prosperity we may feel the imperious pressure of the problem of Evil; and though the age of Death was not one of peculiar suffering, it was one of special suggestion for this side of life.

Probably we have all felt, when an individual human life has ended, distress quite out of proportion to any vacancy caused by the departure. It is not that the lost presence was so specially prized (though the feeling does not arise without love); it is rather the reflection originating in tender memory, " With large result so little rife ! " Our inmost being craves achievement far more persistently than enjoyment, and as long as life hurries on to some goal its bitterness does not pass into perplexity. It is when the movement of life is at an end, when the vague possibilities of the future are cut off, that we are led to the question, Is it worth while ? Few lives bear the question ; perhaps few ages would, if the end of an age were as definite as the end of a life.

When for the first time in the world's history men

---

[1] The second century is the epoch of Gnostic development, and also of the reign of the Antonines ; but the remarks in the text take in a somewhat wider period.

confronted a dead past, they could not avoid this question.
Life for the toiling millions was not then harder than it
had been, but to the thinking hundreds it was darker.
They saw it under an aspect that revealed its nothingness. A pause in all action left them leisure to brood over
the problem, Why did the world ever originate ? The
word Almighty, to most of us so familiar as to have lost
its meaning, represented a new conception to the men
of that day, and the contradiction which we drop out of
sight emerged for them with the distinctness of novelty.
As the first rays of the rising sun even less obviously
bathe the landscape in light than they streak it with
shadow, so when the belief in many gods deepened and
concentrated itself into a belief in God, the world, in its
new character of a *Divine work*, showed forth, as never
before, the flaws and misfits which removed it from being
a satisfactory exhibition of Divine perfection. As a background to the varied movement of human and Divine
activity the world was well enough ; call it the product
of Almighty Will, and it became filled with evil.[1]

Hence it is that from this time two lines of theory
on the origin of Evil are traceable throughout all moral
speculation. On the one hand, the Greek antithesis of
Spirit and Matter presented itself as a symbolic expression
of the contrast of good and evil, which precluded the
need of its being regarded as a problem ; on the other,
to a race for which Sin was the only evil, the Jewish
antithesis of Creator and Creature appeared to offer
some real solution of the problem. Evil to the Greek

---

[1] A sentence constantly quoted from Euseb. (Hist. Eccl., v. 27), πολυθρύλλητον παρὰ τοῖς αἱρεσιώταις ζήτημα τὸ πόθεν ἡ κακία, gives the keynote of all the theological and theosophical discussion of this time. See also Arnobius adv. Gentes, ii. 54, 55, 65 :—" Mala ergo dicetis unde sunt hæc omnia ? " this being evidently the continual Heathen objection, and also the heretical objection. The book, which is a vindication of Christianity from the charge of being re-sponsible for the calamities of the time, was written early in the fourth century.

was what marble was to the sculptor, at once the source
of his labour and the indispensable material of his workmanship; from one point of view it veiled his creation,
from the other that creation was expressed by it. His
ideal lay within the rock; arduous toil was needed to
smite away the disguising material that surrounded it.
But then, from another point of view, the rock lay
within his ideal, his ideal was no more than that which
gave it form. It is the view of a race which looked on
Morality as in the truest sense of the word a subordinate province to Art. Some learned men have imagined
themselves to find a concession to this view in the first
verses of Genesis. "The earth was without form and
void" implies, they think, that the Creator had an
uncreated material for His energy, and therefore an impersonal sharer of His eternity. If it were so, it would
always be possible to a logical mind to see in this
antithesis to God the source of Evil. But it is difficult
even to allow that a Jew saw in this doctrine a conceivable intellectual hypothesis; it is impossible to
concede that Jews felt in it a moral view, explanatory
of the nature of Evil. They had a simpler, not really a
deeper, but perhaps a more natural explanation; Evil,
to their view, was the very opposite of a thing; there
was no possible evil, except in a choice. If to *be* good
means to *choose* goodness, it must be also possible to
choose evil, and evil must be there to choose. The
answer will generally be felt an inadequate one by those
who can see the need of any answer. But the Jew found
no difficulty in this belief, and there must be many who
find none; for the Jewish answer has lasted ever since,
is incorporated in immortal poetry, and is for ever pre-
senting itself to some minds as an original answer to
the ever-recurrent problem of humanity. We find it,
again and again, urged as a great moral discovery that

T

human free will relieves a Divine Creator of responsibility for the evil of the world ; we are continually being led to feel that this thought must have some tranquillizing influence on the heart of man, which cannot be translated into intellectual cogency, and must point to some deep truth which man has not yet learned to express in language impregnable to some objections that are both obvious and forcible.

To the Hellenic spirit this view was inconceivable. Only slightly, and as it were by an intermittent light, did the Greek ever contemplate that which we sum up in the words " human responsibility." All that we mean by human freedom was conceived by his race more vividly than by any other people of the earth. But a variation of dialect may cover a chasm deep as the very roots of human thought. Human responsibility is human freedom contemplated from the point of view of one who believes in Righteousness, who sees Evil as Sin. Some gleams of such an explanation, as of almost every thought that has ever entered the heart of man, may be found in Greek literature ; but all its characteristic expression leads us in a different direction. For the Artist, Sin is no more than the throb of life's pulsation, the warp of its woof, the condition and prelude of all that is desirable and excellent. The evil of Sin cannot indeed be entirely hidden from any race or any individual ; and in a race whose every utterance has the resonance of genius, it will always be possible to find in some undertone a definite protest against a view that excludes a deep part of our nature. But that swift inversion of sympathies which is essential to dramatic genius precludes any deliberate concession that impulses, which fill life with meaning, have no fitting place anywhere. When the Greek had to explain Evil he could not find refuge in human Will. There could be no Evil in Freedom ; Evil

lay in that which opposes itself to Freedom—the world
of Necessity, the absolute antithesis to and negation of
Will, the blind world of Matter. The two theories meet
in sharp, distinct contrast ; the one is the exact contrary
of the other. " Evil begins where Spirit ceases its free
play," says the Greek. " No," says the Jew, when he is
forced to see what the Greek meant ; " it does not begin,
but ends there. Evil can exist only in the choice of a
Mind. Man is created to take the attitude of a Creature, and when he chooses that of an independent
Creator, the result is that which we call Evil."

But let us begin where the Jew began, and understand first the theory which he rejected. When we have
allowed that the fact of man's material organization and
environment is the cause of a large part of what is wrong,
and of a still larger part of what is painful, we appear
to have made the utmost concession possible, from the
modern point of view, towards that identification of
matter with evil which the Greek almost took for granted.
If we were obliged to have any theory on the connection
of the two things, we should be inclined to the very
opposite one. The very sense of necessity involved in
our material environment, which may be called evil, is
to modern feeling a dilution of the fact of wrong. A
starving man steals a loaf; for the good of society we
may think some penalty should be inflicted on the
act, but hunger is allowed to be a palliation of theft ;
and translated from legal into moral language, this
means that guilt slackens as physical impulse becomes
overpowering. We cannot confine our ideas of wrong
to the region of physical temptation. Hatred is an
emotion as purely spiritual as love. Happily it is far
less common. But it is not a feeling that can be left
out of account when we are considering the character of
good and evil. What we call pain of body, which we

should rather call pain from body (since all pain is in a mind), is considered by many to be, when very severe, the worst of all pain ; but it is not considered so by every one, and it is certainly not the only pain.   The Greek thought that the spirit should rule the body as the master the slave.   We can see that that is another way of saying that the body should not be a part of the material world.   There are some forms of inversion of this rightful rule which of themselves we condemn as abnormal ; they should not have been allowed to begin. But so far as any feeling is *natural*, a certain allowance is made for it which is quite incompatible with such condemnation as we give to that which in theological language we term sin.

Yet there must be some meaning in the belief of the greatest thinkers of the old world.   The human race is not more human at one time than another.   Its relation to truth is a permanent one.   It is a futile and sterile method of study (though it be a common one) to fix a date at which thought begins to be either true or false. In some sense all earnest thought must be true ; that which was *meant* by earnest thinkers must be true ; and we may generally discover some part of experience which affords a clue even to the opinions we are furthest from accepting.   It is an important fact, that so far as human beings dwell within the realm of sense, they are to a certain extent necessarily rivals.   Envy, says Virgil to Dante, in the " Purgatory," arises—

> " Because men set their wishes upon that
> Wherein companionship is one with loss."

To some degree this is what no one can help doing. One mouthful of bread will fill only one mouth.   While all beauty, all delight of eye or ear, is common possession to those who are within its reach, the food and garments which form the lowest degree in the scale of need cannot be shared without being lessened. 'This holds good for saint and for sinner, for genius and for idiot, for criminal and philanthropist. All, so far as they are animals, want something that none other can have at the same time ; and all are animals to some extent throughout the whole of their being, and through its earlier stages, when first impressions are received, not much besides, as far as man can see. An animal, so far as it is merely an animal, can do neither right nor wrong; and the not-right may appear wrong as readily as the not-wrong appear right. The animal nature, like some planet which from different parts of our orbit we may visualize in constellations severed by distances imagination fails to compute, may be identified, according to our point of view, with either good or evil. Nor is man an animal only throughout the earlier stages of his life on earth ; he is liable to re-enter this circuit of animal necessity with a hundred accidents to which the best of men is just as liable as the worst is. Whole classes pass their lives in that region "wherein companionship is one with loss," and only under the most favoured circumstances does any one pass through life and *never* feel he must do without something he needs because there is not enough of it for two. The mere fact of man's bodily environment thus becomes a source of separation between man and man, which is perfectly inevitable, and for which no man is responsible ; and while we contemplate that fact and nothing besides, we may call this bodily organization evil.

This connection of the bodily organism with evil is equally evident in experience which has no obvious connection with the external world. It is not the experience of ordinary human beings that sorrow separates us from our kind to the same extent as does

extreme pain of body.   The frame that is racked with
rheumatism or neuralgia is a prison to the spirit in a
sense that no unsatisfied desire of the heart is.   In all
the desolation of bereavement a hungry man is glad of
food, and a half-frozen man of fire ; in a paroxysm of
bodily pain he can be glad of nothing.   From within
and without the lesson is repeated.   As the statesman
knows that hunger is a potent factor in a nation's life,
the invalid feels that even a little pain is imperious, if it
goes on.   We are all forced to feel, sooner or later, that
in man's bodily environment there is an element not only
of necessity, but in some sense even of what appears
like falsehood.   It is as if, with regard to pain, we were
all forced to re-enter that sphere of illusion in which the
vine-leaf is greater than the star which it hides ; and
with regard to pain of body, as if we lost that power of
movement which enables us to catch a glimpse of it to
the right and the left of the obstacle which hides it.
We are obliged to *feel* for the moment as if some sharp
pain which we have to endure for a few seconds were
a great thing, and some large change affecting the permanent fate of millions were a small thing.   It is not
wrong which creates this illusion, it is only the very
nature of our physical organization.

In the grasp on the perennial truth that the world of
matter is the world of necessity we gain a clue to the
temporary belief that the world of Matter is the world of
Evil.   Necessity divorced from Law *is* Evil.   We cannot sufficiently shake off the influence of scientific thought
even to imagine a physical world of Necessity divorced
from Law.   We should first need not only to put away
all scientific conceptions, but also to strip our minds
of all the associations that our commercial and industrial development have interwoven with the very warp
and woof of our intellectual structure.   Human will has

gained a control over the field of Matter of which the ancients knew nothing. Nature is now rather the field where Will finds its exercise than the barrier which forms its limit. We confide an important message to the electric telegraph, and know that it will be transmitted at least to the end of the wire. If we had intrusted it to our best friend he might have forgotten to deliver it. Every time that we cross the barrier between things and persons we are reminded that it is only on the ground of things that we can make our reckoning with absolute security ; our antithesis between the two is between the world of safe anticipation and the world of what we call accident. People are whirled thousands of miles without anxiety or effort, because steam never fails to move what impedes its expansion ; and if they are mutilated or killed on the journey, it is generally because some human being has not done the thing he was expected to do. The lesson that this is not necessarily the condition of human beings with regard to the outward world is enforced by the contrast of ancient and modern thought. A Greek knew no large, familiar every-day illustration of what we may call the convenience of dealing with things. Where we turn to machinery, he turned to the reluctant service of some captive, torn from his home or brought up under the degradation of bondage. All the convenient certainty that we associate with man's control over the forces of nature he associated with the control of one class over the will of another.

This change has revolutionized man's view of the outward world. To modern thinkers Matter is the incarnation of Force ; to ancient thinkers it was the contrary of Spirit. Of the wonderful cycle of laws which it has revealed to us, the only one which they knew (and which no one can help knowing)—gravitation—was supposed by them to be a peculiarity of the only region of space subject to disorder and imperfection. Those silent, ceaseless movements which for our eyes inscribe the midnight sky with testimony to the universal domain of gravitation, exhibited to theirs its narrow limits and eternal opposite. The movements that end and the movements that continue had to their conception nothing in common. Their knowledge was as misleading as their ignorance ; the laws of Space, as they become confused the moment they are illustrated in any material substance, encourage the belief that Matter knows no law. Our modern investigators of Nature would have appeared to the Greek to make exactly the same mistake as a man who cut triangles in chalk to test the problems of Euclid. The world of Matter was the world of multiplicity, of confusion ; truth, if attained here, was attained only by accident.

The Greek had studied the personal to far more purpose than the material world, but his view even of this is different from ours. John Mill has observed— and the observation is important as coming from him, because he would be inclined rather to underrate rather than overrate the truth he there expresses—that we must never think of the cruelties of antiquity as if those who inflicted them were as bad as *we* should be if we did anything of the kind. Napoleon's was a far more cruel nature than Cæsar's, but Napoleon could not have cut off the hands of a whole garrison and left them in that miserable condition, as Cæsar did. He durst not have raised against himself the indignation of the civilized world, which such an action from Cæsar did not raise. The whole moral standard of our day is formed under an attention to individual need that necessarily changes the very character of duty, and affects what men wish to seem, even when it has no influence on what they wish to be. The State—the unit of the classical world—is an unseen being; the individual—the unit of the modern world—is closely connected with the bodily organization; and as the Self becomes more prominent, the body becomes more sacred. Asceticism is no more than this sense of sacredness allied with a desire for sacrifice, and its prevalence in the mediæval as compared with the classical world is an illustration of the new importance of pain. A keen sense of its horror readily passes into a keen sense of its blessing. The nature to which it is comparatively insignificant is equally remote from both.

We can understand that those who saw in the material world all that we see in it of danger, of compulsion, of necessity, and saw in it nothing of law; who felt, as every human being must feel, its wonderful alliance with pain and did not feel the sanctity of the framework which enshrines the Self;—we can understand that to them this formless negative entity became a sort of antithesis to God, a blind sharer of His eternity and a limit to His Will. But why give form to what is evil? Why enter on the work of Creation? It was not a question natural to a race of Artists. Why carve a statue? The question answered itself. And yet it recurred again and again. Plato returns to the suspicion that Creation, in some sense, implies degeneracy. His indifference to the whole physical universe is but the intellectual expression of this doubt. If this world had been, in the full sense of the word, a creation of God, it would have been, as in his view it was not, a worthy object of attention to Man. We sum up his whole view of what we should call Nature when we remind the reader that his account of the material world and its origin is the only work in which he does not take his beloved master as a guide. Socrates appears in the " Timæus," not, as in every other dialogue, as the critical investigator, but merely as the attentive listener. To use his own homely metaphor, he ceases to practise his mother's trade ; he delivers no pregnant mind of nascent truth ; he greets mature opinion ; he does not look for infant knowledge. From the time that Timæus begins his exposition Socrates remains as silent as some modern man of science beneath the pulpit of an eloquent preacher ; there is no occasion for him to bring his *elenchus* to bear on an exposition which expressly abdicates all pretension to bring the mind into contact with knowledge ; which is content with a probable and plausible set of guesses on a subject respecting which nothing can be known. Man cannot know what God has not, in the fullest sense of the word, created. God did the best possible with matter ; He found a Chaos and He left a Cosmos, but the disorder is latent in the order ; ever and anon it recurs, and with it the thought that in some deep sense the world where it reigns, is not the true home of Man.

The very inconsistencies apparent in the various forms taken by this belief in a Fall attest its strong hold on the mind of Plato. Perhaps the work of Creation was given up, at the moment when Man was to be called into existence, into the hands of inferior deities ; or perhaps it is in the course of history that we must trace this degeneracy ; the Creator guided the world at first, but when He let it go, its course was reversed, and it soon forgot His guidance. Or else (and this version of the belief would appear to express his deepest thought) the birth of every human being is a repetition of the Fall ; each soul, as it clothes itself in flesh, descends from Heaven.[1] " Perchance in truth the dead are happiest,"

---

[1] Compare the account of the Creation in the "Timæus," and of what we may call the Fall in the " Politicus ; " the first makes the last unnecessary. For the sense of an individual degeneracy, see the myth at the end of the " Republic," and in the " Phædrus."

he concedes to a scornful antagonist who has made the statement as a jeer; "truly thou sayest that life is an awful thing."[1]   The suspicion led towards a feeling the very opposite of the Greek sense of life ; but for that very reason it was familiar to the race whose whole life knew the rhythm of pulsation.   Inversion, says Plato,[2] is the least change of movement possible. None recognized as the Greek did that the opposite swing was natural—that to feel the brightness of life was but one step from giving a welcome to Death. "The Divinity thus gave a token that it is better to die than to live," says Herodotus, when he has told a bright child-like legend quoted above.[3]

> " Who shall declare if seeming Life be Death,
>   If seeming Death be but the dawning Life ? "

asks Euripides,[4] in hardly more poetic words.   He may here have been thinking of the verse of an earlier poet,[5] who, in describing earth, uses himself the very words applied by Homer to the "joyless abodes" in which Agamemnon sighed[6] for the life of a slave on earth. Life and death, Empedocles thinks, have been inverted ; it is the world of the shades that we inhabit here ; our home is elsewhere.   Earth, in truth, is Hades ; this is the world below ; life and light are to be sought in other realms.   " Our birth is but a sleep and a forgetting ; " it is by a fall that we enter on this realm of death, and that which we call birth, in truth, is dying to the splendour of our original home, and awakening to a dreary exile, to an existence " subject to mad strife." Life in this world is but banishment, and banishment

---

[1] Gorgias, 492.   [2] Politicus, 269.   [3] See p. 122.
[4] In a Fragment quoted by Plato in the "Gorgias."
[5] Empedocles.
[6] ἤλυθες, ὄφρα ἴδῃ νέκυας καὶ ἀτερπέα χῶρον (Od. xi. 94).

must have been earned by crime. What sin did the Spirit commit in its mysterious Paradise that it should be hurled downwards to Earth ? The poet answers this question indistinctly, or at least the fragments we possess of his poem bring us the answer in an indistinct form. It must have been some awful guilt which took the place of Man's first disobedience, and most readers will feel it the more impressive that its character is mysterious. Yet, though more awful than the sin of Adam, its consequences are less dark. The Heaven of which life has deprived the poet is one to which death shall restore him, if the intermediate world of Purgatory be rightly used. "The amplitude of bliss," from which he has been hurled earthwards, lies before him as well as behind him ; he is separated from his past Heaven by a long period of evolution, during which he has traversed the course of animated existence, and has reached the pinnacle of humanity, whence he may take his Heavenward flight. The dream is one of those which haunt poetry in every age, and it is difficult for readers to whom it is familiar in this form to say how much more than poetry it may have been in the early ages when all deep thought naturally took a poetic form.

The Fall of Man thus must be accepted as a Greek idea, in the sense that Greek thought again and again returned to it, and that the deepest minds of the Nation were the most haunted by it. But it is not a characteristic Greek idea. Man a fallen being ! We cannot look at a Greek statue and believe that. He is perfectly beautiful ; he is perfectly satisfied. He seems to need nothing, to remember nothing ; a creature of the Present, at home in the bright world around him, and asking nothing but that it might continue. Even the limitations of Greek art bear witness to this sense of completeness, this satisfaction in the finite. How extraordinary it is to turn to the productions where the sense of beauty breathes through mutilated fragments of long-buried marble, where manhood and womanhood appear before us in a perfection which has given the standard of all time, and to see no trace of enjoyment in the beauty of childhood ! Their men and women were children once ; to our conceptions they must have been lovelier then than ever ; for what beauty, to our eyes, equals that of a little child ? It was a beauty, however, of which Greek sculpture, at its best period, records as little appreciation as does Greek poetry of mountain scenery. All that the Greek seemed to remember about the child was, that he was smaller than a man, or when individual affection brought in more definite feeling, that the curves of the face are rounder ; an inattentive, clumsy chubbiness is the nearest approach the Greek chisel can give to the portraiture of a beloved daughter lost in infancy.[1] Why were the Artist people blind to the beauty of infancy ? Because they had no interest in anything incomplete. They lived in the absolute, the finite, the full daylight of life ; its dawn and its twilight alike were to them uninteresting. They seem to record, for all time, the pride and glory of youth. The Greek, as his sculptured records show him, meets all the perils and disasters of life with a smile— sometimes a pathetic smile, but a smile always. They could not, except in rare moments reached by a few of their deepest minds, contemplate that side of life which approaches the idea of a Fall. They could not be sufficiently interested in the Imperfect to conceive of a higher perfection than that which man had attained already.

---

[1] This must be brought home to all who have enjoyed the beautiful Athenian sepulchral remains, lately made accessible through the photograph. There is a touching relief of a little girl caressing her pet dog, where one is astonished to see the execution of what was evidently a task imposed by loving regret, so clumsy and almost ugly in its result.

When the world, moulded by Greek thought, accepted the faith of Judæa, and the two were blended in a mystic system which we know as Gnosticism, it was in the Fall of God rather than of Man, that an answer was sought to the problem by which the heart of the Greek had never been tormented, and his brain but slightly exercised. But, in truth, it is with Man's relation to the Divine world under the progress of Religion, as with Man's relation to the animal world under the progress of Science. The barrier seems in both cases to disappear. He descends from the Divine on one hand; he ascends from the animal on the other. The endeavour to trace his history on either side shows signs of hesitation as it speaks of origin. We see, when we pursue any moral belief through the course of the ages, that it crosses and recrosses the boundary separating the Divine and human worlds, or rather that it is seen now on this side, now on that, according to the position of the mind that reflects it. Was it a man who fell, or a God? The fact seems more definite than the person. In some mysterious way the Creation was connected with the Fall, and it constantly appears as though the Fall were the earlier event of the two, as if all things earthly had their origin in disaster.

The message of the Jew bearing witness to an Almighty One had come into an atmosphere charged with this deep sense of futility in all things earthly; the old order of things had passed away; no stately civic life awakened enthusiasm, no great ideas kept the mental circulation vigorous. It was just when men were feeling as if the best thing was death, that they were taught that Life was the gift of God. The world was a ruin, and yet the world was a unity. The nations were united in a single whole, but in this vast organism there was no life. It was as if a man had succeeded in unlocking a carefully guarded casket, and found it empty. It was not that the world was then specially bad, but men were taught for the first time to wonder why it was not good. The idea of Unity had never before been brought home to European thinkers; from within and without alike the lesson was now pressed upon them. They saw the world arranged round one centre; they heard of one invisible Author. They saw it for the first time as a whole, and they saw that it was not good.

It is no temporary belief dependent on circumstance which leads men to associate Unity with all perfection. It is a result of principles that lie within the most profound depths that human nature can penetrate. Whenever man turns to the Eternal he turns to the One. Evil is by its very nature multitudinous, and all that is good is convergent. All good unites, confers on him who turns towards it, its own distinctness and purity. All evil distracts, reveals divergence from that which should be the centre of unity, shows will and nature, which should combine in harmony, somehow at strife. Men must have felt this always; when they felt it in connection with the new revelation of one God, and the near recollection of many Gods, they felt it in the clue to the whole meaning of good and evil.

When men were first taught by the rule of the governing race to realize that humanity was one, and by the message of the prophetic race to believe that God was one, while they at the same time looked round on the world with a sense of its evil, they came to feel that Creation was the desertion of the region of Unity for the region of Multiplicity. They identified the Creation and the Fall. The sanction given by Divine, or at least supernatural activity, to the evil world of Matter, took to the imagination of this age the aspect of the Fall of

God.   We cannot better suggest to the reader the imaginative effect of this view than by describing it as the
first sketch for Milton's magnificent picture, the supernatural figures crowding out the natural.   In truth, all
that is merely human in " Paradise Lost " is matter of
secondaryi nterest.   " I beheld Satan fall from Heaven,"
almost the only words in the Bible which give any
groundwork for the poem, indicate its true scope.   Satan
is its hero ; his fate forms the focus of interest.   His
abode is the real world ; it is called Hell, but it is not,
like Dante's Hell, a place of actual torment ; we feel it a
world of exile, but also of grand possibilities of loyal
devotion and of varied aims.   Its inhabitants, though defeated, are still Gods ; and even in their crime there is
something that is majestic and impressive.   Satan is a
kindred figure with Prometheus ; we may even believe
that the poet was unconsciously attracted towards his
theme by the latent sympathy with insurrection which
makes itself felt through his theology ; we feel that his
heart is with the rebels, even while his judgment approves
their fate.   The world itself is in some sense the result
of their sin ; a human race is called into existence to replace a fallen Divine race ; a vast calamity is commemorated in the very existence of this framework of Being in
which man finds his home.   Thus man's very existence
is the memorial of a Fall ; his own lapse is but the echo
and consequence of one of vaster proportions.   The
Spirit who has himself decided it to be " better to reign
in Hell than serve in Heaven," inspires the creatures who
may almost be said in · an indirect way to owe their
existence to him, with vague spiritual ambition, and
throughout the whole poem we feel that the keynote lies
in the ambition and the conquest—for such, in truth,
the world is—of the mighty Tempter.

The myth of Eden holds a perennial truth.   The

Tempter said to Adam and Eve, "Ye shall be as Gods, knowing good and evil," and still speaks thus to every son of man. In the endeavour to know good and evil as God knows them, lies the prelude to a fall. He knows both. Man should only know one; and therefore, in the sense in which we can know nothing till we know its contrary, he should not know even that one. And again, from the Fall comes Redemption; from the knowledge of Evil springs the knowledge of a higher good. We seem to know God and sin together. Here is the perennial paradox of the moral life, ignored or inverted by Science and by Art; but to him who seeks moral rightness above knowledge and above beauty, a permanent high-water-mark of human thought, a limit to its restless ebb and flow, testifying to a vast Beyond, which it confesses while it abjures its right to penetrate. The temptation to know sin *is* sin; yet how can man love Truth and not desire to know? And then, by a strange, sudden, inevitable inversion, the seeker seems to discover that the temptation to know sin is the opportunity to know God, or, at all events, that it is the prelude to the deepest knowledge of God which man is fitted to attain. In the evolution of Christianity this idea expanded, transcending the limits of humanity, and projected itself on a superhuman background. The human temptation in this view reaches to that depth of humanity which seems to need more than a merely human representative. The ideal man, it seemed, must be more than man; if human aspirations have their Divine prototype, so have human temptations. The Fall of man, as it was conceived by human thinkers, was first the fall of a God.

We have already seen how, as the shadow of Greek intellect falls on the faith of Judæa, the awful image of the Divine grows dim; how in this new atmosphere the Absolute Being, as it were, retires, and the Divine agency

U

is carried on by those personifications of the Divine
Powers which clustered round and centred in the Mediator, the Divine ideal of Israel. We have here the germ
of what may be called a new faith ; though, for the
most part, its professors repudiated the name ; their
watchword was Knowledge. Of their teaching we possess only such fragments as their opponents have left
in tearing it to pieces ; we hardly know more of it than
would be known of the science of thirty years ago by
one who judged it from quotations made by the clerical
opponents of scientific men.[1] But one who has followed
the convergent lines of Greek and Jewish thought to
their common ground finds these broken fragments safe
stepping-stones between the mythology of the Old world
and the beliefs of the New. We see the ideas of Philo
blend with the memories of Hesiod ; we watch the Powers
of the Invisible and Formless One take shape in a new
mythology, shutting off the awful abyss of Deity from
any contact with the base world of matter, interposing
an intermediate emanation system whereby the One
should be screened, as it were, from direct responsibility
for the realm of multiplicity, of evil. We see these
strange abstractions hover on the edge of personification, and sometimes pass it ; we have to do with beings
so faintly personal that we may at any moment re-trans-
late them into the language of allegory. If we say that
Wisdom, seeking to comprehend the Absolute, sinks
into a region of confusion, and propagates error, we
speak metaphysics ; if we say that Sophia, presuming to

[1] The authorities for the following sketch of Gnosticism are mainly the
polemic citations in the works of the Fathers, especially Irenæus adv. Hæreses,
Tertullian adv. Marcionem, adv. Valentinianos, de Præscriptionibus Hæreti-
corum, contra Gnosticos Scorpiacum ; Clemens Alexandrinus, Stromata ;
Plotinus, Ennead, ii. 9. The last gives a very interesting picture of Gnosticism
from a Neo-Platonic point of view, showing how large a part of its moral
ground was common to Christianity.

approach the Supreme God, fell from Heaven, and gave
birth to a daughter in the region of darkness into which
she sank, we describe a chapter in the new mythology
of this age, but we have hardly done more than translate
an English word into Greek. According to this mythology the Creator is the son of this lower Sophia. The
Wisdom, even indirectly manifest in the Creation of the
world, is a lower wisdom, inheriting the memory of a
Fall, separated from the region of celestial repose by a
long struggle, and the degradation of an existence begun
in a fallen state, and bearing in its very nature the marks
of disorder and imperfection.

Nothing more marks the difference of Jewish and
Greek feeling than a comparison of this Gnostic Sophia
with the Sophia of the Proverbs : " While as yet He
had not made the earth, nor the fields, nor the highest
part of the dust of the world. When He prepared the
heavens, I was there : when He set a compass upon
the face of the depth : when He established the clouds
above : . . . when He gave to the sea His decree, that
the waters should not pass His commandment : when
He appointed the foundations of the earth : then I was by
Him, as one brought up with Him : and I was daily His
delight, rejoicing in the habitable part of the earth ; and
my delights were with the sons of men." [1] It is almost
as if the Gnostic Sophia grew out of a distinct protest
against Hebrew reverence for the *Creator.* The Wisdom
manifest in Creation was a spirit dating its very existence
from a world of disorder, and inheriting a tradition of
struggle and failure. The Mother of the Creator is already
the inhabitant of a fallen world ; so far must the blunder
of Creation be removed from the Majesty of Heaven. He
inherits unconscious reminiscences of presumptuous aim,
of defeat and despair; these he incorporates in a Creation

---

[1] Proverbs viii. 26–31.

which reflects them—not, indeed, them alone, for a divine
spark is fallen into the dark world, and the Creation is
higher than the Creator. But still it is his work, the
work of a Fallen Deity. The divine Mother has sought
to know God—a presumptuous aim. In her son, this
presumption is heightened into the disastrous ambition
of creating Man.

This new mythology provided for the instincts of
Hellenism and Judaism alike. It gave, however faintly,
the Many to imagination; it preserved, however illogically,
the One for thought. Pallid abstractions as were its
deities, they did yet satisfy, to some extent, the instinct
that craves the Many. The tinge of Greek colouring is
indistinct, to our eyes almost invisible ; it lingers as the
traces of colour discovered by archæologists in buried
sculpture ; yet still it gave some shadow of satisfaction
to minds steeped in Hellenic feeling and yearning after
variety in the Heavens so recently emptied of their
bright inhabitants. It has been called " La dernière
apparition du monde ancien, venant combattre son suc-
cesseur, avant de lui céder le genre humain." [1] The
shadowy and sublimated Polytheism which we learn with
effort and immediately forget does indeed seem a pallid
ghost of that which still glows in immortal poetry and
sculpture ; yet it doubtless had its attraction for many a
spirit hesitating on the borders of the new creed, and
sending looks of backward longing towards the varied
play, the endless dramatic interest of the old. It was
prevalent during the dawn of the modern world, when
the lights of Paganism were growing dim and the light
of Christianity growing strong, and its " endless genea-
logies," carrying on the world of Paganism, doubtless
found acceptance with many minds as a harmonizing
medium between the Heathenism which they had aban-

---

[1] By J. Matter, Hist. Critique du Gnosticisme.

doned, and on which so many of their tendencies had been formed, and the simple, perhaps it seemed to them the meagre, creed which had succeeded it. With the reluctance with which we sometimes greet the morning light that dispels a fanciful dream, many half Christians must have looked up to a Divine world that had suddenly become (as it would seem to them) almost empty, and sighed for the rich plastic variety of an Olympus that mirrored the passions, the instincts, the hopes and fears, that quicken our human world. The strange beings who figure in Gnostic legends formed an 'intermediate mythology, coming between the worship of the Gods and the worship of the Saints, and to men craving after the fulness of a Heaven from which its bright inhabitants were lately banished almost any successors must have been welcome to fill the blank.

But Jewish feeling found a like shadow of satisfaction in this mythology. What the new teachers meant by calling themselves Gnostics was, that they were initiated into the hidden knowledge of the One beyond the Many. That God was One was being taught on all sides ; they inculcated the lesson that, being One, He is hidden in remote inaccessibility ; that the divine world from which this human world has issued is the world of multitude, of division, of plurality, and hence its evil.[1] Nothing can seem more hostile to the spirit of the Hebrew belief, yet it was by a true Jew that this belief had been read into his Scriptures. Philo had discovered, in the first chapters of Genesis, indications that the creation of the

---

[1] Jehovah, the God of the Jews, being identified with the blundering Demiurgus, they were supposed to stand in a special relation towards him. Heathen religions, in like manner, belonged to the dark realm of Matter, while Christianity was a revelation from the Supreme God. Thus the three ideas of Gnosticism corresponded to the three religions of the world at the dawn of our era. Several references in the New Testament suggest Gnostical ideas, e.g., John xii. 31, xiv. 30 ; 2 Cor. v. 4 ; Gal. iii. 19; 1 Cor. ii. 6, 7; Eph. iii. 10.

world was the work of a manifold group, that God was only partially the Maker of so imperfect a being as man. This seemed to him manifest in the expression in which the Hebrew Scripture narrates man's creation.[1] "Rightly is God represented as saying to His subordinates, to whom He deputed the formation of the mortal part of the soul, 'Let us make man in order that the blessings of the soul might be referred to him, its evils to others.'" Something within man, he thought, was created by God, but it would not be true to say that God created him. Man, as he lives in this world, is connected with God only by intermediate emanations; the Divine influence is weakened when it reaches him as that of a magnet through a succession of iron rings.[2] His creator is connected with the Divine world, but is not God. The very conception of creation implies degeneracy—an un-Jewish thought, but yet the refuge of a true Jew, confronted with the omnipotent seduction of Greek culture, under the rule of Rome.[3]

A creator belonging to the world not of the One but

---

[1] Philo, De Confusione Linguarum. See also a passage in "De Profugis," where he imitates a similar passage in the "Timæus" of Plato. Of the *true* man God is the Creator, but not of man so far as he is evil.

[2] *Ibid.*, De Mundi Opificio, 48.

[3] The Gnostical idea of the Creation throws a vivid light on the meaning of the Incarnation. Irenæus, summarizing the Gnostical view of man's creation, says, Ὅτε ἠθέλησιν ἐπιδεῖξαι αὐτὸν (when God willed to reveal Himself), τοῦτο ἄνθρωπος ἐλεχθε (Iren., i. 12, 3). The creation of man was effected through the agency of the Demiurgus, who was not aware that he was copying anything higher than himself, and who was, like Pygmalion, seized with awe at the result. Clement inverts the comparison, καὶ ὥσπερ φόβος ἐπὶ ἐκείνου τοῦ πλάσματος ὑπῆρξε τοῖς ἀγγέλοις, ὅτε μείζονα ἐφθέγξατο τῆς πλάσεως, διὰ τὸν ἀόρατον ἐν αὐτῷ σπέρμα δεδωκότα, τὴν ἄνωθεν οὐσίαν, &c.; so works of art strike their authors with a sort of awe (Strom., ii. 375). This element is supposed to be present in Prophecy. The Demiurgus inspires the prophets of Israel, but he unawares chooses out for this purpose men in whom is a seed of the spiritual life, and who therefore stand higher than himself. John the Baptist "rejoiceth greatly at the Bridegroom's voice" as a representative of the Demiurgus (Clem., Strom., ii. 409).

the Many, and therefore fallible and imperfect—a material in which the germs óf evil were inextricably mixed
—a seed of a loftier nature, divine and imperishable—
these are the three ideas out of which Gnosticism devised a new mythology, satisfying to the needs of the
age. It branched out into a number of separate directions and gave rise to different groups of thought. But
difference between these theories was unimportant in
comparison with their resemblance. They all inter-
posed a long series of Emanations between God and
the Creator; they all assumed an eternal substratum of
creation, independent of the will of God, and an ignorant and blundering Creator, whose mischievous, restless
activity had bridged the gulf separating the world of
Unity or Spirit from the world of mere multiplicity
or matter; and had thus conferred upon this realm a
principle of development which should never have
passed into union with it. And further, all recognized that while Nature is the mere result of this
ignorant activity, in Man there is something higher.
He is the work of the Creator, so far as his bodily
organism, and what we should call his mind, is concerned; but a higher influence has been shed upon the
work, unconsciously to the worker; it is as with those
creations of genius embodying inspiration which their
author dreamt not of, and expressing ideas which seem
to come rather through than from the mind that gives
them shape. The world is the mistake of a mighty
blunderer, but Man has a loftier origin. Like the royal
nursling of the wolf, he owns a lineage elevated far above
all that surrounds him, he dwells as an exile in the only
home he knows, and awaits a mysterious recall to regions
at once strange and yet in some sense familiar. The
Creator, so superior to Man in Power, is in the true
qualities of his inmost being distinctly his inferior. He

is the author of Man so far as Man belongs to the realm of Nature, of which the Demiurgus is indeed the type and representative; but a seed from a higher region is hidden in the nature of Man, and so far he is a revelation to the Spirit of Nature of that which lies beyond and above him, a revelation perfected in the Divine Man— complete only when the Redeemer is revealed to the Creator.[1]

" I feel that I am happier than I know," says Milton's Adam. The Gnostical creator of Adam might have felt that he was greater than he knew. He was the magnified ideal of genius or inspiration, that magic power by which the mind is enabled to transcend its own boundaries, and become the expression and instrument of an influence larger than itself. Its work may be larger than itself, for a higher power is active within it, often unconsciously to the agent. The Jew at Alexandria had already been taught to look for an inspiration in all his deepest utterance, which revealed to him a world beyond himself. "Often," says Philo,[2] " I have found my mind entirely empty and barren when I wished to write, and was obliged to retire without leaving a finished sentence. And often, on the other hand, coming quite empty, I have suddenly been full, thoughts pouring upon me like rain, so that, as by a divine inspiration, I prophesied, and became ignorant of all things around me and of myself." What the Jew felt of himself the Gnostic believed of the Creator. The act of creation was in both cases the revelation of a

---

[1] Αὐτὸν τὸν ἄρχοντα ἐπακούσαντα τὴν φάσιν τοῦ διακονουμένου πνεύματος, ἐκπλαγῆναί τῷ θεάματι παρ' ἐλπίδας εὐαγγελισμένον (Clem., Strom., ii. p. 375). The saying which produced this result is said to be that communicated to Christ at the moment of the descent of the Holy Spirit; and the θεάμα was the glorified appearance of Christ, or perhaps the sight of the dove. The mission of Christ was thus a Gospel for the Demiurgus, who thus hopes for deliverance from the burdensome government of the world.

[2] De Migratione Abrahami.

Higher One. " Let there be light" was not a command, but a prayer from this ignorant blunderer to a Supreme Enlightener. " I am God, and there is none beside me," was an empty boast or a passionate lament, calling forth the revelation from a higher source—a consolation or a rebuke, and perhaps both, as it relieved him from responsibility for the world which he had made. " Speak not falsely, for above thee is the Father of all, and not him alone." How impressive is the dream as a parable of all the highest human work, as a warning against that in man which seeks to be as God, and an encouragement to all that within him which seeks to discover the work of God ! A vision full of instruction for all time as to the meaning of the least imperfect work of Man came to the generation which first conceived it as a clue to all that was imperfect in the work of God.

Nor are the dreams of these forgotten thinkers without their message to our own age ; in some respects they are specially worthy of the attention of our own generation. In them, as they confronted their orthodox opponents, we may discern the first collision of those ideas which we know as Evolution and Creation. The question between the two antagonists was, Is the world the result of an act of Will, or of a process of development independent of Will ? Is it Nature, or God, with whom man has to do ? Beneath all difference of dialect, of illustration, of assumption, the issue was fundamentally the same then as now. They personified Nature, and called it the Demiurgus. We leave it an abstraction ; but when both conceptions are brought into contrast with Divine Will, we see that they are closely akin. The Demiurgus creates the world, but he works upon an existent material ; he is ignorant of the true nature of his work. Creation thus understood is indistinguishable from what we have learnt to call Evolution. "Speak not falsely, for above Nature is the Father of all," seems the fragment from some parable specially devised for a generation which has committed itself to the assertion that in Nature is the Supreme.

When we come to realize the vast influence for evil that lies in ignorant activity, we shall perhaps be surprised, not that this explanation of Evil ever existed, but that it was so much forgotten. It has been revived by an isolated thinker, here and there; and it is curious to reflect that one of those who has seemed most ready for such an ideal impressed his contemporaries as a typical specimen of Atheism. James Mill[1] considered that the aspect of the world was not hostile to one hypothesis of creation; the order of the Universe might, he thought, be conceived as the work of a mighty, but not almighty artist; powers greater than those of man, but not dissimilar to those of man, might be conceived as employed in the construction of this world, and its disasters and failures might conceivably be regarded with a certain sympathy for the Being who was responsible for it, but not wholly responsible for them. We only need to combine such a notion with belief in the malignity of matter to leave space for any amount of evil in the world. It is true that we cannot combine it with that belief which the Gnostics held and Mill rejected. We cannot make room for God behind the blundering Creator, so as to explain why he permitted the elaboration of the evil thing that was to result in further evil. But it is not a small thing that Divine rule should be relieved from responsibility for evil in the same way as human rule is. "An Analogy of Religion to the course of Nature" is always an "Aid to Faith." Throughout the Roman world men every day were accustomed to the ills which

---

[1] See the Autobiography of his son.

were due to the crimes of a subordinate ruler. Cæsar
was guiltless of much that his ministers imposed on their
people. The Roman world in the first ages of Christianity gave just such a combination of the One and the
Many as the Gnostics imagined for the Divine world,
and satisfied the mind of the age with such a harmony
between its inward and outward circumstances as men
constantly mistake for an explanation of both. As a
matter of fact, the worst subordinate might be a ruler
preferable to Cæsar; but when we see how St. Paul
could speak of the dominion of Nero,[1] we must feel that
oneness of rule is an ideal so favourable to all excellence
that it cannot be dissociated from it even by the follies
and crimes of the worst of mankind. And although to
us it is evident that if Cæsar had been omnipotent he
would have been guilty of all that was performed by his
agents, this inference did not trouble the contemporaries
of the Gnostics. Men are slow to perceive an ultimate
difficulty. They state their perplexities in many various
forms before they perceive that they are taking a paraphrase for an answer. They build up long series of the
explanations that move a difficulty one step backwards
before they discover that this retrogression has left the
original difficulty undiminished. And long phases of the
life of thought are sometimes occupied with this translation of some problem into another dialect, under the
belief that it has thus found its solution.

The world began to believe in the Will of God eighteen
hundred years ago, when the nation which had always
believed in it gained an intelligible voice, and when for
the first time the world was one. But men began to
believe in it and to question it at once. The Creator
made the world as a product of Will, but he himself was
conceived of, again and again, as a product of a long

[1] Romans xiii. 1–7.

process of Evolution by which the Spirit approaches
Matter; he was for the Gnostics what man was for the
modern Evolutionists; he was no more than man on a
grander scale, modifying the conditions in which he finds
himself, but not in any true sense an originator of them.
He moulds, he produces, he manages, he creates as the
artist creates, but according to our idea of the word
creation when it is applied to the world, he creates
nothing. We have said that according to the Greek
view there was no more reason that the world should be
perfect than that the Iliad should be perfect, but in fact
there was less. The analogy for the Demiurgus was
rather with Phidias than Homer; he had to use intract-
able material; he worked, as it has been finely said of
the sculptor, with a material which hid his thought.
The Demiurgus, finding formless matter and a disorderly
movement, and leaving an organized Universe and a
set of Divine beings to whom he deputed the creation
of mortal man, left things better than he found them;
he put order in the place of disorder; he reflected on
a colossal scale the work of man in face of a rude
nature, and converted that which was the mere negation of Spirit into an expression of his own artistic,
orderly, harmonious influence. He did as a man does
who, finding a shapeless block of stone, leaves a statue.
But he could only work upon what he found; he did the
best with it; but the best was necessarily tinged with
imperfection, and in the new light falling on the world,
imperfection deepened into evil.

This Græco-Judæic theory of the Origin of Evil would
appear an answer to the perplexities of the world only
to those who confront its perplexities for the first time.
We have been taught by a long series of vain efforts,
that when men seek to know why God made the world
as it is, they are seeking to get behind all the con-

ditions of knowledge. We see that all which explains to us the reason for an earthly ruler choosing any evil is that he must choose some evil, and that when this explanation is cut off from us, there is nothing for it but to confess that we confront the inexplicable. If we start with disorder, we can account for evil. The mind seeks cause only, not reason; asks how the world was developed, not why it was created as it is. We can with difficulty represent to ourselves the condition of those who *for the first time* confronted the belief that the seed of all things lies in the determination of a Mind. We at the present day are familiar with the reasoning of those who have rejected such a belief. But for some purposes those who deny are nearer to those who assert than they are to those who have never conceived of the question at issue. The men of that age never really conceived of what we mean by Creation; the Greek influence was too strong. None who suppose the Creator to have worked upon a pre-existing substratum can believe in Omnipotence; if God has always confronted a lifeless sharer of His own eternity, if there is something that He cannot destroy, His power is bounded. As long as Divine power was supposed to be thus limited, the perplexity of Evil was hidden from the minds of men; and the lingering influence of this view gave an illogical satisfaction to feeling, after it had lost its legitimate hold on thought.

A view which, under the test of a severe Logic, merely moves the difficulty a little backwards, may give the spirit of man all the explanation that it is capable of receiving. It is a deep instinct in the human heart which welcomes any teaching implying, as Gnosticism did, that man's existence in this world is by itself inexplicable. Hope is ready to spring up in the heart on any permission to regard the life of the world as a fragment.

Whenever any form of religion has helped to the satisfaction of that craving which seeks to be assured of the
existence of the Unknown—whenever suggestions are
brought forward which open vistas beyond the life of
man, representing the career either of the individual or
of humanity as an episode in some larger whole, there
Hope finds room to grow.   No other promise so stirs
our human nature as that of *Redemption*.   That pain is
sent and wrong permitted in order to teach the blessing
of healing and of forgiveness, is no answer to the child
who asks why Almighty God could not give the good
without the ill.   But the discovery that some kinds of
blessedness are linked with evil provides a dynamic
impulse in dealing with the evils of the world.   Those
can strive against them best who see some meaning in
them ; to think evils all evil is to feel them irresistible.
The paradox to logic is a victory for life, and as man
seeks to be a Redeemer, he ceases to ask why the world
needs redemption.

    This is a truth for every age, and in a certain sense
and in a certain degree it comes fresh to every age.
But it came home to the age in which Christianity was
born with a force which it could possess for none later.
To that age Redemption was a new idea.   The world
penetrated by Greek thought knew it not.   We, looking back on eighteen hundred years during which men
have professed to believe it, and to a great extent really
have believed and acted on it, have found that any such
embodiment of this ideal as this world presents must be
confessed to be disappointing ; its influence on character
has not given all it seemed to promise, or after eighteen
Christian centuries man would not be what he is.   But
it arose to the contemporaries of the Gnostics as a new
hope ; and among the fragments of Gnostic writing preserved to us in the polemic refutation of the Orthodox,

we find thoughts strangely familiar to Christian ears, expressed with the mingled awkwardness and freshness of a new suggestion. The joy with which Dante describes the souls in Purgatory as welcoming the cleansing pangs of suffering should be, they thought, the animating feeling of all who suffered, even of those who from the world's point of view seemed to suffer unjustly. The world is our Purgatory, and all pain is a heavenly promise. The most perplexing dispensation of earthly events is to be explained really by the need of purification visible only to God, who can call on no soul to suffer that He does not seek to elevate and purify. The sufferings of the world were a proof of redeeming energy, for they could have no other meaning under the dominion of God. And this faith in God implies a faith in man, who was made in His image. The soul of man is invaded by an unseen crowd, through whose lawless sojourn it is filled with pollution, "being like a tavern where all is damaged and defiled by the disorderly dealings of men who take no care of what is not their own;" but they come as mere invaders; and the soul polluted by them shall become holy and resplendent through the influence of the One. There will be a time, says a Gnostic teacher,[1] when those who oppose themselves to "that great and holy Will" shall discover that they have resisted it not in strength, but in weakness and error; when the evil of this world shall be brought to an end, the purpose of purification for which it was created being fulfilled; when old things shall pass away, and all things become new. "And at the establishment of that new world all evil motions will cease, and all rebellions will be brought to an end, and the foolish will be persuaded, and deficiencies

---

[1] This is ascribed to Bardesanes, who may be regarded as the most Christian of the Gnostics. The first quotation is from Valentinus, in whom is expressed the Platonic element of Gnosticism.

will be filled up, and there will be peace and safety by
the gift of Him who is Lord of all Natures."

Gnosticism, embodying as it does the new idea of
Redemption, must be regarded as an imperfect Dualism.
The conception of Nature personified in the Demiurgus,
intervening between Matter and Spirit, essentially embodies a protest against the idea of a blank antagonism
of good and evil.   We thus see all being under a threefold aspect, the good and the bad corresponding to the
realms of Spirit and Matter, and between them the intermediate world of Nature, which was associated with
either side according to the varying point of view.   God
is the Fountain of Unity, and Spirit bears the impress
of that oneness which is complete alone in Him.   His
complete antithesis is the world of dead Matter, in which
Unity is impossible, the world of mere multiplicity, of
confusion opposite to God.   In the midst is the intermediate world of physical life which we know as Nature.
Corresponding to this threefold division of the universe it
was believed there was a threefold division of humanity.
There were some spiritual men—men who belonged
wholly to the realm of Order, of Unity, whose transit
through the confusion of material existence was a mere
excursion into a foreign country ; there were also material men, beings belonging wholly to this realm of Disorder, and incapable of ascending to the realm of Spirit ;
and there was an intermediate race, the natural men,
capable of sinking to the lower or rising to the higher
spheres—occupying, in fact, just that position of choice
which the ordinary view assigns to the whole human
race.   Or, again, these three divisions were applied not
quantitatively to the human race, but qualitatively to
every individual ; in every man, it was said, there was a
spiritual man—a germ of life and principle of immortality,
a seed of God and spark of Divine fire given from the

realms above the Creator ; secondly, a physical or animal man, *i.e.*, the soul, the work of the Creator ; thirdly, material man, the seat of passion, a nature doomed to perish. Gnosticism is thus an incomplete dualism ; it is dualism diluted by the Greek reluctance to confront Evil, softened by the Greek reverence for Nature, which it commemorates in its divine, though ignorant, impersonation of Nature. As such it tends towards a more complete dualism, in which the ignorant Creator, and that whole natural region which is his domain, should disappear, and the world of Spirit should stand face to face with the world of Matter, as Good to Evil.

In truth, as soon as man felt the evil of the world an oppressive perplexity, it was quite as difficult to conceive why a mighty being should have made the world at all as why an almighty one should not have made it better than it is. The act of Creation was the development and organization of that which, if such a thing were possible, had better have been destroyed ; from this point of view the Creator is confused with the Adversary. Here we pass from Greek soil to that of the ancient foe of Greece ; we feel the influence of Persian dualism stealing in beyond the personality of the Platonic Demiurgus ;[1] we lose all Hellenic influence, and feel ourselves overshadowed by some Oriental system in which the keynote is no longer the danger of ignorant activity, the imperfection of the world, but the inherent evil of matter, the primal antagonism of good and evil. The passage from Gnosticism to Manichæanism is the logical completion of this incomplete Dualism. The ancient creed of Persia (at this time lately revived)[2] mingled its

---

[1] The trace of Persian influence is also discernible in Gnosticism, but more faintly.

[2] Mani began to teach about A.D. 270. Zoroastrianism had been revived by Ardisheer 226 B.C. It is said to be the only real revival of an ancient religion.

X

influence with the new faith of Judæa. The antithesis
of Light and Darkness, with all the associations of its
earlier symbolism, pressed in as it were upon the antithesis of spirit and matter, and relegated the material
world to the dominion of an evil being.[1] The Creator
was no longer a Supreme Artist, reducing the imperfection of the world to its minimum ; he gave form and coherence to that which properly belongs to the dominion
of Ahriman. It is indeed a curious inconsequence, when
once the personal and the material realms are divided as
the realms respectively of good and evil, to blur this
antithesis by bringing in a personal representative of
evil ; but the inconsequence is full of instruction. The
explanation of Evil, it was urged sometimes even by
those who did not see that this plea rendered futile every
word of their argument, must necessarily partake in the
confusion of evil. This further development was neces-
sitated by the increased hold which Christianity had
gained upon all thought. Evil could no longer be adequately symbolized, as in Platonic thought, by that which
dilutes and deadens good. Since Plato the idea of Redemption had arisen on the world. The Divine influence
had come into a new relation to evil; men saw it not
as that which stood aloof from what was imperfect, but
as that which opposed itself to what was wrong. The
new idea suggested an antagonist, as the old had suggested an obstacle. But this moral scheme embodied
old and new in an illogical compromise, keeping the
obstacle and adding the antagonist. The principle of
disorderly movement, which seemed dominant in the
material world until men knew that orderly movement
is dominant there, became incarnate in a dark indistinct -

---

[1] This account is taken mainly from two works, Beausobre, Hist. Critique de
Manichée, a storehouse of learning on the subject ; "Mani," by Gustav Flügel,
an account of a fragment from an Arabic manuscript of the tenth century.

being, and Satan appears as the animating spirit of the world of matter, which thus becomes identified with the world of sin. Thus Ormazd and Ahriman confront each other once more, and the primal antithesis of light and darkness returns with fresh associations, and with the old meaning confused by them.

The strange uncouth religion which we know as Manichæanism was the consummation of that tendency towards a Dualism diluted in the Gnostic systems, the natural or psychical region having vanished, and the worlds of good and evil confronting each other in a confused symbolism, mixing up antagonism of light and darkness with that of spirit and matter, so that the contrasted worlds of spirit and matter both occupied space, as the worlds of light and darkness might do. Some internal confusion brought the race of darkness near to the limits of the race of light, and with what is surely a strange inconsistency—for is not the desire of good itself good?—they were filled with a desire to possess this new world suddenly made known to them. In the conflict which ensued Light, or Spirit, was somehow mixed with Darkness, or Matter—it was, says the grotesque allegory, swallowed by the evil race, and the "primal man," called into existence to do battle with these hosts of darkness, suffered a temporary defeat, and was detained in this lower region till delivered by the intervention of a higher Being, the "Living Spirit," or the "Friend of Light." Through this mysterious warfare of the powers of good and evil a seed of the higher life had fallen into the dark world of Matter, and creation is an apparatus for repairing this calamity and recovering the treasure robbed by the evil powers; creative energy is a kind of ransom paid by the world of Spirit to the world of Matter, and marks an episodic confusion in the eternity of distinct dualism from which this mixed world began and towards which it tends. Thus the Creation is here also the result of the Fall. The world of Spirit was un-contaminated by any contact with the world of Matter at the beginning of the scheme which we call Nature, and shall be so again at its end. Nature is the ceaseless martyrdom of Soul, but its martyrdom is its deliverance. Every seed that breaks from the bosom of the dark Earth is an expression of the yearning after escape that pervades the whole world of Growth; the last sigh of the dying is the consummation. The drama of Redemption is represented in a parable which reaches us through the citation of scornful opponents, but even so does not wholly lose its poetry. The waxing of the Moon painted to the Manichæans the gradual filling of a bark with the souls of the departed; when her load was full she bore them to the Sun. And these stages of the departure from the dark world are also stages of purification; in the Moon the death-freed soul undergoes a purification by water, in the Sun by fire; and this gradual trans-ference of the heavenly freight to the region of light repairs the original confusion of Matter and Spirit. When at last this, the last particle of Soul, is disen-tangled from the dark world into which it has fallen, a vast conflagration is to burst forth, which will consume this universe, now a mere husk from which the fruit has been extracted. It endures only as a medium between the dark world of Matter and the bright world of Spirit; when a medium is no longer needed it is to be destroyed as useless lumber. The Creation is a necessary misfortune; it is, to use the metaphor of an orthodox opponent, as it were, the amputation of a limb —a disastrous measure taken only to avert a still greater disaster. The final conflagration is to be the reversal of the original confusion of good and evil. Life, as we see it here, may be regarded as the hostage of a Divine race, held by its deadly foe and ransomed at the price of all this organization given to the material universe which we know as Nature.

Nothing can be more unlike the active, cheerful, hopeful spirit of Zoroastrianism than the timid, scrupulous, pessimistic theory of the world's origin which here appears as its progeny. In place of the energetic spirit of the early belief, which gives honour to industry, which reverences marriage, which stirs everywhere a hopeful activity, we have a timid, scrupulous quietism, a superstitious reverence for all lower forms of life, a dread of all that tends to new life. A new birth is a misfortune analogous to that primæval blending of the worlds of Spirit and of Matter which led to the act of Creation ; death commemorates the escape of Spirit from the chains of Matter. The ideal life, therefore, must hold itself aloof from marriage ; all that tends towards the act by which Man sanctions and perpetuates the indwelling of Spirit in Matter is evil. This ideal makes the centre of a new moral code ; it was soon to disguise itself as Christianity, and in that shape to influence all thought, even down to our own day. But whence its moral contrast to that creed of the past with which it stands in a relation equally close and unquestionable ? Why is the new Dualism in spirit and feeling so unlike the old ?

Because between the dawn of the Persian faith and the attempt of Mani to harmonize it with Christianity a world had come and gone. Zoroastrianism arose in the fresh youth of the world. Manichæanism was the product of the Age of Death. The antithesis of light and darkness, the most striking contrast of the natural world, is in a dawning civilization the natural expression of the contrast of good and evil. It passes easily into the antithesis of Spirit and Matter, and yet with that change its whole meaning is gone. We have quitted the realm of sense for the realm of metaphysics. Darkness to these early races was evil, but Darkness disappeared to make way for Light. Matter was a recondite symbol for evil, and Matter never disappeared to make way for Spirit. The change of symbolism corresponds to an entire change of sentiment. Manichæanism was Zoroastrianism remodelled as an answer to the question, Whence comes Evil? The spirit of that early religion was opposed to anything which takes its starting-point from such a question. But Christianity came into a world overshadowed by the problem, and its struggle with Manichæanism was recorded partly by an acceptance, and partly by a vehement rejection of the Manichæan solution. It was in this form that the vague speculations whose history we are endeavouring to trace were mirrored in the great mind of Augustine, and through his genius they influenced the whole development of religion, and we may add of irreligion. Augustine was first an adherent and then a fierce enemy of Manichæanism, and in him are gathered up those tendencies both of direct influence and of reaction which Manichæanism has left permanently stamped upon Christianity.

The spirit which opposes all natural impulse is a mighty factor in the evolution of moral life. It does more than any other to decide on the character of Posterity. If Virtue mean resistance to Nature, its home is in the cloister. The spiritual man refuses the name of father, and those alone bear onwards the inheritance of humanity who turn from the ideal of Christian purity. The doctrine that Creation was but the prelude to a Fall—even when it disentangled itself from that elder view which made it the result of a fall—this doctrine was commemorated in a profound suspicion of all those impulses by which man becomes in his turn Creator; in an arduous effort after that life which knows nothing of the blending of the spiritual and the material, and endeavours to make man lead the life of spirit here on earth, while it abandons the natural human life to irreligious men, and leaves the world to be peopled by their descendants.

And this, in fact, was the legacy of Manichæanism to its triumphant foe. Manichæans were persecuted, but Manichæanism prevailed. Christians would not allow that the Fall was a superhuman event anterior to the Creation, but they more and more transfigured the simple story of Genesis with supernatural issues, and made the actual constitution of things a consequence of the Fall. What does it signify that God saw all that He had made as very good, if this heavenly creation is relegated to some bygone phase of life, and the world *now* stands under the ban of God's reprobation. Men believed that God made the world, but they behaved as if it were made by a blundering Demiurgus; their aspirations, their condemnations, would have gained coherence and justification if they had been allied with an intellectual scheme which recognized it as a disaster that Spirits ever entered on their tenements of clay. The wide remoteness, the eternal distinction, of spiritual men from all others was becoming more and more a canon of Christian orthodoxy; and although it was a heresy to believe in an embodied Spirit of Nature separate from God, and interposing his organizing power between the sullying world of Matter and the Divine purity, it was more and more the teaching of Christian orthodoxy that all the instincts of Nature were allied with evil. The new creed embodied for a time all that was darkest in the religion of Dualism, and when again the belief of a primal Unity returned as the Spirit of Science, the two beliefs stood face to face as deadly foes, and the battle cannot yet be said to be ended.

CHAPTER VIII.

THE FALL OF MAN.

THE science of our day has taught us to regard the fact of balanced movement as a clue to the most important laws of the visible world. "The imponderable agencies" of an earlier generation; light, heat, and electricity—the metaphysic aspect of a fading polytheism—are for us translated into the positive conception of the swing of atoms; we have exchanged the belief in mystic entities for the idea of that change of place which is the only change we can imagine in the material world. All the most impressive forces of the material universe are explained, so far as they are explained at all, by the rhythm of vibration;[1] when Physical Science has brought us to this point she has reached her Ultima Thule; our next step must be in the realm of metaphysics.

> "What if earth
> Be but the shadow of Heaven, and things in each
> To other like?"

asks the angel who in "Paradise Lost" expounds the system of the world, and the question must often be echoed by students seeking to follow in his track. If there be a law common to the world without and the world within—to the mysterious cause of sensation which we term matter, and to the mind which feels sensation

---

[1] This idea has been worked out by Sara S. Hennell in her "Present Religion."

and originates thought—it is this which in our day has taken such wide extension, and shown us that which makes all else visible as in itself the rush hither and thither of invisible atoms, swaying in rhythmic balance. The scientific interpretation of Light gives a clue to the meaning of Truth, as it is mirrored in human minds. The balanced swing, which gives us the vision of the outward world, represents to us that mental attitude by which we discern the world within ; pause, immobility, is unknown to either region. The history of thought is a continual exhibition of the incapacity of the human intellect to express in any single statement more than half of a truth. Every perplexity which has deeply stirred the human heart seems to need two opposite answers; and for finite beings Truth means rhythmic movement. The spirit which bids us pause at any single vision is that which formerly promised Adam and Eve, " Ye shall be as Gods, knowing good and evil." God knows *at once* what we can know only in successive glimpses at the world of reality ; for us revelation itself implies change of attitude, and there is no conviction that will not become error if, in our attention to it, we stiffen into immobility and lose the palpitating throb, which is indeed the very pulse of mental life.

If this be true of all thought, it is more eminently true of thought which deals with Evil. In this realm of confusion, if nowhere else, Thought moves only by oscillation. No single view can be called true. Wherever we contemplate moral Evil we see something which seems to contain within itself a contradiction, which demands two statements, irreconcilable by logic. Perhaps there never was a crime committed since the world began which would not, to some mind, have taken the aspect of disaster. Certainly there are very few crimes in which the element of disaster can be forgotten without injustice. When we have said all about an action that the Judge cares to hear, we have yet to tell all that, for the ear of sympathy, makes up the true description of that action. The truth is not in either of these mental points of view, nor in a pause at the intermediate point of view, but in a free movement between them. Human justice has no other meaning than a true apprehension of the moment to remember both the inevitable and the voluntary element in wrong; what Divine justice is we must wait to know. At times the idea of responsibility must be discarded from the mind of those who have the firmest belief in human responsibility ; attention must be concentrated solely on the element of the inevitable in human action. And again, no one will be just who *cannot* forget this element. There are moments in which the idea of responsibility flashes through the web of circumstance, and bursts on the intellectual vision of those who have no belief in it ; nay, we may even say that at such moments it is felt that *s'il n'existe pas, il faut l'inventer.* Wherever a man refuses to accept this change of aspect in human guilt—wherever he stiffens into the contemplation of either the circumstance or the choice in which it has arisen—there, however consistent his actions may be with a single point of view, the heart of his fellow-men will fail to recognize justice.

This is not less true for the view that humanity has taken of Evil than for the view that a man takes of wrong. But the race does not err as the individual does ; that vibratory movement of attention which is the duty of individuals makes up the history of moral thought. We have seen how the Greek mind explained the existence of Evil by the very fact of the existence of *things ;* how it emphasized the involuntary, the excusable in all human error and crime, by saying that Evil resides in matter. When we turn to the other moment of the vibration, and note how the Jew, and still more the Gentile mind formed on Jewish belief, explained all evil by the very fact of the existence of *persons*, we realize afresh (what we have to remember in all controversy) that the vibration is never simple. The antithesis is never complete. What one man or one party asserts is not exactly what the other denies ; men are divided not by accepting different answers to the same questions, but by asking different questions. Still, we shall find that no two theories are nearer being antithetic than that Greek belief in the Evil resident in matter—the symbol of necessity, the type of all Evil to the liberty-loving race —and the belief evolved in the acceptance by the world of the Hebrew account of Creation and the Hebrew horror of sin, that the only evil was the choice of Evil.

The belief that the very constitution of our spiritual nature implies the possibility of Evil, was a natural re-action from the belief that the very constitution of our material environment implies the existence of Evil. We see how Personality was made an answer to the un-answerable problem only when we see how the very opposite of Personality had at first filled the place. We understand best the theory that finds the origin of Evil in a choice that may vary at any moment when we compare it with the view against which it was a recoil —that Evil was a definite tangible reality, a thing of a certain fixed compass and amount, which might be shut in within its own limits, and disentangled from its opposite, but which even by Omnipotence could not be destroyed. There can be no reaction more inevitable than that from the spirit which sees in matter the source of Evil, to that which sees the source of Evil in human choice. It was a natural thing to see Evil as the shadow of Liberty, when men had for long seen Evil as the shadow of Necessity.

This belief was specially appropriate to a particular age. But it is the natural refuge at all times for a mind distracted by a view of the eternal opposites, Evil and God. Men find in actual experience that Evil does bring forth a good which, so far as they can see, could never be brought forth without Evil. It is impossible to conceive of courage being exhibited or developed in the midst of safety, of honesty in the owner of boundless wealth, of fortitude amid luxury, of generosity in one who had no opportunity of self-sacrifice. If we are to have any virtues, we must have danger, privation, hardship, difficulty. "A brave man" is an expression that implies peril; we cannot say that any one has shown great patience without also informing our hearer that he or she has suffered great pain ; we could never call any one unselfish who had never been in a position where he might choose the unpleasant for himself in order that he might leave the pleasant for his neighbour. Virtue could no more exist without Evil than light without shadow ; and if Virtue be the true end of Man's being, it was worth the price of its opposite being called into existence at the same time with itself. We cannot invest an angel with the attributes of a hero unless we are prepared to see him converted to a Satan ; and if we are to imagine a hero in the Garden of Eden, we must find the Tempter there.

This belief has always been the refuge of perplexity, and probably it will still dawn upon many a troubled spirit as a discovery that lightens the pressure of the world's great mystery, and points to a possible solution. But in the infancy of Christianity it emerged into a pre-dominance it can surely never regain. We have seen how large a part of the moral energy of men was occupied in the contemplation of evil just at the time when the message of the Jew proclaimed that "God saw all that

He had made, and that it was very good." Evil being the prominent reality to the mind of the age, they had to make room for the belief in a primal excellence, not only as the dim dream of a golden age such as always haunted humanity, and most in its childhood, but in that distinct and emphatic narration with which the Jew described the world as the work of God ; and as the belief in a Fall is the other half of the belief in a golden age, this also came into a new distinctness and a much greater prominence. We may say that the early Christian believed in the Fall as the Jew believed in the Creation. Both believed both, but the change of proportion made the belief itself a different thing. From the collision of Greek and Jewish thought an idea that on each side separately was faint and dim took vast proportions and clear-cut definiteness, and a whole system of theology was elaborated, finding its centre and its form in the belief of a primal degeneration. The Greek had believed in a Fall ; the thought of Greece was haunted by the view of this life on earth as the Purgatory of the soul, the dream that each man who enters on it has fallen from a Paradise to which he may hope to return. The history of the legendary Adam is reproduced in the vision of Plato [1] by the life of every son of man who enters on his earthly career shackled by a supernatural choice, as every son of Adam, according to a later theology, by original sin. Or else there has been a fall of humanity;[2] the race started aright, but either by a sudden change of direction or by a gradual decay it has turned from good to evil, and things are not as they were ; anyhow, man now inhabits a fallen world.

Again, on the page of the Hebrew Scriptures we may find this same varying narrative of degeneration. The

[1] In the myth at the end of the "Republic."
[2] In the "Politicus."

Fall of Adam is but a faint adumbration of the apostasy
of Israel; in varied forms we return upon it, for the
idea immediately grows dim, is forgotten, and needs to
be repeated.[1] The idea of an Omnipotent Holiness was
ever present to the Jew; the idea of human guilt was
only now and then summoned to his mind as the evil
world demanded such a conception. A single page of
the Hebrew Scriptures contains the narrative of the
Fall; the belief that there is no evil but in rebellion
against a Holy Will is stamped on every page. When
Evil became as real as God the proportion of these ideas
was inverted. The doctrine of human corruption was
the product of an age in which any theory that made it
possible to believe both in Evil and God was welcomed
as the satisfaction of its greatest need. The Greek
view, which had made some approach towards this re-
conciliation through the hypothesis of the eternity of
Matter, had become impossible; and the natural recourse
was to its extreme opposite. Evil had been, as it were,
banished from the world of things by the Jewish belief
in Creation becoming the creed of the world, and could
find refuge only in the world of persons. If God made
the world, the evil in it must be the work of Man.
As the Gnostics thought that evil was inherent in the
nature which is purely unmoral, so their opponents
believed it to be potentially existent in the very nature
of a *moral creature*.[2] Moral goodness, it was thought,

---

[1] Apparently in Gen. vi. 1-5.

[2] A good specimen of this orthodox view, as against the Gnostics, is to
be found in the dialogue " De Libero Arbitrio," ascribed to Methodius. The
dialogue is between an orthodox Christian and a disciple of the Gnostic
Valentinus. Lactantius, " De Ira Dei " (about A.D. 321), says that the answer
to the problem of Evil is very simple—" Nisi prius malum agnoverimus, nec
bonum poterimus agnoscere." See also Clementina, Hom., xviii., xix., where
Peter confutes Simon Magus by this argument. One might multiply these
citations almost indefinitely. Augustine, " De Libero Arbitrio," exhibits the
high-water-mark of this line of thought.

means the choice of good, and the choice of good implies
the existence of evil. The one side traced it to what
we might describe as *thingness*, that which we can only
conceive as the opposite of Personality; the other discovered it within the very core of Personality itself.
Will could have no meaning, it was thought, except as
the choice between good and evil. A man who *could
not* err would be a mere machine; goodness, separated
from all effort, would lose its moral character. To
transfer virtue from Will to Nature would be to annihilate it; it means the *choice of good*, and if we suppose
it in the region behind choice it ceases to exist. In
Nature there was no evil; Nature did not admit of evil.
Will was something of which the very essence was its
capacity of manufacturing evil. Man was created free
to choose between good and evil, though evil did not
exist till he called it into being, for the privilege of
remaining the voluntary subject of God implied the capacity of becoming a rebel against Him.

From various reasons this view has faded from the
vision of our day, and in endeavouring to set it forth
we naturally fall into the past tense. Those who represent the thought-life of our day do not confront the
problem which it aims at solving, and if they did they
would not accept the solution. The idea of Omnipotence has faded from the minds even of many who keep
a belief in God; most persons have come to admit a
doubt whether the word be not altogether misleading.
They see neither of the two primal opposites; God
is hidden behind Natural Law; Evil is resolved into
disaster, mistake, confusion. They see no problem to
solve; they feel no bewildering perplexity to prepare
the mind for an eager bound towards a possible explanation. They see evils on every side, but in the progress
of that science which has made in our century such

gigantic strides they see also the remedy for these evils. There is no attitude of mind more adverse to any speculation on the origin of Evil. The Darwinian theory of the origin of species by natural selection opens a view of the whole working of Evil in the world of Nature by which Evil is seen or supposed to bring forth good. " The survival of the fittest " does not, indeed, mean anything more than " the survival of the fittest to survive ; " the resulting good is good merely from an unmoral point of view. But to minds occupied with the part that Evil has taken in fashioning the world as we see it, it is impossible to enter into the perplexity to which the early Christian view is an answer. They cannot see any problem to solve, and the solution, therefore, is to them unmeaning.

And then, again, those who do feel the perplexity find the answer no longer sufficient. It is possible to imagine a world in which no sin and no wretchedness should exist beyond what should be justified by the virtue and the joy visible by its side, but to say that *this* world is one which we can thus explain is merely to invite attention to its failures. If the world were arranged in order that men might see evil and choose good, it has to be explained why men do, on the whole, see good and choose evil. He who arranges any scheme of probation or education in the hope that those subject to his influence will do one thing when in fact they do another, has made a blunder ; and if it is only reverence for infinite wisdom which is to check this criticism on a plan supposed Divine, that reverence had better check the speculation at its origin.

These difficulties were not felt at the dawn of Christianity as they are now. We have seen how, when the City had perished, and before the Nation was born, the individual life of man emerged into a distinctness

Y

that it never had possessed before, into a separateness that it has not retained. It was not only discerned, its independent capacity was enormously exaggerated. All that belongs to the life of Self was for the moment illuminated by the focal light of exclusive attention. In the ancient world Man knew himself only in relation to the State. In the modern world he knows himself in a much richer variety of relations; and though, for that very reason, the word Self has more meaning as a separate reality than it ever could have in the ancient world, yet still the other elements in this relation are objects exacting of attention. That which is *not* man has a breadth, a distinctness, a stately set of associations with all that is orderly and interesting which before the rise of Physical Science it could not have. It was an important chapter in the history of moral thought when it paused between these two phases of development— when between two continents a narrow isthmus shut in the traveller, and leaving him cut off from all that was external to himself, forced him, for the first time, to study the world within. It was the starting-point of a new phase of moral life. Much which then began has lasted ever since. But also by the very fact that this age was a starting-point, much which characterized it has since passed away. The sense of the completeness of the individual life which we meet first in the writings of the Stoics, and which was absorbed and intensified by early Christianity, is not recognized as true by the mind of our day. In looking back on it through the development of subsequent ages we see it to be an illusion— the inevitable illusion of the first embrace with which men greet a new idea. Man is not free as the Stoic thought him free. " The hand cannot say to the head, ' I have no need of thee.' " That is the warning of the first great man whom the world knows as a Christian, but it was hardly realized in the age which followed the preaching of Paul.

We can say of no other age known to historians as we may of this, that whatever was moral in it was also disintegrating. In subsequent ages Christianity has been a strong influence, to bind or to divide, to weld men into groups, often mutually hostile, but always strongly coherent within themselves. But there was an interval during which Christianity seems rather to blend with the mystic, spiritual tendencies of the world than to present any rallying-ground for a new army. A long life in the second century after Christ might have been occupied in watching vainly for any sign that Christianity was to remould the world. Everywhere something like the new faith was prevalent, but perhaps for this very reason that faith itself was stationary. The life of Christ met an aspiration with a narrative, and translated dim unspoken yearnings into a record of the past; these yearnings it found, and did not create. Everywhere in that day men were craving after the hope of immortality. There must have been such a craving always, but average men had been satisfied, in the ages of the past, with a share in the perennial life of the city; they had hardly cared to ask themselves whether their own life was to be perpetuated in any other way. Whatever hopes were commemorated by the Mysteries, whatever yearnings they half expressed, half satisfied, the true immortality for the Athenian citizen lay in the immortality (as it seemed) of Athens. As this membership withered, a new vista opened, and men became conscious of an infinite possibility of hope and fear within the sphere of their own individuality. They felt stirrings of something within to which this seventy years of mortal life was as a flower-pot to a seedling oak.[1]

[1] A noble spirit, says a writer of this period, watches with satisfaction the

They awoke to a fuller consciousness of instincts which would have been cramped and baffled within such a span of life magnified a hundred times. Men must have felt this always, for it is the experience of humanity; but in the great ages of Greece they had no leisure to attend to what, after all, was more or less of an interruption to the interests of political life. When this political life shrivelled, they had leisure to listen to the whisper that is as much a promise as a demand. They heard the voice as something new, and yet as the explanation of something familiar. Apart from Christianity, they had come to recognize an infinite value in every human soul, to suspect that in this was implied an infinite future. Christianity committed itself to a declaration of this infinite preciousness in a form which could be apprehended from the outside, and translated into a dialect comprehensible to those who had no specially spiritual sympathies. And thus, although it held the germ of closer union and fiercer antagonism than any corporation of antiquity, and was to weld men into groups more strongly cohesive than the republics of Greece or the oligarchy of Rome, its influence for the moment was threatening to all corporate life. It gave the separate life a new importance which must dwarf all else, for a time.

The thoughts of men on the mysterious future beyond the grave appear, in our modern world, to have less influence than we should expect. But we cannot, in comparing the different feelings of those who accept and those who reject a tradition of man's immortality, form any estimate of the difference which that belief made when it was a new thing. We inherit a literature

decay of the body, as the crumbling of prison walls (Maximus of Tyre, Diss., xiii. 5). A French translator (who dedicates his work to the First Consul, as realizing the ideal of Plato) accuses St. John of plagiarizing from Maximus, but no one has suspected Maximus of Christianity.

tinged throughout by this belief; we have absorbed
its influence, of which we cannot divest ourselves even
when we deliberately set aside all that it has taught
mankind to expect. When it first came to be preached
—not as a mystic doctrine to be apprehended by a few,
not as a truth for Philosophers, but as a hope which was
to bring comfort to the ignorant, the degraded, the enslaved—it translated a belief into an anticipation, a lofty
ideal, attainable here and there by an Epictetus or a
Marcus Aurelius, into an announcement significant for
every one. However we may explain it, it remains a
fact that the greatest teacher of the Greeks, as he drank
the hemlock, did not believe so firmly that death opened
to him a boundless future as did the ordinary commonplace man or woman when Christianity was new. The
belief in Immortality, as it existed in the old world, was
an *aristocratic* influence. The classical passage in which
is recorded the high-water-mark of ancient hope in this
direction commemorates the belief that *great* souls cannot
perish with the body.[1] When the hope for a few became
the certain conviction for all, it changed its character; it
was no longer a conception of the destiny of genius or
heroism, but of every individual man and woman. The
heir of immortality gained what the member of the State
had lost—a share in a perennial life. The ephemeral
being had owed his moral dignity to his relation to that
which had seemed immortal. Immortality arose on the
horizon of the Man as its last glow faded from the City.
The Roman sailed round the Mediterranean, and recognized that the cities of the past were not eternal, and with
the same waft of conviction came a compensatory belief,
that Eternity was the heritage of every son of man.[2]

[1] Tac., Life of Agricola, 46:—"Si, ut sapientibus placet, non cum corpore
exstinguantur magnæ animæ."

[2] See the letter of Servius Sulpicius to Cicero, quoted p. 205, and compare
it with the letter of Cicero to Atticus, x. 8 :—"Tempus est, nos de illâ perpetuâ

To men inheriting an unalterable conviction that
Liberty was the ultimate good for man and confronting
a world in which it could not continue to mean citizenship in an independent State, the idea of *Moral Liberty*
came with a sudden and partially illusive splendour.
The orb just visible above the horizon looms larger than
in its mid-day career, and all new ideas are expanded in
an atmosphere of intellectual dawn.   Man, considered as
a member of the State, had found Liberty in his relation to that organic whole which explained and justified
his existence.   This ideal perished when the City was
swallowed up in the Empire ; but the aspirations which
it had nourished remained untouched.   Liberty was still
the word of magic import, though the thing that was
meant by Liberty, on the old ground and in the old
meaning, had become impossible.   Around this symbol
all associations of desire had gathered, and from this
they refused to be separated.   And thus the idea of
Liberty, as it was banished from the domain of Politics,
invaded another region.   It quitted an effete and almost
sterile soil to take root in one which was gathering to
itself all fertilizing influences.   It detached itself from
political life just when political life was shedding its
leaves before its long winter, and grafted itself upon that
individual life which was to waken into fresh vigour

jam, non de hac exiguâ vitâ cogitare." The letter was written B.C. 50. I am
aware that some interpret the passage differently. But compare it with the following extract from the " De Senectute," written five years earlier :—" Equidem non
video, cur, quid ipse sentiam de morte, non audeam vobis dicere " (note the tone
of hesitation, as in the enunciation of a new truth).   " Ego vestros patres . . .
vivere arbitror : et *eam quidem vitam, quæ est sola vita nominanda.*" The
strongly personal form of this expression of belief seems to me to justify what
may be called the Christian interpretation of the letter.   See also the " Somnium
Scipionis."   In another direction, the craving after immortality is well expressed
in a passage of that apocryphal literature which, in many ways, best expresses
the cravings of this age, and which was written about two centuries later—the
vivid description of the supposed Clemens Romanus, in the " Clementina," of
his yearning after a certainty of a future life, and the misery of doubt.

and fertility. In trying to account for the evil of the
world by what we mean by Liberty, we are bringing
together two conceptions which will not fit each other;
the lesser thing shrinks and dwindles in the presence
of the larger. But Liberty, stood in these early ages
undwarfed by the neighbourhood of all that was mightiest. There was nothing that it was not worth confronting to make a Commonwealth free. Why should
it be otherwise for a world ?

This belief that Evil was the shadow of Liberty passed,
as Christianity changed from a hope to what must have
been felt by many a disappointing fulfilment, through
two stages, commensurate with the two stages of the
opposite belief that Evil was the shadow of Necessity.
The blundering Demiurgus of the Gnostics was an embodiment of Nature, a principle of error confused with
Evil as the planet with the constellation immeasurably
remote from it. The antithesis of spirit (as good) and
matter (as evil) was thrown into the background by this
introduction of a spiritual being whose activity was pro-
ductive of Evil. Ignorant activity dealing with Evil is
enough to account, as we see daily, for any extension of
Evil, and whatever multiplies Evil will seem to cause it ;
but Evil must in truth be there first. The Creator of
this dark world was the actual cause of the Evil of the
world, but he was also an emanation from the Divine
Spirit, and could not represent Ahriman. That more
complete form of Dualism for which Gnosticism prepared
the way was more distinctly divided from Christianity,
no longer ranking itself among Christian heresies, but
rather an intermediate form between Christianity and
the lately renovated Persian faith, which seems to have
supplied all that was vital in it. Nevertheless, much
that many generations of men have called Christianity
is the descendant of this forgotten creed. It was an

influence both in its direct infusion of belief, and also in the reaction by which it provoked a new assertion of human responsibility, and gave a new meaning to the Fall.

When Manichæanism began to be an influence in the Christian world a change had taken place which had given the problem of Evil a new significance.[1] While Christians were a despised sect, Redemption was of necessity something that chose out the individual from the world, and left the incorporation of the world in the society of the Redeemed as a great future event which should repeat, on a gigantic scale, the renewal of an individual conversion. When this event had taken its place in the past, and the world went on much as it had done, the problem of Evil had to be re-stated in order to adjust itself to a vast disappointment. Redemption, from an experience, became a dogma; from a hope for the race, the privilege of a minority. The glorious promise of "a new Heaven and a new Earth, wherein dwelleth Righteousness," had to fade into a dim, distant Heaven, attained but by few of those who deemed themselves, and appeared to others, its true heirs. The problem of Evil took a new magnitude; it was not only Evil that had to be explained, but triumphant Evil.

No hope that the world has ever known can have been on a level with that which was felt by Christians when first Christianity became the faith of the world. Something faintly approaching it may possibly have been inspired by the dawn of the French Revolution; perhaps something of the same kind is roused in the minds of many by that triumph of Democracy in our day which the French Revolution at once initiated and

---

[1] The treatise of Clement, "Quis Dives Salvetur," seems to me an expression of the new attitude of Christianity to a *stable world*, as compared with the earlier spirit of waiting for the Lord.

delayed. But never since a despised and persecuted
faith was adopted by the ruler of the Western world
was it possible that a change should create such hope
as was felt by the adherents of that faith, for no change,
since then, has been either so wide-reaching or so deeply
penetrating. We cannot say that at any particular point
of time Europe was Catholic and became Protestant, or
that it was aristocratic and became democratic; but we
may say that at a particular time (though no doubt one
less narrowly limited than is usually supposed) Europe
was Pagan and became Christian. Christianity conquered
in a sense that Protestantism never conquered; it was
always possible for Protestants to attribute the un-
satisfactoriness of Protestant Europe to the hostility of
Catholic Europe; but Christian Europe had no Pagan
Europe to contend with. The misery, the disorder, the
baffling tumult of the last hours of Paganism must have
formed to the eyes of Christians a black background,
against which they were at last to behold the image
of triumphant righteousness. The Church was to rule
the world; the reign of disorder and cruelty must be
past for ever. The disappointment which ensued is
the concentration and quintessence of a feeling that
Christians must share, to some extent, at all times.
A Christian thinker of our own time has expressed
the feeling in words which we may take as its classic
utterance for every time. "The world," says John
Henry Newman, "seems simply to give the lie to that
great truth of which my whole being is full, and the
effect upon me is in consequence as confusing as if
it denied that I am in existence myself. If I looked
into a mirror and did not see my face, I should have
that sort of feeling which actually comes upon me when
I look into this living busy world and see no trace of
the Creator." Man still needs a Saviour, though here

and there men have found a Saviour. The redeemed
soul does not inhabit a redeemed world. Centuries of
familiarity almost take the place of explanation ; we are
so accustomed to contemplate life as it is and the hope
of the Church side by side that we sometimes feel as if
they were reconciled. But no such possibility was open
to men in whose time the Church and the world first
embraced. They saw a world farther even than ours
from the ideal of Redemption, and they looked to see
the ideal of Redemption triumphant. Hence the eclipse
of a great hope darkened all their thought, and the
theories which they bequeathed to posterity were coloured
by the need of explaining what seemed to them the defeat of God.

The Augustinian scheme incorporates a disappointment
without parallel in the world's history in a logical and
coherent system. The universe, on which God looked
and pronounced it very good, had no history but that of
disaster ; the very origin of all human activity was a renunciation of loyalty to the Creator. All that man could
ever know of human activity was stamped with evil, for
the initial act of human activity had been to call evil into
existence, and from that moment man was in bondage
to his own Creation. Thus the Creation itself, if it were
judged as any work of human endeavour, must be en-
titled a gigantic mistake ; the creature was a rebel from
the moment of his existence. The belief which we may
thus describe has lasted almost to our own day. But
it could surely have arisen only in an epoch when
Christianity had just acceded to the government of the
world, and men had seen what it could *not* do.

Then it was that a great change came over the conception of man's responsibility.[1] While supplemented

---

[1] There is an interesting passage in Augustine's treatise, "De Libero
Arbitrio," i., xii. 24, where he seems to set his face for the first time towards

by all those vague anticipations which sprang from the very existence of a world awaiting conversion, the moral freedom of man bore the weight of the world's evil as a mere fact of human consciousness. When the conversion of civilized society, as it was known to the men of that time, brought about no transformation of humanity, a new dimension, as it were, was needed for human failure, and then first it was that the shadow of the Fall, in all its depth, was cast upon the path of Man. Men, it was felt, were imprisoned in evil ; yet Man was made by God. Individual choice was too small a thing to bear the burden of a world's despair. It demanded some vast retrospect of guilt, some Titanic exercise of will, some gigantic overshadowing cloud, reaching far beyond the limits of an individual life. Human beings, here and now, were not free to choose righteousness ; every such choice needed a miracle of Divine grace as its source and explanation. But human Free Will disappeared from the world of the present only to appear in gigantic proportions on the dim cloud-land of a supernatural Past. It was raised to a position of prominence and grandeur which its strongest advocates never ventured to claim for it, either before or since, but it was limited to a mere moment in the infancy of the race. *Man* had been created a free being—free in the wider sense of that word which in classical thought was associated rather with the idea of dominion than of the mere absence of restraint. But Man had chosen to invade the preroga-

the idea of inherited guilt, not in the aspect under which he was to formulate it ultimately, as a corporate heritage of the race, but rather as the dream which Plato seems to have borrowed from Empedocles, of a pre-natal fall from Heaven to Earth. It is a question, he says, if the mind did not live elsewhere before its junction with the body. He was then urging the moral liberty of Man, against the Manichæans, as strenuously as he was afterwards to urge the moral bondage of men against the Pelagians ; but his future path seems to have suddenly opened before him, and this idea to have suggested itself as a meeting-point between the two.

tive of God. He had not been content to remain a Creature; he had chosen to be a Creator, and his Creation was the world of Evil. He had used his power to sell himself, and of course his posterity, into slavery. The typical Man had freedom in a sense that no one has ever claimed freedom for the average Man, but the result of his use of it was bondage for the human race, throughout the whole course of history.[1]

This view of human history gathered up that element which had been the strength of Stoicism, and joined it, as no Stoic had done, to a rational view of human nature as it is. As Plato had expounded the scope of human Knowledge, ignoring its limitations and confusing its boundaries, so had the Stoics expanded the scope of human Will. Plato thought that the knowledge of good involved the choice of good. The Stoics thought that the choice of good involved the annihilation of evil. Plato lived at a time when the drama of history forbade men permanently to undervalue the meaning of Will or overrate the importance of Thought. When the time came for an analogous exaggeration, we may almost say that history had paused. The Stoics could say anything they liked about the grandeur of human Will, because human Will had no platform on which its actual exercise would be manifested to the eye of the world. A world without politics is a world which knows less than half the meaning of Will. Humanity, as far as individual experience goes, must at all times be familiar with that sense of failure which, far more than

---

[1] This is the doctrine of all Augustine's anti-Pelagian treatises, and is brought out most distinctly in his "Opus Imperfectum contra Julianum," the refutation which he left unfinished, at his death, of the work of that Pelagian bishop whose protest (though we know it only under this form) against all that was hideous in the doctrine of Original Sin reveals a mind much in advance of his age, and in some respects strikingly in harmony with ours. I wonder that we do not know the movement of thought under his name rather than that of Pelagius.

achievement, conveys true instruction as to the nature
and limits of human volition ; the mournful declaration
that " the things that I would, I do not," is the experience
of men and women in every age. But while it is a mere
individual experience, it can never impress on the human
imagination the inexorable limits of human capacity, the
shadow of necessity that falls on the very source of
liberty. To bring that home to us we need achievements,
disappointments, failures, all on a scale of national life.
The men who lived in the Age of Death were preparing
for the life of the cloister. Their aim was Resignation,
and they were free to imagine, therefore, that the realm
of Will was boundless.

But their theory of human Will, when it came to be
inherited by men who once more knew a corporate
interest, was felt to be a fragment. To be made consistent with the aspect of the world, some addition
was necessary which should explain the paralysis of
that which had been elevated to such a height of sway ;
and this was exactly what Augustine supplied. We can
imagine him taking up a treatise of Epictetus, and making it the text of a sermon. Nothing that the Stoics
had said of the dignity and scope of human Will was
exaggerated, as far as it applied to *Man*. Those only
could regard it as an over-statement who tried to discover
its applicability to *Men*. Man had been all that Epictetus
thought him, supreme ruler over this subordinate world
of good and evil, subject only to those laws of the outer
world which belonged to a realm of indifference ; in all
the region of *desire*, an absolute lord. *Men*, it is true,
were the exact opposite of this. They were in bondage
to that which should have been beneath them. So far
the Stoic and the Christian must be at one ; if any one
thought of humanity as Epictetus did, he must allow
that the men who surrounded Nero could hardly be

taken as average specimens of humanity.   But there he
came to a stop.   He had to recognize a chasm between
typical humanity and average humanity which he made
no effort to explain.   His philosophy contemplated Man
as he is in blank despair, and could be justified only by
the hope of a marvellous transformation in which new
desires, new aims, new fears, should suddenly become
the property of the human race.

Christianity, as Augustine remodelled it, crossed this
chasm between the ideal and the real Man by a logical
bridge, so firm in its construction that it lasted for
centuries, and still remains as a picturesque ruin, a rich
memorial of the past.   The Augustinian theory of the
Fall discovered the Stoic ideal man in Adam, and threw
on all his descendants the shadow of his rebellion, a
state of disaster from which a small minority were
selected to inhabit the City of God.   No antique feeling
was hurt by this heritage of guilt; all antique feeling
was satisfied by this exclusiveness of right.   Turn to
the historian who gives his sympathies to Stoicism.
Read (but it is difficult) the fate of the innocent child[1]
who owed her existence to Sejanus, and you will see
that the condemnation of individual innocence to Hell,
keenly as such a conception revolted the lofty antagonist
of Augustine,[2] had nothing necessarily out of keeping
with the ideal of the past.   On the other hand, his
system wedded Christianity to that ideal of the past.
He lived when, for good and for evil, all the distinctions
which had formed the pride of the old world were

---

[1] Tac., Ann., v. 9 :—" Crebro interrogaret quod ob delictum et quo traheretur *neque facturam ultra.*"   Perhaps the populace, as in the case of the massacre of the four hundred slaves, may have been vainly indignant.   But we have to consider the feeling of the oligarchy.

[2] Julian, the Pelagian, seems to me a Charles Kingsley born before his time. But this estimate must be confessed to be singular.   I have been astonished to meet with no sympathy for him in any account of the controversy.

passing away. A disorderly mob vulgarized the proud ideal of Roman citizenship, a humane philosophy softened the absolute subjection of the slave. But the spirit which the distinctions of citizen and alien, of bond and free, had expressed and encouraged was just as strong as it had ever been. The City of God absorbed all that had been exclusive in the spirit that defended and enclosed the City of man. A State without a background of aliens would have seemed as impossible to the men of that time as a river without banks. The whole theory of ancient politics rested on national antagonism ; if this attitude be changed to one of conciliation, the fabric falls to pieces. The course of history had exhibited just this very fact ; the instincts of a race had been justified by the course of history. As the privileges of citizenship had been cheapened, the life of civilization, as it was understood by the ancient world, had been imperilled. All the teaching of experience seemed to emphasize the exclusive ideal of the old world ;[1] it arose upon the horizon of the inner world as it disappeared from that of the outer, and had hardly ceased to buttress the privileges of the citizen before it was seen in a new aspect, as the peculiar blessedness of the believer.

But Augustinianism satisfied the spirit of the new morality no less fully than the old. It allowed no conception of individual human dignity, such as we have seen in Marcus Aurelius or Epictetus, to surpass its own. All that the slave had conceived of spiritual freedom, all that the monarch had conceived of spiritual dominion, was true of its typical Man. The individual soul had all that completeness which the Stoics had seen

---

[1] The circumstances during which Augustine passed his life were of a nature strongly to emphasize this warning. He died A.D. 430, during the siege of Hippo, his episcopal city, by the Vandals.

in it. It had been created by God in His own image, that is, it had been *created a Creator.* It was endowed with initial power, as real as the initial power to which its own existence was owing. And it is involved in the very conception that if this initial power be misused it will be unchecked. God could, in this view, no more create a being at once free and guarded from the dangers of freedom than He could make two straight lines enclose a space. It was no drawback on His Omnipotence that it was impossible for Him to achieve what in truth stood out of all relation to power.

The typical Adam of this scheme is, in fact, the modern ideal of humanity transfigured and thrown back, in gigantic outline, on an ideal past. Man, we have been forced to repeat again and again, was to the ancient world a part of the State. Man is to the modern world primarily a whole within himself. We do not get at a specimen of humanity by taking the State to pieces; we get at the State by multiplying specimens of humanity. Now Adam, as he was re-created by the genius of Augustine, stood on the threshold of Christian thought; and of all human beings Adam alone stood *out of relation to society.* The modern mind, it is true, does not contemplate Man *apart* from society, any more than the Greek mind did, but it recognizes in him something that social relations do not exhaust; from the modern point of view he is, if we may borrow the language of philosophy, transcendent with respect to the State; from the ancient, he was immanent within it. And the Augustinian image of Adam was no more than this idea detached and magnified. He was the first creation of the new spirit, which dealt no longer with Man, the fragment of the State, but with Man the unit of morality, the molecule of all those spiritual forces which make up the moral world, the integral object of moral attention, the starting-point at once and goal of moral thought.

If the typical Man must be this, the actual Man must be the very reverse. The depth of his fall must measure the height of his origin. No conception that had been hitherto entertained of Divine wrath and human rebellion could match that which should be raised by the legend of Adam when once it was mirrored in a mind that interpreted it, as Augustine did, by the light of a vivid personal experience—by the intimate sense of that *need of redemption* of which it was the logical counterpart. Such glimmerings of the legend as show themselves in Greek mythology do no more than exhibit its loss of all meaning when it is detached from the sense of Sin. Prometheus on his rock is a memorial of the wrath of offended Jove, but he is also a memorial of his impotence, as against the dauntless spirit that dares to defy him ; he is, in fact, like almost all the more characteristic expressions of Greek genius, an expression of the Greek demand for temperance and balance, its protest against unbridled claim, its dread of the infinite. Prometheus and Adam side by side exhibit in their sharpest antagonism the contrast of the Greek spirit with that which has given the legend of Adam its significance and its grandeur. The Greek spirit takes part with the rebel, or rather the antithesis lies between gigantic might and dauntless liberty. We hear the echoes of Salamis ; we are reminded that the poet was also the warrior. But since Æschylus wrote, the whole purport of history was changed. In place of the great King, whose power overshadowed, as a blight, the growing life of a young and vigorous race, was the Emperor of Rome, whose shelter was synonymous with the rule of law, and whose dominion included nothing that had independent life. All ennobling associations had died away from resistance to domination. It had been set to the sweetest melody of national life; it now recalled only the jarring discords of hopeless and life-crushing rebellion.

Perhaps all that is most hurtful in the spiritual history of mankind comes from the endeavour of great men to exhibit the truth that has been felt in experience as part of a logical scheme. If Augustine had been content to utter the convictions of his spirit, untrammelled by the activity of his intellect, he would never have distorted the teaching of Christianity by adding to it the Manichæan dream of a dark world for ever confronting the world of light. He left as a hard dogma, crushing to the spirits of men, and lacerating to their hearts, that belief in a Fall which he felt as a clue to all that was most vital in his own history, because he thought he must complete the Divine message before delivering it. That ambition, which is truly the last infirmity of noble minds, is the ambition of the systematizer. " By that sin fell the angels ; " thereby vital truth is associated with deadly error ; and the permanence of conviction grounded in experience is shared by the product of mere logical activity, unchecked by verification, or by the action of any faculty in man higher than the understanding.

The groundwork of all Augustine's reasoning was that experience which made him regard Redemption as the central truth of the world. This was no logical creation made in the interests of theory, this was a mere gathering up the results of his inmost experience. He passed from sin to holiness as suddenly and as irrevocably as his ideal Adam had passed from holiness to sin. So, at least, he imagined the transition, and for the purpose of history it is his imagination which is the fact. Redeeming power was the thing he was most sure of in this world; Heaven itself could not deepen that absolute certainty; he knew that it was a law of the spiritual world as Faraday knew that electricity was a law of the physical world. Had he been content to proclaim that which he had himself experienced, no man of science would have left less to grow obsolete or unmeaning for subsequent generations. But he was not thus content. He must incorporate his own experience in a scheme of the universe, and thereby he has veiled its significance for all posterity. We have seen how in the primitive Persian faith the world of Ormazd is an actual transcript, on the moral consciousness, of the Heaven of light above us; while the world of Ahriman is a creation of the logical intellect, seeking to give balance and antithesis to the actual immensity of light by an imaginary abyss of darkness. This process is repeated again and again. The Fall was emphasized to explain Redemption. The dark world was an imagined necessity in order to explain the light world. If Adam had not fallen, how could his descendant know a Saviour? Thus the fragment of experience was buried in a world of reasoning, and the truth of one age, striving to complete itself, became hurtful falsehood for all which followed.

The Fall of Man, as the readers of Milton have learnt to think of it, dates from the age of Augustine. But we have seen already that the sense of a Fall is common to both those races whose antithetic feelings and tendencies almost exhaust the range of moral influences which have built up modern Europe. This feeling haunts Greek thought from its dawn,[1] recurring in various forms; to the Greek mind, the conception of Man's whole life on earth as the result of some decadence from a condition

---

[1] See the fragment of Empedocles, quoted on p. 299. It seems to have much impressed Clement of Alexandria, who twice refers to it (Strom., iii. 432, and iv. 479).

of previous splendour was perfectly familiar. And then again we have seen how Jewish thought approached this idea, and yet seemed borne away from it; how evanescent at once and yet vivid was the sense of human failure in the mind that was possessed with the idea of Divine Holiness. But before the complete fusion of Greek and Jewish belief brought this common element into a new activity it was stirred by another influence; Jewish thought, "cross-fertilized" by that of Persia, developed a new phase of the belief in the Fall. It passed beyond the limits of humanity into that world of spiritual beings, which in this later Jewish conception surrounds humanity as the atmosphere the earth. The Fall of the Angels is more closely connected with the system we have set forth than the Fall of Adam is. We may speak of "the first man," but in truth the Adam of Augustine is more than man, coming nearer to the Sons of God, whose fall is narrated in the Book of Enoch,[1] than with the father of mankind as he appears in the Book of Genesis. The story must have taken a wide popularity, since Shakespeare—the interpreter of the vague diffused beliefs of the world—alludes to it before "Paradise Lost" was written.[2] But when he makes

---

[1] The Book of Enoch was probably the work of a Jew writing in the early part of the reign of Herod, *i.e.*, about 40 B.C., and though so little older than the New Testament, was, as we see by its citation in the Epistle of Jude, supposed to be the actual composition of the patriarch whose name it has retained. It was quoted by Tertullian as inspired Scripture, and by Origen as an allegorical description of the descent of human souls into bodies, that being symbolized by the "Fall of the Angels" which it narrates. It is allied to the account of the Fall of Man in Genesis by a great stress being laid on the sin of the Angels in betraying the secrets of Heaven to the women by whose love they were seduced—"Durch dieses Geheimnisz richten die Männer und Weiber viel Uebel auf Erden an" (Book of Enoch, translated by A. Dillman). The legend is thus a link between that of Adam and Prometheus.

[2] And long before Shakespeare or Milton it was dramatized by the monk at Whitby, Cædmon (ob. 680). Milton indeed probably borrowed much from him, but there is some difficulty as to his being able to read Anglo-Saxon, and the "Fall of Man" was not then translated.

Wolsey use it to point his warning against ambition, he follows a different version of the legend from that we find in the Jewish records open to us. The sin of the Angels who fell from Heaven to Earth was indeed the very opposite of ambition; their offence was not the desire to reign in Heaven, but the unwillingness to remain there; it was an incapacity to refrain from desires unsuited to their spiritual condition, a readiness to part with their birthright for temptations no less material than Esau's. The life of spirit was insufficient for them; the seductions of carnal life brought them to abdicate their place in Heaven and descend to life on Earth—to life, and also to death. For it was indeed the yearning of spiritual beings after sensual enjoyment which "brought death into their world, and all our woe." The actions which are innocent in mankind, because they are necessary for the continued existence of mankind, become a deadly sin in those whose eternal life ought to have been enough for them, and in the day when they entered on that lower life they entered on the realm of death.

This legend repeats and varies the fall of Adam in a form which gives us more of the true scope of that event as the centre of a great mythologic system than does the simple narrative which is its actual basis. It shows us the associations of evil with the men of that time; it shows us what temptation was to them the type of all temptation. Sin, if sin exist at all, is surely abdication, the willingness to enter a lower world, to quit the highest plane of being on which existence is possible and choose the good of one beneath it. This is one aspect of sin, as the desire to be as God, knowing good and *evil*, is the other. What we mean when we say that God knows evil we cannot tell, but that God does know it in some sense must be believed by all who believe that God knows anything. What we mean when we say that Man knows evil is that Man has known temptation. He cannot strive to take the place of that which is above him without descending to that which is below him; ambition, in the Angels, *is* abdication. Wolsey could truly say, " By that sin fell the Angels ; " the ambition by which he had fallen was but one form of the sin by which they had fallen. And by a natural parallax of human thought, the narrator of the Fall of the Angels sees that same sin as the very reverse of ambition ; the desire to create new life was inseparable in them from the desire to sink into lower life. There is a deep meaning in the double sense of the verb *to know* as we find it in the English preserved by our Authorized Version of the Scripture; through this we may perhaps come to understand how the Fall of the Angels and the Fall of Man are but two expressions of one dim, large idea, hovering before the mind of men who pondered over their dislocated condition here, and found one side of the antithesis inadequate.

Adam in Paradise, it was supposed by some early thinkers,[1] was a purely spiritual being ; the consciousness of his nakedness was his awaking to the need of that covering which only to a perfectly sinless being could be unnecessary. The clothing with skins was in truth (in this earlier version of the legend) the creation of Man as we know him now, inhabiting a body; and all that went before must be regarded as but another form of that experience which hovered before the mind of the Greek poet when he imagined himself " obedient to mad strife " because in a mysterious pre-natal condition he had disobeyed the law of his being, and was condemned in consequence to sojourn on the Purgatory of this earth. A faint allusion in the Old Testament and an exclama-

[1] Especially Origen.

tion of Christ form the whole Scriptural authority for
the Fall of the Angels, but the legend would explain
the depravity of mankind in a manner more consistent
with subsequent orthodox speculation than does that by
which it has been obliterated—the Fall of Man. We are
more in harmony with that speculation when we represent to ourselves the original disaster as caused by sensual temptation rather than by ambition of intellectual
gain.

For Redemption was to the mind of that age above
all a deliverance from sensual temptation. Augustine is
an inverted Adam ; he shows by the measure of his own
miraculous gain what the ideal Man appeared to him
to have lost at the Fall. When we come to ask what
actually happened, we are, from a modern point of view,
inclined to think that there was as much wrong after
his conversion as before it. We have to take his own
point of view before we can regard it as an instance of
a soul turning from darkness to light. Nothing more
brings out the difference between his view and ours
than the fact that he initiated his Christian life not by
marriage with but repudiation of the woman who had
already borne him a son.[1] Was there, the reader asks,
no pure domestic life in those days ? Doubtless there
is in all ages ; the pieties of the domestic hearth depend on no rule and no religion. Augustine himself
was both a loving son and a loving father, and every
indication of personal feeling as well as of ideal standard
points to a high estimate of family claims, when once
they existed. His mother's love indeed seems to have
taken, to his mind, in a peculiar degree, the typical aspect
of Divine mercy ; the fact that he had known a human
love not earned by merit, not alienated by great demerit,

---

[1] See all that relates to her in the "Confessions." She appears entirely to
have acquiesced in their separation.

was always in his mind when he spoke of the love of
God. But though he knew, in its best form, parental love
from both sides, all that prepares the parental relation
was in his eyes associated with evil. Original sin has
become a mere vague synonym for the frailty of human
nature. In the dialect of Augustine it has a perfectly
definite and consistent meaning. He felt that the clue
to his whole history, and therefore to the history of
humanity, lay in his deliverance from that impulse apart
from which family life would hardly exist. It was only as
an *impulse* he thought it evil ; he would have had nothing
to say against it as a volition. That a man should choose
to be a father by an exercise of his free will, as he might
choose to be a physician or a traveller, presented nothing
evil to his mind ; but family life, as we do actually know
it, lay for him under a curse. The love of man to
woman was incurably associated with that instinct originating new life which he felt to be not only evil, but
the evil. All family life was a commemoration of the
original disaster whereby the body manifested its independence of the spirit. And wherever a new human
life began, there was repeated that initial act of will by
which Man claimed to himself the prerogative of God,
and the creature became the creator. The creature was
in one sense to have been the creator in any case. The
human race was to have been continued through the
instrumentality of Man. But the act of insubordination
by which Adam refused the attitude of a subject and
became "as God, knowing good and evil"—this act
disturbed the whole hierarchy of being, and infused into
the originally innocent and legitimate decision to carry
on the race, and thus share the Divine work, an element
of the dark world known to ancient thought as the
opposite of Personality. As God was to have been
Supreme above all Spirits, so Spirit was to be supreme

above everything material; but within the material framework of Man was something that commemorated the disturbance of this order, and supplied a rebel to his will, as his will had become a rebel to God. He had stood midway between God and the material creation, mysteriously related to both, as far above Matter as he was below God. But Matter always kept its symbolic alliance with Evil, and this alliance, under this line of reasoning, was drawn closer. Man's fall was commemorated in sexual desire, and his regeneration was to be manifested in sexual separateness.

We shall best understand this scheme if we consider where modern sympathy breaks off from it. Animal man, as we have said, is to us neither good nor bad. To bear hunger and thirst is indeed noble, but to feel hunger and thirst is perfectly innocent. It is the cause of much that is wrong; it could not otherwise give the opportunity for anything that is right, but in itself it is neither right nor wrong. Still it is a fact that does inevitably tell upon the desires of man, and therefore, in all but the most heroic natures, on his will. We may account for all the vice and much of the crime of the world by the activity of animal desires, and it is a natural and slight distortion of that truth to say that animal desire is itself of the nature of evil. Hunger and thirst are not merely facts concerning the physical organization. They are facts, and not the only ones, which concern the mental condition of him whom they affect. Such facts represent a certain dominion, so we might express it, of the world of matter over the world of mind ; an inversion which seemed to the men of that age the very essence of evil. They could conceive no greater evil than that the slave should rule. We have come to look on right or wrong, good and evil, with different eyes from those of Augustine and his contemporaries, and only by a great effort see any meaning in this view. We have gone to the opposite pole from the aristocratic ideal of antiquity. The idea that the slave should rule does not necessarily suggest to us anything evil ; it is not the person but the condition which is evil for us. It does not seem to us so very much worse that the slave should rule than that he should obey.

It is impossible for us to subtract in imagination the influence of our environment, so as to conceive what we should be in a universe of pure spiritual emotion, but any approach to such a condition no longer rouses within us an aspiration of desire. Life in Paradise, to the mind of our day, represents itself as coloured by that tedium which drove Rasselas, Prince of Abyssinia, to quit the happy valley and seek the trials and difficulties of the world. It took a different aspect to our fathers. Their imaginations loved to dwell on that state of primæval innocence where all that gives life an object was lacking. They were ready to fill up its details in a way that astonishes us, when we compare the result with the few verses of Scripture whence they took their material, at the large amount of imaginative reasoning implied by those pictures of a lost blessedness. Learned men are not ready to answer, about tolerably familiar periods of history, questions which the men of that time thought any one might answer with respect to the condition of our first parents before the Fall. They imagined knowledge because they felt desire. It was as the inheritance of privileged humanity that they looked for a renewal of the Eden life of the Past.

The Creation had been a failure, and all the varied events in the life of man commemorated that failure. All History was an interruption, a parenthesis, in the far-off Golden Age. Thence human development took its start downward in the Fall; thither human development took its start upward in the regeneration of Christ's new influence on humanity. The light of Eden fell on the path of man in the remote past, and lit up the future of men, as they turned to the near, mysterious Heaven. Between these kindred bursts of splendour lay an interval of deep shadow, shrouding the hopes and occupations that now make up the staple of human interest,—a shadow concentrated upon those emotions which modern reserve indeed shrouds in silence, but in the silence of reverent and fearless sympathy. We may find it difficult to conceive how all that makes up the interest of average secular life should ever have been regarded as a mere interpolation in the sequence of all that is truly significant for man. But we shall never understand the moral life of the past unless we accept the fact that there was a time when, as the refuge from life's ills was actually found in the cloister, so the ideal of life's perfection lay in a projection of cloister life on the background of a fairy-like Paradise.

However strange it be to regard this new morality as one claiming affiliation with the faith made known to us in the Jewish Scriptures, however perplexing its relation to a morality which set the highest honour on family life, and gave a peculiar sanction to the desire for posterity, the rise of such an ideal at such a point in the world's history is clearly explicable. It is the morality of the Age of Death, made logical by an intellectual scheme, and religious by a new mythology. Augustine claimed no greater detachment from all objects of human desire than had been enjoined by Seneca, but the later claim was at once more imaginative and more logical than the earlier. He called in God to enforce this detachment; he remodelled cosmogony in accordance with it. He made the order of things in which we live take its rise in a crime, the shadow of which fell on all subse-

quent exercise of human activity, and was commemorated in every new life. That which was most intensely
original, that in which the whole man, soul and body,
put forth initial energy, was of the nature of sin. Life
was tainted with evil. Death was blessed. The literal
death by which we quit this world was blessed, removing us from a region of possible sin to one of necessary
holiness, from a world overshadowed by a vast initial
calamity to one where the pristine condition of a spiritual
nature should be restored and secured from all further
dislocation. And then the next best thing was to live
in this world as one dead, to give no need to its solicitations, to take no interest in its business, to dwell here as
a Peregrinus whose city was elsewhere. The claims of
family life were all of the nature of temptation ; he was
happiest who avoided all those that could be avoided.[1]
The act which made Man a parent, however innocent,
was a commemoration of sin. The higher life avoided
it ; the soul that had entered into union with God
needed no other union.

Here we have the disintegrating tendency of the new
morality, at its highest point. We are carried to the
extreme opposite of the citizen ideal of antiquity. While
that regarded Man as a part of the State, this regarded
him as—we are driven to the paradoxical expression—
a part of himself. It was not the whole man on which
the redeeming power, as here conceived, put forth its
influence. Man, as he was a part of Nature, was
accursed. Let him, if he would attain his true blessedness, cease to belong to Nature ; let him sever himself from all that owned her sway, let him renounce all

---

[1] See, for instance, the letter of Augustine to Count Boniface, Ep., 220, in
Caillau's edition. Boniface had invited the Vandals to invade Africa, but
Augustine speaks with far greater horror of his second marriage, against a
vow of celibacy.

impulse centripetal within her orbit, then first would the attraction of another centre act upon him unimpaired. So that in the great shipwreck of humanity all was to be cast to the waves except that which was distinctively spiritual. Only a fraction of that which is most intensely personal was to be hallowed with the conservative influence of a new life. Man had been a member of an organism larger than himself, and so he was to continue. But first he must sever his true self from a part of himself, must recognize as a mere accretion that which had seemed the most vigorous outgrowth from his own nature. First he must recognize that which had seemed a part as more than the whole: then he should recognize in the seeming fraction a link to the Infinite. Men were atoms, but each atom was a world; on the stage of each man's Personality was worked out the drama of Redemption. At the core of human individuality Divine power exhibited its marvels, restoring the order that was lost at the fall of corporate humanity, and giving back to Man both his supreme and his subordinate position. What were the rise and fall of States to a drama in which God took part? The soul was the scene of conflicts too tremendous to leave much attention for any struggle that was merely outward, and all ties were outward, except that by which men were bound within the folds of the Church.

The Augustinian scheme, therefore, forms a bridge between the old world and the new, connecting the great central ideas of the classic and the Christian world. While it looked back, in the idea of Original Sin, with a glance of sympathetic retrospect to the corporate morality of Greece and Rome, it gathered up and prefigured in gigantic outline the new man of Protestant ethics. Adam was a magnified image of the new humanity which after a thousand years was to blossom into rich and various development and assert itself in the various conflicts of modern life. This conflict has mirrored itself in the delineations of modern art. The distinctive charm of modern literature, felt first and most in Shakespeare, but more or less in all modern fiction, as contrasted with the great works of the ancient world, is the interest of individuality, the representation of *character*, as an independent subject of attention and investigation. Imaginative genius must, no doubt, always express itself through character; it has no other language. But the interest in a character, as a whole within itself—the interest that we feel in Hamlet, in Macbeth, in the Baron of Bradwardine, in Bailie Nicol Jarvie, in the best creations of Thackeray and of George Eliot—this has no place in ancient literature. Œdipus is as definite as Hamlet; but the crisis of the Greek drama turns on the fate, not the character, of the hero. Achilles, in the tale of Troy divine, is the typical Greek; of Hamlet what can we say but that he is Hamlet? Now this idea of a whole within itself—of Man as a complete being, not claimed and dominated by the State, but independent and deciding by his own will into what relations he will enter with any other being—this ideal is in Adam presented with all the exaggeration of a new conception. We are speaking of the Augustinian Adam, the Adam of " Paradise Lost;" one who read the simple narrative of Genesis for the first time would wonder that it had been made to bear the weight of such significance, and perhaps the reluctance of Augustine to use the name of Adam is a witness to some undercurrent of consciousness that the myth, on which he rested the actual condition of the human race, was hardly suggested in the records whence he had to gather all that he could actually know of the first man. " The abysmal

depths of personality" are prefigured in Adam. All that
romance and essay have imagined of human capacity
is condensed in that ideal of tragic but not despicable
choice. *Will* is exhibited, in that grand drama, as it
never could be again; the ideal of the new world is
cast in lurid relief on the background of all that is
darkest in the actual condition of the old world.

The Augustinian scheme presents us with a new exclusiveness in place of the old. We confront in it a new
application of the aristocratic principle of antiquity to
the grouping of human life. Apart from the Church men
were nothing, just as apart from the City men had been
nothing. Man was, indeed, older than the Church; he
had known an ideal condition in which he had stood
alone, above Nature, beyond Society, and only subordinate to God; but in his actual condition he owed all
his value to his incorporation in a Society inheriting
from the past the boundless claims of the State, con-
ferring the same inestimable privileges, and therefore
repeating the same inevitable exclusions. And the new
exclusiveness was so much more inclusive than the old
that it seemed to include everything. The enclosure
which took in Greek and barbarian, bond and free, seemed
to those who had known these opposites as divided by an
impassable chasm, to be one which had practically no limit.
That which revolts us in what we know as Calvinism,
and what we should know, if we traced the exclusiveness
of Christianity to its true author, as Augustinianism, is
but a transference of the earthly city to the Heavens.
To the eager gaze of Augustine the earthly city had no
other object than a symbolism whereby it prefigured the
heavenly state. The Church everywhere inherited the
legacy of the City.[1] The stately traditions of Rome had

---

[1] See the whole treatise, "De Civitate Dei." It should be compared with
the treatise of Plutarch cited above on the Fortune of Rome.

no other object than to supply, with their pictures of
devotion to an earthly state, reproach or warning for the
less loyal citizen of the heavenly city. The unshaken
fidelity of Regulus, the stern simplicity of Cincinnatus,
the heroic fortitude which triumphed over parental fond-
ness and anticipated in the person of Torquatus or Brutus
the denunciation, " Whoever loveth son or daughter more
than me is unworthy of me "—all this was in parable the
ideal history of the Church. The narrative of what had
happened was an injunction as to what should happen.
Even details which suggest no such typical significance
to our minds, the " Asylum " of Romulus (where a few
robbers, secured by impunity, formed the origin of the
almost immortal state) prefigured that Divine mercy
which in Christ should deliver from the bondage of sin
to the hope of righteousness. " For our sakes this was
written ; " yes, and done also. In the eyes of Augustine,
the majesty of Rome had no value but as a mere symbolic rehearsal of the victory of the Church.

The work which contained this fantastic exegesis of
Roman history was undertaken to refute an opinion
common at the time among Pagans, that the sack of
Rome by the Goths was the consequence of the abandonment of the ancient religion for Christianity.[1] The course
of history of itself so little tended to exhibit the Church
as the ideal State, that Augustine was reduced almost to
refine away the very existence of the actual State in
order to bring the two into relation. It was only by
making the history of Rome a type of the claims of
the Church that he could weld the two in a single
whole ; and when once a divine inner meaning had replaced the obvious significance of outer fact, the calamity,
vast as it was, which put the capital of the world at the

---

[1] Compare it with the treatise of Salvian, " De Gubernatione Dei "—a far
deeper and nobler view of the facts, to my mind.

mercy of barbarians, took a different aspect, and was no longer a break-up of all the hopes of civilized humanity. The downfall of the State might mean the emergence of the Church; and just as Greek implied Barbarian, and the empress city implied a population of slaves, so the City of God must imply a world given over to the powers of evil. Man, not adopted by Christ, must belong to Satan. The corporate life in which he already partook was an evil thing. It included the vast majority of the descendants of Adam, and represented their natural condition. It represented the confusion of evil as contrasted with the distinctness and individuality of original and sinless humanity. The antithesis carried on the one great contrast of the ancient world between freedom and slavery. Adam was the one freeman of the human race; humanity was in bondage. Christ was the liberator; but the deliverance was into an altogether exceptional condition; the natural condition was that of slavery to evil. The first man stood apart from all his sons, as the freeman from the slave. Whatever they were, it was natural that he should *not* be. Hence the aristocratic principle of antiquity passed into a *worship of the exceptional* that characterized modern thought (taking the epithet in its largest sense), until by the natural process of inversion it passed into its opposite—the worship of the universal. The commonwealth was no longer sacred. What was sacred was something taken out of it—something removed from the secular enclosure of national life, and transferred, as it were, from the wreck to the lifeboat. All the arrogance, all the exclusiveness, all the love of privilege, for which the city of man no longer afforded any scope, found a refuge in the City of God.

In this system were thus combined the common exclusiveness of the old Morality and of the new. The Platonic Republic is the ancient state made logical, as the monastic life was the Augustinian ideal made logical. Domestic life, with all that it implies, was equally to be banished from both. From one it was to be banished because the guardian was not to know his own children ; from the other, because the monk was not to have any children.   In both cases equally the common mass of humanity was to be indulged with the ordinary relations that make up the *home*; in both, the saints were called upon to renounce them, to live a life superior to and apparently poorer than that of the common herd.   Augustine and Plato coincided in throwing the shadow of inferiority on all that is symbolized by the domestic hearth, on all private relation, and all the virtues which it elicits and implies. For centuries the holiest men of Europe left no posterity. The holiest men in Plato's Republic would have been obliged to leave a posterity, though they would never have known their own children. But in each case the love of man to woman, of parent to child, was proscribed with equal rigour; in each the ties of kindred were to be stripped of the sanctities of duty, and the object of entire devotion was to be invisible. The Augustinian saint, an actual human being, stood aside from the path of inheritance and left it to the ruffian and the sot to bequeath his evil tendency to his country for ever; the Platonic guardian never existed, but as far as he was a model, the result was much the same. In the one case the man belonged to the State, in the other to the Church ; in both cases men ceased to belong to the family. The moral nature was a mutilated one. That twofold life, in which man and woman became one, was in both a mere concession to the ordinary unblessed, animal desires of the common herd, and all the affections and virtues which find their root on this soil were smitten with the blight of moral neglect.

Man needs Divine sympathy in all his ideals.   If the

Divine act of Creation was a blunder; if the Creation was either the result of, or a mere prelude to, the fall of spiritual beings, then all impulse in Man which tends towards the continuance of Creation is mistaken likewise. If God would have done better not to have created Man, Man would do better not to create Man. Augustine thought that all God's acts were holy, and that therefore the Creation was holy. He believed this firmly, but he did not teach it. His system exhibited Creation as a vast blunder, an exercise of mischievous activity far beyond that of any Gnostic Demiurgus. This consequence of his theology was felt at first, by honest thinkers who perished, as obscure rebels against the truth, and were forgotten. But the idea lived, and centuries afterwards it bore fruit in a renovated world.

In the meantime the sense of the mistake of Creation tinged the whole ideal of Man's moral life. It darkened Earth at once and Heaven; as it lowered the earthly father to a mere animal, it changed the Heavenly Father to a being endowed with cruelty, such as we conceive of in a devil. It gave up earthly love to lawless impulse; it stamped heavenly love with the narrowest partiality, and deprived it in imagination of that expansive power which is of the very essence of love. What we would point out is the connection between these two things. The ban on married love follows, in logical sequence, on the disastrous issue of the Creation. If Creation was a blunder, Procreation is a crime.

The repulsiveness of this whole range of thought, for modern feeling, too much conceals from us a clue to truth. Love is felt by every one to be the spring of all that is excellent in human life. Perhaps it is but following out that belief on its negative side to see that the distortion of Love, which we know as Lust, is not only one of the greatest evils in the human world, but the very focal centre of evil. That impulse, under the control of which persons are treated as things, and human bonds are as fugitive as human impulse, is the very antithesis of all that binds humanity in groups, and forms the school of duty. All that is evil in human relation is at its height when man and woman seek the closest intimacy apart from the resolve, with all its latent self-sacrifice, to make this an exclusive bond. Wherever there is selfishness, wherever there is cruelty, wherever there is falsehood, there is something that is at its height in lust. If anything *of the inevitable* mingles in this temptation to all that is worst—if the mere animal nature, the very type of innocence, be found in alliance with that in Man which tramples on the rights of his kind, which desolates a life to satisfy an impulse, and brings confusion into the very source of family life—may we not say that there, it would seem, is the result of some vast moral dislocation, far transcending the individual life, and needing some redemption equally vast before the life of Man can be purified ?

CHAPTER IX.

THE HERITAGE OF TO-DAY.

THAT which gives life its keynote is, not what men think good, but what they think best. True, this is not the part of belief which is embodied in conduct : the ordinary man tries to avoid only what is obviously wrong ; the best of men does not always make us aware that he is striving after what is right. We do not see people growing into the resemblance of what they admire ; it is much if we can see them growing into the unlikeness of that which they condemn. But the dominant influence of life lies ever in the unrealized. While all that we discern is the negative aspect of a man's ideal, that ideal itself lives by admiration which never clothes itself in word or deed. In seeing what he avoids we judge only the least important part of his standard ; it is that which he never strives to realize in his own person which makes him what he is. The average, secular man of to-day is a different being because Christendom has hallowed the precept to give the cloak to him who asks the coat ; it would be easier to argue that this claim for what most would call an impossible virtue has been injurious than that it has been impotent. Christianity has moulded character, where we should vainly seek to discern that it had influenced conduct. Not the criminal code, but the counsel of perfection shows us what a nation is becoming ; and he who casts on any set of duties the shadow of the *second best*, so far as he is successful, does more to influence the moral ideal than he who succeeds in passing a new law.

Thus it was that while the mediæval and the classical ideal of morality on one side were exact opposites, they had this in common—that they threw discredit on a large part of that which makes man what he is. In neither was there a full sanction to the bond that makes man and woman one. There was, in early Christianity, an emphatic declaration that the bond should be exclusive, but there was an equally emphatic declaration that it had better not exist. Vain is the effort to render pure and orderly the life which is thrown into shadow by the consciousness of an ideal towards which it is not tending. The magistrate may regulate such a life, the legislator may concern himself with its details, but that in man which seeks rightness will turn elsewhere.

Man is the member of a society to which he is joined by the principle of resemblance, and of a union to which he is joined by the principle of difference. He has fellow-citizens, to whom he is bound by common interests and duties; he has a family, to which he is joined by reciprocal and correlative duties. We cannot, indeed, group any human relations in sharply antithetic divisions —the citizen must recognize special claim (though less and less with the progress of ages); the brother knows common interests and the bond of resemblance. But these are the exceptional elements respectively of civil and family life. The duties of the father are not the duties of the son, and the charm of conjugal happiness would be gone if husband and wife received from each other nothing that he or she was not prepared to return. All that makes up the poetry of the mutual love of man and woman is an expression of the fact that it contains something which is not mutual, something which does not merely invert all self-centred feeling and teach men to turn the passive desire into the active exertion, but which supplies self with a complement and teaches men concession to needs they do not feel. Each of these relations is incomplete without the other. In all human relation, it is obvious, men need to treat each other from some points of view as beings of similar nature and equal claim; this is true even in the mutual relation of adults and children. But also in every human being as compared with every other there is something of which the duties of sex, the duties of differing age, are the true type. In the most ordinary, the most commonplace man is something that his brother man does not share and cannot estimate. Civil life ignores this element. It was not so in the ancient world. Status was a fact of which ancient law took cognizance, of which modern law is only at this hour ceasing to take cognizance. But the whole development of modern life is towards that view of things in which men recognize no duty that is not mutual, no need that is not common. This was always to a great extent the civil basis of life; it is so now entirely. As a citizen a man is blameless if he give his brother man what he claims himself. This is justice on this plane of being, and we must ascend to a higher if we would understand any other justice.

But how poor, how meagre were our moral life if this were all! How poor were even the typical life of equality if it caught no reflected lights from the life of inequality! It is the relations of family life which make up the focus of rightness. Family life may no doubt, when this principle is forgotten, become a mere magnified selfishness. When two become one, and imagine that they keep their original separateness, their dual selfishness far exceeds the worst selfishness of an individual. For what keeps down the selfishness of an individual

is surely the consciousness that every other man is a
" self ; " and if those whose needs are identified with our
own are allowed to count as *others*, the double pull of
vicarious and natural selfishness locks up all attention.
When the most unselfish of men looks upon his care for
wife and children from this point of view, he multiplies
unawares his own claims, and flatters himself that he
has given much, when he has merely transferred something from his right hand to his left. The Family thus
becomes a disguise in which selfishness invades the army
of the virtues and paralyzes their movement. Nevertheless it is the non-mutual relations which call out the
larger part of man's moral nature, and give the Conscience and the Will their fullest exercise. Where men
cease to speak of rights, there Right finds its centre.
While no service to the State can make him a good
citizen who bequeathes to his posterity the influence of
a bad father, the man who is faithful to one woman,
who has brought no children into the world without
endeavouring to ensure their welfare, who has paid back
to his parents that tribute of protection and care he has
received from them—such a man may be counted by the
State among her true sons, though he have contributed
no service beyond mere obedience to her laws. The
realm of civil right, contrasted with that of conjugal,
paternal, filial duty, shows how all that is most truly
moral in our nature demands the life of contrast, the
presence of that element in character which claims and
exercises Faith.

This life it was that fell into shadow, when Christian
faith was a vivid, dynamic reality, remoulding the world.
All lofty spiritual impulse passed it by, all fervent desire
for the Divine life hurried away from it ; its neighbourhood was drained of all that elevates, purifies, and spiri-
tualizes humanity. When a man sought to complete

his life by that union which gives the world its true moral unit, he was taught to regard himself as a mere animal; and that which should have been the school of the Conscience was abandoned to lawless impulse and unhallowed desire.

One tribe alone in our race has fully recognized the place of the Family in the moral education of Man. We are occupied, through perhaps the most interesting and important stages of the history of Israel, with a mere family narrative; and the lives of Abraham, Isaac, and Jacob take more space than many centuries of the later history. The Jew could never ignore the bond of family life. It lay at the root of his history. Where other races traced their course backwards in a genealogy that, ending in some deity, threw a shadow of repudiation on the bonds of mere human kindred, this people found their national records occupied with the relations of a husband and wife whose fears, jealousies, and affections might be paralleled in the most insignificant of their descendants; and the last word of their Scriptures was the promise that a representative of their nation should turn the hearts of the fathers to the children, and the children to the fathers. But Christendom, which should have inherited the lesson, has been, in some sense, even a loser by the lesson of Judaism. Refusing to recognize that the object of its reverence, whatever else he was, was a typical Jew, it has missed the meaning of a teaching that has thus been violently dissevered from all that it implied as its groundwork. A mournful declaration of the inevitable has been interpreted as a precept,[1] a sense of the expansion needed to keep an ideal alive has been taken for a rejection of that ideal, and that

---

[1] Luke xiv. 26. Compare xii. 49-53, a passage apparently spoken shortly before, and turn to the passage which our Lord is here quoting from Micah vii. : " Woe is me! for I am as when they have gathered the summer fruits . . . the good man is perished out of the earth . . . Trust ye not in a friend . . .

consecration of all family bonds which was a part of the
religion of the Jew has been ignored or defied by what
should have been the expansion and fulfilment of Judaism.
To our generation Christianity seems associated with the
sanction of all the ties of kindred, especially the conjugal
bond ; but many generations would need to pass away
before the natural bonds which man at once finds and
chooses could be hallowed by a Christian association as
deeply rooted in the past as that which opposes it ; and
the protest thus stirred up, like all protest, must intensify
what it opposes. It is not the fierce recoil from asceticism which brings us near the true union of the sexes ;
that, though a necessary preliminary in the history of the
race, of itself adds to the disorder which it finds. The
element of protest, inevitable in all moral evolution, is
always distorting, and no other phase of the moral life is
so much distorted by strain and stress as this, The
protest must die away and be forgotten before a true
ideal of marriage can spring up and ally itself with all
that is holiest in man.

The great teachers of the mediæval and the classical
world left their descendants a mutilated ideal of humanity ;
not only an incomplete ideal, but one that was cut off
from its natural expansion. In that fractional ideal
which all are compelled to choose who refuse to regard
the bond which unites man and woman as sacred,
Augustine and Plato each took the ideal of a different
sex. Plato set his seal on the virtues of the man,

keep the doors of thy mouth from her that lieth in thy bosom ; for the son
dishonoureth the father, the daughter riseth up against her mother, the daughter-
in-law against her mother-in-law ; a man's enemies are the men of his own
house." Is it possible to doubt that the lament of the earlier prophet was
echoed by Him who saw that these ills were the inevitable result of His own
claim, knowing that human beings confuse the gradation of love with hatred?
See for a similar confusion Rom. ix. 13, and the passage itself which St.
Paul is there quoting, Mal. i. 2, 3, also Matt. vi. 24, which seems the quotation of some familiar expression.

Augustine on those of the woman. The guardian of the Republic was to be courageous, patriotic, energetic, resolute; the monk in the cloister was to be chaste, meek, obedient, self-denying. It seems strange that when a man traces all evil to the attraction of woman he makes womanly virtue his ideal. And yet it is natural. All that is moral in human nature finds its focus in the relation of man to woman, and sooner or later we shall exaggerate the scope of whatever we refuse to acknowledge in its own proper place. The teacher of mediæval morality, seeking to dissever the influence of woman from the character of man, did actually effect, so far as he impressed his ideal on mankind, that the virtue of the man should be none other than the virtue of the woman. The worship of the Virgin is but the expression, on the side of art, of this mediæval ideal of humanity; the love of woman, denied its natural scope, avenged itself by invading a foreign domain. Manly virtue was as much lost to the aspiration of the age as womanly virtue had been to that of an earlier age, but never in any previous age had human excellence been contracted within limits so narrow.

How eagerly, after centuries of this frost, must the human spirit have turned to the sunshine of Greece and Rome, when it broke anew through the clouds! All that is extravagant in that revival is explained when we see what had gone before. Men had been taught for hundreds of years that a man's life was the lower life; they suddenly found themselves in contact with a literature which exhibited it as the only life. They had been taught to look upon nature as something evil; they saw it suddenly rise and expand to something Divine. All impulse had been allied with sin; all impulse was now shown as portrayed in glorious art, and of itself the creator of a noble world rich in beauty and variety, and needing no re-

demption. We think of science and literature as hostile,
but, though foes now, they were nursed in one cradle.
The release from one cramped, unnatural attitude set
free the spirit of man to enter for the first time into the
study of nature, in all its aspects—nature in man, and
nature in the world; wearied with the keen knife-edge
antithesis of Truth and Error, it turned with rapture
to the gentle slope of gradation that severs Knowledge
from Ignorance. Men looked on the world with new
eyes, and for the first time they saw it as it was. " And
lo! Creation widened to man's view." The universe
expanded. Earth lost her central place, but found herself one of many earths; the sister worlds seemed
to inscribe the nightly skies with their lesson of the
heavenly in the earthly. For as Heaven disappeared
from the vault above, it reappeared, in some sense, on
earth. This dark earth became a star, taking its place
in the bright choir that had seemed the ideal home of
purified spirits. As this antithesis vanished—as earth
changed from the dark, motionless centre of the universe
to one of the host of Heaven—its own expanse widened,
new realms opened in the west, man's home became a
boundless estate for the expanding human race, and yet
was seen to be a mere speck in the universe. Man
entered on a double inheritance—new worlds in the
Heavens, new lands beyond the seas. A boundless universe opened upon him on every side, to explore with
eye or mind, and unexpected aid sprang up in every
quarter. Even the weapons of mutual slaughter afforded
patterns of the heavenly movements,[1] while a new vehicle

[1] Those speculations on the laws of motion which attained their culminating
point in the Newtonian astronomy appear to have received much stimulus from
the study of projectiles, which occupied many mechanicians of the seventeenth
century, as, *e.g.*, Anderson, "Art of Gunnery" (1674), Blondel, "Art de Jeter les
Bombes," 1683. The true theory of projectiles was somewhat delayed by an excessive deference to Galileo, who had overrated the analogy of their movement
to that of the planets. See Whewell, "History of the Inductive Sciences," ii. 56.

for the record of thought gave thought rapidity. Man
entered upon the rehabilitation of nature. His home
was no longer overshadowed by the recollection of a pristine crime. It was a glorious palace, and its inhabitants
must be a regal race.

It is by no fanciful association that we may see in the
new astronomy a type of the development of thought by
which the life of Man became vivid, various, dramatic.
"Heaven and Earth" was originally a description of
the ideal Universe. When we turn to the poem of
Dante, and mark the prosaic, consistent literalness with
which he conceived the material framework of his imaginative creation, we realize that he was not building
up a new universe to suit his poetry, but merely giving
definiteness to the ordinary and familiar conceptions of
his contemporaries. The world was all, so to speak,
laid out to fit the drama of judgment. Heaven was
above our head ; Hell might well be below our feet ; the
earth itself, the centre of the universe, had nothing in
common with

> " The wandering fires which moved
> In mystic dance, not without song "——

When once Galileo and Newton had forced the world to
recognize that Heaven, if it was anywhere, was everywhere, then morals took a new direction. The antithesis
of Heaven and Earth vanished from the inward as well
as from the outward world. Human nature became interesting for its own sake. The stress and strain of
a conflict between the powers of darkness and of light
vanished, to make way for the development of various
aims, of many-sided feelings, of hopes in which there was
no edge of terror, of interests which, instead of merely
emphasizing the common attitude of different spirits to
the Eternal, brought out and stimulated their differences,

and developed all that was individual, all that was specific, in each.

"If any one doubt the connection of this new interest in character with the new interest in science, let him turn to Bacon's Essays. There he will find an attention to the specific tendencies of the human mind, apart from all preconceived ideas of what that inquiring glance should discern, which is the true attitude for the investigator of nature. "A mixture of a lie doth ever add pleasure." "There is no passion in the mind of man so weak but it mates and masters the fear of death." "Chaste women are often proud and froward, as presuming on the merit of their chastity." "Men of noble birth are noted to be envious towards new men when they rise, for the distance is altered, and it is like a deceit of the eye, that when others come on they think themselves go back." "The wiser sort of great persons bring in ever upon the stage somebody upon whom to derive the envy that would come upon themselves." That is criticism of character in the spirit of the observer of nature. Men are regarded not as righteous or wicked, but as formed by circumstance, as the result of natural law. We have returned to the Greek sense of variety ; we have lost all remembrance of a great division-line separating the travellers to Heaven or Hell. We are already in the modern world of secular, scientific interest ; we observe moral tendencies as facts just like any other facts ; they have lost their overwhelming significance as hints of an eternal distinction. It is difficult for us to realize that this ever came upon the world as a new thing. It is the spirit of art at all periods of the world's history, and it is also the spirit of science. But as a broad, catholic influence it came upon the world in the breath of the Renaissance, and buried germs of life felt the influence and rushed into the genial air.

In this sunshine of a new life sprang up the luxuriant and various vegetation of modern literature—literature as it is impressed with the revival of classical life, as it bears still the character given it by the rebound from a gloomy and mutilated theology. The modern drama commemorates the reawakening of individual human interests after their long sleep, the sudden influx of sap into the withered boughs that had felt the frost of the long winter. The love of woman changes from the centre of human temptation to the centre of human desire. A halo of romance succeeds a shadow of sin. Human passion gathers up all the associations of poetry and drama; it appears in connection with whatever is stately, whatever is vigorous, whatever is pure. Man's spirit is no longer a battlefield for the contending forces of Heaven and Hell. It is a rich and varied landscape, full of beauty, full of interest; its qualities cannot be tabulated under antithetic heads of good and evil; they are various, and interesting for their own sake. Once more, as to the Greek, Nature becomes sacred; her laws succeed her deities. Gravitation binds the world in a golden chain, and in its completeness prepares men's minds to be satisfied with all the wealth and variety contained therein, and to cease from all striving towards that which lies above and beyond it.

This line of development could not be followed out unbroken to our own day; if we were to keep it so we should have to ignore the Reformation. Protestantism is a revival of Augustinianism; though Augustine was the great Doctor of the Roman Church, his true successor is Luther. That crisis in the history of a man which we call Conversion—a crisis which we may find in the lives of some men who care nothing for religion— is not a natural, not at least an inevitable incident in the life of the member of a Church. The fact of a relation and the consciousness of a relation are indeed two things, and the fact that when Augustine lived Baptism was still an expression of individual conviction—that the new member of the Church was not an unconscious babe, but a man or woman desirous to enter its fold—this fact prevented, at this time, any discernment of the inchoate divergence between two systems which were not logically irreconcilable. But the Church, which sets her seal on every unconscious infant, demands no spiritual crisis as the pledge of membership, and cannot emphasize the emotion which testifies to a new perception. The doctrine that man is justified by faith—that an inward emotion sets each individual in his right place, and that this is a transaction between the soul and God—this view is not obviously harmonious with the ideal of a Catholic Church. Catholicism had developed the corporate element in Augustinianism ; Protestantism went back to its individual element. These two were harmonious in the mind of Augustine, but they diverged with the progress of the ages, and the two divisions of Christendom have divided the two elements between them.

Protestantism, therefore, which is often regarded as a step forward in the progress from the age of undoubting faith to the age of critical reason, was in reality a step backwards. Or perhaps, rather, it was an excursion away from the path. It gave new vitality to the doctrine of the Fall. That doctrine, though accepted by the Catholic Church, is not a distinctively Catholic belief. We find scarcely a trace of it in the poem of Dante, where our first father, with a few selected spirits alone of those who knew not Christ, is to be found in Paradise. The Catholic Church remembered only that man was the member of an organism ; she never taught that man must in his own history reverse the part of Adam. Protestantism took up this lesson, and gave emphasis to the doctrine of the Fall by the doctrine of individual Redemption. But Protestant and Catholic, deadly foes as they were, might have joined hands against the Renaissance, if they could have understood the path of History. They were like Athens and Sparta, wasting their strength in internecine combat, in presence of the growing power of Macedon ; their differences vanished before their common interest, in the presence of a common foe.

A new epoch was at hand, in which the struggle should be transferred to other issues than those which divided Protestants from Catholics. The French Revolution took up the lesson of the Renaissance. It received its heritage, not from men who dethroned an infallible Church to make way for an infallible book, but from men who taught that nothing was infallible but the spirit of universal humanity. It proclaimed the sanctity of nature. It repudiated the doctrine of the Fall. The repudiation was too complete to be conscious. But the ideal of Democracy, started by the American, and made emphatic by the French Revolution—what is it but the doctrine of Original Sin inverted ? Man's nature is corrupt, said Augustine, education should be the victory over Nature. Man's nature is holy, said Rousseau, education should be the victory over all that is artificial. The strange hankering after savage life which distinguished the eighteenth century and found its interpreter in Rousseau, was the reversal of the doctrine of the Fall. Those who most dwelt on it may never have heard of the doctrine of the Fall ; none the less the whole meaning of the second doctrine depends on the meaning of the first. The Rights of Man, the Goddess of Reason, the worship of Humanity—all are the sonorous, the emphatic, the passionate unsaying of the doctrine of Original Sin, the Fall of Man, the evil of Nature ; and, lastly, in our own day, the Darwinian theory of the survival of the fittest and

the origin of humanity by natural selection, has come to
bind the scientific and the moral members of this new
development into a complete whole.   Nature had been
the invading, disturbing influence in Creation : she is
now enthroned as the Creator.

We underrate the power of reaction in thought.   We
seldom give an adequate place to that element in all
assertion which is truly denial.   God, says an Indian
sage (and he repeats the phrase more than once), is only
to be described by No No.   That is, so many of Man's
thoughts of God are unworthy, that the true doctrine
concerning Him is largely made up of protest.   The
" No No " may be heard in every earnest doctrine.
How much of modern science is made up of it we
are hardly yet able to appreciate.   The men who give
attention to Nature, as to something Divine, may be
even ignorant that there was a time when Nature was
traduced as something almost Satanic ; but they are
none the less protestants against that belief.   The conscious participation in thought and feeling granted to
every son of man is but a small part of that which he
truly *is*.   Far below the stratum of consciousness in each
one of us lie the unsounded depths of a heritage we can
as little abjure as discern.   In some mysterious thrill,
in some strange unintelligible foreboding, in some vague
unexplained ecstasy of hope, the struggles of our fathers
make themselves felt in our hearts.   And what for a
thousand years men believed leaves its record for centuries in a protest after it has ceased to exist as a creed.
The doctrine owes all its distinctness to what it has over-
thrown, even when that is, in the mind of the teacher,
utterly forgotten.

It is by a vain and shallow explanation of that great
reaction of thought against Christianity characteristic of
our day, that men would trace it to any discrepancy

between the account of the genesis of things contained
in the Hebrew Scriptures and that which is the result
of modern research. A divergence setting men's feet
in paths which increase their remoteness at every step
could never be removed by omitting a few lines from a
narrative. The men of our day turn away from Christianity not because it is committed to any assertions
about the beginning of things, but because the idea of
Evolution, as they hold it, implies a sanction on all desire
and choice, and bars the possibility of any relation
between Man and his acts in which he should stand outside them as the Creator from the Creation. All that
Man does is from this point of view but a part of Man,
and any demand that some part should be renounced,
that the true Self should be disentangled from elements
which yet are torn away with more sense of severance
than those in which the true Self is found—such an
attempt revolts the instincts that are bred of exclusive
attention to the external world. When a man thus
formed uses the old language and speaks of God, he
means something quite different from the God of Christians. He means the sum of things, and whatever that
principle is which lies at their root—that principle which
explains them as gravitation explains the movement of
the planets, and is exhausted by such manifestation. It
was possible, in former days, for Faith to slumber in
some closed chamber of the mind while the logical understanding seized on all present event as its exclusive
property, and felt that its negative conclusion could not
touch God. Now that we see every moment to be as
full of Him as any moment ever was, we must trust Him
infinitely more, or must cease to trust Him at all.

The Science of our day stands towards Time as the
Science of the Renaissance stood towards Space. As
the astronomers of the seventeenth century, in destroy-

ing the old cosmogony of the earth below and the
heavens above, discovered a new star in this seeming
dark earth, so the men of Science of the nineteenth
have discovered in the seemingly undivine processes
of all growth the work of the Creator. The six days
of Creation have expanded to take in the course of
all the years, as the realm of Heaven expanded to
take in the orb that holds all that is known of life.
Yet the men of the seventeenth century recognized
with glad reverence that their discoveries were but an
enormous expansion of the Divine, and the men of
the nineteenth deem that their discoveries eliminate
the Divine from the realm of all that man can know.
Whence this vast difference of spirit in two revolutions
identical in principle? Why was it easy to recognize
the Divine influence throughout all Space, while it seems
impossible to recognize that influence throughout all
Time without a degradation and dilution of the meaning
in what is Divine that practically leaves men, as far as
consciousness goes, superior to the force which they
know, while it cannot know them?

Our aim is history, but if history land us on a problem, we cannot conclude our review without attempting
to suggest the direction in which the answer is to be
found. Such an attempt, made in face of a problem
so vast and so ancient, can be but little more than
an indication of tendencies inadequately recognized, and
truths obvious indeed, but not obviously connected with
the questions which give them their most important illustration. The contrast between the earnest and devout
astronomy of the seventeenth century and the irreverent
and narrowing physiology of the nineteenth seems to us
explained, so far as it is explained at all, by the far
greater stress on Faith which is demanded by an extension of the Divine Agency to all Time than to all Space.

Time is the common element of the inner and the outer experience.   Space belongs only to the last.   We cannot think, we cannot feel, we cannot dream, without some change, imperceptible as it may be, and inadequate as it may seem to its content, of the shadow on the dial.   To be told that the Divine working is *now*, is a far greater revelation than to be told that the Divine Presence is *here*.   It forced men to a recognition, immensely and immeasurably greater, of that distinction in the Divine Agency which separates the manifestation of Divine Will from the manifestation of Divine Character.   It did not introduce that distinction.   When men believed that the tiger's claws and the sensitive nerves which feel lacerated flesh were the work of a moment in the sixth day of Creation, they did not feel it impossible to say, "The infliction of pain, apart from penal decision, must no doubt be accepted as a decision of the Creator, but indications of His character must be sought elsewhere." They find it impossible to keep hold of this conviction when the sharpening of the claw and the increased sensitiveness of the nerve is exhibited as a gradual process, part of the whole course of things which, as far as concerns what we call Nature, was in the beginning, is now, and ever shall be.   Nothing is brought before them but a change concerning time, but what seems to have happened is, that God has been dethroned to make way for Nature.

The fervour of modern Democracy is explained, as well as the fervour of modern Science, by their common recoil from an abandoned creed.   This doctrine we have been studying, which called itself Christianity, was in its whole political aspect a *worship of the exceptional*.   The ordinary course of things was unblessed ; salvation was a setting aside the ordinary course of things, an escape into some realm that was no inheritance of humanity.

In our day, on the other hand, if any desire is widely felt, that fact is supposed to establish its legitimacy. We imagine ourselves to approach the ideal of government in proportion as we give a larger number of individuals a chance of influencing government. The divine right of kings has been succeeded by the divine right of multitudes. There is a virtue, it is thought, in multiplication. If each individual wants something wrong, they cannot all together want something wrong. Human nature is elevated into a sort of Divine rule, regulating the disorders of individual will. The worship of the exceptional is changed into the worship of the universal, even at times into the worship of the average. The " worship of humanity " by a small but influential sect among us is but the caricature of what is felt by all who exercise an obvious and lively influence on our own generation.

It may thus seem at times as if the epoch of individualism, which began with the modern world, were at last at an end. We are apparently returning towards the ideal of antique life, according to which the unit of moral thought was not the individual but the group. Modern Democracy, with its bias towards Socialism, its deference towards " the masses," appears to revive the classical reverence for the State at the expense of the individual. Modern Science, with its great idea of Evolution, opens a backward vista in the history of every man which exhibits his seventy years of individual life as an insignificant fragment of all that makes up his true history, and thus arresting all judgment until his moral biography be completed by all its ancestral preface, returns towards the Augustinian idea of Original Sin, seen under the fainter light of a day which knows only evils and not Evil. Yet all, probably, which is vital in this revival of a past ideal, is of the hour. Never can a

principle of incorporation which depended for its life on
repulsion widen to include the human race. And then
again never can the Individual lose the indefeasible claim
that Immortality has symbolised for mankind. Science,
explaining every man's life by a finite prelude, cannot
undo the work of belief in an infinite future ; it is not
anticipation alone which has been affected by that belief,
nor may its influence be banished when it is itself rejected. Men and women may refuse to regard themselves as heirs of immortality, but they can neither
abdicate nor refuse to concede the claims which only
began to exist with that high anticipation. The words
" for ever," uttered by lips on which they were a hope or
a fear, do not lose their meaning as they fall on ears·
which receive them as a mere fiction. Those who deny
must explain them, and whatever the explanation, it
must involve a consciousness in man—were he cut off
from all political grouping, were he alone in Juan
Fernandez, never expecting to look on the face of a
fellow-man again — of something that seems eternal.
The eternal can never be subordinated to the perishable
—even though the eternity be but a hope, and the
transient far outlast the span of man's sojourn on earth.
The questions that concern the being in whom an
infinite hope has arisen can never again be subordinated to those which concern the framework of his life
in this world, however inferior be the span of his own
life here, and however faint and dim the hope of any
other.

We have seen how the evolution of the moral life of
Humanity passes in throbs of antagonism from race to
race, and how yet this antagonism is never a mere recoil ;
so that, when the Persian Dualism arose to protest against
the confusion of Good and Evil in the Indian Pantheism,
this dualism held some hint of an ultimate Unity, which,

as the goal of all existence, must also have been in some sense its starting-point. And then, again, we have seen how, when the process was reversed, and the rich variety of the artist people was exchanged for the monotony of the world's lawgivers, there was yet a sort of escape from that monotony in the influence which made of Rome the mediator of the nations, enclosing in its hard frame-work the variety of the Greek world. No stage of thought, in an individual life or in that of the world, can be a mere unsaying of what has gone before. Yet thought progresses by a continual turn towards such an unsaying. When the consciousness of the race passed from that conviction which was the groundwork of all ancient morals, that the State was a unity, to the double conviction that the individual is a unity, and that the human race is a unity, it made an advance which could never again be lost, but which with the progress of the ages withers into as exclusive a doctrine as that against which it was a reaction. Man, to the old world, was a mere fragment of the Republic. To the modern world the starting-point of thought has been the individual man. Perhaps no greater revolution ever moved the world of thought than that which effected this change in its moral unit; it has needed nearly two thousand years to work out its consequences, and exhibit the morality of the "Self" as the classic world exhibited the morality of the citizen. And now, it would seem, a new epoch of expansion dawns on the world. Science has given the word Self a new meaning; in the light of Evolution it is seen to contain as a part of its very being a relation to the Past. We need to carry on this expansion into a different direction. What each man means when he says "I" is but a fragment. The true I is made up of relation to something larger than itself; its instincts are centrifugal as well as centripetal; it has not to create bonds with other personalities; it need but recognize those which make up a part of its own being. Personality is the very source of Unity; but it has been the constant temptation of human beings to impoverish this Unity, to refuse to recognize its organic relational character, to ignore the multiplicity which lies at its base. We shall discern this multiplicity when we discern the larger Unity which encloses it. We shall see that Self means relation to Man when we see that it means also relation to God.

All the strength of ancient life was wrought up with its exclusiveness. A few persons were welded into a closer unity than that attained by any modern State, because a number of persons, quite as necessary to its existence as any of its members, were treated as things. Towards this unity we can never return. We cannot so unlearn the lessons that we inherit with our bodily structure as ever to combine in a conscious unity which is to shut out others of our kind. We have no antagonistic pressure to supply limits from without; our oneness must come from a universally felt attraction towards something within. Men think in our day that this centre can be found in the ideal of Humanity. They have yet to learn that no ideal is possible if that which is idealized know no Beyond. These pages have been occupied with an effort to illustrate from the history of moral thought the belief that Man can strive towards no virtue in which he does not feel the sympathy of God. He must feel himself in some sense a fragment, if ever he is to discover his true oneness. Virtue must be a refracted ray from something above Virtue; duty must be the aspect, visible in our dense atmosphere, of a higher excellence extending far beyond it. And they who would deny this, they who feel that Nature exhausts God, that the summits of human virtue are the summits of moral excellence, that reverence is the provision for inferiority, and fades away before Man reaches those heights towards which he is always striving—they can find in the moral thought of the Past little but a collection of errors. Man, if we judge him by history, knows himself only so far as he turns towards the eternal Other of the human spirit; he finds his true Unity only as he finds a larger Unity which makes him one with himself and with his brother man.

[IT has been pointed out to me, by a reader of the first edition, while these sheets were passing through the press, that the true analogue for the Venus of Virgil, as a type of the Divine Mother, must be sought in Thetis rather than in Aphrodite. I think any one who will compare the freakish whimsical result of the appeal of Thetis to Zeus—the lying dream sent to Agamemnon, the purposeless pretence at a wish for a return, &c.,—with the whole action of the Æneid, wherever Venus appears in it, will allow that the contrast between Venus and Thetis illustrates the remarks in the text almost as well as the contrast between Venus and Aphrodite. No doubt Venus is just as *partial* as Thetis is, (and so is the Mediæval Virgin). But the difference in their dignity, and their connection with the plan of the world's history, seems to me immense.]

INDEX.

THE END.

www.ingramcontent.com/pod-product-compliance
Lightning Source LLC
Chambersburg PA
CBHW030825110726

47900CB00006B/1747